I0782079

DARK BEAUTY

Blake Rudman

A HellBound Books Publishing LLC Book
Houston TX

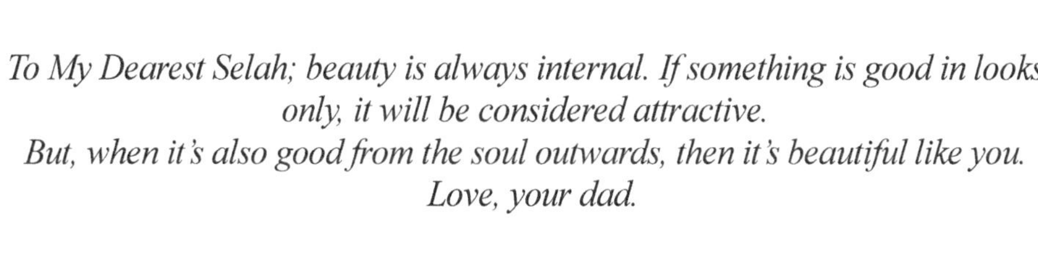

To My Dearest Selah; beauty is always internal. If something is good in looks only, it will be considered attractive.
But, when it's also good from the soul outwards, then it's beautiful like you.
Love, your dad.

DARK BEAUTY

Act 1
Yin and Yang

Chapter One

Tessa Morgan was the happiest woman in the world. Mostly.

She was beautiful. She was famous. And now, at the age of twenty-five, she was a movie star. Better, she was a critically acclaimed actress. She stood in the middle of a party being thrown by Alexei Dvorak, the director of her new film, *Dark Beauty*, while celebrities swirled around her—*other* celebrities, she reminded herself. These people she had watched from the outside all her adult life now seemed to accept her as one of them, and today, she was the center of their attention.

It was puzzling. Even a little disconcerting. Still a bit alien.

The one source of unmitigated joy was that her fiancé, Daniel Takashi, was somewhere nearby in the company of her parents, Jennifer and Kenneth Morgan. She and Daniel had been moving toward marriage since college; him proposing at the film's wrap party and putting a ring on her finger had been a mere formality—a ritual. Daniel had been a constant through the journey to this point in her life; she doubted she would have gotten through the last several years in one piece without him.

She checked to see where he was in the expansive great room at the rear of the Dvorak home. He wasn't in the room. Searching outside the floor-to-ceiling windows that formed its exterior wall, she saw him on the broad patio that overlooked the Dvoraks' gardens and pool, chatting with her mom and dad. Amid a nebula of fairy lights, the three were seated at one of the small round tables that dotted the terrace and the pool surround, smiling, laughing. They had known each other for years and their affection was mutual. That simple fact made Tessa smile and long for her first family holiday with Daniel as a bona fide member of the Morgan clan.

Top of the world. That was where Tessa Morgan was currently residing. She had no way of knowing that, somewhere in that world, an invisible clock was ticking.

"You were wonderful in that film, kiddo."

Tessa turned to see a striking young redhead in a saffron-colored designer dress that was as simple as it was stunning.

Her admirer raised a champagne glass. "It was like *A Star is Born* but in real time. Kudos to you, and I hope we get to work together. Soon. You got 'it,' girl."

The woman needed no introduction. This was Audra Alexander—at thirty-four, the most popular and sought-after actress in the world. She'd done everything from blockbuster superhero movies to deeply thoughtful Oscar fodder. And she was talking to Tessa as if she were a colleague, an equal, someone whose craft she respected.

Tessa's smile felt like it originated in her soul. "Thank you, really.

That means so much, coming from you."

Steve Fields, Audra's startlingly handsome boyfriend and the star of what had just become one of the highest-grossing films of the year, nudged his significant other aside with a mild push. Audra scowled at him comically.

"Don't hog the woman of the hour, babe," he said, flashing his trademark crooked smile. "Tessa, I have a project I'm working on with Legendary Pictures, and I'd like to talk with you—"

"Nobody talks to Ms. Morgan about projects without first talking to me."

The short, stocky man with the round, bearded face who'd appeared at Tessa's side was her agent, Jerry Lance, one of the most powerful men in Hollywood. He could have easily played the part of a well-groomed and nattily attired Santa Claus except that he behaved, on occasion, more like Santa's evil twin. He was magical, in any event; the man could do with a simple phone call what most agents couldn't do with a bribe.

"Tessa's in great demand right now, as you might imagine," he said in a voice that was more growl than purr, his white brows all but head-butting over the bridge of his nose. "Any projects she takes on go through me."

"We'll have our agent call yours," Audra told Tessa, pointedly ignoring the man. She turned on her heel and walked away. Steve shrugged apologetically and followed, making the universal "call me" sign at Jerry. Tessa turned to look at her agent. "Wasn't that unnecessarily rude?" she said, honestly perplexed.

"Honey, this is a rude business. It's my job to protect you from leeches. They don't want to work with you because they like you or think you're talented. They want to work with you because there are more dollar signs on your face than tinsel on a Christmas tree. And I'm making sure those dollar signs stay in place. You represent the next wave of Hollywood talent. They want to make sure they catch that wave."

"Isn't it my talent that puts the dollar signs there?" She drew a circle around her face with one finger.

Jerry gave her a patronizing smile and patted her arm. "You," he said, "are such an adorable newb. You need to trust my instincts, not yours."

"Of course," she said, only half meaning it. Jerry was a great agent; he was just calibrated differently in the way he dealt with people. "I need to find Kristin," she said and excused herself.

After searching for several minutes, fielding congratulations and kudos, Tessa finally spotted her sister in an alcove behind a staircase that spiraled up to a second-floor gallery. She was surrounded by men, as usual. Tessa could see from Kristin's posture that she was ignoring them, also as usual, staring at her iPad, a scowl on her face. She was clearly in a bad mood—not unexpected, though, since she'd been in a perpetual bad mood since before the movie had finished shooting.

As Tessa waffled about whether or not to approach, Kevin Salinger, *Dark Beauty*'s producer, entered the alcove; the other men in the alcove fled. He stood close to Kristin and spoke to her, but Kristin froze him out as well. He wandered away, disappearing quickly among the other guests.

Tessa had taken one step toward the alcove when someone grasped her arm. Before she could protest, Gianni DeLuca, the fashion photographer who had made Tessa and Kristin famous, drew her in the opposite direction. "Where are we going, Gianni?" Tessa asked, glancing back at her twin.

"My exhibition." He said the words with the slight Italian accent that Tessa knew for a fact was cultivated. He'd been born in Cincinnati to Italian parents and had once vacationed in Milan when he was a child. She supposed the accent was intended to lend a certain European flavor to his dark good looks. It said, *I'm mysterious because I'm not from around here.*

He propelled her out of the great room into the massive foyer, bringing her to a halt before a fifteen-foot-long velvet-covered panel tucked to one side of the circular room. A bevy of lights and video cameras had been set up in front of it, and a crew was fussing over the equipment.

"This is your exhibition?" she asked, staring at the black-and-white reproductions of the most famous pictures DeLuca had taken of Tessa and her twin.

"This is all the room that Mr. Dvorak would allow me," he said wistfully. "But it will have to do."

Director Alexei Dvorak was one of the few people that Gianni DeLuca, whose ego was even more massive than the display of black chest hair he was exposing through the open buttons of his silk print shirt, genuinely held in awe.

"It will look bigger on television, of course," he mused. "The media are here. Where is that sister of yours? Off bewitching the boys again?"

"I don't think she's in a particularly bewitching mood."

"Mood?" Gianni growled. "That woman is a prickly cactus tree of moods. I shall personally drag her here and pose the two of you in front of my photos—the photos," he emphasized, "that put you where you are now."

Tessa had stopped reacting to the reminder, which Gianni made as often as he dropped names and business cards. "She's in the little lounge alcove behind the spiral stair," Tessa said, gesturing in that direction. DeLuca stormed off through the kinetic thicket of guests.

Tessa scanned the display of photos. She remembered every one of them. One hanging with a spotlight on it was of the first cover that she and her sister had done for *Vogue*. Surrounding that one were several images from their first photo spread for *Cosmopolitan*. She smiled at the poster that had introduced them as spokesmodels for Robeson Cosmetics, the one for which Kristin had first dyed her hair black to contrast with Tessa's natural blonde. The sisters had gone from identical twins to Yin and Yang, light and dark, and their hair colors had come to define them. That poster had been all over Los Angeles, on billboards along freeways, plastered in monstrous proportions on the sides of buildings. Tessa and Kristin had been mirror-images of one another until Kristin had made them opposite sides of the same coin. Kristin still dyed her hair to further the image of the sisters as opposing forces.

Tessa turned her back on the display and gazed longingly through the great room's western-facing windows to where she'd last seen her parents and Daniel. If she could teleport, she'd be out there with them in the mild Malibu evening, admiring the view and listening to the heartbeat of the Pacific Ocean. Beyond the infinity edge of the pool, the ocean's seemingly endless expanse sparkled in the light of a full moon. The setting was breathtaking. Tessa's house in Marina del Rey would fit into the first floor of the Dvorak home twice over and afforded her a view of the ocean only over a clutter of rooftops.

She sensed someone peering at her from off to her side through the hedge of cameras and photographers. She turned her head and met the gaze of a young man who blinked and started when their eyes met. He pretended to be staring at something else, seeming awkward and out of place. His face was unshaven—not stylishly so—and his longish hair looked like it hadn't been combed in a while. His faded jeans had seen better days and appeared even worse accompanied by the leather jacket a size too big for him. An odd choice for such a warm evening, she noted. "Sorry," he mumbled. "I thought I knew you. I mean, I thought you were ..." He trailed off and made a shambling retreat. "Here she is."

Gianni was back, dragging Kristin behind him like a recalcitrant mule. She glared with an unadulterated hatred that would have frightened a mass murderer. She avoided Tessa's gaze, choosing instead to scowl at the blank space a few feet in front of her.

"And look who I found mingling with the glitterati!" the photographer added, giving Tessa an overly big smile as he motioned with his head back toward her twin.

Alexei Dvorak stepped from behind him, smiling at the twins. He had the slightly geeky look of an aging film-school student, a Steven Spielberg doppelgänger who, at the ripe old age of forty had close to as many hit films behind him as Spielberg had at that age.

"Always happy to pose with my stars," he said, smiling.

The cameraman from the TV show *Hollywood Deadline* stepped behind the camera and signaled his crew to turn on the lights and activate the sound equipment. Tessa winced at the sudden brightness.

Elle Greenwood, the blonde, blue-eyed cohost of *HD*, stepped in front of the camera with Tessa and Kristin beside her and Dvorak sandwiched between the twins. DeLuca tried to muscle his way into the shot but was pulled aside by a staffer.

"More photos after," the guy told him.

Taking her place in the lights, Greenwood raised her microphone and smiled for the cameras. "We have a special treat for our viewers tonight: Tessa and Kristin Morgan, stars of the brand-new Alexei Dvorak film *Dark Beauty*, which opened in theaters this weekend and is already projected to have one of the biggest November openings in Hollywood history." She held the microphone out toward Tessa. "Tell us, Tessa, were you as thrilled as I was to see your performance on-screen?"

Tessa laughed. "Actually, I hate watching myself on-screen. Every flaw I've ever had gets blown up to the size of a blimp. And hearing my own voice? Yikes."

Greenwood laughed. "You'd be surprised how many stars say that. But let me tell you, Tessa, you don't have any flaws. Other famous actresses—and I'm not naming any names here—have flaws, but you're something new. You're as close to perfect as any actress I've ever seen since Michelle Pfeiffer. God, what I wouldn't give for your complexion." Tessa blushed with an embarrassment that reached her toes. She'd never seen herself as extraordinarily beautiful and certainly never as perfect. Her nose was too long, her lips too full, her breasts too small by current standards. Only now was she actually starting to believe that the telecaster's words might be true—and even as the thought occurred to her, she pushed it away. It was vanity.

Worse, it was tempting fate. And fate was easily tempted. Tessa didn't realize how easily. The invisible clock was still counting down.

Greenwood turned the microphone to her sister. "How about you, Kristin? How did you feel about working with Alexei Dvorak?"

Kristin shrugged. "It was okay."

"Okay?" Greenwood said with mock disbelief. "Alexei Dvorak is the most successful director in Hollywood right now. There are major stars that would kill to work with him."

"Oh, there are easier ways than killing," Kristin said.

Tessa cringed, watching Alexei turn and walk away, a resigned look on his face.

"Really?" said Greenwood. "What do you mean?"

Kristin grabbed the microphone and shoved it in Greenwood's face. "Forget it, bitch. You put on this act like you know how things work in Hollywood and you have no fucking clue!"

She turned her on heel and stormed away, vanishing into the crowd. "Well, shit!" Greenwood exclaimed. She turned to the crew. "Cut that bit. Just cut it right out and put it on the staff blooper reel so we can all laugh about it at the Christmas party. We're staying on Tessa."

When the interview was finished and the crew began removing their equipment, Gianni DeLuca shouted after them. "My photographs! You never showed the sisters with my photographs!"

"Your photographs will be here all night, Gianni," Greenwood told him. "I'm heading for the bar."

Tessa ignored them and dashed after Kristin, working her way through the crowd, giving quick but hurried smiles to people who gave her congratulatory pats on the back; she recognized some of their faces but had little recall on any of their names.

Alexei Dvorak caught up with her as she was entering the great room. Tessa turned to see whose broad hand was touching her shoulder, unable to hide the crease lines in her forehead.

"You might not want to interact with your sister right now," he said. "She's been reading entertainment reviews all evening and they're all telling her that you eclipsed her. You're the real star of *Dark Beauty*, Tess. She isn't blind to that. She's your sister and I know you love her, but I think there's a lot of jealousy there. Jealousy she may take out on you. I'm thinking you may not be the best person to try to talk to her right now."

"But someone's got to—" Tessa protested.

Alexei squeezed her shoulder. "Listen to me, Tess. I think you need to be careful with Kristin right now. She's ... she's not in a good place. I know that sounds cliché—"

"No. I know what you mean. She's more fragile than she seems. I know she always acts like she's sure of herself. But she's not. I grew up with her, Alexei. I've seen how she breaks a little bit every time life shows her it can't be hacked or rigged in her favor." She said the words without rancor or disdain.

Alexei shook his head. "You're a wise young woman, Tessa Morgan. Just don't let Kristin's anger dampen your enjoyment tonight ... or ever.

Which reminds me, you should be getting the script for our next project this coming week."

She tried to smile. "I look forward to reading it. I think a fantasy film would be a lot of fun. I ... don't suppose there's a part in it for Kristin." She already knew the answer, but thought if she asked ...

Alexei lowered his eyes. "No. There isn't. She's beautiful—she's your identical twin, so how could she not be—but she sabotages her talent with her lack of dedication. If she were half as hardworking and collaborative as you are, I'd be happy to work with her again, but you remember what it was like on the set. You gave everything your best; she gave ... I'm not sure what she gave. It was like she was intent on sabotaging the project ... or herself."

Tessa felt tears welling up in her eyes. It was true. Every last word of it. And he was being kind, at that. "I ... I have to find her. I think she might need me."

Dvorak nodded. "I'll see you later. Just be careful. She's in a foul mood. Whatever she says, don't believe a word of it."

As the director moved away, Daniel appeared, taking his place. He was smiling at Tessa in that way he had that made her warm all over. She wanted to take his hand and lead him back out among the fairy lights where they could listen to the heartbeat of the Pacific, but she couldn't, because there was Kristin, who had disappeared into some dark recess and who needed her.

"Sorry about that scene back there," Daniel said, glancing toward Gianni's exhibition.

"You saw that? I'm so sorry."

Daniel shook his head. "Don't apologize to *me*, Tessa. I'm just hoping it doesn't throw a damper on your evening."

"Little bit," Tessa said with a forced smile. "Listen, I've got to—"

"I know. You go find Kristin. Maybe give her a little tough love. That girl holds way too much inside. Of course, this is probably neither the time nor the place to talk it out, but invite her for a walk by the ocean or something."

Tessa gave a resigned shrug. "I'd really like to tell her what a great job she did in the movie, but I doubt she'd buy it."

"Yeah. It's hard to find more than a handful of bright spots in that performance." He leaned in and kissed her ear, and whispered, "Go get 'em, tiger. Love you."

"Love you," she told him and planted a kiss on his lips, marveling anew at how utterly at home she felt with Daniel.

Kristin was still in the little half-hidden lounge she'd been ensconced in previously. Isolated from the great room by the metal and wood staircase that bisected its threshold, it contained a gas fireplace faced in tiny glass squares of gray and white and surrounded by a set of four matching gray club chairs and a pair of black side tables. The plush area rug was cream colored.

Kristin was seated in one of the chairs, glaring at her iPad as if it had done something reprehensible. Fury blazed in her gray eyes and drew her brows down over the bridge of her nose. She didn't glance up as Tessa approached.

It was shocking to Tessa that someone who was physically identical to her could look so very different, could be so unrecognizable to her. The differences went beyond the hair color. She was certain she'd never worn that expression on her face, not even when—

She choked the thought off. She did not want to go into a possible confrontation with Kristin with *that* at the back of her mind.

"Sitting around reading on our big night?" Tessa made a wry face. "I thought you loved parties. Why aren't you out there dancing, flirting, doing Kristin things?"

Kristin snorted. "Are you kidding? You think I'm going out there where half the people have also been reading *this*?" She held up the iPad.

Kristin was clearly not going to be jollied out of her mood. "Come on, Kristin. It doesn't matter what they're saying. You know how critics are. They always have to find something to nitpick."

"Nitpick?" Kristin snapped angrily. "You call this 'nitpicking'?" She waved the iPad in Tessa's face. "Look at this review from the *New York Times*. 'When Kristin Morgan isn't sleepwalking through her role like an extra from *The Night of the Living Dead*, she pinballs through it like a greyhound on speed. A performance that erratic leads this reviewer to the inescapable conclusion that the young actress is bipolar. It's hard to believe a veteran filmmaker of Alexei Dvorak's caliber would have *directed* her to give that performance. At least in her more wooden moments, she could have been wrangled by the set crew.'"

Tessa swallowed. Why did critics have to be so brutal? Couldn't they just say that a performance was uneven but that the performer had had her moments? And she *had* had her moments, but getting them out of her had taken a toll on Alexei's legendary good temper and patience. Tessa realized she'd intentionally forgotten what Kristin had been like during production.

"Maybe …," she said now, "maybe the reviewer was just in a bad mood. Remember that guy who said I was pretty but had all the presence of a Barbie doll? He compared me unfavorably to a Disney princess."

"Yes. But he said you were 'drop-dead gorgeous' and had all the presence of a Barbie doll. I also remember that he later admitted he'd been blubbering drunk at the screening and was hungover when he wrote the review." Kristin closed the *Times* review and swiped to one from the *Washington Post*. "'What saves the film is that Kristin Morgan's scenes are mercifully brief. Apparently, we have someone in the cutting room to thank for that.'"

"You can't take this stuff too seriously."

"Oh, can't I? Here's what the *Post* has to say about you. 'Tessa Morgan may be the greatest discovery since Jennifer Lawrence. She rivets the eye and she riveted this reviewer's mind. Her scenes blaze and smolder like a firestorm.'"

She threw the iPad to the plush carpet and fixed Tessa with a stiletto gaze. "I don't know how you did it, Tess, but you managed to sabotage me. Were you sleeping with Dvorak?"

Tessa cringed. Alexei had been right to warn her about the venom that Kristin might spit at her. Not that she didn't already know the sort of tactics her sister was willing to use to achieve her own ends.

"Or maybe not," Kristin went on. "I tried that, but he just ignored me. Ignored. *Me.*"

She'd tried to seduce Alexei? Maybe Daniel was right. Maybe tough love was what was needed here.

Tessa faced her sister directly. "You were on drugs, Krist. They yanked you from one extreme to another. You could see it on the screen."

"I needed those drugs!" she snapped so loudly that several of the partygoers who had gathered at the base of the spiral staircase stopped talking and turned their heads. Kristin lowered her voice, though not by much. "I wasn't sleeping. Could hardly eat. I needed them to get me through that movie."

"Why? It was what you wanted. What you'd worked for. Harder than I did. I didn't need drugs."

Kristin's expression turned to a mocking grin. "Oh, yeah. My good little sister. You were always the perfect one, the fucking …"

Suddenly she paused, staring over Tessa's shoulder. "Oh, for the love of God. It's Kurt Morrison. How the hell did he get in?"

Tessa turned to see the unkempt young man she'd caught staring at her earlier. He was heading straight toward them, his fists clenched at his sides and a hard, determined look on his face. He shoved his way through the little knot of guests around the stairs and stood, trembling, facing Kristin across the cream-colored area rug.

"You haven't been answering my calls, Kristin," he said. "I've called every day, several times. I guess you were too busy making your movie debut."

"No, I was just ignoring you," Kristin said. She picked up her iPad and stood. "I thought by now that brilliant mind of yours would have deduced that I didn't want to talk to you. How did you get past security, anyway?"

"The key grip owed me a favor and I called it in."

"You mean he owes you for drugs, right? Doesn't he know they sell better quality shit right on the Paradox Studios lot?"

"I'm not here to sell you drugs, Kristin. You know why I'm here."

"To sing me a rousing chorus of 'Baby, Come Back?'"

"Kristin ...," murmured Tessa, praying her sister would just shut up. "I'm here because I love you. You know that. I've told you in every message I've left. Every text I've sent."

"I've been deleting your messages as soon as they pop up. I didn't want to hear that whiny voice of yours. In my ears *or* in my head."

"Kristin!" Tessa shot a glance at Morrison. The rage in his eyes made her tremble. He was breathing in short, tight gasps, as though he was prepping to spit words at Kristin like machine gun bullets. But as Tessa watched, the fire in his eyes banked down to smoldering embers and his breathing steadied.

"Well, it's too bad you didn't listen to those messages, Kristin. Because then you might not have to hear what my whiny voice has to say now."

"Oh, and what is that?"

"That if I can't have you, nobody can," he said finally, his voice surprisingly steady. "Of course, you'd argue that sounds like a line from a bad movie. From what I saw this afternoon, you know a thing or two about bad movies."

I should leave, Tessa thought. *I should just turn around and find Daniel and my parents and leave.*

Kristin's voice lowered to a feline growl. "Go fuck your hash bong, Kurt. It'll make you come faster than I ever did."

His face tight and pale, Kurt Morrison pulled something from the pocket of his leather jacket. Tessa stepped back in horror, afraid he had a gun, but no. It was a plastic flask roughly the size of a large bottle of vitamins.

"Last chance, Kristin," he said.

"*Fat* chance, Kurt," she told him and took a step as if she meant to make a grand exit past the spiral staircase and its gawkers.

Everything after that took place in slow motion, or at least that's how Tessa would remember it later. Morrison uncapped the flask and flung the contents directly at Kristin's face. Tessa watched the stuff ripple through the air in a weightless stream. She had no idea what it was, but instinct told her it was not benign.

Her reaction was automatic. She lunged toward her sister to push her out of the way, but there wasn't time. The liquid moved faster than she did, and arrived just as she got her hands on Kristin's shoulder. Kristin had raised her iPad to shield her face, but the liquid would reach her before the device would offer much cover.

The spray caught Tessa on the right side of her face. She reflexively screwed her eyes shut, but she was showered with pain so intense it blocked out any further thought. She had once accidentally placed her hand on a hot oven burner; this was a thousand times worse. She could feel her skin sizzling like a steak in a frying pan.

She crumpled to the floor in agony. She wanted to reach up and wipe the acid away—for that's surely what it was—but she could only huddle on the carpet, screaming and crying and feeling her skin burn. There was nothing to be done but let darkness wash over her with the sounds of Kristin's hoarse screams in her ears.

The invisible clock had struck midnight.

Chapter Two

Tessa Morgan lived in a universe of gray gauze. She was swaddled in it. Worse, it lived within her, seeping into every fiber of her being, permeating every corner of her mind. It was numbing, suffocating. She couldn't even see.

Am I blind?

She eventually realized that bandages covered her eyes and that a tiny bit of light oozed through to illuminate the dense fog. Not completely blind then.

She was pretty sure she was drugged. She could feel needles in her arm, pumping fluid into her veins, and heard the steady, quiet beeping of machinery. Voices floated in and out of her awareness, but she could barely understand what they were saying. They were too soft to make out words, then too loud to comprehend. She thought she heard her mother, her father, her fiancé, but she might have dreamed it. It hardly mattered. If they were really there, she had no way to speak to them.

She struggled to block out recollections, to hide in the recesses of her own mind and forget how she had ended up where she was, but the memories refused to go away. They haunted her, waking or dreaming, ghastly hallucinations made all the worse by the knowledge that they were rooted in reality. She remembered the searing pain vividly. It had scorched her face, but more than that, it had burned her very soul. That had happened. That was why she was here.

Now, lying in a hospital bed, she wasn't certain which was worse, the pain or the numbness that had followed. All she could do was float in a cloud of gray, fearing both darkness and light.

Chapter Three

Tessa Morgan was eighteen.

High school graduation was only one week away, and she, along with her best friend Sarah Hernandez and others, was helping to decorate the school gym for the Mar Vista High senior grad party. Tessa had brought crepe paper to be strung from the rafters in flowing rainbows, something that symbolized the promise of the future and the happy anticipation she felt at moving on with her life. High school had been a wonderful experience for her. She had friends, she had teachers who had come to respect her intelligence. She had a life. But it was a life she knew she had to leave behind.

The thought of graduating made her both happy and sad. She would miss her friends, particularly Sarah, but she had college to look forward to, new friends to meet, and a future that could be anything and everything she wanted it to be. She had that future all planned out. And she was ready for it.

She peered up at Sarah, who was on a ladder attaching one end of a blue streamer. "What do you think? A little to the left?" Sarah jiggled her head to move a lock of dark hair away from her eyes.

"No. Right there is good!" Sarah was a go-getter like Tessa. She had plans to go to CalTech and study engineering. The two girls were opposite in looks—the tall blonde alongside the petite brunette—but they had forged a tight friendship since childhood and had spent many hours laughing and studying together.

"I think we could design the setup of these decorations better," Sarah said, climbing down the ladder. "What if we—"

"You are definitely an engineer, girl! All right. Let's hear it!"

"Tessa," a brusque voice interrupted, "put these name tags into the plastic holders."

The speaker was Brenda Hutchens, the student who had spearheaded the organization of the grad party. It was the perfect job for her, Tessa thought wryly, because she loved to bark orders. The expression on her broad face was always dour and often critical. Everyone agreed that someday she would either be CEO of a major corporation or would hit the glass ceiling and end up as a night-shift manager at a burger joint.

"Uh, sure, Brenda. Hold that thought, Sarah."

Sarah smiled and strolled a few feet away, studying the layout of the decorations and clearly determining a way to arrange everything more efficiently.

"Doing Brenda's scutwork, huh, sis?"

Tessa's twin, Kristin, was sitting three rows up in a section of bleachers that had been pulled out, sipping punch she was openly spiking from a bottle in a brown paper bag. She was surrounded, as usual, by her posse of mean girls, none of whom were even remotely as attractive as Kristin and every one of whom craved her approval. She'd once told Tessa her selection of friends operated on the theory that if she surrounded herself with girls who were average or ugly, she'd always shine brighter in comparison.

"Yeah, Tessa," said Jill Tillwood, a pretty-eyed blonde with a crooked nose who sat next to Kristin on the same bench. "Brenda's making you her bitch."

Kristin turned on her with a fiery glare. "Shut the fuck up, Jilly-Tilly! That's my sister you're talking to."

Jill's eyes opened wide and she straightened with a start but didn't respond. Sarah shook her head at the exchange. Sarah knew Tessa's sister nearly as well as Tessa did ... and avoided her. Tessa cringed a little inwardly. Her twin had always been protective of her. Born fifteen minutes before Tessa, she sometimes pretended to be an older sister than she was. Tessa was the only female student in or out of Kristin's tiny clique that Kristin had never mocked or treated unfairly. Although Tessa didn't approve of her twin's imperious attitude, she was a good sister. Mostly. At least in private.

"Hey, look," a girl with a wide mouth said. "There's Brittany Stamper, folding napkins. I'm telling you, Brittany. You'll have a great career in food service."

Brittany wisely ignored them.

"Why don't you guys come down and help?" Tessa asked.

The other girls looked at Kristin askance but kept their mouths shut. Kristin raised her punch glass and said, "Because it's too much fun to sit back here and cheer everybody else on. We're just rockin' that old school spirit!"

"More like *mockin'* that old school spirit," Tessa said wryly. Kristin saluted her with the punch glass and took a swig. "Hey! You! Morgan!"

The voice came from behind Tessa. She turned to see a short, chubby Asian girl making a beeline across the gym's shiny floor, her dark, intense eyes piercing Tessa's soul. The normally timid girl had apparently psyched herself up for something and was not about to back down. Tessa took a couple steps back, unsure of what was happening. The girl never broke eye contact and, when within reach, stopped and slapped Tessa sharply across the face.

"Ow! What are you doing?" Tessa attempted to grab the girl's arm before she swiftly pulled it back.

"Hey!" yelled Sarah, running over to help.

"That's for the time you called me 'Piglet' in front of my friends. Guess you'll never get the chance to do that again." She hiccupped, tears starting from her eyes, then turned and stormed off.

"That wasn't me!" Tessa objected. "I'd never—" Tessa shot a glare over at her twin, then turned back toward the dark-haired girl who was already nearing the exit. Tessa paused for a second, redirecting her anger at being slapped, and shouted out to the girl before she was gone, "Wait! Hey!"

The girl pivoted, keeping herself a safe distance from the girl she hated.

"Come back. Please," Tessa requested.

Sarah turned her head swiftly toward Tessa and gave her a wide-eyed stare as if to say, "Are you sure? This girl just *slapped* you!"

Tessa motioned to Sarah that all was good.

"Wh—" the girl began, but Kristin, who had witnessed the whole exchange, cut her off.

"Oops!" called Kristin, faux-covering her mouth with one hand. "My bad! That *might* have been me." She finished with a grin and an exaggerated shrug.

The girl's eyes widened as she slowly retraced her steps, glancing back and forth between Kristin and Tessa. Tessa met her halfway so the two could speak out of Kristin's earshot. "Oh, God, I'm so sorry I hit you! I've heard about twin swaps, but ... I hate to say it, but your sister is a ... a ... well, it rhymes with *witch*. I'd go over and slap *her*, but she has bodyguards. The coward." She glared at the girls sitting up in the bleachers.

Tessa could empathize. There were times she wanted to slap her twin upside the head, herself. "I'm sorry. My sister is, well, complicated. Say, I don't even know your name. I'm Tessa."

"Yeah. I get that, now. I'm Melinda Chao ... not that anybody in this room cares who I am." She quietly mumbled the last part of the sentence.

"That's not true, Melinda."

Melinda's eyes suddenly welled with tears. She stared at her feet, clearly embarrassed.

"Oh, come on, it's okay." Tessa squeezed the girl's arm. "Really. High school is almost over. I'm sure the real world will be much better."

"Yeah. I suppose," said Melinda, clearly not convinced.

Tessa quickly thought of an idea. "Hey, you know what? I just saw these super funny memes today. How about you give me your Snapchat and I can send them to you?"

Melinda looked up and cracked a small smile.

"You'll love them. I promise! Some are about graduating high school, and others are funny ones with cats. Do you like cats?"

"Yeah," Melinda answered. "I love cats."

"Maybe we can even get on a streak!"

Melinda was now clearly trying to hold in her smile from becoming too large. "Okay." The girls exchanged information.

Tessa heard Kristin's exaggerated groan from across the gym and knew she was rolling her eyes. She ignored it.

"Thank you," said Melinda. "You're actually really nice, Tessa. Not like ... well, you know."

"Kristin's not that bad when you get to know her. She just doesn't let a lot of people get to know her."

Melinda lowered her voice to a murmur. "I know a lot of people who don't *want* to know her. They get out of her way when they see her coming."

Tessa chuckled. "I completely understand why. Well, I'll send you a Snap later today. And good to meet you, Melinda."

Melinda left the gym with a hop to her step she hadn't had previously.

As Tessa turned to go grab some more streamers, she nearly bumped into another girl she knew named Haddi. "Hey, Haddi! I haven't seen you around for a while."

During Tessa and Kristin's growing-up years, they had each struggled through finding their identity—like everyone did—but with the twist of having a double. When they were third grade and younger, they often dressed in matching outfits in different colors. But then they each reached an age where matching was no longer acceptable. In fact, they strived to be as different as possible. Kristin went out for volleyball and softball; Tessa chose soccer and dance. Kristin took guitar lessons; Tessa enjoyed playing saxophone in the school band. And they even developed different friendships that seldom overlapped. Tessa's best friend was Sarah, and Kristin's was Haddi.

Tessa liked Haddi and thought she was a quality friend for Kristin—much better than the caliber of friends Kristin now hung with. But at some point, Kristin refused to see Haddi anymore. Tessa never knew why.

"Yeah," said Haddi with a shy smile.

Not knowing when she'd get the opportunity to talk to Haddi again, Tessa asked in a low voice, "Whatever happened between you and Kristin? You two were such good friends."

Haddi glanced over at Kristin. Tessa saw that as soon as Haddi and Kristin's eyes met, Kristin looked away and started up some conversation with the girl next to her.

Turning back to Tessa, Haddi said, "I ... uh ... don't know." Tessa was silent, hoping for something more.

"I mean ... I truly do not know. One day we were friends, and the next ... we weren't. I would like to know someday what I said or did. But I probably never will. I'm ready to get beyond high school at this point."

Haddi's friendship with Kristin was clearly a sore point. Tessa made a mental note to try and get something out of Kristin later regarding what had happened. She hadn't realized the break in their friendship had been so sudden. Tessa glanced across the gym at Sarah, who was still working on streamers, and felt renewed appreciation for her friend.

"Well, I gotta go," said Haddi.

"Okay. Sorry about ... whatever happened. See you at the party tonight, hopefully!"

"Yeah maybe. Or at least I'll see you at graduation."

###

The festivities kicked off at seven thirty p.m. with the gym disguised to look as much as possible like a night club ... or a fairy's lair. Fake candles were displayed on the tables (the only kind the fire marshal would allow), and sprays of lights and even a disco ball hung twinkling from the ceiling. Brenda Hutchens and her lieutenant handed out name tags at the door. The punch bowl in the back of the room quickly became the most popular place in the gym, though Tessa was pretty sure the punch wasn't spiked like her sister's was earlier in the day. It would be a pretty wild party if that happened. Thank God for adult chaperones. Who wanted their grad party to be shut down by the local PD?

The evening was a blur. Students that Tessa only vaguely recognized approached her with their yearbooks and awkward smiles, asking her to sign them. She learned the names of the classmates she didn't know from other signatures on their pages, not wanting to admit that she didn't know someone's name. She hung with Sarah as much as possible, wanting to appreciate her waning high school days as much as possible. Meanwhile, Kristin and her coterie prowled like a pack of animals, even growling at students who seemed intimidated by her throng and then laughing when they reacted. Tessa never saw Haddi; she must have chosen not to come. Tessa's date, Andrew Shankman, attempted to entertain her by telling funny stories and showing her amusing cat videos on his phone. She appreciated that Andrew included Sarah and her date, Jed, in the conversation. Tessa didn't know Andrew well but giggled at his humor. Sarah seemed to find some of the cat videos truly hilarious. Tessa hadn't dated much in high school, despite many offers, because she had preferred to use her time to study and was a little leery of the guys who'd approached her after one told her she looked just like a woman in a *Playboy* centerfold. She'd gone to the movies with him once—but he'd had "expectations."

In contrast, Andrew was a sweet boy, skinny but cute; she'd accepted his invitation to the party. She wondered if she'd ever see him again.

Kristin controlled her behavior better when her date was near her. Ryan Bautista, the captain of the football team, was a muscular, handsome eighteen-year-old with a cocky smile. Kristin dated him because he was the most popular boy in school, and that made them a prestige couple. After graduation, when Ryan was no longer a star football player, he'd be gone. Tessa knew Kristin was a firm believer in catch and release.

Halfway through the party, the lights dimmed and the disco ball began to turn, spotlights striking it from three sides. Bright points of light dappled the room and its occupants, and the dancing began in earnest, spurred on by a local DJ. Andrew grabbed Tessa's arm and pulled her to the dance floor in response to the opening notes of the "Cupid Shuffle." He turned out to be unexpectedly good on the dance floor, and Tessa laughed as he spun her around, making her dizzy and happy. The other dancers seemed to glide around her like horses on a merry-go-round. Tessa saw Sarah throw her head back and laugh during the BUM BUM BUM part of "Sweet Caroline," clearly enjoying herself. Kristin even looked happy dancing with Ryan, even though he seemed to think dance was merely flexing his biceps in time to the music.

The evening flew past quickly. After the last song, students filed out the doors, calling out to one another their goodbyes or locations for post-party meetups. Tessa was exhausted and ready to go home. She hugged Sarah goodbye and then waited at the door for Andrew to grab the car. Meanwhile, she scanned the crowd for Kristin and Ryan, who had ridden with them. When Andrew pulled up, she slid in the passenger seat. They waited several minutes before spotting Kristin, who arrived at the car with her column of acolytes. They wound through the parking lot behind her like one of those Chinese dragons—all they needed was the costume. Kristin turned and gave Ryan a big, lingering kiss, which Tessa suspected was more for the benefit of her girlfriends, who swooned over Ryan and clearly were imagining that they were Kristin. Then the two of them clambered into the back seat.

For her part, Tessa planned to give Andrew only a light peck on the cheek. She didn't want to give him false expectations that they might have a future together. As they pulled away from the school, Kristin's friends stood and waved.

Tessa and Andrew were forced to be quiet on the drive home, as Kristin's raucous laughter—about who knew what?—was too loud to attempt conversation. She definitely sounded drunk.

When Andrew pulled up in the girls' driveway, the sisters hopped out and Ryan switched to the front passenger seat. He winked and mouthed *see ya* at Kristin. He had a surprise coming, Tessa was pretty sure.

The twins' mother, Jennifer Morgan, was waiting up when the girls entered the house. She was an elegant and attractive woman in her forties who hadn't yet begun to dye her hair, though silvery strands were starting to appear. She smiled warmly back at her daughters and asked, "How was the dance?"

"It was really fun," Tessa said. "I think it was the best time I've had at a party."

"Not that you'd know from parties," Kristin said. "You've always got your nose buried in a book. Your idea of a good party is three textbooks and a glass of OJ."

"Tessa works hard for her grades," their mother said mildly, the (accurate) implication that Kristin didn't. "How did you like the dance, Kristin?"

"It was great," she said, smiling. Then she caught herself, lost the smile, and added, "Actually, it sucked. Every dance in this shit hole high school has been crappy."

"Kristin!" her mother exclaimed, but then she settled back into her leather recliner with a sigh of resignation. She'd almost given up trying to get Kristin to temper her language.

Their father, Kenneth Morgan, entered the room, a late-night snack of crackers and cheese in his hand. He had clearly heard the exchange but offered no comment. He was of the opinion Kristin was just "spirited" and had been pleased with her choice of party date. He was a former football player himself, gruff but soft-hearted. Kristin was still a little miffed that he hadn't let the girls drive his BMW to the dance. But his one hard-nosed rule was that nobody else drove his BMW. It was his baby. Neither girl had ever been allowed to drive it, even under supervision. Mom had confided laughingly to Tessa that she'd never even asked.

Their home was a three-bedroom bungalow in a quiet suburb on the edge of Marina del Rey and only two miles from Venice Beach. Their house looked much like the others on the tree-lined street, except for a ghastly McMansion somebody was building on a corner lot. The Morgan house was unpretentious by upper-middle-class Los Angeles standards, but it had a great backyard with the obligatory pool and orange tree. Besides the three bedrooms, it had a large den a step down from the small kitchen, a living room that her parents used for entertaining, and a dining area big enough to hold the family's eight-seat table.

Their father went directly to settle into his favorite armchair while Tessa and Kristin took the sofa, Kristin picking up the TV remote.

"So, Tessa," her mother said, perching on the arm of Dad's chair, "now that the senior dance is over and high school is winding down, UCLA is only three months away. How does that feel?"

Her father beamed at her, also awaiting her answer.

She hadn't thought about college all day and wasn't eager to have a conversation about her future, preferring to soak in the fun of the dance and time with friends. But as always, she indulged her parents. "I'm excited," she said. "It's still school, but different. I'll have to be more ... self-motivating."

"Oh, yeah," Kristin said. "Like motivation is ever a problem with you. Seven years of college and medical school, studying until your brain pops. You'll be like a pig in sh—"

"Kristin!" their mother said reflexively, frowning. Then she turned back to Tessa. "You'll make a wonderful doctor, Tess. I know it's what you've wanted since you were able to say the word 'doctor.' Most kids change their minds about what they want to do with their life a hundred times before they settle on something." She tilted her head to one side and gave her daughter an assessing look. "I've heard that roughly sixty percent of college kids switch majors before they graduate."

"I won't," Tessa said with complete certainty. "I know what I want: a medical degree from UCLA's world-class neurology program."

"Jesus," said Kristin, rolling her eyes. "I want a drink." She heaved herself dramatically from the sofa and went to the little liquor cabinet that occupied the wall between the entertainment center and the back door. She pulled out a bottle of Scotch and poured some into a shot glass.

"Kristin, that isn't for you!" said their father. "It's for guests!"

"Take it away from me then," she said, knocking the Scotch back in a single gulp. She winced and made a face, but she swallowed and gave her father a smug look. "Guests, my butt. I know you'll be guzzling this as soon as we go to bed."

Her father glared at her. "With reason. Look, Kristin, I realize you're just flexing your adult muscles, but—"

"Is that what I'm doing, Daddy?" Kristin asked with mock sweetness. She set the glass on top of the cabinet and started to flounce toward the staircase.

"Dishwasher, please," Mom said.

Kristin turned and locked eyes with their mom, her mouth open to retort. Tessa knew the look in her mother's eyes: disappointment. She cringed. She'd do anything not to be the cause of that *look*. She remembered a time when Kristin had felt the same way. Her gaze was drawn to her sister's face where she watched a subtle battle taking place. At the end of the skirmish, Kristin crossed back to the liquor cabinet, stowed the Scotch bottle, picked up the glass, and carried it to the kitchen where she rinsed it and put it in the dishwasher.

"I'm going to bed. I'm exhausted," Tessa said, rising. She hated to admit it, but Kristin's unexpected outbursts were more draining than any party she'd ever attended.

"I'm not," Kristin said. "I think I'm going to borrow Mom's car and hit the Hollywood strip."

"No, you are not," their father said. "Especially not after that Scotch."

"Then I'll go to my bedroom and hang out on the internet. Have you seen some of the things they do on those porn sites? I didn't even know it was possible to put—"

"Stop it," their mother snapped. She rose from her chair, her expression way past disappointed and into scorched. "I know you just love to play 'little bad girl' and rile up Mommy and Daddy. Ooh, rebellion. I get it. But your life with us is coming to an end, baby girl. So maybe back off the bitch routine once in a while and find a way to enjoy being eighteen *without* hurting other people's feelings." Mom was out of the room and up the stairs before Kristin could do more than close her mouth.

"Whoa," she said, finally, with an exaggerated raising of her eyebrows. "What brought that on?" She looked from Dad to Tessa as if seeking support.

Dad ignored her and licked the salt from the crackers off his fingers.

Before heading up to bed, Tessa had a sudden urge to peek out the back sliding door into the big yard—to recall happier memories with her sister. She made her way over. A streetlight from the next street over cast light on the dark backyard, and Tessa could make out the outline of the swing set that she and Kristin had played on a decade earlier. It was faded and probably starting to rust, but their parents hadn't been able to part with it. She recalled how she and her sister would play games in the yard when they were young, tumbling on the ground and laughing. They had made hours of happy memories in the pool as well. She sighed and realized that the images were beginning to fade like the paint on that swing set. Those past moments were frozen in time.

Kristin had been so sweet then, before adolescence had set in. Puberty seemed to have changed her. She'd always been more outgoing than Tessa, and the recognition of the effect that her beauty had on others had excited her in ways Tessa didn't understand. In fact, Tessa sometimes thought it was that discovery that had catalyzed the changes. Tessa, more inclined to introspection and curiosity about things beyond herself, couldn't begin to comprehend the impulses that drove Kristin. She knew only that she missed the sister she'd once had.

She shook herself out of the unhappy reverie, recalling something her dad had told her when she'd asked about his brief career in football, which had ended in a knee injury. "Nothing lasts in this world, sweetheart. You either accept change or you get stuck in one place, unable to move forward." Tessa had always thought those were the wisest words her dad had ever given her; she had plenty of plans for moving forward.

She turned and crossed the room, heading for the staircase, pausing only to land a kiss on the top of her father's head. He smiled and said, "'Night, Tess." She whisked past Kristin, giving her an eye roll, and took the stairs two at a time up to her room.

Entering the room that she had called her own for as long as she could remember, she closed the door and paused for a moment to view the space with fresh eyes. She was, after all, now a young woman who was going to be attending college in the fall, rather than a high school kid. Noticing the poster on the wall for her favorite band, a local folk group that played clubs nearby, she realized she wouldn't be bringing it with her. Not because Kristin had deemed the band too cerebral but because Tessa's ideas for room décor would be different in college.

She glanced at the shelves filled with books, mostly science and medicine ones that she had read. The rest were science fiction, fantasy, and mystery novels—a mixture of new works and classics. She wouldn't have room to bring all of them to campus in the fall. Maybe it was time to load some new books onto the iPad her parents had given her for graduation.

The sound of her door opening interrupted her reverie. She knew instinctively it was Kristin.

"So, you're really going through with this medical school thing, huh?" Kristin asked, her tone an ambiguous cross between wistfulness and sarcasm.

"No, I thought I'd join the circus. Of course, I'm going to medical school, you dope. I've wanted it since I was, like, five."

"Well, I have bigger plans, little sis. Plans that are a lot better than anything college can help me with."

According to Kristin, she hadn't even applied to any colleges for the reason she'd just tossed out: bigger, better plans. Tessa wondered if the real reason wasn't that she was afraid she'd be rejected.

She turned and sat down on the foot of her bed, attempting to give Kristin the benefit of the doubt. "Really? And what do those plans involve, exactly?"

"Look in the mirror, Tess. Better still, look at me, because I *am* your mirror. We're beautiful. We were the most beautiful girls in our high school. Nobody else even came close."

"Uh-huh. So?"

"So ..." Kristin came to sit next to Tessa on the bed. "So, we can become models. Photographers will *beg* to take pictures of us."

Tessa laughed. "I don't know if you've noticed this, but LA is a mecca for beautiful women. They flock to it in droves."

"But they aren't all the perfect height, and they aren't twins. That's a killer gimmick, Tess. You and I on camera together. That's going to be a hard combination to beat."

Tessa made a face. Kristin was dreaming, talking like they would actually do something that crazy. "There are other twins in town."

"None of which are as gorgeous as we are."

"I wouldn't bet on that."

"I would. Besides," Kristin said with a wicked smile, "we have a secret weapon. Me."

Unsure where Kristin was going, but afraid she was hinting at something illegal or immoral, Tessa joked, "You're doing witchcraft now? Voodoo? Should I tell Pastor Avery?"

"Ha. It's not witchcraft ... exactly. But you know how persuasive I can be." Something hard and cold glittered behind Kristin's eyes.

Tessa realized her fears about her sister were grounded in reality. Suddenly uncomfortable, she attempted to end the conversation. "Maybe so. But I don't have time. I'll be at school five days a week and I'll need to spend most of my free time studying. I'll even be studying over the summer. Maybe *next* summer we can—"

Kristin's eyes flared with anger. "We're eighteen years old, Tessa. We'll never be this beautiful again in our lives. If we don't act now, we miss our window of opportunity."

Grasping that her sister was serious, she replied, "*Our* window? You can't be serious. I don't have a window of opportunity and I don't want one. You do what you want and I'll do what I want: med school. Now, I really want to go to bed."

"That's your final decision?"

"Yes! That's my final decision."

Kristin shrugged. "Okay. Say goodbye to fame and riches. You'll regret it."

"No," Tessa said. "I won't."

Kristin flounced to the door, then glanced back with a grin. "I'm willing to bet you'll change your mind about that."

She closed the door quietly behind her.

Chapter Four

Kristin ate the painkiller like it was food, food she desperately needed. She had to. She could feel the needles pumping medications into her veins, and she knew the drugs had painkillers in them, but she had too high a tolerance to meds for them to have much effect. Even the morphine, which she could trigger at intervals by pressing a button next to her pillow, barely gave her a ripple of relief. She pressed it every five minutes, but it refused to vomit out its contents until the full time had passed. Were they worried she'd become addicted? She was already addicted, to practically every drug she could coax from sleazy Hollywood star-fuckers. She suspected it was the withdrawal from those drugs that made the pain even worse.

She would have to channel the pain—redirect it into anger, into spite, into vengeance, where it would be useful.

The thick gauze on her eyes prevented her from seeing, but she knew that her mother and father had been there. And the nurses, the fucking annoying nurses, who wrapped blood pressure cuffs on her arm, clamped blood oxygen meters on her fingertips, and were only useful when they were changing the bag of chemicals on her IV drip. Put in something stronger, she wanted to tell them, but her upper lip was a numb knot of reconstructed tissue, and only nonsense syllables came out.

Tessa hadn't visited. At first Kristin hadn't understood why. Then, when snatches of conversation began to make sense, she understood; her noble sister had tried to charge in like the fucking cavalry to save her and had gotten caught in the crossfire. Her gut had roiled when she first realized that. It felt like guilt, which she hated, hated, hated. That made her angry, and she turned her anger on both the pain and the guilt.

Pain could be useful. She'd known that for a while now—at least since the ninth grade. The world had hurt her. Fine. She'd hurt it back. "Kill it with fire"—she liked that saying. And this new kind of pain would make the best fuel for her personal conflagration.

Chapter Five

THEN ...

Kristin breezed through Culver City toward Santa Monica, with the top down on her mother's convertible and her hair flying in the breeze. Her mother didn't know she had the car, but she'd be so busy with her damned book club that she wouldn't even notice her daughter was missing. Her mother rarely left the house, even to buy groceries. She ordered them over the internet, from a service that brought boxes of food from the local supermarket that dear old mom only had to unpack and stuff into the kitchen cabinets. Kristin could only figure she must have inherited her work ethic from her father. He was an executive at some company that apparently paid him well enough that they could afford to live in Los Angeles, which was becoming a more expensive proposition every day. She knew his company was a service organization, not a producer of products but an information broker. Other than that, she had no idea what her father did.

She was passing through what she considered the real LA—not the glamorous city of TV and the silver screen but row after row of strip malls, where trendy restaurants nestled wall to wall with tattoo parlors and "adult" shops where you could buy dildoes, vibrators, and poppers.

Some parts of LA were nice, but this wasn't one of them. It was a tacky suburb that called itself a city, fashioned in a cheap replica of Spanish architecture. At least the air was nice. The famous Los Angeles smog had gotten much better on most days, ever since the government had instituted strict pollution controls on vehicles. Now you could drive in a convertible without your eyes watering and burning.

One day Kristin would live in one of the really nice parts of LA, where you could see the ocean from your bedroom window. She would wake up every morning and show her perfect breasts to the blue waves of the Pacific Ocean ... and whatever guy she happened to be sharing her bed with.

She pulled up in front of a four-story office building, the kind of blocky white structure that architects turned out when their clients needed something quick and cheap. Legos for grownups. She parked the car and entered the lobby, glancing at the directory next to the elevators. The Ultimate Modeling Agency was on the third floor. It sounded like a good place to start. She'd found it on Craigslist, and they claimed to have plenty of open jobs. You had to start somewhere, she thought, and this looked like as good a place as any.

When she reached the third floor, she followed the room numbers down a hallway to the right. The office was at the far end and had a single door, with the name on a standard brown plate. She knocked, but there was no answer, so she pushed the door open.

A bored-looking girl sat behind the front desk, chewing gum and reading a *People* magazine with a reality show star on the cover who Kristin wasn't familiar with and didn't want to be familiar with. Reality TV was for the imagination challenged. The girl tucked the gum to one side of her mouth and said, "Yeah?"

"I'm Kristin Morgan. I have an appointment at one."

The girl glanced at a ledger in front of her and waved Kristin toward a door. "Okay, go on in."

"No waiting?"

"Slow day."

The sign on the door read Martina LaVecque, Talent Coordinator. A woman. That was disappointing. Kristin stepped inside anyway, hyper- aware of how damn good she looked. She'd worn a short teal skirt and a yellow tank top with a row of tiny fake pearl buttons down the front. The outfit showed off the golden tan of her skin, the gleaming gold of her hair, and plenty of cleavage and leg.

From behind a neat desk with Ikea vibes, a woman with makeup that looked baked on assessed her with a wry smile. "You must be Kris Morgan. I'm Martina. Have a seat." Martina waved at a faux velvet–covered side chair that looked like she might have stolen it from a tacky Vegas hotel.

Kristin didn't miss the appraising way the woman watched her as she sat and perused the office. The wall displayed framed headshots of both men and women, presumably the models they managed. Other frames surrounded clippings from magazines showing attractive people who also presumably worked for the agency. That was a good sign, though the clippings looked mostly like they came from clothing catalogs.

"So, you want to be a model, Kris?" Ms. LaVecque said, her gaze now on Kristin's face.

"It's Kristin," she said. "And I'm here, aren't I?" She shook her thick, wavy blonde hair, loving the feel of it on her bare shoulders.

Martina looked at her for a few seconds more. "Well, I can see that you have what it takes. You're a very attractive and charismatic young woman."

"That's damning with faint praise," Kristin said. "I'm gorgeous."

The agent's eyebrows rose. "And you have self-confidence. Also a good quality."

"So, when do I start? Can you get me an assignment today?"

Martina chuckled. "It's not quite that simple. There's a lot more to modeling than being gorgeous and confident."

"So ... what? I have to give someone a lap dance?"

The woman raised her eyebrows, simultaneously rolling her eyes. "That's not how it works. There's a process. Modeling is a skill, and a skill is something you have to learn."

"How much skill do I need to hold a bottle of perfume and smile for a camera?"

"A great deal more. You need poise. You need to understand how the camera sees you. You need to be able to follow a photographer's instructions."

"I've taken a lot of selfies."

Martina's lip twitched, alerting Kristin to the fact that she was inwardly laughing at her. "Well, I'll note that. But before you start, you'll need to take some courses. Our clients expect expertise, and that's something we can teach you."

Kristin, nettled by the older woman's attitude, wanted to say something scathing about the slim likelihood that a woman obviously in her fifties with a face that looked like a drag queen had died on it could teach her anything about how to be beautiful.

She didn't. She bit her tongue and said, "Okay, when are the classes? Can I take them online?"

The woman pulled a booklet from her desk and placed it where Kristin could reach it. "This is our list of courses. You'll need to take all of them before you can go out on assignment."

Kristin stared at the book. "There are a lot of pages in that."

"If you have trouble reading ..."

"I read just fine," Kristin said, snapping up the book. It began with some pages of bullshit about the modeling "art" and the many advantages of working with the Ultimate Modeling Agency. Finally, she came to the list of courses. There were fifteen of them, each described in great detail. The Camera and You. How to Use Makeup to Your Advantage. Photographer Knows Best.

Then she looked at the prices. Each course was $200 plus sales tax. In LA, sales tax was something you needed a separate bank account for. She did the math and calculated that the courses would come to well over $3,000.

"Are you freaking insane?" Kristin said. "Why should you be charging me when I could be out there now making ten times this much for you?"

"I told you. That's not how it works, Kristin. You think you have what it takes, and you do. But you're raw material. We'll mold you into something perfect, someone who's worthy to be on the covers of magazines."

"I don't see any magazine covers on your wall. Just some ads for underwear and kitchen products."

"You'd be very good in ads for underwear."

"Honey, a picture of me in my underwear would give the cameraman a boner. Hell, it would give the *camera* a boner. Neither of them would survive the shoot."

"You know, there's such a thing as overconfidence."

Kristin threw the booklet back down on the desk. "This is total bullshit. I'm ready to start modeling right now. And you damn well know it."

Kristin expected an explosion, but it never came. Martina LeVecque's lips twisted sardonically, and her eyes glittered with suppressed emotion that Kristin couldn't read. Maybe she just didn't want to ruin all that makeup.

Kristin stood up and headed for the door. "You're making a huge mistake." She tossed the words over her shoulder.

"And you have a lot to learn about how the world works," the older woman said.

Kristin paused at the door to scoff. "I'm gonna learn how the world works from your stupid courses?"

"Whether you take our courses or someone else's, you need to learn marketable skills."

"No, *Martina*. I've *got* marketable skills, and you're letting them walk right out your door."

Martina shrugged. "Then don't walk out."

Kristin laughed and left the room, not even closing the door behind her. The girl at the front desk didn't bother to look up as she sailed past.

In the hallway, Kristin leaned against the wall for a moment, fighting her anger under control. The nerve of that bitch. Asking somebody like her to pitch in $3,000 just so she could do underwear ads. She was better than that. She was so much better than that.

She strode back to the elevators and pushed the down button. A middle-aged man in an expensive suit walked up beside her and grinned.

"I saw you coming out of the Ultimate Modeling Agency."

"Oh, no. Now the whole world knows."

"They're a scam, you know. They'll take anybody. They don't make money off the modeling. They make money off the courses."

"No, really?" She slathered the words with sarcasm.

"They don't have any credibility. You'd have to hustle up the work on your own."

"Happens I'm good at that."

"I bet you are," he said, leering a little.

Okay, that was creepy. "So, where do you recommend I go?"

"Skip the agencies. Go directly to a photographer. I think you could convince one to work with you. Hell, if I were a photographer, you would have convinced me by now."

"So, who's the top photographer in town?"

"Oh, you don't want to go to the top. Those guys already have stables of models."

"Then they can add a new horse to the stable. A thoroughbred." She struck a pose, head up, chest out.

"You're pretty sure of yourself, honey. Fine. If you think you can pull it off, then go to Gianni DeLuca. He's the biggest name in the fashion business right now."

"DeLuca, huh? You wouldn't happen to have any connections with him."

"Sorry. Wish I did."

They got on the elevator together. When they got off in the downstairs lobby, he cleared his throat and said, "Do you have plans for dinner tonight?"

"Yep. Kung Pao chicken straight from the microwave."

"Well, I do have some pull at one of the best restaurants in town. I can get us a table for this evening. What do you say? Have dinner with me as a favor for telling you about DeLuca?"

Kristin looked him up and down. His hair was thinning and the skin around his mouth was starting to wrinkle, probably from too many cigarettes. Kristin made a mental note to stop smoking dope. Bad for the skin. Oh, and he was wearing a wedding ring. She felt her skin crawl.

"Okay, I'll do you a favor," she said. The man's face brightened.

"Look me over real good." She turned slowly around, turning the movement into a sinuous dance.

"Oh, I am. I like what I see." He grinned at her with undisguised lust. "Now you have my permission to think about me when you fuck your wife tonight." She gave him a little wave. "Buh-bye!"

Chapter Six

NOW ...

Tessa was aware of movement. She was lying on a gurney being wheeled down a hallway. She heard the rhythmic thrum of the wheels, saw fuzzy pulses and streaks of light overhead as she passed beneath light fixtures. She was either on her way to another surgery or on her way back from one. She'd lost track of her own comings and goings.

She tried not to imagine doctors hovering over her, cutting into her face, removing pieces, rearranging them, repairing and reattaching nerves. Despite their work, the entire right side of her face was numb—or absent. Maybe nothing was left of it. Could sulfuric acid do that? She didn't think so.

Her face was likely numb from the medication, the anesthetic. At least that's what she told herself. She'd heard the doctors say that nerves took time to repair themselves and reestablish their networks. Or she thought she had. She might just as easily have recalled it from a lecture or a textbook ... or a science fiction movie.

She was acutely aware that when the local anesthetic wore off, the vaguely remembered pain might return. She hoped it would. Anything would be better than this wretched numbness she'd been feeling for what seemed like an eternity.

Was it spreading? Was it moving from the right side of her face—the side the acid had splashed—to the left? Would it eventually take her tongue and her voice box, her heart and her lungs? If it did, would she die? She almost hoped that was the case. Better dead than life without feeling.

She chastised herself for the dark thoughts and tried to shut them down. She imagined they were a tap she could twist closed, cutting off the chaotic flow. They were replaced by questions: Where were her parents? And Daniel? Surely, they'd been to the hospital to visit her.

And Kristin. Where was Kristin? Had she done enough to save her?

Wracking her brain, she tried to remember the acid attack, to strip it of its nightmare quality. How much of the corrosive liquid had reached Kristin? She couldn't recall, but she feared that her sister was also somewhere in this hospital, every bit as helpless and confused as she was.

Chapter Seven

THEN ...

UCLA was everything Tessa had hoped it would be and more. She stood on a high stone terrace looking down on a large quad covered with carefully trimmed grass and elegant trees, crisscrossed by walkways. The open area was surrounded by gorgeous Romanesque buildings—the original center of the campus that dated from 1929. There was so much history here. Or at least as much history as you could find in Los Angeles, where the 1950s were considered the classical period.

Tessa had been stunned and fascinated when her family had visited the East Coast to find still-existing Civil War battlefields and buildings from Colonial times. Even more intriguing, a friend who had visited England told her about seeing graffiti dating from the 1500s and putting his hand on a pub, still in use, built in 1350. LA clearly didn't compare to that, but its history was fun to absorb anyway.

Below her, in the quad, students strolled or hurried to their classes. She hefted her stack of textbooks and hurried down to join them—very carefully. She knew she was carrying too many books and should have bought a backpack or some kind of courier bag to lug them around. The backpack she'd used in high school was old and frayed and announced that she was a Hufflepuff. She'd be embarrassed to be seen on campus with it.

Halfway across the quad, the pile of books teetered, and her biology text fell off the top. As she was trying to decide how she could pick it up without dropping the rest of the books, someone stooped down and picked it up for her.

Her helper was a strikingly handsome boy about her age whose graceful features were Asian blended with something else—Caucasian or Latino, maybe—a fairly common circumstance on the West Coast. When he smiled at her, she noticed he had nice dimples. "Biology major?"

"Uh, yeah. I'm in the premed program."

"Wow, planning to be a doctor. I'm impressed."

She liked his voice. It was a warm tenor, confident without sounding macho or cocky. And the hint of shyness in his eyes made her feel comfortable.

"So, what are *you* majoring in?" she asked, hoping to keep him talking while she walked several steps onto the grass to find a tree to lean her stack of books against, relieving her of some of their weight.

"Engineering. I plan to go into the tech industry when I graduate. Here, give me a couple of those books while we're chatting. They look heavy."

"Thanks," she said as he took the top three books off the stack. "You could get a job with Elon Musk."

He laughed. "Oh, I plan to *be* Elon Musk." His eyes twinkled when he said it, so it didn't seem arrogant.

"My name's Daniel Takashi," he said.

"Tessa Morgan." They giggled as they shook pinkies because that was all they could manage, given the stack of books in each of their arms.

"What class are you headed to, Tessa?" he asked.

"Professor Torres. Principles of Mathematics."

He broke into a wide grin. "That's where I'm going too. Mind if I tag along?"

"Not at all. Race you to the lecture hall?" she said with a twinkle.

He gave her a narrow-eyed glance. "I would love to see you run while carrying that stack of books. Better idea: how about if I walk with you and help you get your books to class. Then, in the future, you might want to consider getting a backpack." He smiled light-heartedly.

"Yes. Got it. A backpack is on my list of things to get. And thank you." He took a couple more books so he had half of the stack, and they walked briskly past the classically designed Royce Hall to enter a more modern building with open-air staircases and walkways surrounding the rooms. The lecture hall was large, arranged like a movie theater with arching rows of seating. It was also mostly full. Tessa spotted a single seat down front—her favorite place to be in any given classroom.

Daniel caught her eyeing it and grimaced. "You're a front-row creature too, aren't you?"

"Afraid so," she told him.

"I'd offer to thumb wrestle you for the spot, but I'm too much of a gentleman. You take it. I'll find something up here." He gave an exaggerated sigh, handed back Tessa's textbooks, and scooted into the third row from the top.

"Thanks again!" Smiling, Tessa hurried down the stairs to snag the coveted seat. She set the books on the floor, imprisoning them between her legs.

Professor Torres looked to be in his early fifties, and his lecture style was dry but clear. She found herself struggling to keep up with him as she typed notes into her iPad. She noticed that several students had placed their phones or other devices next to the podium to record the lecture so they could transcribe it later. She'd have to try that next time. Her typos were multiplying like bunnies.

Her mind kept wandering to the boy she knew was sitting eight or nine rows above her. Daniel Takashi. He was really easy on the eyes, but that wasn't what had captured her attention. She felt as if she already knew him. Maybe he felt the same way about her. She rejected the thought—drop-kicked it right out of her head. She was being overimaginative. It was her first day in a strange environment; she was just looking for an anchor, that was all.

Having almost succeeded in banishing him from her thoughts, she was surprised to find Daniel waiting for her outside the lecture hall.

"Got another class?" he asked. "I mean, next period."

"No," she said. "I've got a free period before biology."

"I've got some time too. Want to grab something to eat or drink? There's a coffee house just past the library."

"Actually, I was planning to go to the library and study."

"The café has baked goods."

"Oh, well, baked goods ... forget studying," she said and grinned. The Kerckhoff Coffee House was a venerable establishment of the UCLA campus. It had baked goods galore, plus sandwiches, salads, and a plethora of coffee drinks. Daniel got a croissant and "candy coffee" as he called it; Tessa indulged herself with a cinnamon roll and plain iced coffee. "I shouldn't do this," she moaned, biting into the gooey, sweet pastry. "I'll have to give up lunch."

"Nonsense," said Daniel. "You're going to be walking miles every day just to get from one class to another. This is a huge campus. You could probably eat three more of those and still not gain an ounce."

She nodded, gravely. "I'm going to choose to believe you, Mr. Engineer."

He rewarded her with a smile. He had an amazing smile.

They sat together for a full hour. Tessa found Daniel easy to talk to, knowledgeable, and willing to listen. He seemed at least as interested in what she had to say as in talking about himself, and she learned that she was right about his genealogy; his dad was of Japanese descent, and his mother was second-generation Polish-American. He had grown up in the San Fernando Valley and had been a marching band geek who still played a "mean tenor sax."

"Hey, I played saxophone too!" said Tessa. "Alto sax, though. And I don't play it so much anymore. But I do still have my saxophone at home somewhere."

"Duet!" cried Daniel. The two of them laughed.

When they finished, compared schedules, and noted that they had only the one class together, Tessa picked up her stack of books and said, "I guess I'll see you Friday in Torres's lecture."

Daniel eyed the stack critically. "You've got a bit of a walk to biology. I'm gonna suggest we stop in at the campus store over there and get you that backpack. If you can't afford it," he added quickly, "I can front you the money and you can pay me back."

"Oh, I couldn't—"

"It's either that or I help you schlep these weighty tomes to your next class ... which will make me late to mine, which could halt the progress of Western civilization."

She laughed. "Plan A then, I guess."

He didn't leave it at helping her pick out a backpack; he then asked her if she wanted to go to a movie that evening. "The film department is having a Hitchcock festival. Different movie every Wednesday night. They're showing *Vertigo*. Have you ever seen it?"

"No."

"Then you have to. It's one of Hitchcock's best films."

"I love *The Birds*, so ... yeah, sure."

They exchanged phone info and Tessa waved goodbye. Despite the weight of her textbooks, she found herself smiling all the way to her biology lecture.

###

A week and a half later, Tessa came home from school to find Kristin in a frenzy, dancing around and practically bouncing with excitement. She had spread several rows of magazines atop the living room coffee table. "I've done it, Tess," she crowed. "I've nailed us a spectacular future."

Tessa set her backpack on one end of the sofa and sat down next to it. "I told you, Krist. I already have a spectacular future planned."

"Not like this, you don't. I've gotten us an audition with Gianni DeLuca."

"Johnny who?"

Kristin rolled her eyes, then grimaced and admitted, "Okay, I didn't know who he was at first either. But look at his work. He's the greatest photographer in the world."

"I doubt he's as good as Ansel Adams."

"I have no idea who that is." Kristin picked up a copy of *Vogue*. "Look at that cover. Gianni photographed it."

Tessa gave Kristin a coy look. "Wow, you're on a first-name basis and you've only just met the guy."

"Tess, *look* at the *cover*."

She did. It was impressive. Striking, even. "It's very nicely done." Kristin grabbed a copy of *Elle*. "He did this one too."

"Also very nice."

"These are more than nice. They're art. Fashion art. He's worked with Iman."

She flipped open a copy of *GQ* to a spread of black-and-white photos of men modeling clothing. "He did all of these pictures. Look at the poses, the lighting, the composition."

"Guy clearly knows what he's doing. But it's clear he has his pick of models."

"Not like us. Not twins. We have to be at his studio at ten in the morning."

Tessa laughed. "I can't. I have a class."

"So, skip one tomorrow. This is too important."

"We're not likely to get a job out of it anyway. And even if we did—" Kristin did a full body shrug. "You're too negative. Think positive!

We're going to get this. I promise."

"How can you promise something like that?"

"Let's just say I did a little networking. You're going to thank me for this."

"Kris, I *can't* ..."

"Yes, you can. I don't want to have to beg you, Tess, but this is very important to me. As much as you want to be a sawbones, I want this. You can help me get it." Tessa opened her mouth to protest, but Kristin bulled her way through. "C'mon, Tess. Help me get my foot in the door. Then once I'm in, you can go back to playing doctor."

Tessa didn't bother objecting to the idea that she was *playing* doctor. Kristin could be so frustrating. But she was also persuasive. She always had been. Right now, she was giving Tessa her patented This Means Everything To Me facial expression and, for one moment, she reminded Tessa of a younger Kristin. The Kristin who'd seemed like the other half of her own self.

"All right. I'll cut English class in the morning and get the assignment from the teacher later. But you'll owe me a favor."

"This *will* be the favor. You'll see."

Tessa grimaced. "I need to grab a quick shower. I have a date tonight." Kristin cocked an eyebrow. "With a boy?"

"No, with a howler monkey. Yes, with a boy." She had told only her mom about Daniel, and Mom knew how to keep a secret.

"You got asked out a lot in high school, but you didn't date much."

"High school boys didn't interest me ... possibly because *I* didn't really interest them, if you know what I mean."

"Is he cute?"

Tessa grinned. "Yeah. Very."

"I'm happy for you, Tess," Kristin said, but then she gave Tessa a stern look. "Don't stay out late, though. You've got to look good for the audition. And"—she shouted after Tessa as she turned and headed for the staircase—"do your best makeup tomorrow!"

As Tessa and Daniel left Royce Hall, she was literally spinning with excitement. "That movie! It was so ... so romantic!"

"If you say so," Daniel said, laughing.

She swatted him, then indulged in a few more pirouettes. "And that final scene, with Cary Grant and Ingrid Bergman, where she's sick and Cary picks her up off the bed. Hitchcock *spins* the camera around them so you can see how close their faces are to each other. They never even kissed, yet it was the sexiest thing I've ever seen!"

"Agreed. That scene was a trick Hitchcock used to get around the film code. There was a limit on how long you could hold a kiss, but by not letting their lips touch, he was able to linger on the shot as long as he wanted."

"It was amazing. The chemistry between Grant and Bergman was like nothing I've ever seen. It just oozed off the screen." Tessa stopped spinning and slipped her arm around Daniel's waist. "Thank you for taking me to that. It was the best movie I've ever seen. I like *Notorious* even better than *Vertigo*."

They're showing *Rear Window* next week."

"Is that sexy?"

"Not as sexy as this, but it's a pretty good film."

"Then we'll go. I think you're going to turn me into a film buff."

"You *should* be a film buff. Everybody who lives in Los Angeles should be a film buff. You know"—he averted his eyes briefly—"you're every bit as beautiful as Ingrid Bergman."

Tessa felt her face flushing with heat. Impulsively, she gave Daniel a quick peck on the lips. "That was for Cary Grant and Ingrid Bergman. Who never got to kiss."

Chapter Eight

NOW ...

I n one of her waking moments, Kristin had made the mistake of mumbling something to her surgeon about hearing the whir of the bone saws and the clicking of the scalpels in the OR. The doctor had patiently explained—as he would to a small, dimwitted child—that under general anesthetic, she would have heard nothing. She didn't contest that, but she knew he was lying. Men always lied to women.

They'd given her a local anesthetic after the surgery to help with the pain that the other drugs didn't seem to touch. Yet somehow, she missed the pain. It had become a friend to her, a companion. She recalled a line about saying hello to darkness and calling it your friend. Wasn't that a line from an old song? Who was it—Simon and somebody.

She wondered why they were even bothering with another surgery now. Clearly it wasn't working. Doctors were all quacks, incompetents who claimed to understand mysteries other people didn't. Tessa had planned to be a doctor. If Tessa could become a doctor, anybody could.

Fucking Tessa.

The pain had tightened Kristin's resolve, focused it on the people she wanted to hurt for hurting her. She would have hurt the doctors if she could have seen them. If not for the fact that the upper part of her face had been ruined, if her eyes weren't still swaddled in bandages, she would have struck out at them for keeping her in so much pain. She only knew she'd escaped complete blindness because she could see light seeping through the gauze. So, they had saved her sight. Big deal. She was still certain these doctors were incompetent.

She added them to the vengeance list she'd been compiling, definitely in the top ten. Kurt Morrison was at the top of the list, along with Alexei Dvorak and his executive staff, but over the hours she'd spent making the list, one name had slowly made its way toward the top, where it would share a throne with Kurt.

Fucking Tessa.

Tessa, who'd never wanted a life in fashion or movies to begin with, had somehow managed to take Kristin's prize and sabotage her yet again. With her sparkling talent, with her stupid I-can-have-it-all naivete. If Tessa hadn't ...

She was confused for a moment about what it was Tessa had done, then she remembered: They'd made an agreement. Tessa would help Kristin get her foot in the door, then she'd go back to school and her insipid boyfriend. But she hadn't done that. She'd stuck around long enough to become a star in her own right. In Kristin's book, that was a betrayal.

Chapter Nine

Kristin arrived for DeLuca's audition at nine forty-five a.m. and counted seven women who had gotten there before her—seven beautiful women sitting nervously or confidently or hopefully in folding chairs set up along the wall. Kristin defined beauty relative to herself; by that standard all of these women were Plain Janes.

She was annoyed that Tessa wasn't there yet. Probably coming by Uber. She'd no doubt been in class when Kristin had borrowed her mother's convertible and driven to Beverly Hills. Damned if she was going to let Tessa's study habits hold her up. Who the hell has a class at eight-freaking-thirty in the morning anyway?

DeLuca's studio was in a large loft, or what passed as a loft in Los Angeles, which is to say a large, square room with floors of polished concrete and water pipes and steel beams deliberately visible in both walls and high ceiling. LA lofts were modeled after New York lofts, which came by the name honestly; they were literally constructed in the loft or attic space of turn-of-the-twentieth-century buildings that artists had made trendy by turning them into inexpensive studios. DeLuca's fake loft had probably cost a fortune.

His had a large platform in the center of the floor, with several backdrops positioned strategically across it and lighting equipment mounted at every conceivable angle. A team of assistants were positioning cameras and setting dimmers to what Kristin assumed were DeLuca's preferred brightness levels. God forbid that an artist of DeLuca's stature should do grunt work.

Tessa burst through the door at four minutes before nine, a backpack slung over her shoulder and her hair artfully windblown. She was, Kristin noted approvingly, wearing the clingy mini dress Kristin had insisted on. With a front zipper and a low, square neckline, it matched her own in all but color. Hers was teal; Tessa's was a deep plum. Back to the matchy-matchy days of primary school—but this time for a distinct reason. Tessa dropped her backpack beside the last of the folding chairs, next to the one Kristin had staked out, and proceeded to pull a large textbook out of it.

"That had better be the *Dummies Guide to Modeling*," Kristin growled. "Who brings a textbook to an audition?"

"A college student. It's my biology text. I've got required reading." Kristin peered at her sister as though she were a biology specimen. "Focus, Tess. Our job today is to look beautiful, not like you've got an actual brain in your head. One that you use."

Tessa looked at her for a moment, then tossed her head with a chirpy, "I'm not *really* a dumb blonde. I just *play* one on TV. Uh-yuh?" The wisecrack was delivered with an exaggerated Valley Girl accent.

Before Kristin could recover from her surprise, the man himself appeared from out of a back room. The time was exactly ten a.m. He wore a tight, open-necked shirt calculated to show off his muscles. Gianni DeLuca's glare of deadly seriousness only enhanced his Mediterranean good looks. He walked to the front of the platform and stared out over the aspiring fashion plates. His perfect upper lip curled. "*Buon giorno*, ladies," he said, his voice booming and fierce. "I know that you think that you're the luckiest women in the world because you're auditioning for me. Well, I have bad news for you. Most of you are going to be crap. You think you're beautiful, but you're only average here. This is Los Angeles, ladies. Women who are merely beautiful end up becoming waitresses and escorts. You either steam up my camera lenses or you go find a photographer who specializes in catalogs for housewives. I wish to work with only the finest models in the world."

"We wasted our time coming here," Tessa murmured, looking up from her book.

"O ye of infinitesimally little faith," Kristin murmured. "We'll do fine."

"I don't know where you get your confidence," Tessa said. "And I don't know where you get your pessimism."

Kristin crossed her legs and waited impatiently. Naturally, DeLuca called the first woman from the opposite end of the row to go before the cameras. He snapped a few pictures of her on a digital camera and reviewed the results on a small monitor.

"You have the presence of a horseradish. Get out of my studio. Don't come back."

Looking as though her dearest friend had just died, the young woman ran from the stage, scooped up her purse, and headed for the door, hugging it to her wounded heart.

Tessa gaped at the photographer with a horrified expression on her face. "What kind of monster is this guy?"

"The best kind of monster," Kristin said. "The kind that makes people famous."

Tessa turned her glare on Kristin. "That woman isn't going to be famous. She's going to go off and slit her wrists."

"She'll get a job doing underwear ads," Kristin said ironically. "I hear they're big business now."

The next woman stood up and went through the same process. DeLuca crushed her with another withering put-down and sent her from the room, literally sobbing.

"This is how you want to make a living?" Tessa asked. "Having your ego crushed by a human steamroller? Or watching him crush other people right in front of you?"

"I don't steamroll easily. Trust me, Tess. I've got this covered." One by one the women stepped up on the stage, and one after another

DeLuca sent them away in various stages of borderline psychosis and rage. One started berating him so vehemently that DeLuca had a pair of assistants physically remove her.

"You're a pig," she snarled as they herded her to the door. "I bet you treat your mom like this."

DeLuca was unperturbed. It was obviously something he was used to doing and also something he seemed to enjoy doing. It was like an episode of *American Idol* when Simon Cowell had been a judge. The withering dismissal was his joy in life.

Finally, and inevitably, he arrived at Kristin and Tessa. Kristin hung back a bit to let him get a good look at her sister, then followed at a leisurely pace to stand beside her. DeLuca appraised them at some length, his brows disappearing beneath the lock of raven hair that fell across his forehead.

"So, a twin act. Unusual ... but not unheard of."

He gestured for his assistants to arrange the backdrops to accommodate both girls at once, then adjusted his camera for a wider angle shot. "So, come on up," he said with none of the brusqueness he'd shown to the other model hopefuls. He gestured at the low stage.

Kristin caught the surprise on her twin's face and smiled secretly at it.

"Stand next to each other over there," he said, gesturing at the backdrop. "Just look at the camera. I want to see how you look together." Kristin and Tessa did as told.

Kristin's inner confidence was aglow, and she hoped that some of it would warm Tessa's mood. Her sister already seemed to be more relaxed as DeLuca snapped several photos, then paused to peer into the camera's view screen.

"Yes," he said. "It is remarkable how much alike you are, feature for feature. And yet, there are these subtle and telling differences. Your eyes are the same color, your mouths the same shape, yet you are ... different. A paradox. One steel; one ... velvet."

"Is that bad?" Tessa asked.

"Not at all," DeLuca said. "It's the sort of thing that will keep the viewer staring at the photograph and wondering how identical twins can still be unique individuals. In fact, I'd like to exaggerate the contrast between you. You on the right—Kristin, isn't it?—show the camera that you distrust it, even disdain it. And you, the other one ..."

"Tessa."

"Tessa, show the camera that you see a breathtakingly full moon in its lens ... or a breathtaking man, as you prefer."

Kristin gave the camera a face of sheer contempt. This expression was something she was very good at. She'd been perfecting it for years. She glanced at Tessa, whose face combined wonder and joy. DeLuca had certainly chosen the right expressions for them.

He snapped several more pictures, then studied the viewer closely. "Yes, yes, wonderful contrast. It's amazing. You are like two sides of the same coin. This, I could find useful in my work."

Kristin gave Tessa a sidelong glance and was delighted to see frank amazement on her face. Maybe she would trust her big sister's instincts after this.

"Now wrap your arms around each other like lovers," the photographer instructed. "Intertwine. You are a two-headed beast, your eyes filled with passion."

"*That's* ick—" Tessa started to say, but Kristin cut her short.

"Do what the man says, Tessa. The photographer knows best." Kristin smiled internally at the irony that she had actually learned something from that stupid model agency she'd visited.

Kristin faced Tessa, draped her arms over Tessa's shoulders, and wound her right leg around Tessa's left. After a moment of hesitation, Tessa wrapped her arms around her sister's waist.

"Look at me!" DeLuca commanded, then snapped a series of images. "Look at each other!" he cried and snapped some more. Then he lifted the camera off the tripod and moved about them; *click, click, click, click, click*. When he was done, he stared at the viewer with what Kristin interpreted as naked lust. She felt laughter building in her throat and swallowed it.

DeLuca was nodding, smiling, all but licking his chops. "Oh, yes, *yes*. The sensuality is almost shocking. *I* am shocked. And I am, you know, a connoisseur of the sexy, the arousing. You girls are not merely hot; you are volcanic. Even fully clothed."

Tessa had stepped out of the embrace and looked like she was ready to vomit. "Is that something we'd have to do—"

Kristin cut her off. "What my sister is saying is that we'll do anything you ask of us, Mr. DeLuca. We admire your work very much and trust your instincts. If you'll have us."

DeLuca looked offended. "How could I not have you? You are perfection like I've never seen. You will work for me and exclusively for me."

"We ... we will?" Tessa stammered. "I'm in college. I don't know if I can ..."

"Tessa's a college student, but she won't let that stop her from working with you, Mr. DeLuca. I guarantee it." She turned her eyes to Tessa. "I know my sister. She's reliable as reliable gets, and a total work horse."

DeLuca laughed. "You call your beautiful sister a horse? She is a gazelle. And your guarantee is good enough for me. I will try to accommodate your schedule, Tessa, but you will have much work to do here. I have a vast number of things to teach you. You know I work with many star models, but I think you and your sister could eclipse them all. Now, you may go back to your ordinary lives and I will assemble a schedule of shoots to build your portfolio." He made a shooing gesture. *"Presto! Presto!"*

Tessa wandered back to her seat in a daze with Kristin trailing her and grinning from ear to ear. "How did that happen? Those other women were all gorgeous. They were every bit as beautiful as we are."

"No, they weren't, and you know it. We have that special something, Tess. We have 'It.' We've always had it. I see big, beautiful, bright things in our future."

Tessa picked up her backpack and looked inside. "My biology textbook. It's gone."

"Guess somebody stole it. Probably the competition. Though God knows why anybody would want to read about blood and guts."

"It's about cellular metabolism and proteins—"

"I don't really give a fuck. Pick up another when you get a chance."

"Do you know how much those books cost?"

"Do you know how much we'll make working with DeLuca? Buy out the whole biology section at the school bookstore."

"I have to get to class," Tessa said, turning.

Kristin felt a prickly ball of irritation form in her stomach. "Hey, look happy, damn it," Kristin said, placing a hand on Tessa's shoulder. "We just became professional models."

"Maybe, but I still plan to become a neurologist. Hey, maybe I can model in a lab coat." She offered Kristin a conciliatory smile.

Kristin shrugged. "Yeah. Like modern Barbie."

Tessa hefted her backpack and rushed out the door. Kristin calmly reached into her oversized purse and pulled out the biology text. She heaved it into a trash can.

"Kristin," DeLuca said from behind her, "come into my office, if you would."

"Of course, Gianni."

Tessa followed him through a door with a frosted and pebbled glass panel that bore his name in large gold letters. The room behind the door was equal parts office and parlor—luxurious, if a bit cluttered. Photo books and journals, fashion magazines, and models' portfolios were stacked on the huge kidney-shaped desk, strewn across the identically shaped coffee table and arranged haphazardly on shelves alongside antique cameras.

"Close the door, won't you?" He moved languidly to sit on a large, ornate love seat in the parlor section of the room, then leaned back with a smile and spread his legs. He gazed up at Kristin with desire glazing his dark eyes. "I believe we were going to resume where we left off yesterday."

"Of course."

Kristin moved with a cat's grace to stand in the middle of the compass rose carpet that marked the center of the room. She unzipped the front of her dress and pulled the straps off her shoulders. Then she let it drop smoothly onto the floor. She was completely naked underneath, her skin golden in the light of the absurd chandelier directly overhead and a trio of wall sconces.

She let DeLuca stare at her for a long, admiring moment. His eyes were hot with lust, and she could clearly see the erection growing under the zipper of his pants.

Kristin smiled. That had to be painful. "Believe me, Gianni," she said. "This is going to be even better than it was the last time."

Chapter Ten

NOW ...

Tessa lay in her hospital bed in the Johns Hopkins burn clinic in Baltimore, half dreaming, half conscious. That seemed appropriate, as she had half a face. She could see out of one eye now, though the drugs made her sight wonky and foggy. Gauze still covered the right side of her face. Her cheeks were no longer completely numb, but whatever feeling she had was uneven and uncertain—as if some of her skin had been replaced with latex or Silly Putty.

She was horrified by the sudden impulse to giggle at the image. It wasn't funny. She'd lifted her hand to the pressure mask exactly once, and the contours seemed all wrong. The right side of her nose didn't match the left, and her lips were puffy and swollen with collagen. What was under that mask wasn't her.

She was half Tessa ... and half not Tessa.

"You'll get more sensation back as you heal," the head of her surgical team in the burn unit had told her. "Nerves automatically begin to rebuild and repair their networks, and with the new methodologies, you'll be able to grow a great deal of new skin on your own over the scaffolding the surgeons created."

I don't believe you, she thought but didn't say the words out loud. Her parents were there and she didn't want to upset them. She wondered idly how long she'd been in the hospital; her sense of time had become unmoored.

"What if the ... the scaffold process doesn't work?" That was Mom. "If that doesn't work, the doctors can return to traditional skin grafts using skin from her thigh. That would require another surgery, of course," the doctor explained. "But I wouldn't worry about that. We're already seeing good progress."

"Then," said her mother, "she'll look like she did before? The right side of her face will match the left?"

"No. That's still a bit beyond our reach. The acid destroyed enough tissue that we had to remove cartilage from that side of her nose. The cosmetic surgeons did a great job of replacing it, but there will always be some irregularities and scarring and some ... lines of demarcation between the natural skin and the new growth."

Lines of demarcation? A sudden image flashed through her mind of herself as the Bride of Frankenstein with a crazy quilt of stitches and scars around the new tissue. The image was equal parts horrifying and ridiculous. Again, she fought the impulse to giggle ... and sob.

"The good news is," the doctor went on, her voice buoyant and positive, "her body will produce that new skin, so there's no chance of rejection."

Rejection. The word lodged in Tessa's mind like a splinter. She did not deceive herself; she would face rejection. Not from her mom and dad, of course. They would always love her and even find her beautiful. That was the nature of parenthood. The acid might have destroyed half her face, but it had not touched her soul. She was still Tessa Morgan, but she was no longer Tessa Morgan the model, the actress, the star.

The idea of being rejected by Hollywood did not frighten or disturb her nearly as much as the knowledge that when the bandages finally came off, she would have to face being rejected by Daniel. She doubted he would want to marry a half-Tessa, nor would she want him to.

Chapter Eleven

Walking into a lecture hall was usually a thrill for Tessa. Walking into her biology lecture ten minutes late made her wish that she had Harry Potter's Cloak of Invisibility. She'd find her seat, then pull off the cloak and pretend she'd been there all along. The thought made her smile. But, lacking the famous cloak, she gave up hope of taking her usual seat down front and instead slipped quietly into the back row, uncomfortably aware that Professor Arnett looked directly at her as she sat down.

When the class was over, he dashed any illusions she may have had about invisibility.

"Ms. Morgan, do you have a class to get to?"

That stopped her in her tracks. "Uh, no sir. I have a free period."

"Good. Please come see me in my office."

Tessa's nerves were already on edge from the audition, despite it having been successful—or maybe *because* it had been successful—and now she was buzzing with a weird mixture of excitement and anxiety. She shouldn't have cared about the damned audition or the arrogant photographer or the idea of being a fashion model, yet on some level she did. The idea was disquieting. Maybe she was vainer than she'd realized.

The professor gave her a stoic glance as she followed him into his office. He sat behind his desk and looked up at her over the rims of his glasses, his long, angular face absurdly sober. Lugubrious. That was the word. He was like Eeyore from Winnie-the-Pooh, but with wire-rim glasses.

"Miss Morgan, your participation and work in this class so far have been an early bright spot in an otherwise gloomy landscape. I was beginning to hope I saw potential in you. Please, tell me this tardiness is not the beginning of a slide into mediocrity." His deep, slow baritone was as Eeyorish as his face.

Stunned, Tessa stammered out an apology. "I ... I'm sorry, Dr. Arnett. But I was off campus. I'd promised my sister I'd help her with a ... a job application."

That had the virtue of being mostly true. She *had* been trying to help Kristin get work. She wasn't about to mention what kind of work or what their "job application" had consisted of. He'd think she wasn't serious about her education.

"Ah. A noble cause," he said, sounding as if he didn't find it all that noble ... or simply didn't believe a word of it. He did not quite roll his eyes. Absurdly, Tessa half expected him to launch into Inigo Montoya's soliloquy on true love from *A Princess Bride.* She fought to keep from grinning.

"I don't take attendance, strictly speaking," her professor went on. "This isn't high school. You're an adult now. Attendance is your responsibility. Do you understand?"

"Yes, sir."

He studied her for a moment, and she was struck by how different his regard was from Gianni DeLuca's. He sighed. "I understand that a young woman of your attractiveness must have an exciting social life. For the sake of your grades, don't let that get in the way of your studies." Well. Prejudices apparently came in all forms. Tessa opened her mouth to say, "I won't, sir," but what came out was. "Sir, I assure you my social life consists of one male friend and a sister who ... well, let's just say she's high maintenance. I don't party. I don't do drugs. I don't drink. Bingeing, for me, means maxing out my library card. If I was the

kind of book my 'cover' suggests, I wouldn't be at UCLA. Sir."

She took a step back, aghast at what she'd somehow found the temerity to say.

The professor's expression didn't change, except for a tiny ripple of his impressive brows. "So noted. You're premed. That's very ambitious. And I've seen your transcripts. Your high school grades are impressive, and the notes from your teachers are all glowing."

"I strive to do my best, Professor."

"Then keep striving and you'll do fine." He settled back in his chair, seeming to relax. "College life gets the better of too many students. Despite rumors to the contrary, I was young once myself, and I remember what it was like. There's so much going on, so many distractions. But UCLA's medical school has stringent requirements. You'll need strong grades and recommendations from your teachers to get into it."

"I know, sir."

"Forgive me, Ms. Morgan, if I've underestimated you. But I'd rather nip carelessness in the bud and risk alienating you than watch it become a pattern of behavior. I've been at this post for thirteen years. I've seen too many good—even great—students fail because they let themselves get distracted. The world demands a great deal of doctors. You will be taking the lives of patients in your hands, making a difference in the world. If you find undergraduate work tough, you'll find med school even tougher. And being an intern at the hospital will be even more demanding still."

"I know. I've been prepping for this since I was about seven. I understand how grueling it can be."

"I doubt anyone understands it," Dr. Arnett said, "until they're in it." He made a gesture at his office door. "That's all I wanted to say. Thank you for coming in. I trust I'll see you Friday on time."

"Absolutely, sir."

Tessa left Arnett's office feeling at once vindicated and guilty. *Oh, what a tangled web we weave ...* She'd walked for five minutes, her eyes downcast, her mind a noisy conflict of priorities, before she remembered that she was supposed to meet Daniel for a 'tween-class rendezvous in the sculpture garden near the library. It was a lovely public space where students went to read books, eat lunch, and occasionally dodge clumps of tourists who'd been seduced by Yelp's description of the many charms of the Franklin D. Murphy Garden. It was home to more than seventy statues and was roughly at the midpoint between their classes.

Tessa checked her watch. She was about ten minutes late. Daniel was probably wondering if she'd stood him up. She turned and hurried back the way she'd come, hoping he hadn't given up on her.

She realized she *needed* to see Daniel. She was certain he was the antidote to her current untethered feeling. He wasn't hard to find. They'd arranged to meet by Gerhard Marcks's classic nude, *Maja*, and he'd managed to stake out a much-sought-after cherry tree near the statue. Sitting on a picnic blanket beneath the tree, he was waving at her enthusiastically, holding up a bag of sandwiches from Kerckhoff's. On the blanket he had placed iced coffee drinks in a cardboard take-out tray, straws sticking jauntily out of the lids of the cups.

"I hope you like bears." He gestured at the blanket. It was brightly colored and covered with pictures of the UCLA mascot. "It was all they had at the campus store."

She tried to smile. "I like them now."

He studied her face. "What happened? You look like your dog died."

"I don't have a dog. We have a cat. Maeve the Magnificent."

"Then your sister ... oh, my God, is your sister okay?"

"She's fine," Tessa said, plopping herself down on the blanket. "Better than fine. It wasn't anything, really. I just got a lecture—a personal lecture—from Professor Arnett about being late to biology class. He was nipping carelessness in the bud."

"You were late to class? That doesn't sound like you."

"It isn't. Usually. But my darling sister got us an audition this morning with a big-name photographer, Gianni DeLuca."

"Johnny who?"

"That's exactly what I said. Anyway, this guy is a big deal. He takes photographs for all sorts of high-end magazines and fashion campaigns and works with only the top models. And now, apparently, Kristin and I are joining their ranks."

Daniel's jaw dropped. "You got a job as a *model*? Congratulations!"

She laughed. "Yeah. Stop drooling, you raging stereotype. Next, you'll be asking if we're going to be in the *Sports Illustrated Swimsuit Issue*."

Daniel stared up at the *Maja* with an exaggeratedly dreamy look on his face. "*Sports Illustrated Swimsuit Issue*. Mmmmm ..."

"Oh, cut it out! Anyway, he'll be taking photos of us, I guess."

Daniel dropped the act. "Seriously, I'm thrilled for you. But ... how are you going to work that in with your studies?"

"That's sort of what Professor Arnett was wondering. Well, except he doesn't know about the modeling gig. He thinks I was just helping Kristin get a job ... which is technically true. It's not like I would've gone out and done this on my own. It's all Kristin. To me ... honestly, I don't know. I think this whole modeling thing may be a huge mistake."

"I can help you," he said. "We can study together."

She gave him a quizzical expression. "You're going to help me study modeling?"

"Academics, smart ass. I'll drill you on potential test questions."

"That's great, but we're not taking all the same classes. Math, yeah, and English Comp, but you're not taking biology. That's the big one."

"Then I'll learn biology. I'll buy the textbook. I'm a quick study. And I read fast."

Tessa stared into his gorgeous brown eyes with a kind of awe. "You'd do that for me? Even if it cuts into your engineering studies?"

"Hey, who needs sleep?" Daniel said. "It's highly overrated. It's not like you can die from lack of sleep."

"Actually, you *can* die from lack of sleep. Your brain goes first, then your organs shut down."

"Oh. Well, I'll just have to catnap then. Maybe during my more boring classes."

Tessa laughed out loud. "You're incredible. You're wonderful."

"I'm hungry," he said. "Let's eat." He handed her a Monte Cristo sandwich with Swiss cheese, ham, and turkey, all battered and fried. "I'd better eat only half. If I start getting fat, DeLuca will probably fire me." Which would not be an entirely bad thing, she thought. Maybe she should put on a little weight, but not until Kristin was safely ensconced in her dream job.

"Don't go all anorexic on me," Daniel said. "Eat the other half later. I like you the way you are, and so apparently does this Johnny guy. What's he like? Is he, like, a hunk?"

Tessa made a face. "He's in his late thirties, I think. Dark and handsome, if you're into that Latin lover thing—which I'm not, for the record. Knows he's good-looking and has the ego to show for it. Kinda creepy, a little bit of a bully. Not my type."

Daniel nodded thoughtfully. "Good to know. So why don't you come by my apartment this evening? We'll start your new study routine. I'm going to get you through this semester even if I have to flunk my own classes."

Tessa stared at him in horror. "Oh, God, don't do that on my account."

"Don't worry," Daniel said, tapping his head. "Remember, I'm smart!"

Daniel, being a sophomore, lived just off campus in a four-story apartment building. It had the standard Spanish architectural trim of the area, but also spacious balconies with a view of the Santa Monica mountains over the one-story houses on the opposite side of the street, and an awe-inspiring glimpse of the futuristic J. Paul Getty Center that perched on top of a peak overlooking the city.

The place looked expensive. Tessa felt she didn't know Daniel well enough to ask, but she suspected that his parents had money. That would be useful for somebody who planned to become the next Elon Musk, especially if he planned to do it straight out of college. Even Musk had needed to create PayPal before he could start his career as the modern Nikola Tesla.

She mounted the steps to the broad veranda and pushed the button next to the front doors. Daniel buzzed her into the building. His apartment was on the top floor and he'd left the door open. The first thing she noticed was that it was spacious and just messy enough to look as if a college student was in residence. The second thing she noticed was that he had a dozen textbooks open on the hardwood floor.

"I'm ready to start quizzing you on biology," he said with a grin. "You can start with teaching me some first. You've probably read more of the textbook than I have."

"And," he added, standing up with a graceful flourish, "I have popcorn in the microwave all ready to pop. Perfect for a girl on a diet."

"You might want to try an air popper. That's even better for a girl on a diet."

"Siri, add 'air popper' to the shopping list," he shouted.

"I've put 'air popper' on the shopping list," said a smooth female voice from a tall cylinder on his desk.

Tessa giggled and collapsed onto his sofa. "I think you have twice as much energy as I do. After that audition and four classes, I'm ready just to eat the popcorn and call it a night."

"Then I'll have energy for the two of us." He turned on the microwave, grabbed the biology textbook from the floor, and sat down next to her while the popcorn popped. "So you know what the citric acid cycle is, right?" He began firing off a series of questions on basic biology principles— basic, that is, if you were taking a college-level course in introductory biology. Despite the dryness of the subject matter and not just because she was filling her stomach with fresh popcorn, Tessa felt a warm glow growing inside her. Daniel was so enthusiastic, so smart, so ... handsome. She had to stop staring into his eyes—which she'd just realized were dark hazel, not brown—just to remember that she was supposed to *answer* the questions.

After a couple of hours, even Daniel's energy seemed to flag. He leaned back on the sofa with a long, satisfied sigh. Tessa had answered every question correctly—or at least to Daniel's satisfaction. Of course, they'd get to tougher questions at a later occasion and they hadn't even touched on any subject except biology yet, but they'd cross that bridge when they came to it. With Gianni DeLuca expecting her to return to his studio with Kristin at the end of the week, that bridge was starting to look longer and longer, but Tessa decided not to think about that and just enjoy the moment.

Daniel seemed to be enjoying the moment too. They began to talk about school and her impressions of UCLA after her first two weeks of classes. Two weeks! Tessa couldn't believe that she'd only known Daniel for two weeks. It already felt like they'd known each other for eons and that they'd been really happy eons. He was so easy to talk to. They shared so many interests and agreed on so many things. And where they disagreed, both of them were amicably willing to not insist on having the last word. Daniel had been moving closer and closer to her as he quizzed her, not flirtatiously but so that they could both see his copy of the textbook, where he'd done extensive highlighting. Yet she suddenly, electrically, became aware that his leg was pressed up against hers. It felt good. She hadn't realized how much she'd yearned for the warmth of physical contact with him. Her head began to swim with thoughts beyond studying and talking about college.

"Tessa? Tessa? Are you still with me? I was wondering what you thought about Professor Torres's math class."

"Oh," she said, having to bring herself back into the real world for a moment to remember who Professor Torres was. "Right. Yeah, he's kind of boring, don't you think?"

"Oh, God, yes," Daniel said, laughing. "And I actually *like* math."

Daniel had his hand on the open pages of the textbook, which was half on Tessa's lap. Without thinking, she placed her hand on top of his and, magically, he stopped talking. They gazed into one another's eyes with the dazed look of two people who had just realized their entire lives had changed in a heartbeat. Tessa lifted her chin, and Daniel brought his lips down to meet hers. For a moment they lingered like that, and then the kiss became more passionate, more urgent. Daniel's arms slipped around her back and she laced her fingers together at the nape of his neck.

You've only known him for two weeks, Tessa thought. The fact that her grandparents on her mom's side had known each other that long when they married helped her objectivity not one bit.

Daniel raised his head. "I have to ask you something," he said. "Okay."

"Are you ... are you a virgin?"

Tessa felt a chill. She wasn't sure Daniel would like the answer. "Yeah, I am. You probably think that's lame, but—"

The look in his eyes surprised her. It was relief.

"Well, if you're lame," he said, "so am I. I don't have condoms stuffed in my pockets or stocked up in my bedside table. Not yet, anyway. I mean, I wasn't planning on falling for someone like you two weeks into the school year."

Falling for? Was that what this was? Were they falling for each other?

Sure felt like it from her end.

"I was hoping," Daniel said, "that you and I ... that we'd become a *thing*, but ... Wow. I'm *so* not good at this."

Tessa laughed in relief and delight. "Me neither." He wasn't going to make fun of her because she was eighteen and still a virgin. He wasn't going to think she was some sort of religious kook.

"Look," Daniel said, "I'm pretty sure there's no law that says we have to ... to sleep with each other, like, right now. I want to, but I think maybe we need to do some, uh, lab prep before we ..."

"Take the big biology exam?" Tessa said.

Daniel nodded. "If that's where this is headed, yeah. I really would like to kiss you again, though. I don't think that requires any ... special precautions."

"Maybe just a few science experiments?" she suggested, and kissed him.

Chapter Twelve

Kristin had come to a decision. A life-changing decision.

Through the pain of withdrawal and the seemingly endless surgeries (she knew Tessa had been done with surgeries weeks ago), she had finally managed to achieve something like peace. She had done it by hanging onto something her twin had quoted to her, allegedly from their father: "Nothing lasts in this world; you either accept change or you get stuck in one place, unable to move forward."

Hard to believe the old guy capable of that deep a thought, let alone being right about it, but there it was. And he was right. Nothing lasted. She had spent years relying on her beauty to propel her forward through the world. Her beauty was the key to her fortunes; it had supplied her with the means to get what she wanted. She'd known, on an abstract level, that it wouldn't last forever, but she'd figured she'd have years in which to exploit it, years in which to build a life and live off the residuals.

She'd been wrong. Deep beneath the bandages and whatever drugs they had tried to numb her with, she knew she no longer had those years. Her beauty was gone. Her face was an unknown land mass, a jagged terrain of misshapen landmarks to which she had no map. They'd offered her a mirror to let her see the "progress" she was making. She'd refused. They thought she was afraid to look. She wasn't afraid; she was pissed because they kept telling her the secret to her recovery was time, and she knew she'd run out of it.

They had repaired her eyelids in the first surgery, rebuilt the cartilage in her nose in the second, and covered it and her upper lip with their so-called scaffolding in successive trips to the OR. She was supposed to wait now. Wait for it to heal.

It will heal, they kept telling her, but she knew it would never heal to the point where she would be Kristin Morgan again. Yes, her foray into acting had been a disaster, mostly caused by her betraying weasel of a sister, their egomaniac director, and their holier-than-thou producer, but up until the time that Kurt Morrison had flung that acid in her face, she'd had a fallback position: Go back to modeling.

Now, she had nothing, and no amount of healing of this Frankenstein's monster mask would make her whole again—make her herself again.

If that was the change that she had to accept before she could move forward—then she was going to accept it all the way. Waiting for healing that would not restore her to even a semblance of her God-given beauty was weak, ineffectual.

There was a phrase they'd used back in high school: *The Lord yeeteth and the Lord yoinketh away.* He'd damn well yoinked everything she'd earned.

She'd actually done the exercises they'd given her to build up the tiny muscles around her eyes so she could open them enough to see her IV stent through the translucent lightweight netting that covered her eyes and forehead. Now, she sat up in her hospital bed and clawed at the tape that held the IV in her left arm. She pulled the stent out, then ripped the gauze off her face. She couldn't feel much, but she imagined her distorted features crumpling, tearing away, leaving only raw disfigurement behind. As the last pieces of gauze and netting dropped into her lap, she called out for her nurse to bring her clothing. She was leaving. She wasn't going to waste any more time in this hospital.

Her nurse, a middle-aged woman named Yolanda, came rushing into her room, panicked and angry at the same time. "Ms. Morgan! Kristin! You're not ready to leave. You need to heal!"

"I need to get out of here."

The woman glanced at the door. "You *need* to calm down. I'll get Dr. Sorenson."

"To hell with doctors," Kristin said. "You're all afraid I'm going to become a monster. Well, it's too late. I've already become one."

The nurse went from commanding to conciliatory. Making a placating gesture with her hands, she murmured, "You're not a monster, Kristin."

"Bullshit. You're a lousy liar, Yolanda. I see the way you're looking at me. I disgust you. I'm a one-woman horror show."

"Kirstin, if you'd look in a mirror, you'd see—"

"I'd see a monster. Let. Me. Leave."

The nurse hesitated for a moment, then said, "Fine. I'll get Dr. Sorenson to check you out." She left the room.

Kristin watched her go, wishing she could be a little spider on the wall and see the look on the stupid woman's face when she and Doc S got back and found her gone.

Act 2
The Road to Hell

Chapter Thirteen

Kristin stepped out of DeLuca's office and into his studio, settling her skirt around her hips. She and Tessa had been working with the photographer for four months now, and Kristin's obligation to satisfy his sexual needs had gotten old. He was a selfish lover—which meant he was no lover at all. He expected Kristin to do all the work while he lay back and enjoyed it. Typical.

Of course, she had no more desire for any kind of actual relationship with him than he had for a relationship with her, but it was about time he appreciated what she and Tessa could do for him professionally—more than what she could do for him on his office couch or in his party-sized bed.

On the studio walls hung framed blown-up photographs of quite a few high-profile models, all executed with DeLuca's usual artistry, but the prime spot across from the entry was now occupied by the fashion spread that he had done of Kristin and Tessa for the latest issue of *Vogue*. That alone should be enough to seal their relationship with him on a professional level. The twins were already starting to get some recognition in the tightly knit world of fashion modeling, and that gave them professional capital. The next time he asked her for a blow job, she might just turn him down.

They were approaching the tipping point where he was going to need them more than they needed him.

Tessa burst through the door of the room, looking harried. As usual, she had a backpack full of books with her, which infuriated Kristin to no end. Her sister was going to have to make a decision at some point, even if Kristin had to make it for her. She could become a doctor or they could become famous models, living rich, luxurious lives. Kristin had no intention of letting Tessa be a doctor. She just had to figure out how to change Tessa's mind.

"Always with the books!" DeLuca declared, emerging from his office. His staff was already arriving to set up the lights and cameras for that day's shoot. "Why do you need to read those books when I can teach you all that you need to know? I've already given you the skills you needed to get into the pages of *Vogue*. Of course, without my brilliant photographic skills ..."

Yada, yada, yada, thought Kristin. They could probably go to any other photographer in LA and get work that afternoon. Not that she wanted to, but she was getting sick of the taste of DeLuca's dick.

"I've told you, Gianni," Tessa said. "I'm working on a premed degree. I have to keep studying."

"Why in the name of God do you want to be a doctor?" DeLuca said with a moan. "The world already has enough doctors. Do you want to charge exorbitant rates for popping pimples or do you want to be one of the most famous faces in the world?"

"I'm studying neurology, not dermatology."

Gianni made a dismissive gesture. "Never mind. I have something that may chase all those silly thoughts from your mind. Have you heard of Robeson Cosmetics?"

Kristin's heart skipped a beat. Robeson was one of the most famous cosmetic companies in the US—one that advertised exclusively in high-end fashion and women's magazines. Their products sold only in brand-name boutiques so upscale that Kristin had never been in one.

"Robeson Cosmetics?" Kristin said. "God, yes, I know who they are. Are they ... ?"

"Auditioning for new models? Yes. Always." DeLuca took a press release from his equipment table and held it up with a flourish. "Robeson Cosmetics is holding auditions next week to find a spokesmodel for their new line of hair care products."

"We've got that in the bag!" Kristin declared excitedly. "How could they resist having a pair of gorgeous twins as their spokesmodels?"

"It is true that you girls have beautiful hair," DeLuca said, "but do not get your hopes too high. Even with my magnificent work behind you, you will have competition from all over the world for this role. It will be difficult for you even to get an audition. Perhaps it will be impossible."

"Nothing's impossible," Kristin said.

"Sometimes you frighten even me, Kristin," DeLuca said. "But if you think you have a chance for this, by all means, you should—how do you say?—go for it."

Tessa's face turned white. "But I have my classes, my studies. Finals are coming up."

"Oh, Tessa," Kristin said with a sneer. "You wouldn't recognize the biggest break you'll ever get in your life if I didn't shove it in your face."

"You have already assumed that you will get this break, my cocky little prima donna," DeLuca admonished. "Now, would you two stop bickering and get to work? We have a photo shoot to begin."

Oh, we'll get this break, Kristin thought. *I can get anything I want. All I need is a plan.*

That afternoon, Kristin sat in her Lexus ES 350 on a side street off Sepulveda in Westwood. She'd bought the car with the income from the last four months of modeling. She would have preferred a Maserati, but that was still a bit above her pay grade. If things this afternoon went as planned (and of course they would because *everything* Kristin Morgan did went as planned), that was going to change.

She had eyes on the corporate LA headquarters of Robeson Cosmetics and felt like the star of a detective series—a femme private eye just doing a little surveillance. The three-story building in front, with its graceful Spanish architecture, housed the administrative and design studios; the larger two-story brick building behind it was home to the production lab for the high-end cosmetics line. The manufacturing hub for the hair care products was somewhere down in Oxnard. An asphalt parking lot stretched along one side of the lab, but from her vantage point, she could see the entrance to an underground parking garage, most likely for the upper crust administrative and design staff and execs.

She picked up her cell phone and brought up her contacts list, tapping on a number she had purloined from Gianni's phone.

A husky female voice answered. "Robeson Cosmetics. How can I help you?"

Oooh, bedroom voice. Is that how it is? "I need to speak with George Robeson. It's important."

"Is he expecting your call, Miss ...?"

"I'm sure he is. I'm calling from Studio DeLuca and I have a portfolio of photos from Gianni that Mr. Robeson wanted delivered ASAP."

The woman paused. "Mr. DeLuca usually delivers the photographs himself when he meets with Mr. Robeson."

"Mr. DeLuca is tied up at the moment, but he made it clear that Mr. Robeson expected to get these photos right away. Can you tell me when he'll be available?"

"He's in a meeting right now. You can drop the photos off downstairs at the front desk."

"I'm sorry," Kristin said, "but Mr. DeLuca was very specific about having the photos hand-delivered to Mr. Robeson in person. It's related to his current model search. So if you'll just tell me when he'll be available ..."

"I'm afraid he'll be in the meeting all afternoon. He won't be out until five at least, and then he's going home for the evening."

"This can't wait until tomorrow," Kristin said, letting a little panic slide into her voice. "If I can't deliver these photos, both our bosses are going to be angry. Do you like your job? Because I sure like mine."

Following a moment of hesitation, the other woman said, "If you're in the office a bit before five, you should be able to catch him as he leaves the meeting. I can text him to expect you and let the receptionist downstairs know you're coming if you'll give me your name."

Kristin grinned. "It's Tess."

With that handled, she checked her watch. It was three thirty. She had some time to kill before her date with Mr. Robeson. She thought she'd use it to get the lay of the land in case it was necessary to come up with a plan B. To that end, she took a walk around the perimeter of the Robeson campus, mind-mapping various employee entrances and noting where trucks loaded and unloaded. The fact did not escape her notice that the parking garage was protected only by one of those automatic gates no doubt activated by company-issued ID cards. Good information to know, in case she needed it.

She returned to her car after her little walkabout and sat listening to music and daydreaming about her future as a Robeson spokesmodel.

At four forty-five, she climbed out of her car, carrying the sleek leather portfolio in which she had placed a selection of Gianni's best photos of the Morgan twins. Because she thought they were provocative and sexy, she had included the ones he'd taken during their audition—the ones in which they were entwined in apparently incestuous passion. She thought of them as the Twin Sin series. She had, in fact, put the most artfully provocative one of those near the top of the stack, just beneath the *Vogue* cover.

She strode up to the front of the Robeson building with the portfolio tucked under her arm, watching her reflection in the tinted glass of the building's front doors. In an electric blue suit coat over a dove gray miniskirt, she radiated confidence. A bit of silvery gray lace peeped above the lapels of the suit coat. She knew how to dress for success ... and, she thought wryly, how to undress for it, which was far more persuasive.

In her experience, men had two drivers: success and control. Every relationship boiled down to how well they could manipulate others, especially women. She'd been only fourteen when she'd gotten a face full of that reality, and she'd spent most of her time since learning how to turn the tables.

She entered the building and strode immediately to the reception desk that sat at the center of the lobby against a cream-colored pony wall. On her way, she flicked oblique glances at the security guard seated behind his own desk to the receptionist's left. To her right, a red tile staircase with a black wrought-iron rail rose to the second floor; between the receptionist's desk and the staircase, a broad hallway ran toward the rear of the building. A pair of elevators was tucked beneath the staircase.

Kristin approached the receptionist with a brilliant white smile. "Hi, I'm Tess, from Studio DeLuca. Was it you I spoke to earlier?"

The young woman behind the desk was disconcertingly pretty. If she was the standard for a receptionist, what must Georgie Boy expect of his models?

She returned Kristin's smile. Kristin noticed that the receptionist's teeth weren't as white as they could have been. "No, that would have been Mr. Robeson's executive assistant, Violet Hollister. She's expecting you. The elevator is just over there. Mr. Robeson's offices are on the third floor. Ms. Hollister's desk is right across from the elevator."

"Thanks!" Kristin turned on her heel and dashed to the elevator, slanting a look behind her to see if the guard had noticed. He had, of course. She shot him a smile over her shoulder.

The upstairs lobby was the same basic footprint as the one downstairs, but as the receptionist had said, the executive assistant's desk was directly across from the elevator where the steely-eyed Ms. Hollister could eyeball anyone entering her domain. Ms. Hollister was a couple of decades older than the receptionist but still a strikingly good-looking woman with olive skin and hair the color of mahogany that she wore center parted and coiled at the nape of her neck. Kristin was willing to bet she was a cougar.

She crossed the reception area with a snap in her step and a smile on her lips. "You must be Violet! Hi, I'm Tess. I spoke to you about these." She untucked the Studio DeLuca portfolio, making sure the gleaming gold leaf of the title was clearly visible.

"Yes, of course. Mr. Robeson is in the main conference room." She nodded toward a pair of ten-foot-tall distressed oak doors to Kristin's left. "You can take a seat here, if you like."

Kristin assessed the lay of the oval room. Dark wood chairs and low coffee tables were strategically placed around the perimeter of the lobby, none of which would have put her directly in Robeson's sight line when he emerged from his meeting. She could take the one with the best location and stand the second the doors opened, but ... At the rear of the lobby, facing the conference room doors, was a long hallway lined with executive offices.

"I assume he'll have to return to his office before he leaves for the evening," Kristin said. "Why don't I just wait for him there?"

Violet the Cougar shook her lovely head. "I'm sorry, I can't allow anyone access to the executive offices. The chairs are really quite comfortable, and you won't have that long to wait, I'm sure."

Kristin bit back her annoyance, smiled, and took a seat, picking up one of the fashion magazines that littered the low tables between pairs of chairs. At five p.m., the doors of the conference room remained resolutely shut. At 5:10, Violet closed up shop and left for the evening, telling Kristin, "I'm sure he'll be right out."

When the admin was safely in the elevator and on her way downstairs, Kristin left the lobby and headed down the hallway, checking the name plates by each door. Robeson's office was the last one on the left and was unlocked. Kristin slipped in, allowing herself a moment to be impressed with the size and decor, which included rich fabrics and generous amounts of dark wood.

She staged herself carefully; seated on his desk, facing the door, suit coat unbuttoned to show her camisole and ample cleavage, legs dangling. She held the portfolio between her thighs, the gold-leaf lettering proclaiming this package to be from Studio DeLuca accented by the warm light of the overhead fixture.

At 5:20, Kristin heard George Robeson approaching his office, conversing with someone.

Shit. He'd brought someone to his office with him! Her adrenaline spiked. She'd have to bail on plan A, damn it. It would take only a second to look circumspect; she hadn't taken off any of her clothing, except her panties. Just slip off the desk into the chair where she'd left her purse—

She'd started to move when she realized that the conversation was one-sided. Robeson was on the phone and had paused just outside the door to complete the call. She relaxed.

You got this, Morgan.

The door latch turned and George Robeson entered his office, pocketing his phone. He was of average height—maybe five nine or five ten—but there, the average ended. A trim, fit-looking forty-five or so, she figured, he was dressed impeccably in a charcoal gray suit with a spring green tie. He had gleaming black hair, thick and wavy, with silver at the temples; he probably used his own hair care products. When he saw her, his gray eyes processed a swift series of reactions—surprise, disorientation, confusion, wariness, affable puzzlement—when his eyes finally lit on the portfolio between Kristin's thighs.

"You're ... the girl from Gianni's studio? Tess, was it?"

"That's me." Kristin smiled, her eyes inviting. He might be more fun than Gianni.

"He sent you, himself?" He made a broad gesture at her, his smile tentative. "Is this a new pitch strategy?"

"Sure, let's call it that. I brought you a present." She wiggled her hips, making the portfolio dance.

He stared at the leather folder, a red flush rising from his collar. "Really?"

"Come take a look."

"I'm not sure ..."

"I don't bite. Promise." She almost added, "Unless you ask," but thought better of it. The guy looked uneasy, and she wanted him to be easy.

"Oookay."

He closed his office door, and Kristin thought she heard the click of the lock. That boded well for plan A. Plan B had been to ambush him in the parking garage and go for it in his car, which, depending on what he drove, could be awkward and potentially embarrassing. The idea was to make the guy feel studly and desirable, not ridiculous.

Robeson crossed to the desk, scanning Kristin as if he suspected a prank. She followed him with her eyes, catching every stray glance that made it that high. He sent back high-voltage looks that told him how much he wanted her.

"Am I supposed to take this?" He gestured at the portfolio. "As you wish, Mr. Robeson."

He lifted the portfolio from between her legs and opened it without looking past it at Kristin. She was a little pissed by that. He was supposed to have noticed that she was naked and exposed beneath her rucked-up skirt.

Fine. Whatever. We'll do this the long way if we have to.

She stayed perfectly still, legs still spread, and waited.

He was studying the *Vogue* cover, still looking puzzled, but not in a bad way. "Wait," he said. "You're one of the twins Gianni's been crowing about? I thought maybe it was a publicity stunt—photoshopped."

"No, sir, we are the real deal. Identical twin models."

He flipped the *Vogue* photo over. His face when he saw the Twin Sin pic was a study in male psychology. Surprise, admiration, discomfort, lust. Kristin couldn't contain a chuckle. Robeson merely glanced at her before he flipped that page too.

He looked through the entire portfolio, then went back to the top of the stack. "So, this is Gianni's flamboyant idea of an audition, is it?"

"Mine too. I'm all about rockin' that first impression." She shrugged her shoulders, and her suit coat slipped to the desk top. Her camisole made it halfway, exposing her breasts to the cooled air and the man's gaze.

Now he looked at her. Now, he registered that the woman perched on his desk was not only exposed from the waist up and naked beneath her minuscule skirt, but primed and ready to go. She read the shock in his gaze; it was a definite turn-on. She could almost hear the well-oiled gears in his head turning—see the slipping of fantastic thoughts behind those fine gray eyes.

He was most definitely *thinking* about it. Okay, well, that was just the tiniest bit insulting, but he was a man with a lot to lose. Time to give him a little push. She lowered her eyes from his face, slowly scanning the length of his body until she came to his groin. She could see his erection clearly through the fabric of his trousers.

She smiled. "You poor thing. That must really hurt. Let me help." She was off the desk with catlike grace, bringing their bodies together, meeting his eyes, and cradling his erection in her hand. He quivered but didn't pull away. He looked ... scared. She loved the fear in his eyes. It was heady, powerful.

She found his zipper, lowered it with practiced ease, and slid her hand in, past his briefs, seeking his heated flesh. It was her touch that broke him. In mere seconds, she was perched on the desk again, with him inside her, rocking to his rhythm. He held her waist; she grasped his shoulders, making tiny, appreciative noises.

He was the silent type—no grunting, no panting, just intentional, purposeful thrusting. Probably the same method he'd used to build his cosmetics company. He'd closed his eyes. She wondered if he did his wife this way. The only sound he made was when he came—a low half grunt, half growl. Kristin liked it so much, she came too, then laughed, surprised at herself. The growl didn't stop until he was spent.

"GR, you really know how to rock a girl's world," she told him, murmuring the words in his ear.

He was sweating when he pulled out of her. Sweating and pale and uncertain. She smiled, hiked up her camisole, pulled her suit coat back on, then slid off the desk. Grabbing a handful of tissues from a box next to his laptop, she wiped herself, tossing the wad into a wooden wastebasket by the desk.

"You can keep the portfolio, GR. To remind you of our little pre-audition audition. *I* won't tell Gianni, if *you* don't tell your wife."

He was still looking dazed and gutted when she gathered up her purse and straightened her skirt, checking to make sure there was nothing incriminating on the front of it.

"Well, I'll see you soon, Geo. And you might want to have someone clean that up." She gestured at the pool of semen she'd left on the desk. "Or, I dunno, maybe you'd rather clean it up yourself. Wouldn't want anyone to think you'd had an embarrassing accident."

She gave him a finger wave and strode out of the room, heels clicking on the tile floor. She was surprised, though, to realize that he hadn't locked the door after all. She wasn't sure whether to be insulted by that or proud that she'd overcome his pathetic attempt at resistance.

She opted for pride. She'd had to work harder than she'd expected for the payoff, but ultimately, she'd won the match of wills. Once he'd double-dipped his dick, the calculus was simple. If he tried to charge her with extortion, he'd have to admit that there were grounds for extortion. That was not going to go down well with the beautiful wife and the three doting children she knew he had. And Tessa thought Kristin never did her homework.

She was looking forward to working for Robeson Cosmetics.

Chapter Fourteen

Tessa stared at the math textbook in her lap, trying to make sense of differential equations. Daniel had drilled her on them for weeks, but they were still as opaque to her as they had been from the first day of class. She had no trouble with basic algebra. She could solve quadratic equations in her sleep. But differential equations were slippery, scooting around like insects that defied her every attempt to swat them. Solve for the value of one variable, and the value of another variable changed. It was like trying to solve a Rubik's Cube, the difference being that a Rubik's Cube actually could be solved, while differential equations seemed to be something that only a computer could penetrate. Maybe that's why Daniel, the computer genius, seemed to be so comfortable with them.

She had no idea what good all this would do her as a doctor, but it would be on the final exam, which was only a few days away, and passing her finals would make all the difference in the world to her career. They'd determine whether she would actually have a career in the first place. So she stared at the examples on the pages and ground her brain against them until her frontal lobe felt like it was going to implode.

She was almost relieved when her phone rang and she saw Kristin's name appear on the screen. She felt relief right up until she heard what Kristin had to say.

"I got us an audition with Robeson Cosmetics. It's on Thursday of next week. This is it, Tess. This is the big time! We're there!"

"No," Tessa said. "No way. I have my last two finals that day." A hard, cold knot settled in the pit of her stomach; she was already cringing in preparation for what she knew would come next.

"What do you *mean*, 'no way'?" Kristin went from chirpy to harpy in less than a second. "Didn't you hear me when I said that this is the big time? This is what we've been working toward for the last four months!"

Tessa kept her own voice low and firm, willing Kristin to understand that no meant no. "It's what *you've* been working toward, Krist. *I've* been working toward a premed degree. And my finals begin on Tuesday. Thursday is out of the question."

"Forget about finals! We've absolutely got this. I've made sure of it!"

Tessa had no doubt that Kristin had made sure of it and equally certain she didn't want to know how Kristin had made sure of it. Kristin had long viewed herself as the Irresistible Force, but Tessa was determined to be the Immovable Object in this equation. Her career as a doctor came first. It always had. She'd been crystal clear about that. As much as she liked the financial benefits of their modeling work (which she'd put in savings toward buying a car), she felt the time for her to pull out of modeling was drawing near. Kristin was established with Gianni; there would be no shortage of work for her. One more job like the *Vogue* cover and Kristin would be established.

Tessa had bent her schedule for her sister as long as possible, but missing finals was another order of magnitude. Her work thus far had been iffy enough; she'd struggled to meet the demands of her professors on one side and of Kristin on the other. If she flunked finals—or, worse, didn't show up for them—she could kiss any chance of getting into medical school goodbye.

"No," Tessa said again in an end-of-discussion voice she never knew she had.

"You can't do this," Kristin barked. "I've done everything possible to make this happen for us, and you can't say no to it. It's too late. You're committed to this, Tess."

"I'm committed to my education. I'm not going to be there. You can do this on your own." Tessa terminated the call.

Not surprisingly, Kristin called back five seconds later. Tessa didn't answer. She leaned back and closed her eyes. She had to get away, go somewhere she could study in peace, where she could *think* in peace, with her phone turned off. There was no point in going to her teachers and asking if she could postpone her finals. At one point or another that semester she had asked every one of her teachers for favors because of work. They were sympathetic to students who held down part-time or even full-time jobs to be able to afford school, but she had scored a hefty scholarship and lived at home. She didn't know if any of her profs knew that, but all of them had made one thing clear: The future of her education at UCLA hinged on her passing the finals, on time and with a grade of at least a B. Anything less and she could kiss med school goodbye.

She called Daniel and arranged to meet with him after his last class that afternoon. She took a quick shower, pulled on her UCLA sweatshirt, grabbed her keys, and left the house, heading to her brand-new Prius plug-in, which was charging from a bulky electric charging station her father had installed just outside the garage. Before she drove off, though, she made an impulsive phone call to a friend.

Sarah Hernandez, Tessa's best friend from high school, squealed with delight when she saw Tessa standing at the door of her parents' house, where she lived in the finished basement. "Tessa! It's been almost two weeks! But I figured I might not see you for a while with finals coming up. Or is the boyfriend keeping you busy?"

"Mostly helping me study," Tessa said as she entered the apartment. "It's good to see you, Sarah."

"I just made some cookies," Sarah said, heading for the tiny galley kitchen her parents had installed. All part of their campaign to keep their daughter at home while she studied at CalTech. "Want some? They're still warm. Peanut butter chocolate chip."

Tessa smiled but waved her friend away when she came out of the kitchen with a plate piled high with fragrant, seductive cookies.

"As much as I want to, I can't eat those," Tessa said, grimacing and rolling her eyes. "I have to watch my weight. The job, you know."

Sarah seated herself on a Mission-style love seat in the cozy living area and set the plate of temptation on the coffee table. She waved Tessa to the matching Morris chair opposite.

"I saw you guys in the latest issue of *Cosmo*! You're famous now, Tessa! You've got it all: Scholarship to a prestigious school, dreamy boyfriend, beauty, stardom. Can I just be you for a while? Just to find out what it's like?"

Tessa laughed. "Sure. If I can be you and know how to bake cookies and code software. But I'm not sure you'd really like being me."

"What's not to like? Your life is perfect. What could possibly be wrong?"

Tessa looked down at her hands, toying with the little braided bracelet that Daniel had made for her. It had two beads on the free end—a gold one to mimic her hair, and a jet one to echo his. He'd given it to her the night they'd made love for the first time, or as Daniel said, they'd "taken their biology exam." For two virgins, they made damn good lab partners. The experiment was a success by any measure.

"Well," Tessa said, "my sister, for one thing. I told you how she dragged me into modeling in the first place."

Sarah frowned; it wasn't a natural expression on her pert face. "Yeah, I remember—the Wicked Witch of West LA. Everyone in our high school knew her reputation."

Tessa took a deep breath, trying to dispel the tightness in her throat. "That's what I've always believed. Kristin used to be so sweet. She was sassy and a little rebellious—dyed her hair this awful shade of green her sophomore year of high school—but she was never mean. Now ..." Tessa looked up at her friend. "Sarah, she's starting to scare me. She's determined that we make it big at this modeling thing, and she'll go to any lengths to make that happen. I'm not even sure I know what those lengths are. She's obsessed with her power over men, but it's only because it gets her the things she wants. She doesn't seem to care for any of them." Following a hesitation, she added, "She's always made fun of me wanting to be a doctor, and now she's started taunting me about Daniel, telling me how stupid I am to be in a committed relationship at my age. I know I just turned nineteen, but Daniel's parents were that age when they married."

"Maybe she just wants love," Sarah said. "That's why I'd want to have power over men. Or, well—a man, singular."

Tessa smiled. Despite being a grade-A computer science student and a seasoned "code monkey," Sarah was big on romance novels. A little pile of mostly paperbacks sat on one end of the coffee table, their spines broken from reading and rereading. They had titles like *Code Me a Hero* and *User-Friendly Warmware.* Sarah called them nerdmances, fantasies for women who wanted to believe that even the ungraceful and unpopular could find perfect love.

Maybe, Tessa thought, that's what she'd found with Daniel. But that wasn't Kristin's fantasy. Tessa wasn't even sure that love factored into Kristin's cold equations. She hated to be so cynical about her own sister. She wanted to understand what had changed her. She'd read articles on the psychology of twins, but in all her reading, she'd never found anything to explain the person Kristin was, more and more, revealing herself to be. "I don't think she'd be envious of me, if that's what you're thinking," Tessa said. "Kristin's not much for romance. I think she's in love with power and success. That's what has me worried. Kristin does not want me to have the kind of success I want. She wants me to have the kind of success *she* wants."

"Why does that matter?" Sarah asked. "She can't tell you what to do with your life. If you want to be a neurologist, then that's what you should be."

Tessa smiled at Sarah with honest affection. "Thanks." Sarah shrugged. "For what?"

"For being my Greek chorus. For telling me what I already know but need to hear from someone who's as levelheaded and pragmatic as you are. Kristin looks at the world through the lens of her physical attractiveness, and it's hard sometimes not to get sucked into it. I have to tell you, I've had a professor and at least one counselor who's treated me differently because ..."

"Because they think you're a dumb blonde?"

Tessa nodded. "Yeah. They've questioned my commitment. They've shown surprise that I actually study. One of my high school teachers figured I was getting As in her class because I was cheating. She spent a semester trying to catch me. It's disheartening, that kind of prejudice. You know what I'm talking about."

"Flip side of my tale of woe," Sarah said, nodding. "Because I'm short and stout and nerdy, guys friend-zone me, like, all the time. Meanwhile, my male peers tell me I've got the wrong chromosomes to be a real, honest-to-Jobs programmer. I don't listen to those voices. You shouldn't listen to hers."

Tessa felt a rush of certitude, dispelling the lingering fear that she was being a bad sister. "You see, this is why I wanted to see you, Sarah. I need you, girlfriend. You believe in the power of dreams."

"I thought your dreamy Daniel had a lock on that territory."

"He does, but he's also infatuated with me. I'm not always sure that, as brilliant as he is, he can see me clearly. You see me clearly and you tell me what's what."

"Tessa," Sarah said, "here's what: If being a doctor is what you want, then don't let Kristin tell you otherwise. And if Daniel is *who* you want to be that with ... well, I'd love to see you become one of those women who really does have it all."

"I think they only exist in romance novels," Tessa said, nodding at the pile of paperbacks.

Sarah cast a wry glance in that direction. "Yeah. Those guys are like unicorns; I doubt they even exist. Most of the alpha nerds I've met in class are so insecure they don't even know what to do with me ... except ignore me, tell sexist jokes, or theorize that I'm really a guy who doesn't know it yet." She shrugged. "But I suppose there's always hope, right? Oh, and for the record? I'm pretty sure Daniel is way beyond infatuation and into true love territory."

Tessa laughed and jumped up to give Sarah a spontaneous hug. "Thank you, Sarah. That's what I needed to hear."

"Good. You just stand your ground. Don't let anyone take away the things that are important to you. Including that little voice in your head that says you're not worthy. I hate that guy." She grinned.

"So sayeth the Greek chorus," teased Tessa.

"I prefer to think of myself as the *geek* chorus. Sure you won't have one of those cookies, future Dr. Morgan?"

"You know what? Hang the skinny. Give me that big one, there on the top."

Daniel was waiting in the sculpture garden when Tessa got back to the UCLA campus. She found him sitting in what had become one of their favorite places—the edge of a long, rectangular fountain that featured a gargantuan steel sculpture by Richard Serra. Daniel thought the sculpture, from which recycled water was delivered to the pool, looked like a robot from a grade-B science fiction movie.

"One of these days," he'd joked, "the aliens are going to come back, and when they do, that old boy is going to wake up and have words to say."

Today, when he saw Tessa approaching, he grinned, nodded toward the sculpture, and said, "I think I saw him move!" When she didn't toss him a quippy comeback, he stood, scanning her face.

"Kristin problems?" he asked.

She reached him, dropped her backpack on the lip of the fountain, and plopped down next to it. "Am I that transparent?" she asked. "Yeah, it's Krist. She's determined that I cut finals to attend an audition for a cosmetics company."

"Not an option," Daniel said, reseating himself next to her. His face was completely and uncharacteristically solemn. "I hope you told her that."

"Oh, I told her that, all right. I'm pretty sure she just decided not to hear me."

"Well, at least you're ready for the finals. And"—he cleared his throat with mock humility—"I think I've done a better-than-adequate job helping with that."

She took his hands in hers. "I feel like I'm in one of those cartoons where there's a devil sitting on one shoulder and an angel on the other."

"I hope I'm not the devil in this equation. I mean, I did lure you into my laboratory." He said the last word like Bela Lugosi ... or Count Chocula.

She slapped his hand gently. "You know that's not your role in this little cartoon. Kristin is the devil. You're my angel. You've been my angel since the day we met."

He smiled all the way up to his tilted hazel eyes. "You know that even if, God forbid, you don't make it through the finals, I'll still love you."

Tessa froze, gaping at him. "I don't think you've used that word before."

Daniel looked uneasy. "I ... I've almost said it—God, every day since we first met. I've been thinking it, I just didn't know if ... if you'd be frightened, or if you'd feel suffocated or overwhelmed or ..."

"I like the word," she said, leaning in so that their foreheads were nearly touching. "It's a good word. It's the word I'd use. I love you, Daniel."

He leaned back, a little bit dazed, a little unsure, maybe. "You love me. You're drop-dead gorgeous and you love *me*. Weird, nerdy Japanese- American guy."

"Brilliant, devastatingly handsome, weird, nerdy Japanese-American guy, you mean. Yeah. I love that guy." She kissed him, then said, "We've both got a free period. Why don't we go back to your apartment? We can run an experiment ... or study, if you'd rather."

They were undressing each other almost before Daniel had his front door locked, and left a trail of clothing from the door to the fluffy faux-fleece area rug that decorated the hardwood floor in front of the apartment's tiny gas fireplace. They were both completely naked at that point and agreed, by silent consensus, that there was no need to proceed to the "lab."

Stretched out on the fake shearling with Daniel lying close beside her, Tessa gasped softly as he ran a hand lightly over her body—along her thigh, over her stomach, then smoothly up to cup one breast. He dropped hummingbird kisses on her tightened nipples as if sipping nectar, his tongue flicking gently across her flesh in a way that sent electric bursts of pleasure through her entire body. Then he did something he hadn't before. He kissed and nibbled his way down her body until his mouth found the well between her spread legs. Her mind went completely blank, and she found herself writhing in mindless, overwhelming sensation.

"Now," she whispered. "*Now*."

He knew what she was asking for. He pulled himself up between her legs and mounted her, sliding in, then moving gently within her. The first time they'd done this—the first day she'd been ready to trust her birth control pills— it had been at night in the darkness of Daniel's bedroom. Now, they coupled in the light of day, their eyes locked as intimately as their bodies. Daniel was beautiful in the warm light filtering in through the trees in the front yard of his apartment building, and the look of ecstasy on his face, the passion in his eyes, made Tessa's pleasure so intense she nearly cried.

Her orgasm was almost painful, so fierce it triggered Daniel's. It was like having a second heart pulsing inside her; the beating of it went on and on, suspending Tessa in a bright bubble of sensation. She was certain every single atom of her body was lit up, that Daniel had touched and illumined every single one.

She was still in the throes of orgasm when he collapsed on top of her. They lay conjoined for long moments, breathing in harmony, until Daniel put his hands around her face and kissed her on the lips again.

"That was ... inspiring," she murmured when he lifted his head.

He smiled down at her. "You're just so beautiful. You inspire me too. I guess we have a mutual inspiration society."

A tiny, dark ghost laid a spectral land on Tessa's heart. "Would you still ... be inspired if I weren't beautiful? Would you still love me?"

He gave her a what-madness-is-this look. "Of course I would," he said, kissing the tip of her nose. "You're just as lovely on the inside as you are on the outside. And I don't mean that in a sexual way. I mean you're sweet. You're funny. You're smart. You fit. *We* fit. Together."

"And you didn't mean that in a sexual way either?" Tessa asked, teasing.

"Actually, I think that works any way you want to look at it. Maybe we're just made for each other."

Tessa felt a soft movement between her legs as he slipped out. "I hope we didn't mess up your fleece."

"I think I can throw it in the wash." He made a wry face. "I guess there's an upside to condoms. I've got some now. I wasn't sure if—"

"No," she said, running her hands softly up his arms and over his shoulder blades. "I like how you feel. And since we've only been with each other ..."

He smiled again. "As you wish—which, as everyone knows means 'I love you.'" He kissed her, more deeply this time. She felt another stirring against the inside of her thigh.

"Mmm," murmured Daniel. "I'm starting to feel inspired again."

Chapter Fifteen

Kristin stood in the shabby hallway of the low-rent apartment building, trying not to smell the stink of chemicals rolling out of apartment 412. She'd been directed there by one of her old high school buddies—a guy who'd occasionally sold her some recreational goodies, pot and hash, mostly, though she'd tried Ecstasy once. She hadn't liked it. It made her feel woolly and out of control. She had to be careful about what she imbibed. She'd seen how hard drugs could screw up a woman's looks. She wrinkled her nose and wondered if she was going to age on the fumes alone.

She knocked twice; after long seconds the door cracked open a few inches. A scruffy, unshaven male face glared out at her through a bleary eyeball.

"Kurt Morrison?" she asked. "Who wants to know?"

"The best thing that's ever happened to you," Kristin said. "I hear you sell drugs."

"Whoever told you that didn't know what they were talking about."

"Half the kids I knew in high school bought drugs from you. Brandon Epps told me to come here. That reliable enough for you?"

"Yeah, I know Brandon. He's a shit head and a douche. He owes me. If you're one of his friends—"

He started to close the door, but Kristin stopped it with a straight arm, catching him off guard. She was able to push hard enough to slide one bare leg through the aperture, hitching her skirt up so he could get a good look at her from ankle to thigh.

"You sure you want to shut me out, Sparky?"

He clearly wasn't sure, which made it easy for Kristin to push the door all the way open while he gaped at her. She slipped into the room and closed the door behind her. The apartment was larger than she'd expected and frankly, not as wretched. The building was old, but Kurt Morrison had decorated his space (if you could call it decorating) with strands of orange and purple LEDs, an array of colorful scarves and throws strung along the walls, and a mismatched array of pillows on the floor. There was a tiny kitchen to the right of the door, and beyond it, a door she suspected led to the bedroom. That seemed to be the source of the chemical odors. That there was a mattress on the floor in one corner of what could only charitably be called a "living room" substantiated the belief that Kurtie had converted his bedroom into a drug lab.

"So, let's get down to business. I need some drugs ... for a friend."

He was ogling her, thoroughly, if wryly. "Yeah, that's what everybody says. I bet your 'friend' looks an awful lot like you."

Kirstin laughed out loud at that. "You're right. She does. But the resemblance is only skin deep. Under the skin, she's like Dorothy or somebody. I need something to send her to Oz."

She gave Kurt a quick once-over. He wore a faded pair of jeans that she was sure had come by their rips and tears honestly, and a short-sleeved plaid shirt that was unbuttoned down to his breast bone. He had several days' worth of scruff on his chin and long hair that hung in ragged curls, unwashed and uncombed. He looked as if he might be producing some of the chemicals in his scrawny body and just sweated them out.

"So, what do you want?" he asked.

"Something that'll mess someone up a bit. Just short term. Just for a day or a couple of hours."

"Most of what I've got'll do that. You'll have to be a little more specific."

"I want something that'll make a person think they're going a little nuts. Hallucinations would be a nice touch."

"LSD. Aka, lysergic acid diethylamide." He shrugged. "Or just have 'em eat curry on an empty stomach. That'll work too."

"Show-off. Do you have any LSD?"

He gave her a smug grimace. "Does a cow have milk? Of course, I've got it. How much do you want?"

"Just enough to freak somebody out. It's not for a pleasure trip."

"So just a tab or two, then," he said.

There was a spice rack sitting on the kitchen peninsula—the kind that had a magnetic backing with the spices contained in round metal containers. He moved to it, popped one of the containers off the rack, then pulled a tiny manila envelope from a little wooden box on the counter. He opened the metal container and shook two minuscule squares of a translucent gray substance out of it into the envelope. Then he held the envelope out to Kristin.

She peered in at the little gray squares. "This is LSD?"

"It's called Windowpane in that form," Kurt told her. "'Cause that's what they look like and"—an artless shrug—"they let you see the world through a different window, I guess."

"So, what—I dissolve this stuff in water?"

"You could, but it's better if you slip a square under your tongue."

"She's not going to take it willingly. It's sort of a prank."

He made a frownie face. "Some prank. Will there be chlorine in the water? Carbonation?"

"Just the stuff that comes out of the refrigerator. Or bottled, maybe."

"So, filtered. Yeah, you should be able to put it in that. But it should be consumed quickly. It degrades fast."

This guy really did like to show off his chemical smarts. She was willing to bet he didn't do that with all his customers. He wanted to impress her.

Kristin reached for the envelope, but Morrison pulled it away from her. "That isn't free," he said.

"Oh. I thought maybe we could barter for it." She smiled to convey exactly the sort of barter she had in mind.

He apparently missed her intent. "I've got bills to pay. My little chemistry set isn't cheap and I have to pay rent on this place."

She reached for the top button of his shirt, but he stepped back. "I'm serious," he said. "I need cash. In real Treasury Department bills. Do you have money?"

"I've got something better," Kristin said, reaching for his crotch. He pulled away again.

What the hell? thought Kristin. *Is he gay?*

No, from what she'd heard, he was definitely not gay, but he was the supplier for several strippers at LA dance clubs who needed his products to keep them going through long nights of lap dancing. Maybe he was getting all the female attention he wanted. The thought nettled Kristin. She wasn't some pock-marked, pot-headed show girl.

She banished her annoyance with an effort. This was going to take a different approach. She had money, but she didn't want to spend it on this. She glanced around the room, looking for ammunition. Sitting on a table next to a rattan chair was a stack of comic books. *Samantha Solar*, Issue #115. She knew almost nothing about comic books, but Morrison was apparently into them.

Maybe that was the way to his heart—and other organs. Something the strippers couldn't give him. A woman who liked comic books.

"Hey, you've got the latest issue of *Samantha Solar*!" Kristin exclaimed, feigning excitement. She wasn't sure it was the latest issue, but it looked crisp and shiny, fresh off the shelf, so she knew it must be recent.

Morrison looked surprised. "Yeah, I don't miss an issue. Do you read it?"

"Wouldn't miss an issue either," she said. The cover showed a dark-haired, curvaceous woman in a remarkably scanty spacesuit fighting off some sort of octopoid creature floating against a background of stars. "I mean, a woman who can kick ass in outer space. How cool is that? Sam's my hero."

Morrison gave Kristin a more serious look, starting with her legs and moving up to her breasts and finally her face. "Now that you mention it, you sort of look like her. Your hair's even the same color."

Damn, Kristin thought. *Talk about serendipity.* She'd only just dyed her hair a Robeson color called Midnight at the Oasis two days earlier. And, wouldn't you know it, Kurt was starting to get a boner. She could see it bulging the crotch of his faded jeans. He was just the sort of guy who would get off on the idea of fucking a comic book heroine.

"Maybe we can work out a deal after all," he said. "I've always wondered what Samantha Solar would look like naked. One second."

He crossed to a bookshelf that held more of the magazines, some action figures, and some cosplay gear. When he turned back to Kristin, he was holding a Samantha Solar headdress—a half-mask, the upswept temples of which merged into an iridescent gold sunburst.

You have got to be kidding. He has cosplay shit. Of course he does.

Kristin decided she might as well assume the role. She tossed her raven locks and fixed him with a penetrating gaze. "So, you've discovered my secret identity, human. Give me my sun crown. I need it to return to my full powers. I've been in this mortal form too long."

He held the headpiece just out of her reach. "No, Solar, not unless you agree to join with me. If you refuse me, I will destroy your crown and you will be stuck in this weak human form forever."

She glared at him, then held out her hand. "Agreed. Give me the crown and I will submit to you."

Was that the way superheroes talked? She had no clue, but he seemed to be digging it. She took the headpiece, then struck a pose and fitted it over her hair. Looking out through the eye holes, she could see the effect it was having on Morrison. He was practically panting. Kristin took off her shirt, unbuttoning it slowly, letting him get a good look at her breasts framed in the lace of her bra before she undid the front clasp and released them to the air.

His eyeballs almost did a cartoon "aah-oo-gah!" as he took her in. She felt her nipples contract as they always did when a man admired her breasts. She gave him a solemn, superheroine look and dropped her skirt.

He drew in a sharp breath when he saw that she was wearing nothing beneath it.

"Wow," he said, looking her up and down. "I knew you'd look good but not *this* good. Everything's different in 3D."

Kristin rotated her hips, a long, slow movement that held the guy's gaze as if in a vise. She ended the movement with her pelvis thrust toward him. "I can feel the heat of your desire, human. It burns my flesh. I can hear your thoughts. You have long wondered what it would be like to bed Samantha Solar."

He swallowed hard. "Every hour of every day."

Ew. She suspected those magazines had seen a lot of time in the bathroom. She shrugged off her disgust. "You shall achieve your desire," she said. "And I shall achieve mine—I will regain my full strength and be released from this mundane form."

Not a bad improv, she thought. *I should try acting.*

Blinking, Morrison led her toward his mattress. She didn't want to know the provenance of any of the stains she could see peeking from beneath the wine-red velour coverlet. There was no way she was letting that mattress get anywhere near her skin. She stopped, pushed Morrison to the bare floor, and straddled him, ripping his shirt off so violently, buttons went flying. That's what a superheroine would do, right?

"You have fallen into my trap, villain! You will now discover how Samantha Solar feeds her superpowers!" She unzipped his jeans and pulled both jeans and underpants down to his knees. Boy, was he ready. "Call me Xanagar," he gasped. "You know, the head of O.R.I.O.N."

"Xanagar, you fool," she said, though she didn't have the foggiest idea what O.R.I.O.N. was. "You won't escape me this time. I'll drain your life essence dry."

He didn't make any attempt to escape. He just groaned, "No, Solar, you super bitch. Not that. Anything but that!"

She mounted him quickly and rode, keeping herself stiffly upright. It kept her further from his general grime and allowed him an eyeful of her "girls" bobbing above him. At one point, he reached for them with both hands, but she grasped his wrists and pinned his arms down so the worst he could do was grab her thighs.

Kristin almost laughed, wondering what the hell Morrison's neighbors must think of all this ruckus. She wished there was a mirror in the room so she could see just how ridiculous they looked: Him thrashing violently beneath her, panting and moaning and gibbering incoherently as if she were torturing him, and she sitting astride him, stone faced and erect, like a queen on a wild horse, her crown gleaming in the glitter of his Halloween lights.

"Solar, you demon! I'll—!" He gasped and came explosively, his body quaking and his eyes rolling back in his head.

Shit! Kristin was afraid for two seconds that he was having a seizure and she'd killed the golden goose. She jacked herself off of him and stood, wondering what to do next. Call 911? Grab some more Windowpane and maybe some other stuff and split? But in a moment' he seemed to recover, breathing heavily but chuckling under his breath.

Relieved, Kristin moved away from him, knocked some comics off the rattan chair, and seated herself in such a way that he could see where he'd just been. She had another deal in mind.

"Now, Xanagar," she said, "the next time I come to you for sustenance, will you submit willingly?"

Morrison shook his head. "No, Solar," he whispered. "I will not submit. You'll have to take what you want. Do your worst."

"You wouldn't survive my worst," she told him.

He took a couple of deep breaths then sat up. "Wow. That was intense. I mean, I've never … Wow."

Kristin pulled off the cosplay headgear and fluffed her hair. "Does that pay for the LSD?"

"Yeah," he said, grinning now. "Yeah, it does."

"Okay," Kristin said. "Look. I know I said I didn't want anything for myself, but I've got an important audition coming up next week and I need something that will give me a little extra confidence."

Morrison staggered to his feet, pulling his underpants and jeans back up. "You, um, you seem pretty confident already, Samantha. I know that's not your real name—"

"It'll do. I just need a little extra something for this one."

"Like a-an acting gig? You an actress? Or, uh"—he licked his lips, his eyes dropping to the glistening spot between her legs—"something like that."

He thinks I'm a porn star. She smiled. "It's not important what kind of audition it is. You're the expert. What do I need?"

He stumbled over to his spice rack, opened a container, and withdrew a plastic pouch full of white powder. "Cocaine. The breakfast of champions. How much do you want?"

"You tell me."

"I dunno. For a kick in the confidence, maybe a quarter of this."

"Great. Wrap it up."

His eyes widened. "Do you know what that much coke is worth?"

"Maybe an additional battle with Samantha Solar would cover it?"

She read his face. "*Several* additional battles ... Xanagar?"

"I think several ..." He swallowed. "Here. I'll show you how to use it."

He laid out two lines of cocaine atop the peninsula, then handed her a straw. "Put the straw in your nose and snort about half a line. If you've never had any before, that's all you'll need."

Kristin, still naked, bent over the table and did as he suggested. She could almost feel him staring at her ass. For a few minutes she felt nothing and then experienced a rush like nothing she'd ever felt before. It was like she was two feet off the ground, looking down over the world like she owned it.

This must be what Samantha Solar feels like, she thought. *Floating in space wearing a skimpy spacesuit.* She decided she'd have to look into getting a complete Samantha Solar costume for her capers with Kurt.

"Oh, this is good," she said. "This is really good. I might need more than that little pouch."

"Take it easy. You don't want to overdo it. Even Samantha Solar would have a fatal heart attack from too much coke."

"I'll take it easy," said Kristin. "Just not on you, villain. Does your lair have a decontamination chamber?"

"A ... what?"

"A shower, Kurt. Try to keep up." If she was going to play games with this guy, he was going to have to bathe.

Chapter Sixteen

Tessa had read that suicide was the most common form of death among college students and that the deaths peaked around exam time. Standing outside the lecture hall where her first final was about to start, playing with the tail of her braid and shivering a little in her UCLA hoodie, she could understand why. She felt a heavy weight in the pit of her stomach and, though she'd studied intensely, she was still afraid the test would have questions she didn't know the answers to.

The Getty Center, perched high in the Santa Monica mountains, appeared serene and distant. She wondered what it would be like to jump off one of its ultramodern balconies, then chided herself for the thought. She didn't really want to die, yet at the moment it seemed like a more appealing prospect than entering the exam hall.

Daniel rushed up with a backpack on, probably filled with books that he'd be studying between exams, and a familiar-looking water bottle in one hand. He stopped and caught his breath. "I got hung up at the library," he said. "I was afraid I'd miss you."

"I'm still here," Tessa said. "I'm afraid to go in. This is my third final and I'm more nervous than I should be."

"Tess, you're a good student, and you've been studying medical lore since you were in grade school. This is in your wheelhouse. Besides, you did great on the practice exams I gave you."

She laughed, catching the double entendre. Visions of the hours of practice made her feel warm in places she found distracting. "Yes, but your practice exams are rigged. And what if they ask questions we didn't cover?"

He sobered. "I asked every question I could think of. You'll be fine."

"I know. It's just ... I'm starting to panic. I know it's silly. I never felt like this in high school. Not even in the honors classes."

He put a hand on her shoulder. "Relax. It'll go great. Just take a deep breath and go in there. You can do it."

Tessa took several deep breaths. "Okay, I feel better. I'm gonna go in there and pass that test with flying colors."

"Atta girl," Daniel said.

They kissed, lightly at first and then passionately. Finally, Daniel pulled away. "I'd like to do more of that, but we'll have to wait for tonight." He glanced at his watch. "Almost time."

A bell rang, summoning the students inside. Tessa started for the door, but Daniel stopped her.

"Wait, I almost forgot to give you your water bottle." He held it out to her.

"Where'd you get that? Did I leave it at your place? I'd swear I brought it home last night."

"Man, you really are nervous. You handed it to me before the library gobbled me up and told me to give it to you before the exam in case you forgot it."

"I ... I did?"

The bell rang again. No time for puzzles or time travel paradoxes.

She grabbed the bottle and dashed for the door.

"I'll see you afterward," Daniel said. He tilted his head sideways and made a wry face.

"What?"

"You. You're all nervous about this test, but you took the time to braid your hair in the last hour."

"You're weird," Tessa told him, blew him a kiss, and hurried through the door. She grabbed an empty seat in the lecture hall between a skinny girl with beads around her neck and a big, buff guy who looked like he probably got into UCLA on a sports scholarship. A graduate assistant began passing out the exam materials, a sheaf of papers stapled together with questions on them and a small booklet for them to write their answers in. She put the water bottle at her feet and lay the materials on the fold-down desk in front of her.

She had been up late studying the night before and was pretty sure she knew the material, but still ... The graduate assistant announced that the exam was beginning and set a timer for 110 minutes. As reluctant as she was, Tessa had no choice but to open the exam. She took a swig of water to steady herself and stared at the sheaf of paper.

The first question was multiple choice, about base pairing in DNA molecules. Tessa began to relax. That was a simple one. Adenine pairs with thymine, and cytosine pairs with guanine. Tessa checked off the answer and began to relax. Maybe the test wasn't going to be so tough after all. The next question was on mitochondrial DNA, and that was easy too. She took another swig of water and felt her panic ebbing.

After the first hour of the test, Tessa knew that she was going to pass. Daniel was right. She had the answers down cold. He'd been good at predicting what questions the professor was going to ask and had quizzed her so relentlessly on them that ...

Whoosh!

The oddest feeling raced through her body. She felt lighter than air, as though she were rising off her seat and floating away toward the ceiling. She reached down and examined the chair to make sure she was still sitting on it. She was. Maybe she hadn't gotten enough sleep the night before. Maybe she was dehydrating and needed to drink more water. She took a long drink from the flask and looked at the next question.

It was on protein synthesis. That was a funny term, she thought. She knew that proteins were a type of molecule, but ... suddenly it struck her that the word could also refer to somebody who liked teenagers. Pro-teen. She knew a lot of people didn't like teenagers, which must make them anti-teen. Or maybe some antigens were anti–Gen X ...

Oh my God! she thought. *What am I thinking?*

If she didn't know better, she'd think Daniel had put something in her water bottle to try to make her relax. He said she'd given it to him earlier. She didn't remember that, but then she'd been consumed with dread over this test. High school AP and honors classes were one thing; premed college courses were something else again.

She shook herself and tried to focus on the test. Protein synthesis. Absurdity struck again and turned the phrase into Pro-Teen Sin

Thesis. Maybe she should take a course on philosophy the next semester and make that the subject of her thesis paper.

No. No. *No!* That was absurd! Why in the world couldn't she focus? She trained her eyes on the test booklet and lifted her pencil to check an answer, but the little square boxes were moving. They danced, they spun, they refused to stay still.

She turned to ask the skinny girl with the beads how she could make them hold still, but the girl was in the process of morphing into something strange and alien. As Tessa watched, her neck stretched to nearly a foot long and her lips extruded from her face like an insect's mandibles. She gave off a soft, orange glow. Tessa recoiled in horror, slamming her shoulder against the large boy on the other side of her. When she turned to apologize, she realized that he had changed too. He was an ogre—an immense, vividly green Shrek lookalike with a head twice the size of a normal Shrek and massive, scowling features. He turned toward her and opened his mouth as though to shout angrily at her for interrupting his test ... or eat her.

Something was terribly wrong. Was the wrongness in her head, or had she somehow become trapped between alien creatures in the middle of a UCLA lecture hall?

Tessa stood up, flipping the fold-out desk in front of her into the upright position and scattering her exam papers onto the floor. Was this a nightmare? Was she not really on campus? Was she still lying in her bed at home, having her own twisted version of a not-ready-for-the-test nightmare?

The room around her seemed to be growing larger, turning from a lecture hall into a massive cavern. Streaks of blue and gold ran across the walls and ceiling, and the place seemed to be breathing or pulsing. Panicking, Tessa tried to slip past the ogre toward the aisle, but she stumbled over his legs and landed in the next student's lap. This student, too, had morphed into something otherworldly with pointed ears and fangs. Certain he was going to start counting at her in a cartoon Slavic accent, she picked herself back up and scrambled toward the aisle again, climbing over legs that turned into coiling snakes at her touch.

Tessa screamed. Every head in the room turned toward her, but they had become distorted, like figures in a cubist painting. And the sounds they made— the barrage of shrieks and moans and growls were deafening. Was this hell?

When she reached the end of the aisle, Tessa rushed toward the doorway, but the distance to the door grew faster than she could run. She tried to run toward the doorway, but the walkway kept stretching longer and her legs wouldn't move. Escaping the building took forever. Once outside, she found herself in a strange world surrounded by towering, enigmatic buildings under a dark and foreboding sky, roiling with dark blue clouds. Snow fell softly from the sky.

Snow! It never snowed in Los Angeles! She looked around for somebody who could tell her what was going on, but the monstrous creatures that surrounded her just stared, as though she were the monster.

"Help me!" she wailed. "Somebody, please help me!"

One of the monsters, a tall, white-skinned creature with pale green hair, reached toward her with skeletal arms and said in a remarkably human voice, "Is something wrong?"

She pushed the thing away and screamed again. The monsters gathered around her and she began sobbing hysterically, shoving her way through them. She stumbled over a concrete curbing that she hadn't seen and sprawled on the grass, landing painfully on her hip. She tried to stand back up, but one of the monsters grabbed her. This one looked like a wolf. It had a long snout with sharp teeth.

"I think you should lie down," it said. "I'm an intern at the hospital. You're hallucinating, miss."

"No!" Tessa cried. "This is a nightmare. You're not an intern. They don't let werewolves be interns."

"Werewolves? You're hallucinating. It's okay. Help is coming."

The monster sat her down on the grass and kept her from standing up. Was it going to eat her? How could a wolf speak English? She knew a vulpine mouth and vocal cords weren't even capable of forming human speech. But, of course, it was a werewolf, and therefore supernatural, and therefore not bound by the laws of physics.

None of that matters. I have to get away before it bites me or I'll be a werewolf too.

The werewolf claimed she was hallucinating. If that were true, then it was most definitely *not* okay. Dreaming. She had to be dreaming. She was still in bed. Still at home. This was just stress. If she ignored this, it would go away and she would wake up and then everything really would be all right.

"I'm dreaming," she murmured. "I'm just dreaming."

She went limp then, relaxing back into the blue grass and looking up past the kindly werewolf to the boiling, blue clouds. *Steven Spielberg skies.* That's what she'd called them ever since she'd seen *Close Encounters.*

I'm having a close encounter, she thought as she was lifted from the ground or levitated. She had no idea which. *I'm just having a close encounter with my own fears. This is okay. I'll get it out of my system, and when I really do take the test, I'll be fine.*

She disengaged from the nightmare then, watching the weirdness slide by her, occasionally giggling at some of the things she saw and heard. Eventually, she heard a high, keening sound close by like an angry clarinet and some strange, blurry beings who smelled like disinfectant and sunscreen. They strapped her to a flying carpet, put her in a metal box, and transported her somewhere. Following a tiny, sharp pain in her arm, she relaxed further into the dream.

She was looking forward to waking up. She'd tell Daniel about her nightmare and they'd laugh about it together.

Chapter Seventeen

Tessa woke up in bed with sunlight streaming through her window. She smiled at the absurdity of the dream, of which she retained only murky memories, and blinked at the view through the blinds.

My bedroom doesn't have blinds.

A spike of adrenaline brought the surroundings into hard focus. This place wasn't her room; it was a hospital room. How in the world had she gotten here? The clock on the wall said two forty-five. Was that afternoon? Early morning? Light came from the window, so it must be daytime. She sat up but was hit with a wave of vertigo. Even when she lay down again, the bed seemed to be moving slowly beneath her.

Spotting a call button hanging on a cable over the bed's guardrail, she pushed it. Nothing happened for a good ten minutes, long enough that Tessa was about to press the button again when a nurse with dark hair and brown eyes appeared in answer to the summons.

She smiled. "Hello, Tessa. It's nice to have you with us again."

"How ... how do you know my name?"

"We checked your purse for your ID. You left your personal items behind in the lecture hall; one of your classmates made sure they made it into the ambulance with you."

"I need the purse back," Tessa said. "And my backpack. I need to get back to school. I have another exam at three thirty." *But wait. If she'd taken the biology exam this morning, if that hadn't been a nightmare ...* "I'm really confused."

"I can only imagine." The nurse gave her a sympathetic look. "Was that your first time?"

"My first time with what? Oh. No. I had my English comp and history exams Tuesday. It was biology this morning. I don't think I've ever been so nervous."

"I see," the nurse said, though Tessa wasn't sure what it was she saw. "Where am I?" she asked.

"UCLA Medical Center."

That was a relief. "So, we're close to the school. I can make it back before—"

"You really can't leave, Tessa. Your parents are on their way here. The doctor will release you then."

Her parents? Oh, dear lord. She suddenly recalled the incident in the lecture hall in a series of freeze frames. If it hadn't been a nightmare, what had it been? She'd never experienced anything like it.

"What's wrong with me?" Tessa asked. "Was that some sort of anxiety attack? Or a seizure? Am I sick?"

The nurse shook her head. "I can tell you that you're not sick. Your attending physician will be in to see you in a few minutes. He can answer any questions you have."

The doctor arrived roughly thirty minutes later. He was an older man with graying hair and wire-rim glasses. He bent over Tessa with an otoscope, shining a bright light in her eyes and examining her pupils. Then he had her open her mouth and examined her lips and gums with a gloved hand.

"Classic symptoms," he said.

"Of what?" Tessa asked. "The nurse said I wasn't sick, but something was horribly wrong with me this morning. It was absolutely terrifying."

The doctor gave her a disconcertingly direct look, as if he was trying to read her soul. "Don't you know what was wrong, Ms. Morgan? What did you expect—dropping acid before a major exam?"

"Acid?"

"LSD. When I was a student, back in the seventies, it was a trendy thing to do, and it seems to be making a comeback. But before an exam? That wasn't very smart."

"I've never used LSD in my life," Tessa said. "Or any other drug."

"You did this morning, apparently. If you took it while on campus, that was a major infraction of university rules."

Tessa thought her heart was going to beat its way out of her chest. "But I didn't take anything. I didn't even eat breakfast this morning, I was so nervous about the exam. All I had was water—"

Tessa stopped in midsentence. The water flask had been given to her by Daniel, who'd said she had given it to him earlier. But she hadn't even seen Daniel earlier. If she hadn't been in such a panic over the exam, she would have realized that the flask had come from a different source, one that looked just like her. Except for the newly dyed locks. That made semi-sense of Daniel's comment about braiding her hair. Kristin must have plopped a blonde wig on her head, but she couldn't have known that Tessa would braid her hair rather than take the time to wash it. Kristin had pulled a twin switch!

She groaned aloud. "Doctor, if someone put LSD in about a quart of water, would it ... would it work? Even if you didn't drink all of the water?" His eyebrows rose toward his hairline. "It would depend on how much was in the water to begin with. You're saying you think the drug was in your water flask?"

She nodded, still pondering the imponderable. "My boyfriend handed it to me as I was going into the lecture hall. He said I'd given it to him earlier in the day. I didn't think of it at the time, but I hadn't seen him earlier in the day. And I thought the flask was in my backpack. I put it there last night."

The doctor fixed her with a sober look. "You think your boyfriend put LSD in your water flask?"

"No. My twin sister. I didn't give Daniel that bottle; she did."

"You have a twin sister?" He sounded a bit skeptical.

"I do. And she's dead set against me pursuing a career in medicine." She looked at the doctor. "Could a lab test the water in my flask for LSD?"

"In fact, our lab did test for it. And found it." He gazed at her soberly for a moment. "If, in fact, you are telling the truth about this twin—" Tessa felt tears start from her eyes. "*Cosmopolitan* magazine, Doctor.

There's probably five or six issues in most of your waiting rooms. Our picture is on the cover of the November issue." She took a deep breath. "I did not willingly take LSD. Please believe me."

He frowned, and she thought she read sympathy in his eyes. "It doesn't matter whether I believe you, Tessa. UCLA will make the final decision as to whether you violated campus policy. Drugs are a major problem here. Unfortunately, if this was actually some trick that your sister pulled on you, the burden of proof is going to be on you. The campus authorities aren't bound by any legal obligation to find you innocent until proven guilty." He hesitated, as if wanting to say more, then added, "I'm going to sign you out, Tessa. Your parents should be here soon."

Tessa lay her head back on the pillow. Her entire core had turned to ice. Kristin. She'd been trying for days to convince Tessa to blow off finals so that she could go to the audition on Thursday.

"Tell them you've injured your hand and can't write," she'd suggested during her last attempt, "or that you—I dunno—got a mild concussion in a horrific sex accident."

If Tessa had wanted a career in modeling half as much as her twin did, she might have actually done something like that. It had the virtue of offering a reasonable excuse to postpone the test and giving her extra time to study. But she didn't want a career in modeling; she wanted a career in neurology—a career that now might hang on getting Kristin to confess to slipping LSD into her water flask.

As if. Kristin was probably gloating right now over how well the trick had worked. Tessa wondered now if Kristin had hung around outside the lecture hall to watch the meltdown.

She was pulled from her chaotic thoughts when her mother came into the room, followed closely by her father. The look on her mother's face was a combination of confusion and worry, but her father appeared ashen and frail, as if someone had knocked his legs out from under him. He placed a hand on her forehead, and Tessa noticed a slight tremor. "How are you doing, my girl?" He then plopped into a visitor chair near the bed, as if the effort of standing was too much. "Okay now. I'm still not sure what happened."

Then he got right to the point. "They said you were high on drugs," he said, shaking his head slightly. "That there was LSD in your water flask."

"There was. I just found that out myself. Kristin put it there."

"You must be mistaken," her mother said. "It was an accident, right? It must have been. Kristin wouldn't—"

"It wasn't an accident," Tessa said, her voice sounding raw and harsh in her ears. "She did it on purpose. She took my water flask out of my backpack last night, put LSD in it, and then handed it to my boyfriend to deliver to me right before the exam."

"Maybe it was your boyfriend—" Dad started to say.

"No. Daniel would never do anything like that to me. He loves me."

"How can you be sure—"

"There's nothing Daniel wants for me that I don't want for myself. Kristin wants what she wants and to hell with me."

"What does Kristin want?" Dad demanded. "I don't understand. Why would she do something like this? She loves you too."

"Because Robeson cosmetics is looking for new spokesmodels, and she set up an audition for us on Thursday. I have finals that day. I suggested she reschedule, but she talked about how hard she'd worked ... how hard *she'd* worked! Like she gives a crap about how hard *I've* worked to ... to get into *this* school ...” She couldn’t finish the sentence. Her voice got louder as she vented, and angry tears streamed down her face.

Mom looked stricken. Dad, as if she’d spoken to him in Swahili. “I don’t understand,” he repeated. “I’m sure she didn’t mean for you to just walk away from a scholarship.”

“The last time we spoke, she said I should pretend to have injured my hand so I couldn’t write, or fake a concussion or something so I could make the tests up.”

Dad shrugged. “And you couldn’t have done that? Gone the extra mile for your sister?”

“Dad!”

Her mother turned on him as well. “For the love of God, Kenneth!”

Her dad blinked, looking miserable. “Krist doesn’t have the prospects that you do, Tessa.”

Tessa’s laugh was brittle. “You mean the prospects I *had*.”

Her mom came and put an arm around her. “You’re a good student, sweetie. You always have been. Without a spot on your record. I’m sure they’ll take that into account. We’ll talk to the university board or whomever we have to. You’ll see. It will work out. Right now, let’s get you home.”

Several hours later, after enduring the discharge process from the hospital, Tessa felt like a sleepwalker as she entered their house leaning on her mother’s arm. Kristin was standing at the bottom of the staircase to greet her with smug satisfaction in her gray eyes.

“I’m shocked, Tess,” she said, barely managing to keep a straight face. “I really thought you were the good girl in the family.”

Dad shut the front door quietly behind him before saying, “She *is* the good girl in the family.”

“Well, gee, thanks,” Kirsten snarked. “I guess I’ll just go up to my room and sulk.”

“No, you’ll go up to your room and pack,” said Dad. His voice was like ice, his eyes hundreds of degrees colder.

Kristin cocked her head and gave him the big, pouty eyes. “What?”

“I want you out of this house. Now. Today.”

For mere seconds, Kristin’s face showed a flash of unguarded shock.

Then she retrieved her “cool” and grinned. “Nice one, Daddy.”

“I’m not joking, Kristin. I have finally had it with your cavalier behavior. You’ve done a lot of incredibly fucked-up things, but this takes the cake. Get. Out.”

Kristin shook her head, looking affronted, confused, disbelieving. She turned to their mother. “Mom, you’re not going along with this—”

"You heard your father. Go upstairs, pack some things, and get out of here. You've been earning enough money to afford a car, expensive clothing, and drugs, apparently. So you can surely afford an apartment. When you've got someplace to live, you can get the rest of your things out of our house. Your father is right; you have crossed a line. That you could do something like this to your sister ..."

"I have no idea what you're—"

Dad completely lost it. "GET OUT OF MY HOUSE! NOW! And don't come back until you can do something to earn Tessa's forgiveness."

Tears that looked real streamed from Kristin's eyes. She dithered on the staircase for a moment, looking uncharacteristically lost. Then she shrieked, "Fuck you, old man!" and pounded up the stairs.

Mom guided Tessa up to her room, hugged her for a long moment, then told her to rest until supper. When Tessa emerged an hour or so later, Kristin was gone.

###

Wednesday morning the college decided that the presence of drugs in the water flask was a clear violation of policy and suspended Tessa pending review of her case. She would miss her finals, and even if the college should happen to decide in her favor, ultimately, she would have to make up an almost impossible amount of work.

She'd taken refuge in her room where she collapsed on the bed and cried until she'd spent every tear she possessed. Her cell phone rang. Daniel was calling, but she didn't answer. She couldn't bear to speak with him right then. After some passage of time, which could have been minutes and could have been hours, so deep was Tessa into her reverie, she sat up and looked around. The textbooks on her shelf, the science books that she'd collected for years, seemed to taunt her. She'd read them lovingly, over and over again, and now she felt as though they had abandoned her. UCLA had abandoned her, at least temporarily. Would it have killed them to let her finish her exams? They would have until after the new year to render a decision, but until they did render a decision, she was stranded.

She finally sat up, took a deep breath, and decided she needed to seriously consider the possibilities for her future. She could apply to another school in California. But now with a "history" of drug use, would she be accepted to the better schools? And anyway, today's date was likely too late to be admitted by next semester. So, what would she do, sit around until the following fall? School was definitely a possibility for the future. But for right here, right now. Likely not.

And what does a person who doesn't go to school do with their life? Well, they get a job. She hated to admit it, but she did enjoy the modeling, and it paid far more than anything else she could possibly do. Her long-term goal still had to be to become a doctor. No way would she give up on that. And modeling could be a way to pay for future med school. It was common knowledge that med school was expensive.

But then there was her pride to consider. Kristin had engineered this circumstance! How could she let Kristin "win"? Simply thinking about Kristin, she felt the anger building, even verging on rage. Yet she had never been a vengeful person.

She stopped and took some more deep breaths. She knew Kristin better than anyone else. And although she had been unsure of Kristin's motivations for several years, she loved her sister. She also recalled a promise she had made to herself during her teens that she would never hold a grudge. Harboring a heart of unforgiveness was the source of all sorts of angst and physical pain for the one who refused to forgive. She knew that. Even so, forgiveness was not going to happen immediately, but she also knew it would come at some point. Living otherwise was not an option for her.

She thought wryly that there was nothing keeping her from going to the audition the next day. Was Kristin sitting by the phone, waiting for her to call and say she would, or would she call and try to talk her way back into Tessa's good graces? She sensed in her heart a decision that she would go to the audition. But it would be on her own terms. And she would let Kristin know, in no uncertain terms, how much pain she had caused. Kristin called late that afternoon, sounding a little tipsy. "Hey," she said, her voice more subdued than Tessa had heard it for years. She almost sounded as if she was taking something seriously. Getting thrown out of the house, maybe.

"I figured I'd be hearing from you," Tessa said dully. "What's your sales pitch today?"

"Yeah, I get that it was a bitch thing to do. And I hope the school decides to drop the charges or whatever."

"Really? Are you willing to tell them what you did?"

Kristin snorted. "Well, that'd be stupid. Robeson wouldn't even consider us if I copped to that."

"Thought so."

"Look, if they decide to let you stay, it's all water under the bridge, right? But if we get this gig, if I can establish myself in the industry, you can write your own ticket. Take it or leave it." After a moment of silence, Kristin added, "I'm not like you, Tess. I don't have your smarts or your willpower or your drive. I have nothing but a perfect face and a perfect body. Help me do this thing. There's nothing keeping you from it now."

"Thanks to you."

"I'm begging, Tess. If the school doesn't expel you—"

Tessa took a deep breath and let it out. "Yeah. And if they do, I guess I'm going to need a plan B." She paused. "Okay, you lying bitch, what time do the auditions start?"

"Nine o'clock sharp. With us looking sharp. I'll come pick you up." She sighed. "All right. See you then."

"Oh, by the way," Kristin added, just before Tessa tapped the end call button. "Your boyfriend is an awesome kisser. I'd totally bang that." Tessa sucked in a sharp breath, stinging, hot words leaping to her tongue. She didn't say them but instead ended the call and called up another number. *Why did Kristin have to be so cruel?* she thought as the phone rang. Tessa couldn't even comprehend the way her sister thought. She considered for a moment not showing up for the audition. That would burn Kristin. But it would also be inconsistent with her own character; she knew she would be at Robeson precisely at nine sharp. "Hello," Sarah answered.

"Sarah! Please help me. I need your wise words or I might just murder my sister."

Chapter Eighteen

Time was a funny thing, Kristin thought. When you're young it feels like a month is a year and a year is an eternity. Yet when you get older ... *Time flies like an arrow. Fruit flies like a banana.* That was a joke her agent, Jerry Lance, had told her. It was from somebody named Groucho Marx. Kristin had laughed hysterically when she first heard it, even though it wasn't really that funny. But the part about time flying was all too true.

Five years had flown by since she and Tessa had won the audition to become spokesmodels for Robeson Cosmetics. Five years since they had become two of the most recognizable faces in the fashion industry. And all that time had passed in a blur. At first the blur had been from the drugs that Kurt Morrison was giving her, but she'd gotten off them after the first year, in part because of his whining about how much coke she was snorting.

"It's going to age you, Kristin," he'd told her. "You don't want people thinking you're Tessa's mom."

That had hit home and, despite getting clean, she'd kept seeing Kurt, because she'd found that a little coke went a long way to grease the skids with people for whom sexual favors weren't practical. Besides, he'd cleaned up well. He'd started showering every day, grooming himself, and even dressing better. Turned out, underneath all the grime was a good-looking guy with a riot of dark blond curls and penetrating green eyes. She'd actually begun to enjoy their X-rated cosplay ... until he got clingy. Kristin was sure he was falling in love with her, which gave her the creeps.

No attachments. That was her rule. Attachments held you back. They kept you from making decisions that needed to be made. They conditioned your responses to everything. She'd broken off their relationship almost two years ago.

Still, she was grudgingly glad he'd nagged about the effect of drugs on the body. As much as she loved the rush, she'd curl up and die if she ever saw a crow's foot anywhere near her eyes. The working life span of a model was short enough as it was, and she didn't want to make it any shorter. She'd made plenty of money in the last five years and owned a mansion in Malibu overlooking the Pacific—something she'd always dreamed of—but fame was even more important than wealth because it was the source of wealth. If you had fame, you were a wealth engine. Once she stopped being a model, her fame would evaporate like the evidence of a Los Angeles rainstorm. A few rays of Southern California sunshine and it was gone.

Kristin liked to exercise her fame the way someone else might exercise a dog. She took it for walks where it might be recognized and commented upon. Just now, she was standing in a Robeson Cosmetics boutique, counting the number of times her face appeared on boxes, displays, and art posters. The largest and most striking of these last items were the yin/yang shots she and Tessa had done when they'd first started working with Robeson. They'd become a branding icon, repeated on a variety of product displays, but none so prominently as for the new line of Robeson hair colorants, touting the vividness and range of the brand's offerings. *Robeson: The Difference Is Like Night and Day.*

The iconic image had spawned a myriad of spin-offs in the other market segments in which the girls modeled. For cosmetics, Tessa and Kristin were exclusive to Robeson, but the twins' images also advertised watches, jewelry, and clothing. Inevitably, Tessa was arrayed in the colors of the sun and vivid blue skies and bright spring greens, while Kristin's on-camera wardrobe seemed to have less variety than Morticia Addams's—blacks and midnight blues, purples, deep reds, and twilight mauves. The closest thing she had to a daylight getup was a Bob Mackie gown she'd worn for a *Cosmopolitan* spread—a shimmering silvery-white piece of gauzy silk that George Robeson said made her look like she was drenched in moonlight.

Her relationship with George was pretty weird, she thought. After avoiding Tessa as if she was a plague rat (something that must surely have confused the crap out of her sister), he'd finally figured out that Kristin was the evil twin. Now, whenever they shared a room, she'd catch him staring at her, his brow furrowed in thought, his desire like a hot white spotlight gliding over her skin. But though she'd tried to manipulate the situation, he'd never allow himself to be alone with her for more than the time it took him to escape a room. Too bad, really. She could still remember their one and only encounter vividly, and sometimes imagined repeating it, sending him steamy thoughts that failed to penetrate his reserve.

An older woman in a red Christian Dior suit looked up from the hair color display and said the same words Kristin had heard hundreds of times before: "Oh! You're one of the Robeson girls!" Then a brief pause, followed by the tentative question: "Aren't you?"

Kristin tossed her glossy black mane, laughed with all the sincerity she could muster (which wasn't much), and said, "Why, yes. Yes, I am."

"Are you doing a promotional event here today? I didn't see any ads for it."

"Oh, no. I just always shop at Robeson's for my cosmetics." Bald-faced lie. At that moment she was wearing Pat McGrath eyeshadow and Charlotte Tilbury foundation and setting powder. Only her hair color was a Robeson product.

The woman fumbled in her Hermes purse for a pen. "Could you autograph my hair coloring?"

"I'd be delighted." Kristin gave her a huge white smile.

The woman handed Kristin the pen and a box of product she'd been holding (one she hadn't even purchased yet); Kristin scribbled the name *Taylor Swift* on it, then added, *JK, Kristin Morgan.* She returned the box to the woman. "Anything for my fans."

"Oh, thank you!" the woman gushed, not even looking at the sig- nature. "My husband will be so thrilled. Don't tell anybody, but he has a pile of magazines in his den with your pictures on the cover."

Kristin felt her smile lock into place. "Really?"

The woman chuckled conspiratorially and lowered her voice. "I think he finds them ... stimulating, if you know what I mean."

"Stimulating," Kristin repeated. *You mean he jerks off to them.* "You don't seem to mind."

"Dear girl, I have no complaints. After all, when he comes to bed, you're not there. But *I* am." She smiled and swung around to stride off on her Louboutin shoes, flashing the patented red soles.

Kristin watched her go, bemused. She'd never thought of it that way before. She wondered if Georgie R had a similar stack of magazines in his office and if his wife was the beneficiary of their effects. She decided it was time to have another go at George. A serious go. He needed to understand that his aloof and principled behavior was having a negative impact on his star model's self-esteem and that it would be a shame if she ended up in therapy having to spill her guts to some shrink.

She smiled, already considering where and how to arrange the encounter, and left the store, stepping out into the sunshine of a typical coastal SoCal morning. The two-story Robeson showcase was on the Third Street Promenade, a swank outdoor pedestrian mall in Santa Monica, and she could feel a cool ocean breeze wafting up from the beach four blocks away. The morning sun warmed the pavers under her feet and sparkled off the waters of a nearby fountain. She looked around to see if anybody else recognized her, but at nine thirty in the morning, few people were around. Spotting an old-fashioned newsstand near the center of the mall, with magazines and paperbacks displayed in rows, she wandered over to it and looked for the ones with her picture on them; most also included Tessa. Several had their images, but of course no labels identified them as the Morgan twins. To find their names, you had to read the fine print at the bottom of the photo spread, and it was really fine print. She doubted that Dior Woman's lustful hubby even knew who the hell was winding him up. That bothered her a little. She supposed some people could keep straight that Tessa was the White Swan or whatever they called her, and Kristin the Black Swan or The Raven as she'd been hashtagged on Instagram and Twitter.

"Nevermore," she croaked, not sure how she felt about being associated with a bone-picking bird that was only one step up from a crow.

Maybe she'd throw on a bikini and head for the beach. That could be fun. She was supposed to be at Gianni's for a photo shoot in ten, but she was in no real hurry to get there. Still ... she called for an Uber on her iPhone and strolled down to Santa Monica Boulevard, turning right toward the beach and continuing west while she watched the Uber change routes to keep up. Let him chase her, she thought. He should have to work for the thrill of giving her a ride.

The driver finally found her standing alongside Ocean Avenue studying one of the ubiquitous billboards, the white sands of the beach behind her. He stared at her as she slid into the back seat and finally said in a thick Pakistani or Indian accent, "Don't I see you somewhere?"

"Well, there was that torrid night on the sands of Manora Beach."

She and Tessa had done a photo shoot there once, with armed guards standing watch just outside of camera range. She'd hooked up with one of them after and discovered that sex, sand, and saltwater don't mix nearly as well as the movies say they do.

"No, no, I'm sure I see your face before."

She pointed up through the window at the billboard she'd been looking at when he'd arrived.

A delighted smile spread across his face. "You're that blackbird girl from the magazines. My wife has very many of them."

That blackbird girl from the magazines. That anonymous girl from the billboards.

"Yes, but do you know my name?"

He shrugged. "Your face, I know. But your name ..." He shrugged again.

Kristin was suddenly sick of being a face with no name. How bizarre was that? She was famous and anonymous at the same freaking time. "Tell you what," she said. "Tell your wife that you met Rihanna today."

"Rihanna? No. She is a Black actress. You are not Black."

"Really? My mistake. I must have me confused with someone else."

He laughed and pulled out into traffic, leaving Kristin to lean back in her seat, a sick feeling in the pit of her stomach and an old America tune running through her head with a sarcastic parody lyric supplied by her cynical imagination: "I ride through the city, just a face with no name. I've discovered anonymous fame ..."

Don't give up your day job, said a snarky little voice from somewhere in her carefully partitioned brain.

She ignored it. *You should be happy,* she told herself. *This was what you wanted.*

Yeah, but now I want more.

Tessa had once told her—in one of those blindingly boring history lectures she loved to give—that, according to legend, some Macedonian guy named Alexander had had a nervous breakdown after he conquered the world because he had nothing left to accomplish. Kristin knew exactly how he'd felt. She had no worlds left to conquer.

Fine. She'd just have to find a new world to conquer, set herself a new goal. Something even bigger and better than getting Geo Robeson to shag her again in his office or on his dining room table.

The Uber driver dropped her off at Studio DeLuca. Tessa was already there, of course. She'd probably arrived half an hour early, not because she was all that enthusiastic about the job but because she had to be perfect at everything. They had long ago reconciled over Kristin's little stunt with the LSD, or at least the subject had finally stopped coming up, but Kristin still felt a certain resentment over Tessa's compulsion to overachieve. Why work so hard when they were already at the top of their profession? She was convinced that her sister was doing it just to make her look lazy. DeLuca strode into the studio with a wide grin on his face. He and Kristin had stopped having any kind of sexual relationship some time ago, as the horny goat had moved on to newer, younger, more impressionable models, which was just fine with Kristin. Keeping him sated had become a chore.

Now the sisters kept him satisfied by bringing him in mountains of money for taking their pictures for a wide array of clients. His attitude had become more protective, almost fatherly. Kristin had almost forgotten what it was like to have a father. Her own was a distant stranger. Neither he nor her mother had been able to let go of their absurd conviction that she'd robbed her sister of something. They called Tessa "sweetheart" and "baby" to this day; she was just Kristin. No endearments.

That embargo had extended to Tessa as well; though she worked side by side with Kristin every day, it had taken a couple of years after UCLA pulled up the drawbridge before she called her her sister again. Even now, she was sometimes withdrawn and wary.

That was okay. Gianni called the sisters "his girls" and "his darlings." She was his Starry Sky and Tessa his Golden Sun. He sent them expensive presents on their birthday and on holidays. Sometimes he sent them jewelry just because he thought it would look good on them in photos. Tessa called him Saint Nick. Kristin bit her tongue every time.

Saint, my ass.

"I have news, ladies," DeLuca announced. "There will be no shoot today."

"You couldn't have called to tell us that?" Kristin asked.

"That is not the news," DeLuca said. "The news is that your agent believes he can make a deal for you that does not involve my superb photography."

"Why would Jerry tell you and not us?"

"He *will* tell you. We were chatting just now, and he happened to mention this certain deal, and I pleaded to be the one to tell you of it."

"What kind of a deal?" Kristin demanded. "And could we do without the cheesy Italian sausage–speak?"

Gianni ignored the insult but dropped into a perfectly SoCal speech pattern, sans Italian accent. "Jerry spoke with Alexei Dvorak this morning. You've heard of him, I imagine."

Kristin felt her heart leap into her throat. "*Heard* of him? He's only, like, the most famous director since Steven Spielberg!"

"I don't get it," Tessa said. "What does Dvorak want with us?"

"What do you think he wants? He wants you to be in a movie!"

Kristin was speechless. She and Tessa just stared at each other for what seemed like an entire minute before Kristin fixed the photographer with a fierce glare. "So what's the catch, Gianni?"

"There is no catch, Krissy. You won't have to ... entertain him. All you'll have to do is take directions from him. Apparently, he has a movie script for which a set of twins as different as night and day would be perfect. He thought he would have to 'manufacture' them using sleight of camera and CGI when he saw you two doing that little devil and angel skit Dolce & Gabbana cooked up for Halloween last year. He also caught several of your interviews, liked your on-camera chemistry, and decided you might just be able to act. He wants to see if his instincts are on the money ... quite literally. So you have an audition to prove you can act the part of twin sisters. How cosmic is that?" He affected a cheesy grin. "Cosmic," repeated Tessa, shaking her head. She seemed bemused.

Kristin froze, a sick, slimy panic rising up from the pit of her stomach. "Act? I ... I ..." She caught herself. She'd wanted a new goal—some new territory to conquer. This was it. And it would put a name to her face. "Of course, I can act. What's there to prove?"

Gianni gave her an uncharacteristically stern look. "This is Alexei Dvorak we're talking about here, my girl. If I were you, I'd be grateful to have an opportunity to prove myself to him. Jerry's hiring acting coaches for you, and there will be screen tests. All a formality, of course, because I am sure you will both be brilliant." Cheesy grin again.

Tessa seemed lost in thought. "There are books on acting, right?"

"Yeah," Kristin said. "We could start with *Acting for Dummies*."

"Oh, God, there's so much I have to learn," Tessa murmured. "You do that, Tess. I'll start learning in my own way."

Gianni looked at Kristin as though trying to penetrate the enigmatic look on her face, but Kristin just winked at him and left the studio.

###

The chemical smell was much the same as Kristin remembered—sharp, pungent, and obvious from the moment she reached the fourth floor of the shabby apartment building. Kurt Morrison had once told her that the only reason he didn't get raided by the police was that he had so many cops for customers.

"Did you think they stay up all night on coffee and donuts?" he'd asked her, laughing.

Kristin knocked on the door, prompting a series of strange whispers, growls, and grunts from within. She put her ear to the door and knocked again. This time she heard swearing, and a male voice yelled, "I'm busy!"

Kristin grinned. She suspected she'd caught Mr. Chemist in the throes of crazy sex. She knocked a third time.

"C'mon, Taragon, or whatever. It's your old pal, Sam Solar. Answer the damn door, lover boy."

Following a flurry of rustles and thuds, a female voice whined, "But I'm not done!"

In the relative quiet that followed, more rustling was followed by the sound of footsteps. The door swung open to reveal Kurt wearing a silk robe that looked very last century. His unshaven face telegraphed shock and even alarm. Behind him, on the other side of the room, a naked woman lounged fetchingly atop the comforter on his mattress. The glare she leveled at Kristin might have scalded most women; Kristin was not most women.

"Wow," he said finally, the stunned expression on his face unchanged. "It's been awhile."

"Yeah," Kristin said. "I was hoping you'd remember me."

"Of course, I ... What do you want?"

She shot a look past him at the skank on his bed. "Not something I care to discuss in front of present company."

The woman's glare sharpened. "You heard him, bitch. We're busy. Get lost."

Kurt turned his head toward the naked woman without quite looking at her. "I need you to go, Fay. I've got business to do."

"What the hell?" the skank said. "Business? *I'm* your damn business, boyfriend. And I ain't come yet."

Kurt swung around, went to his spice rack (his new and improved spice rack), extracted a baggy filled with white powder from a container, and tossed it at the woman. "Go buy yourself a vibrator."

"Fuck. What's got into you? Who is this bitch?"

"Fay ..."

"Whatever. At least let me get my fucking dress on." She stood, grabbed a short yellow dress that had been flung over the arm of a chair, and shimmied into it. Then she slipped her feet into a pair of high-heeled sandals and click-clacked her way to the door. She paused to give Kristin the stank eye, no doubt registering her perfectly made-up face. They also registered something else.

"Hey, I know you. I've seen you in *Elle* hawking perfume. You're a model."

Kristin felt as if icy fingers had wrapped around her heart. *What is this— a fucking object lesson? Careful what you wish for, you might get it?* The one time she didn't want to be recognized ...

"Right. Like a model would be caught dead here. The name's Sam, sweet cheeks, and I'm a stripper. But I get told I look like one of those Robeson girls all the time. Day Light and Fright Night, or whatever they call 'em."

"Go on, Fay," said Kurt. "I'll see you later."

Fay shot a look at Kurt over her shoulder. "Maybe. Maybe not." She slithered past Kristin and disappeared down the hallway.

Kurt opened the door wider and let Kristin into the apartment. The room wasn't much different than the last time she'd seen it, except that the rattan chair was gone, replaced by a chair like the one in her dad's home office. What'd he call it—a wingback. And a cheap little electric fireplace had been installed on the left-hand wall with a braided rug in front of it. The place still smelled of chemicals, but with an overlay of cologne or body spray and incense.

Delightful.

"So ... what are you doing here?" Kurt said tonelessly. He'd backslid a bit since she'd seen him last—his hair was an unruly mop, but it looked fresh washed; he had stubble on his cheeks and chin, but he was clean.

Be thankful for small favors. "I need a little confidence booster," Kristin said aloud. "Very little. Nothing like what I was doing before."

He didn't react to that but just kept looking at her as if trying to memorize her face. "I kept waiting for you to call me," he said. "I thought ... I thought we had a connection."

He was looking all puppy-eyed again. Kristin choked back her revulsion and smiled seductively, lowering her gaze to his groin. "Wanna find out if we still have it?"

He looked wary. "How do I know you're not just going to vanish on me again?"

"Because I've missed you, honey. I never should have fallen out of touch, even when I stopped doing drugs. You know how at NA meetings they tell you to stop seeing the people you used to do drugs with? Well, I guess that's what I did."

"We were an item for years after you stopped using," Kurt observed dryly.

"I didn't *want* to leave you, and now I realize it was a terrible mistake." She made her voice low and wistful as if tears weren't far away. *Hell, yeah, I can act.* She moved closer to him and ran her fingers through his wild hair. "I was hoping ... we could get something started again."

He started to say something, then stopped and swallowed hard, his lips pressed into a grim, straight line. She moved in still closer, draping her arms around his neck and kissing the corner of his mouth (the mouth he'd no doubt had all over the bimbo who'd just left).

Finally, he reacted, though not quite the way she expected. He grasped her wrists, pulled her hands down, and stepped back. "I take VISA now," he said, turned his back to her, and returned to his spice rack. "Just tell me what you want. And don't say, 'I want you, Kurt,' 'cause I think we both know that's not true."

Kristin wavered just inside the door for a moment, bemused and annoyed. Okay. So, the little shit was going to play hard to get. Fine. She'd always liked a challenge. And one way or another, she was going to get what she wanted.

Chapter Nineteen

"You've got this in the bag," Jerry Lance murmured, eyeing the stunning collection of tall, slender young women—identical twins, all—with which they shared a large Paradox Studios conference room. They were all about Tessa and Kristin's age and seemed to represent every ethnic group from Hollywood and beyond. To a woman, they were staring at scripts and silently mouthing lines as they paced the floor.

Jerry's fireplug body was nattily if casually attired in a navy Ralph Lauren shirt, athletic jacket, and chinos. His neatly trimmed beard was a shade between silver and snow and reminded Tessa of Christmas. As persuasive as she knew Jerry was, she was amazed he'd been able to pull this audition out of his bag of presents.

"Dvorak can see star quality from a mile away, and he thinks you've got it, Tess. These other women are just plan B. But they're going to be very disappointed, because he's not gonna need a plan B. You and Kristin are gonna ace this."

He flashed Tessa a beatific grin and pulled a long gold tube out of his jacket pocket. He withdrew a $150 King of Denmark cigar and started to light it, but a woman in an elegant pants suit pointed to the No Smoking sign on the wall. Jerry reluctantly tucked the cigar back into his gold-plated case and sighed. "What's Hollywood coming to when a man can't even smoke a cigar in peace?"

Tessa smiled. She'd always thought of Jerry as unflappable, but the fact that he'd tried to light up in an enclosed space he didn't own was testimony that he, too, was suffering from a bout of nerves.

Daniel appeared, carrying a pair of chicken-salad sandwiches, one for him and one for Tessa, that he'd purchased in the studio commissary.

She waved hers away. "Oh, I can't. I'll eat when this is all over."

"I'll take it," Jerry said, grabbing it from Daniel's hand before he could object. "But you shouldn't be nervous, kiddo. You got this."

Daniel sat next to Tessa. She felt a warm glow knowing that he had taken the day off for her. Having gotten dual master's degrees in engineering and business from UCLA, he was in the throes of establishing a tech startup in Silicon Beach, the high-tech mecca around Venice, California. Daniel's startup involved self-driving cars and other AI tech and was already attracting attention from venture capitalists. Between Tessa's modeling career and Daniel's eighteen-hour-a-day job at his own company, they barely seemed to see one another anymore, but Tessa knew that was going to change as soon as Daniel felt secure about his income. That they would marry was a foregone conclusion; the only open question was when.

"If Jerry says you've got this," Daniel said reassuringly, "then you've got it. You have the best agent in the business. My fiancée is going to be a movie star before the year is out."

"Listen to the kid, Tessa," Jerry said. "You've got a real smart guy there. And try to relax."

Tessa was finding relaxation difficult, but she used the breathing exercises their acting coach had taught her. "Focus on the air moving in and out of your lungs," Olivia had said during their last session. "You've got your dialogue down cold, and your line readings are flawless. Just walk onto that soundstage and become the character."

Piece of cake.

She glanced up to where Kristin, standing against the opposite wall, was poring over the script. Jerry had gotten up and was giving her a little pep talk. Kristin nodded but otherwise ignored him. She was still memorizing her lines—something their acting coach had repeatedly told her to do in advance. Her expression was downright grim. Tessa wasn't used to seeing her sister like that. Kristin was the assertive one, the one who always had a plan, the mover and shaker.

She doesn't look like herself.

There was more to it than that, though. Kristin seemed to have an extra edge to her energy these days. Tessa had first noticed it in their early sessions with their acting coach. Tessa worried that she'd gone back to using cocaine, something she knew had gotten her twin through the early days of their modeling career. She prayed that she was wrong, that the excess energy was just from excitement, nerves, and all the caffeine Kristin was consuming. If it was coke or some other mood enhancer, there was nothing Tessa could do to stop her. One thing she had learned the hard way was that when Kristin wanted something, she was unstoppable. The woman in the pants suit reappeared, calling "the Morgan twins" to the studio. After a quick kiss from Daniel and a thumbs-up from Jerry, Tessa and Kristin followed the woman down the hall. Their escort smilingly ushered them into a soundstage that reminded her of Gianni DeLuca's studio, but the man sitting in the director's chair was Alexei Dvorak.

Dvorak wasn't exactly handsome, but at a youthful forty-one, he exuded a comfortable warmth that immediately put Tessa at ease. He had curly red hair that was fading toward strawberry blond, and green eyes that seemed to smile even when his mouth was serious. He was, Tessa thought as she shook his hand, a man who seemed completely at ease in his own skin. Kristin shook his hand as well and smiled as if she were posing for a beauty shot. Then, an assistant director led the sisters onto a set with the decor of a high-end kitchen, offering Tessa a copy of the script for the film, which she'd left behind in the Green Room.

Tessa shook her head. "I don't think I'll need it," she said.

Kristin shot her a dirty look and mouthed, *show-off.* "I think I'll hold on to mine."

"Now, just relax," Dvorak said. "We'll do the real work here. The lights are set up and the cameras are ready. We'll do the scene where Lenora—that's your character, Kristin—realizes that Caitlin—that's you, Tessa—has murdered her husband. We'll start with the camera on Tessa. Kristin, you'll feed your sister her cues. Then we'll do it again with the camera on Kristin. Your marks are on the floor: Tessa's in blue; Kristin's in red. Cheat a little toward the camera, Tessa, so we can see your face." Tessa stepped onto the blue mark, facing her sister at a quarter angle.

"Ready? ... A-and *action.*"

Tessa slipped into the character of the scheming sister and began delivering her lines from memory, letting her facial expressions and body flow from the situation and the character profile they'd given her.

"Xander was standing in your way, Lenora, but you just couldn't see it. You have to understand, I did it for you. He was destroying your life, taking a wrecking ball to your career—to everything you'd worked so hard for. He was wrong for you. He had to go, Len. There was no other way to save you."

"*Save* me?" Kristin shouted, her fists clenching around her script. "I didn't need your saving, you mercenary bitch!"

Tessa was caught off guard by the ferocity in her sister's voice and the ad-libbed insult. She could see the weird, frenetic energy flashing in Kristin's eyes like bolts of lightning. Her expression was frightening—and yet Tessa suspected it would be effective on camera.

"I've called the police," Kristin went on, glancing down at her script. "I hear the sirens now. Don't you? You won't get away with this."

"I don't have to get away with anything," Tessa said quietly, stepping slowly toward her sister.

"Oh, because you're going to run? Well, you'd better run fast, because I'm going to send the police right after you."

"No, you're not. You're not going to betray me. You're my sister, Len. You're my *twin*. That's a bond unlike any other." She stopped moving. "And you know it. I can see it in your eyes."

As she spoke the dialogue, something magical happened. She could hear her character, Caitlin, speaking the lines inside her head. When Tessa opened her mouth, it was Caitlin's voice coming out. She felt as though she were sitting in the back seat of her own body, letting the character drive. Her acting coach had told her this miracle could happen, yet she hadn't fully believed it—until now.

When the scene was over, there was a moment of silence, and when the AD said "Cut!" the small crew spontaneously burst into applause. Tessa had never experienced anything like that in her life. For a few minutes she had become someone else, and the feeling was exhilarating. With the camera turned on Kristin, they repeated the scene; Tessa could see something similar happening to her sister. But her performance was exaggerated by that sharp, artificial edge. She snarled and sobbed her lines as if possessed, her acting as powerful in its own way as Tessa's had been, but from where Tessa stood onstage, it bordered on parody. Every word, every expression, every gesture of her delivery had a quivering, frenetic energy.

Cocaine or nerves? Tessa prayed with all her might it was the latter.

Thankfully, Kristin also got a burst of applause from the crew, and when the screen test was over, Dvorak hugged both of them.

"You girls have real talent," Dvorak said. "I can't say anything until we've finished testing everyone, but we'll contact your agent whether you get the roles or not." He winked. "I wouldn't wander far from your cell phones tonight."

###

They got the parts. Jerry called that evening, his voice slightly slurred with what had clearly been several celebratory glasses of champagne. He sounded as excited as Tessa had ever heard him. Daniel was with her at her

126

house in Marina Del Rey when she got the call, and when she called her parents, they revealed that they'd already half planned a celebratory party for the weekend. They intended to invite Kristin back to visit their home. It would be the first time since the UCLA incident.

"If you're all right with that, sweetheart," her mom said. "What Kristin did was unforgivable, but if this movie deal is something that will make you happy ..."

"It does make me happy," she said. "Acting in front of a director and stage crew ... I've never felt anything quite like it. It was ... magic. So, of course Kristin should be there. She's part of this."

Tessa thought about that after she hung up, cuddled up to Daniel's side on her sofa. She'd always believed that even the darkest moments and the starkest setbacks often yielded even brighter consequences. She recalled a classic Arabic poem she'd studied in her senior year lit class that told of a man named Majnun (which meant "crazy") who'd lost his beloved in the city. Seeking her one night, the poor man was pursued by a nightwatchman intent on arresting him, believing him to be a thief. He ran and ran and eventually ended up at the foot of a great wall. Cursing the watchmen as demons, he climbed the wall and toppled to the ground on the other side.

He looked up to find himself in a garden, blinking in the light of a lamp ... a lamp that was in the hand of his beloved Layla. And so, through what Majnun was certain was his doom, he'd found the object of his quest. In the aftermath, he reflected that if he had been able to see the end in the beginning, he would have praised the watchmen as angels of opportunity, not cursed them.

Yes, Kristin had put her through hell. That was true by any measure. Tessa had felt, at first, as if she'd lost everything that mattered to her. But that wasn't true. She hadn't lost her parents or Daniel, and she had one career—if not the one she'd planned—and the beginnings of another. And ironically, her family was being stitched back together by the success that her twin had brought about, for all the wrong reasons and in all the wrong ways.

"Penny for them," Daniel said softly, wiggling the shoulder her head was resting on.

She laughed, realizing that she was just sitting there smiling like—like a madwoman. "You ever study the poem about Layla and Majnun?"

"No, but I think Eric Clapton wrote a song about it. Or about somebody named Layla anyway. Why?"

"I was just having my own personal Majnun moment." She looked up into his eyes. "Meaning I was counting my blessings. Even the ones that came through a lot of hurt."

"Those can be some of the best," he said and kissed her.

Chapter Twenty

It was the first day of shooting for *Dark Beauty*, and Kristin was so excited she was bouncing off the walls—almost literally. Giggling with excitement and the rush of cocaine, she was dancing around, naked, inside her dressing room, knocking objects off the makeup table, stumbling into anything in her path, and picking herself back up to dance happily some more.

Jim Parkinson, a member of the movie's crew, was also naked and lying on the dressing room couch, watching her with amusement. "I told you it was good coke," he said.

Kristin had quickly sized up Jim to be the local source of drugs, and it had taken mere minutes to seduce him into giving her some in exchange for a blow job. Jim was clean-cut and a lot more presentable than Kurt Morrison had been and didn't seem to be interested in any relationship that extended further than his dick could reach, which fit Kristin's needs perfectly. No attachments. No moony Kurt Morrison. And better drugs. Much, much better drugs. These left her feeling stoked, not cranked. The edge without the burn.

Parkinson got up and yanked on his pants and shirt. "My break's over. You'd better get dressed too. They'll be calling you in for the table read."

"I'm gonna set that place on fire!" Kristin shouted happily. "I'm going to light up the screen! I'm going to light up Hollywood!"

He gave her an appreciative, if wry, once-over. "Well, watch out for the electric cords or you're going to light up your dressing room. And not in a good way."

Kristin fell back against a table, giggling. "I'll blow 'em away! I'm going to give a performance like they've never seen!"

"You gave a pretty good performance just now, I have to say," Jim told her, smiling crookedly. "I'd sure hand you an Oscar for it. But you might want to grab some food at the commissary so you'll have enough energy for the read."

"I've got plenty of energy," Kristin declared. "I've got enough energy to blow the roof off this building."

He shook his head and tucked his shirt into his jeans. "Yeah, that's the problem. You need to dial it back a bit."

"Dial it back? Why would I want to do that?"

"Because you need to control the high or it will control you. Burn itself out and . . ." He pantomimed a plane crashing.

She giggled again. "What?"

Jim shrugged. "You'll find out." He gave her a cocky salute, pushed open her door, and stepped out into the hallway.

Kristin shot a dirty look at the back of his head. Dial it back? Dopey idea. She had so much energy she'd blow away every other actor at the table. Including her sister. She looked at the little baggy of cocaine peeking out of her makeup kit and wondered if she should do another line. But no, she was good. She'd save it for later. She tucked the baggy out of sight, then closed and locked the kit.

There was an insistent rap on her door. "Ms. Morgan," a woman's voice called. "The table read is in ten minutes in conference room two."

"I heard you," Kristin said, slightly irritated. She was ready to get out on the soundstage and show them what she could do, but she could as easily impress everybody simply by reading the script. She looked around for her dress, found it on the floor under the couch, and slipped it over her head. Then it occurred to her to look for her panties. She failed in that endeavor and was forced to go to the read sans underwear. That was good, she thought; it gave her an additional charge of self-aware freedom.

Mr. Dvorak's production company, Dove Rack Productions, was the most illustrious of Paradox Studio's denizens. She'd thought Dove Rack was a weird name for the company until Tessa's boyfriend Daniel had pointed out that it was a tongue-in-cheek reference to the way people slaughtered the director's last name when they'd never heard it pronounced. Daniel could sometimes be a real prick. He seemed to like to remind everybody how smart he was or how smart Tessa was. They were like two peas in a pod. She'd toyed with the idea of breaking them up, which she figured she could best do by pulling the ultimate twin swap and setting up Tessa to find them in bed together. She got hot and bothered just thinking about it; Daniel was a really good-looking guy. Yet, she had this niggling fear in the back of her head that he'd be able to sense she wasn't Tessa.

Plus, she had no idea what their relationship was like on the inside or how they acted around each other when they were alone.

Improv was just another aspect of acting, right? Plus, she figured there was a good chance he'd go for it even if he knew he was screwing the wrong twin. Men loved that sort of danger.

She shelved the idea, reasoning that it would be sort of her nuclear option. Something she'd do only if Tess or Daniel seriously pissed her off.

The young woman who had knocked on Kristin's door led her to the conference room, which was across the hall from the office Dvorak used when he was at Paradox. Most of the actors, Dvorak himself, the screenwriter, and several producers were sitting around a long conference table. Kristin sat next to Tessa, who smiled at her as she joined them.

Poor Tessa, Kristin thought. *I'm going to blow you away.*

An assistant passed out the scripts and Dvorak said, "Okay, we'll begin with a series of establishing shots, setting up the small suburban neighborhood where Lenora and Xander live. Terrence, can you read the descriptions?"

Terrence Mallory, the assistant director, read the narrative text from the script as the others waited for their parts. "Night: Fade in on an upscale suburban neighborhood in Northern California. A car enters the driveway of a large ranch home, parks, and two people get out, Lenora Lawson and her husband Xander. They've just returned from her first, very successful gallery showing in San Francisco."

Kristin smiled. Lenora was her character, happily married and a successful artist. She felt a thrill run through her just hearing the character's name. The plot was a slow burn as the couple shared early moments of seeming domestic bliss before the plot took a turn toward the bizarre. She was the one who got the first line of dialogue.

"Xander, don't you think this house is a little too big for us?"

Dvorak held up a hand. "Kristin, could you tone that line down a little? She's musing, not accusing."

Well, that was a little annoying, but if that's how Dvorak wanted it played, she could go with it.

"Sorry," she said. "Just excited."

"No worries," Dvorak said, smiling. "Try it again."

"Xander," she repeated, trying to control the energy pressing to burst out, "don't you think this house is just a little too big for us?"

Dvorak didn't give her a thumbs-up, but he didn't say anything.

Kristin assumed that was a good sign.

Fredrik Halvorsson, the gorgeous Swedish actor playing her husband, responded in a perfect American accent, looking mildly surprised. "Is this your way of telling me you're pregnant?"

"No, silly. I just ..."

"You just what? Let me guess: you want to sell it and move into a garret where we'll live on bread crusts and love while you paint and waste away. I know you need to suffer for your art, but I don't think I'm the garret type."

"Oh, shut up, you Philistine," Kristin read. "It's just ... I got a call from my sister this morning. She needs a place to stay and, well, we do have a couple of spare rooms. She'd be here by Thursday ... if you're okay with it."

Halvorsson paused for a beat on his next line. "I was hoping we could spend some time alone after all the hubbub around your gallery opening and gala. I've got a week's vacation coming up."

"That would work. She could come on Thursday and settle in; you and I could go off the following week, which would give her some time to adjust. She won't be here long, Xan. It's just that she's still in shock from Ben's death and needs a little time to get her head together before she looks for a new home ... God, Xander, I can't even imagine what she must be going through."

Dvorak paused her again. "Not quite so perky, Kristin. Lenora is legitimately sad that her brother-in-law has died and she's imagining losing her own husband. She shouldn't sound so ... casual."

Kristin stifled her annoyance again. She wanted to argue the point, but common sense prevailed. She bit back her irritation, smiled, and nodded.

They read on. When the sister, Caitlin, arrived at the house and it came time for Tessa to read, Kristin chuckled inwardly.

Let's see how you handle Dvorak's incessant interruptions.

But the director seemed pleased with the way Tessa read her lines and paused her only once to ask her to leave a beat between two lines. At first, Kristin was irritated, but then she thought she understood what Dvorak was doing. He must clearly see that Tessa lacked Kristin's confidence and was being careful not to step on her. She was playing the role too soft, Kristin thought. Where was the sense that she was the evil twin, only pretending to be good? This was a woman who'd turned grief over losing her husband into a vendetta against her own sister's happiness.

She flip-flopped between two poles throughout the read, first believing Dvorak was just being kind, and then that his lack of commentary on Tessa's performance meant he thought everything she was doing was too perfect to criticize. Nor did he let up on Kristin. He stopped her several times more to ask her to change her tone or her pacing, while leaving Tessa almost entirely unscathed. He stopped her once to ask that she deliver a line with "a little more ambiguity"—whatever the hell that meant. By the end of the read, Kristin was fighting the urge to snort the whole baggy of coke the moment she got back to her dressing room. She hated feeling like this. This was not the way the morning was supposed to have gone. Before Kristin could stalk off back to her dressing room, after the table read, Terry Mallory stopped her in the hallway. "Mr. Dvorak would like to speak with you in his office," he told her.

"Oh, he didn't complain enough during the read?"

Mallory ignored the comment. He directed Kristin to Dvorak's office, which turned out to be surprisingly cluttered. Scripts were piled on every flat surface, and the walls were lined with bookshelves stocked with titles like *Fahrenheit 451, Dune*, and *The Anubis Gates.* She recognized those titles from Tessa's library, but Kristin had never paid attention to them because they looked boring and she wasn't much of a reader. Clearly, though, Dvorak was a fan of science fiction and fantasy—not surprising, given that he had made a number of highly successful films in those genres.

The director was thumbing through a script, but he looked up when he saw Kristin. "Kristin! Good to see you."

"Are you going to critique my half of our conversation?"

Dvorak made a bemused face and chuckled. "No, not at all. This is just an informal ... pep talk. I wanted to discuss your performance at the table read. I know how nervous you girls were."

"I wasn't nervous. I was just excited." She decided to go all soft and cuddly and fixed him with her best "mouse" look. "You didn't like it."

"It's not that. You just seemed a little ... wound up. That's understandable. You're new at this. It's natural to be excited when you first read a script out loud. I just wanted you to know that it's perfectly okay to relax. Give yourself a moment to get into character and into the emotional content of the specific scene. Pretend you're just play-acting at home alone or in the shower or whatever helps you let go of the jitters. The cast and crew are your friends and family. They're on your team."

"Are they?"

"Absolutely. Everyone wants to see you succeed."

"Not everyone," murmured Kristin.

"Excuse me?"

"Nothing. Is that all?" Kristin asked.

"Sure. I just wanted to help you relax and feel good on the set."

"Yeah? Are you going to give Tess the same pep talk?"

He read her for a moment, then said, "If I need to. She seemed pretty comfortable and relaxed in there. But trust me, if I see signs that she's struggling, I'll speak up."

"Struggling," repeated Kristin. "Is that what I was doing?" Dvorak leaned forward in his chair and laced his fingers together atop his desk. "Kristin, this was the first time you've done anything like this. Give yourself a break. You're good. You just need to relax, which I'm sure you'll do when this starts to feel normal to you."

Kristin nodded and turned to go. At the door, her hand on the knob, she paused. "Is she better than I am?" She tried to control her voice but knew that the underlying angst was coming through.

"Apples and oranges, Kristin. Your roles are polar opposites. Tessa's just more relaxed in her approach. Like you'll be, once you get used to the process."

Kristin fumed for a second but said nothing. Then she went back to her dressing room, again contemplating that she might just snort every ounce of cocaine left in the bag. She settled for a short line and one of the beers she found in the mini-fridge under the makeup table. The beer took some of the edge off the coke. It was good.

She went into the afternoon table read feeling a little better. Maybe Dvorak was right. Maybe she just needed to let go of the jitters. Still, she needed the energy she got from the cocaine. She'd be careful, she told herself. She'd just balance the highs with a little alcohol.

Chapter Twenty-One

They rehearsed for three weeks before they began shooting, with Dvorak taking them to the various sets on the soundstage. They were starting with interior shots; they'd do location filming after. He blocked each scene move by move. A member of the set crew placed tape marks on the floor where each actor was supposed to stand and what direction they were to be facing. As during their screen test, Kristin's marks were red; Tessa's were blue.

Dvorak started with one of the most crucial scenes in the film, the one where Lenora discovers that Caitlin has been pulling a twin swap and sleeping with her husband during those times she was in the throes of a new painting out in her studio.

Kristin suspected that the director was testing her, to see how well she'd handle the dramatic moment, but her paranoia had a chemical edge to it. She'd fucked her way to another bag of cocaine from Jim Parkinson the night before, and she'd already done about half of it, which left her floating in a cloud of energy and confidence.

When Tessa's Caitlin slyly revealed that she'd been playing lustful wifey and lapping up Xander's delight at her new adventurous side, Kristin exploded. She roared her lines with the rage she thought a woman would express if her man cheated, turning red-faced and threatening.

"Let's pause for a minute," Dvorak said. He stood and walked onto the set. "Kristin, I'm getting rage, but no sorrow. No shock. No disbelief." The flush of anger beneath Kristin's skin inhabited her to the core, her flesh burning like she was standing too close to a fire. "I think this is the way I'd react if my sister fucked my husband pretending to be me." The fact that she'd thought of doing that to Tessa with Daniel intruded sharply for an instant. She shoved it aside.

Dvorak nodded thoughtfully. "Yes. I don't doubt that's true. But what we're looking for is how *Lenora* would react. She's not you. Remember, you're playing the sane sister. A woman who has it all and knows how fortunate she is. She's been living in heaven, and what her twin has told her has just thrown her down to earth. It's new and shocking and hard to absorb. Think of it as an emotional gut punch. You're gutted, disbelieving—how could your sister do that to you, to Xander? How could Xander not know he was making love to the wrong twin? Is there a chance he *did* know?" He paused for a moment to read her, then said, "Right now, you're acting as if you already know what Caitlin is going to tell you. You don't. Give your character time to hear and confront each of these thoughts and emotions. Give Lenora time to arrive at an awareness of the enormity of what her sister has done. If you explode instantly with rage, you'll lose the audience, because they won't have time to process what's happened.

"And the goal, always, is to take the audience with you to your pain and your anger and your sense of betrayal."

Kristin knew he was right, and that his words, which were delivered in a gentle, guiding tone, should have resonated. She understood them, even agreed with them. But her anger was like a living thing, overwhelming her, taking up every bit of her emotional landscape. It rose up from a wound so deep inside that she'd lost conscious awareness of it—a wound that had been ripped open by the chemicals interacting with her brain. Through her distorted senses, Dvorak's face, hidden meekly by dorky, steel-rimmed glasses, appeared almost satanic, a leering villain mocking the perfection of what she'd just done on the soundstage.

How dare he think, for one second, that she wasn't good enough for him—for his stupid movie? She was a natural for this part.

"Are you telling me I can't act?" she shouted, her voice piercing even the softened acoustics on the area off-camera. "I'm the actor. Aren't I the one who makes those decisions?"

Dvorak looked taken aback. "It's more of a collaboration, Kristin. I don't like to tell actors how to deliver their lines. But I do sit down with them and discuss the character—which I've done with you and Tessa and everyone else I've put in front of the camera. You don't seem to have heard me. Lenora isn't a powder keg primed and ready to go off. She's a creative, happy, well-adjusted woman who's just been presented with a situation she's had no reason to believe existed. And if you asked Angelica"—he nodded at the screenplay writer who was sitting next to the AD scribbling notes on her iPad—"she'd tell you the same thing. I took a chance on you, Kristin, because you were perfect for the role in many ways."

"Well, if I'm so fucking perfect," Kristin snapped, "let me go back and show how perfect I can be."

"All right," Dvorak said, his voice infuriatingly gentle, "but this time remember what I just told you. Give Lenora time to *hear* what Caitlin is telling her, process it, and react to it." He made a fist. "Gut punch, right? You're winded, trying to make sense out of chaos."

Kristin went back to her initial mark and they began rehearsing the scene again. She started the scene at a lower volume, though her performance was more seething fury than gutted shock, but by the midpoint she had doubled down on her intensity, screaming the lines in defiance of Dvorak's instructions. It was a big "fuck you" to the director for telling her how to interpret the character and to the screenplay writer, who was sitting in her little director's chair looking like she was having kittens. Kristin's smug lack of repentance only wavered when she saw Dvorak turn to his assistant director and murmur something that she couldn't hear. A moment later he turned back to the actors. "We'll work on this reveal tomorrow. Right now, let's move on to Tessa's scene at the supermarket. We won't need you for the rest of the day, Kristin. Your call is at seven a.m."

The stinging words that Kristin was about to fling in Dvorak's direction caught on her lips. He was letting her go for the entire day? "What the hell?" she said. "You're throwing me out?"

"I'm not throwing you out. I just need some time to decide what to do about your lines."

"Good," Kristin snarled. "I think maybe Angelica needs to do a rewrite so that Lenora's reacting like a *real* woman, not a candy-ass."

She was so blindly enraged that she barely remembered going back to the dressing room, snorting more cocaine, hopping into her car, and driving to a pub near the studio that was frequented by industry types. She just seemed to find herself there on a stool in a dark corner at one end of the long bar, her eyes blinking at the neon piping that ran above the bar and behind the racks of bottles and glasses. There was a drink sitting in front of her. She tasted it. Rum. Really good rum.

Inevitably, a man came up and sat next to her; that was a given whenever Kristin went into a bar or a restaurant on her own. Somehow, they all seemed to believe no beautiful woman could possibly be content in her own company. That she needed a male to admire her, to make her feel useful, or valuable, or even alive. They couldn't leave her fucking alone. "I'll have my usual," the guy said to the bartender. "And bring her another."

Kristin raised an eyebrow. "That'll be the most expensive rum in the house. And a shot glass of schnapps."

"Interesting combination," the man said. "Can you afford it?" Kristin asked.

"I'm pretty sure I can," the man said. He looked like he was in his late thirties, early forties, maybe, wearing a stylishly cut suit but with no tie. He was tall, handsome, and clearly worked out. His hair was thick and wavy and curled around his ears. She couldn't tell what color it was because of the neon and the semidarkness. Ditto on the color of his eyes. She thought they might be hazel. He looked vaguely familiar.

"You look familiar. Are you one of those guys that likes to hang around movie sets?"

He smiled. Nice dimples. "I am, indeed. I'm Kevin Salinger. I'm producing the film you're in."

She covered her surprise and sudden discomfort by giving him a long, assessing look. Easy on the eyes, for sure. If he really was who he said he was, it would be useful to know him.

"Saw you had a little dust-up with Alexei Dvorak just now," he observed.

"You saw, did you?" Kristin asked. "Did you follow me here?"

"Yes."

Honest. "Why?"

"I thought, given as I'm your producer, I ought to get to know you better."

"You ought to check up on me, you mean," Kristin said.

He made a wry face. "I wanted to see how you were doing, yeah."

"And what have you seen?"

"I see you drinking schnapps and rum at eleven in the morning."

"I got the day off," Kristin said. "Director's orders."

"I saw. Thanks," he added to the bartender who brought the drinks.

His was a mixed drink in a glass mug that looked as if it had orange juice in it. Gin fizz, Kirstin thought. Kind of fussy for a dude.

"And you want to have sex with me," she said.

He didn't even blink. "Perhaps you've mistaken me for Harvey Weinstein."

She offered him a cockeyed smile. "Hell, no. You're good looking."

"I'm also in a position of power over you. That puts you off limits, Kristin."

She swiveled her stool and leaned back on her elbows against the bar, a move that put her breasts front and center. "And if you weren't in a position of power over me?"

"Things might be different. But they're not different. So, whether I find you attractive or not is a nonfactor."

She swiveled the stool to face him. "If you're not nosing around for sex, what do you want?"

"I want to make sure you're okay. I think you have some things you need to work out."

"Oh, thanks. Now I'm a project?"

He laughed. His laugh was warm and came from deep in his chest. "Maybe. But I think mostly what you are is a beautiful, talented young woman with very little self-esteem and a lot of anger. I think if you could work those things out, you'd be—"

"A better actress?"

"A happier human being. Which would, in all likelihood, make you a better actress. I saw your screen test, Kristin. You have natural talent. But you're standing in its way."

She took a gulp of her schnapps. It burned all the way down. "No," she said. "That'd be my sister Tessa."

He sat back on his stool and fixed her with a long, searching gaze. "Tessa's not the twin who's holding you back. I think, on some level you know that."

"Why are you telling me all this? Afraid I'm going to cost you money? Dude, I'm gonna *make* you money."

"It's not the money, trust me. It's what you're doing to yourself. I've been there. Coke and alcohol, right? Heady combination. I crawled out from under it years ago, but I know the look." He took a deep breath, then said, "You were fighting Alex tooth and nail today. You've been fighting since that first table read. Why?"

She slid off the stool and stood, shakily, but she stood. "I don't like this line of questioning, Mr. Salinger."

"I don't doubt it. And call me Kevin."

"I don't like this line of questioning, *Salinger*."

"Who hurt you?" he asked. "Or do you even know?"

She just stared at him, then turned and headed for the door. She'd made it about halfway there, when a strong hand took her by the elbow and guided her out into the parking lot and all the way to her car.

"Keys," he said when they reached her Lexus. He held out his hand.

She glared at him for a moment, then realized this was his play. He'd take her home, get her into her house, and then give her his best Harvey Weinstein impersonation.

I know you, she thought. *You don't fool me.*

She grinned and gave him the keys. He got her into the car, then took the driver's seat, popping his phone into the dash mount and calling up her address on his GPS.

Figured. She gave him a knowing grin. *Prick.* "Oh, I'm no Harvey Weinstein," she parodied. "I care about *you*, you pathetic little girl. I think you're special. You've already got my address in your damn phone."

He turned to look at her. "I have the contact information for everyone involved in the film in my phone. Frankly, if any of them were lighting themselves up with coke, then putting out the flames with rum and schnapps, I'd be driving them home too."

"Fuck that," she told him. "What's your angle?"

He didn't respond, just shook his head, started the car, set it in motion, and drove her home. By the time they reached her Malibu mansion, she'd come up with a new plan. Once he'd parked her car inside the security gates, she let him guide her into the house. She overdid the helpless, drunk female routine just a bit, whimpering a little like she might start crying any minute, yet laughing on the inside.

Standing between her foyer and living room, he asked, "You live alone or is there someone here who can help you?"

She turned to face him, not touching him but with only inches between their bodies. "There's no one here but you and me," she told him wryly, giving him the full-on ragamuffin look. "I don't have anybody in my life. Just work and a sister who hates me. I'm so fucking alone, I sometimes wonder why I even get up in the morning. You may not believe this," she added, forcing her voice to break just a bit, "but it's been ages since anyone made love to me."

He looked down at her for a long moment, then swept her up into his arms. Kristin was hot with exultation and anticipation as he carried her to the long sectional sofa in her living room, laid her gently on the cushions, brought his face within inches of hers, and looked deeply into her eyes.

She lifted her chin, parted her lips, and closed her eyes, anticipating his kiss and the weight of his body on hers.

He put his lips to her ear and murmured, "Now, if you could bring that to your role in *Dark Beauty*, you'd be a shoo-in for an Oscar."

Then he was gone. Just like that. It didn't register how gone until she heard the front door close.

Any inebriation Kristin felt seemed to burn away in the heat of her humiliation and anger. She had never, *never* had a man reject her so glibly. Even Kurt had blown her off in a fit of wounded pride, but Salinger had no such excuse. It galled her that she'd been given a timeout by two men today, while Tessa was still at the studio, flogging her lines like a good little trooper, winning the undying regard of Alexei Dvorak with her good twin routine.

Well, fuck that. Tessa thought she had it all. Well, there was something Kristin could do about that. Something she could take away.

She checked the time. It was lunchtime for most people; possibly that included Daniel Takashi. If it didn't, she was pretty sure she could convince him to take a lunch break. She donned one of the blonde human hair wigs she wore for the film, then took a Lyft to Tessa's bungalow. She had the driver wait outside. She had the security app and the passcode to the place, just as Tessa had hers, so getting in was not an issue. She raided Tessa's closet for something relatively sexy—a short, teal, off-the-shoulder summer tunic with matching shorts—and shoved her feet into a pair of Tessa's strappy sandals.

She had the Lyft drop her in front of Daniel Takashi's offices. They weren't flashy, but sleek, modern, and eloquent of high-tech. She was waved in by the security guy in the small foyer, merely shooting him a brilliant smile. A minute later, she stood in Daniel's office, turning that smile on him.

He looked up, reacted with surprise, then favored her with a look so full of gooey appreciation that she almost rolled her eyes.

"Tess, sweetheart, what are you doing here in the middle of the day?"

She shrugged, causing the shoulder of the shift to slip farther down her arm, exposing the curve of her left breast. "I'm taking a long lunch and I thought, who better than to spend it with than you." She tilted her head and gave him a look calculated to set his pants on fire.

He bit his lip. *Actually* bit his lip. She'd never seen anybody do that before.

"I wasn't planning on taking lunch today," he said slowly. Then, "But, you know, I am feeling a little peckish. What would you like to eat?" She moved closer to the desk, put her hands on it, and leaned forward, all but exposing both breasts. "You. I was thinking we could go back to my place and—"

"Conduct a little science experiment?"

Seriously? Did they really refer to sex using a freaking metaphor, or were Daniel and her sweet sister into some sort of kink? His smile was crooked and quite attractive. This might be interesting.

"As you wish, Professor Takashi. You can *sexperiment* on me any day of the week."

He stood, then cocked his head to one side. "What did you do with your hair?"

She shrugged. "Just some movie magic. This is my look for the scene we're shooting this afternoon."

They took his car; she claimed hers was in the shop. Kristin used her phone again to unlock the front door of her sister's bungalow. She entered first, leaving Daniel to follow.

She started peeling off her clothes the moment she stepped through the door and was totally naked except for the sandals by the time she reached the living room. She didn't look back once but simply walked away from Daniel, swinging her hips as she let each garment fall to the floor. She still had her phone in hand; she planned to take some dynamite selfies.

She heard him behind her. "Ah," he said, his voice dwindling to a husky whisper as he followed her into the room. She lost track of his footsteps when he hit the Berber carpet but kept walking, fluffing the wig over her shoulders, running her hands down her bare flanks. She stopped at the grouping of living room furniture to consider her options: Carpet? Sofa? Coffee table?

"Where do you want me?" she asked. "Or should I ask *how* do you want me?"

He didn't answer.

She turned to look at him, expecting him to be as naked as she was, but he was standing at the edge of the carpet, still fully dressed, watching her.

"Why'd you change your outfit?" he asked. That was out of left field. "What?"

"This morning you were wearing jeans and a Griffith Observatory T-shirt."

She made a face at him. "Dude, you're going to go all fashion police on me while I'm standing here naked?" She put her hands beneath her tits and boosted them up. "Come eat your lunch, Daniel baby."

He looked at the floor and shook his head. "I'm sure you can catch a ride home, Kristin."

He turned on his heel and left her standing, naked and trembling with humiliation and growing fury, in her sister's living room.

Chapter Twenty-Two

Kristin arrived at the studio for her seven a.m. call exactly on time. Her hangover was in a pitched battle with her most recent dose of cocaine, the terrain in dispute being her brain. On the one hand she felt energized by the drug, confident that she could handle anything Dvorak could throw at her; on the other, she was still feeling the sting of yesterday's rejection hat trick.

The PA met her in the hall outside her dressing room and asked her to join Mr. Dvorak in his office.

Shit. She was clearly going to get a good scolding for her behavior yesterday. She could either react with the fury of a woman scorned or play the penitent. She decided on the latter. She'd promise to be a good girl. Anything not to have to endure one of those patient Mr. Rogers lectures.

She entered the office with an apology on her lips and was appalled to see Kevin Salinger sitting in one of the side chairs next to Dvorak's desk, smiling at her. She was more than a little pissed. Most men were ready to hop in the sack with her if she so much as looked at them cross-eyed. But *this* guy— this suave, witty, intelligent, good-looking, nice guy (also dripping with money) was the Lone Fucking Ranger.

She watched him from under her lashes as she wavered in the doorway, her game plan all but blown out of her head. He was just playing hard to get. That was it. He was one of those guys who loved to be pursued. Or maybe he was gay and just hid it well.

"Have a seat, Kristin," Dvorak said, gesturing to the chair next to Salinger.

She seated herself and was gathering her wits and forcing the words "I'm sorry" to her lips when Dvorak said, "I want to be up front with you, Kristin. Yesterday I thought I was going to have to fire you—"

"*Fire* me?" Kristin repeated, her voice oozing out in a stunned whisper. "How can you fire me? I'm—I'm part of a matched set. That's what the whole movie is about. You *need* me."

"We could have cast Tessa in both roles. With optical tricks, a body double, a split screen, and some CGI, it would have been almost trivial, though it would keep us in post-production longer. And I have every reason to believe that Tessa's performance would be a tour de force."

Kristin tried to get some air back in her lungs, steady her voice. "So why didn't you do it?"

He glanced at Salinger. "It seems you have a guardian angel. Kevin convinced me that you could handle it and that he'd help you give the performance we need. Exactly how he intends to do that I'm not sure, but he's an old friend and he produced my last seven films, so I trust him."

For once, Kristin couldn't think of anything to say. Why was Salinger willing to stick his neck out for her like this, when they hadn't even—? "I do have a question for you, though," Dvorak continued. "Are you doing drugs?"

Kristin's blood ran cold. Her mind was racing on a combination of chemicals, even now, but damned if she was going to admit it. "That's none of your business."

Dvorak leaned forward, hands clasped, his face and his voice with more steel in them than she'd ever seen or heard. "I'm your boss, Kristin. Anything that affects your performance in my film is very much my business. I don't like meddling in the private lives of actors. It's not my business to save you from your own bad habits. But your behavior has been ... erratic, to say the least. Those frenetic, overblown readings you've been giving, the way you spoke to me yesterday, suggest that you have a problem, and whatever that problem is, you aren't handling it very well."

She could only glare at him, trembling with emotions she couldn't name.

"You have a week," he told her. "If you continue to refuse to take direction, I will insist that you submit to drug testing—and if the results come up positive, you're off the film."

"You have no right to do that to me," Kristin blurted. Tears stung her eyes.

"If you really believe that," Salinger said, speaking for the first time. "Then you're living in an alternate reality. You're doing this to yourself, Kristin. But if, as I suspect, anger is your way of processing criticism of your perceived failures, then I can help."

"You're going to stop him from firing me?"

"I'm going to help you not get fired. We've got a twelve-step group right here on the lot."

"You mean I'm not the only problem child?"

"Hardly. I can go with you to meetings so you'll feel comfortable. Or not, if you'd prefer."

"I'd prefer not to go at all."

"That isn't an option, Kristin," Dvorak said solemnly. "The most important condition of my agreeing to keep you in the part is you getting your head on straight. And because we don't have time to put you in rehab, you're going to have to do it around your working schedule."

Kristin rolled her eyes. "I have a life, you know."

"Not for long, if you keep this up. While you're a part of this movie, you'll be getting that life back together."

"Does Tessa know ... any of this?"

Dvorak shook his head. "At this point, there's no need to tell her—or anyone. But if this doesn't work ..."

"Don't worry," Salinger said. "I've been through this myself. It's a little intimidating and uncomfortable at first, but you'll relax after a couple of meetings."

"What was your drug of choice?" she asked him.

"Alcohol. Alexei suggested I could do with a little less of it." He glanced at Dvorak.

"What about the gin fizz you had yesterday at Tully's? Your usual?" Dvorak gave Salinger a raised eyebrow.

"*Virgin* gin fizz," Salinger said. "Orange juice, cream, vanilla, and a bit of soda water."

"Fine," Kristin said, surrendering. "When do I start?"

"Today. There's a meeting around one o'clock. We can grab lunch at the commissary first."

"Are you always this full service a producer?"

"I want this to be a good film. And I don't want to see you blow your big chance."

Disappointing. "So, it's not because you like me?" He quirked a smile. "Maybe that too."

The chemicals doing a feisty tango inside Kristin's skull somehow combined to produce a burst of self-loathing. "Well," she said, "that's only because you don't know me very well."

###

The 12-Step meeting was in one of the smaller buildings on the lot, behind a door marked Employees Only. Salinger opened the door with a keycard and led Kristin inside. The room wasn't impressive. There were some plastic chairs arranged in a semicircle on the hardwood floor with a desk at the open end. Kristin recognized a couple of the seven people sitting in the chairs. A pot of coffee was brewing in the corner.

"Want some?" Salinger asked, nodding toward the pot. "Does it come in a grande half-caf macchiato?"

He smiled. "No, just straight brewed coffee. They've got cream and sweetener. And half-caf is for wimps."

She made herself not smile. "I think I'll pass."

A balding man whom Kristin recognized from the studio's human resources office sat at the desk and passed some laminated sheets of paper to a few people. One of them began reading aloud from a list called the Twelve Traditions, which sounded about as interesting to Kristin as an Ikea instruction manual, and probably a lot less useful. The third tradition was "The only requirement for membership is a desire to stop using." That almost made her laugh out loud, but she stifled herself for Salinger's sake, since he'd seemed so sincere about saving her soul.

The group's leader, Bruce—Salinger called him a facilitator—left the desk to sit in one of the chairs. He handed something to the young man in the chair next to him, and the younger guy started to speak. His name was Peter, and he was a stunt double. Clutching the object the facilitator had given him, he spoke for a few minutes about his struggles that week to resist using the opioids he'd gotten hooked on after a bad fall injured his left knee. At the last moment he had invoked something he called his "higher power."

The rest of the circle was the same deal: The "baton"—a half-size replica of the Maltese Falcon—passed to the next person, prompting them to give an update. When the stupid thing came to Kristin, she simply muttered, "Pass," and handed off to Salinger, who just said, "Status quo" and gave the falcon to the next penitent. Kristin didn't feel too awkward; two of the others also elected not to speak. At the end of the meeting, which seemed to last hours, everybody stood up, held hands in a circle, and recited a generic prayer.

What the fuck? thought Kristin. She'd heard this wasn't a religious organization. She bowed her head, not wanting to look like she wasn't willing to play the game. After the "amen," everyone suddenly did a move Kristin had always thought of as jazz hands and chanted, "Keep on keepin' on! It works if you work it!" Even Salinger. The man seemed to have no shame.

Kristin rolled her eyes. Salinger, seeing her skepticism, leaned toward her and whispered, "You'll get used to it. Just keep coming. If nothing else, it's an hour when you aren't contributing to your premature aging."

Dickwad. Making a direct appeal to her vanity.

For the remainder of the day, when she wasn't on camera, Kristin turned ideas over in her head about how she could contrive to get Kevin Salinger into bed. If nothing else, it would give her a shit load of leverage. At the end of the day, she let it be known that she was exhausted and didn't feel safe to drive. He, playing his role to the hilt, offered to drive her home.

Score one point for Team Kristin, she thought.

At her house, she took the second step in her plan and invited him in. "Dvorak gave me some really weird homework," she said. "He said I should see the way Deborah Ann Woll played Karen Page in *Daredevil*, of all things. Something about her character arc leading up to her killing a guy?"

Salinger nodded. "Alex has been known to do that. I think I know the episode he wants you to watch. Season one, episode eleven, right?"

"Yeah, that one." Dvorak had written it down *and* he'd texted it to her, but she'd had no real intention of watching it ... until now. "I think it's on Netflix. Watch it with me?" She gave him a look she'd copied from Tessa's face.

When he agreed and suggested they order dinner online, she was sure she'd come up with a winning strategy and began to fantasize about an evening of "Netflix and chill"—a term her high school cohort had used as a euphemism for having sex with the TV on. She'd snuggle up to him and he'd put his arm around her and they'd make out on the sofa like a pair of school kids. When they'd cranked it up to eleven, she'd pull away and lead him to her bedroom where they'd have slow, languorous sex on her silk sheets.

To her frustration, they actually watched the entire episode on her eighty-six-inch wall-mounted OLED television while they munched on Thai food. Afterward, Salinger helped her clean up the takeout mess and put away the leftovers, then said they both had an early day tomorrow (well, duh), and got up to leave.

"Really?" she said. "You're really just going to skedaddle?" Salinger raised his eyebrows. "Skedaddle? Who says that?"

She bit her tongue. "My dad said it when I was little. I guess you remind me of him."

She'd meant the crack as an ego crusher, but he just chuckled and said, "I'm glad to hear that."

He turned toward the door, but she put herself right in front of him and put her arms around his neck. "You're not getting out of here without at least a kiss."

He darn near rolled his eyes. "Kristin, we've been over this."

"Yeah? I'd like to see you be over this," she said, and planted a kiss on his mouth.

His lips were warm and soft, but they didn't open and they didn't move. She kissed the corner of his mouth, then gave it a flick of her tongue, knowing that some guys just couldn't resist that move for some reason. He was apparently not one of those guys.

She slid her tongue along his lips and tried to slip it into his mouth, but he gently pushed her away from him, his expression as cool and collected as if he were not face-to-face with a woman whose image thousands—maybe millions of men—took into the bathroom with them on a regular basis.

"Are you gay?" she asked bluntly.

He laughed out loud. "No. No, I'm most definitely not gay."

"Show me," she insisted and reached for his groin.

He pushed her back again, then made an exit while she stood there fuming and frustrated.

Five minutes after the front door had closed and she had thrown every pillow in the living room at it, Kristin called a guy she'd met at a little dive down on Wilshire Boulevard a couple of weeks earlier—he called himself Mad Wolf. They'd done a thing in the unisex bathroom that she'd found kind of exciting. She wondered if he'd like to try his moves in her stupid large shower. Turned out he would.

Mad Wolf was at her place in less than ten minutes and on her before the door had quite closed behind him. He was wild and hungry, fucked with abandon, and recharged faster than any guy she'd ever done. He also bit her a couple of times, which she worried would show up on camera. Fortunately, the bites would be hidden by costuming or she'd have gone nuclear on his cute ass. As it was, she laughed and slapped him and called him Bad Dog, and he growled something about a full moon.

When they were both spent and a bit too drunk, she found herself lying in bed, staring at her bedroom ceiling and wondering what sex would be like with Salinger. Nothing like Wolf, here, she was sure. Wolf was too easy. Salinger was a different sort of beast. He was a challenge that she would handle like any other challenge she'd ever faced: Attack from every conceivable angle, cheat if necessary, and keep at it until the immovable object surrendered to the irresistible force.

Chapter Twenty-Three

She was back in rehearsals the next day, and Salinger showed up afterward to remind her about the five o'clock NA meeting. If he noticed Wolf's bites, he didn't say anything, which was disappointing. She considered accidentally intentionally showing them to see how he'd react.

They settled into a routine by the end of the week: Rehearsal, NA meeting, dinner after, home to bed—alone. Also disappointing, but after a week of this routine Kristin found herself falling into it. She even spoke in NA when she got the falcon on occasion, but she kept her comments brief and nonspecific. She knew several of the people in the room; a couple of them were working on her film. She didn't want details finding their way back to Dvorak.

She had flushed what cocaine she had down the toilet, but she knew where and how to get more if she needed it. She had craved the drugs all week, but when the cravings started to pass, something unexpected replaced them: a warm, euphoric glow, like she was on some new, better drug. She hadn't found her "higher power" yet—she was pretty sure she was never going to—but now not using the cocaine was starting to feel good. Not just normal, not just a return to sobriety, but like she was experiencing actual joy. She found herself happily engaged in rehearsal, no longer resenting the notes that Dvorak gave her. She thought Tessa was getting just as many, and Kristin's weren't sharply critical, just comments about how she should pause at certain moments or what direction she should turn her head when she delivered a line. Maybe she didn't need drugs for this acting thing. Maybe it was going to work out after all.

"You're in the pink cloud," Salinger told her when she talked about it at an NA meeting.

"What the fuck is that?" she asked.

"It's your brain cells waking up as they start functioning without the chemicals. Your endorphins go into overdrive and you feel like you rule the world."

"I *do* rule the world! Bow before your queen, unworthy vassal."

She drew a laugh from the rest of the group, but they sobered quickly and were quick to assure her that the cloud would eventually dissipate.

"It can last for weeks or even months, but it doesn't last forever," said Peter, who was coming up on his one-year anniversary for sobriety.

Salinger added his own cautionary testimony. "Don't be so quick to stop going. For one thing, it's still a condition of your employment, and you'll find that when the pink cloud starts wearing off, things can get dicey."

Not this time, Kristin thought. She felt it with a certainty she'd never had about anything. *I'm gonna ride this all the way through production.*

###

The night before filming began, Kristin felt like the Queen of Hollywood. She wanted to share the feeling with Salinger, but she knew he wouldn't go for it, so she called Mad Wolf. Their evening together was a kick; they did everything everywhere with increasing recklessness. It was always something new with Wolf, and she'd enjoyed it. It was adventurous, riotous, top-of-the-world sex ... until he pulled a studded dog collar out of a jacket pocket and demanded that she submit to wearing it.

She laughed. "That's fucking backward, dude. The doggie wears the collar."

"I'm not a doggie, bitch. I'm a wolf. You're the prey. So, I truss you up and prey on you. Just, y'know, a little role-playing game. You be Red Riding Hood. I be the Big Bad Wolf."

"Some other time," she told him. "I'm all played out."

"C'mon, baby," he'd wheedled. "You'll like it, I promise. You like the things I do to you. You'll like this. It'll be a little rougher—"

"Do *to* me?" she repeated, her feeling of power and control slipping away. "Is that what this is about? What you can get me to let you *do* to me?" It was as if a doorway had opened, revealing the progression of her sexual encounters with Wolf; what had begun as fun on both sides had somehow morphed into a studded dog collar and a man's agenda. She felt as if a lead weight had dropped into the pit of her stomach. She began to tremble. Suddenly,

152

she was back in her freshman year of high school with one of two boys with the same name—a name she told herself she couldn't remember. With those two boys was the first time she'd felt like this. Like someone had been playing her, manipulating her, coaching her to do what they wanted her to do—what they had *planned* to have her do.

"Get out," Kristin said. "Bitch, don't be a bitch."

"Get out," she repeated. "Take your dog collar and your alpha male attitude and get the hell out."

"I haven't done anything to you that you didn't want—"

"I'm a model and an actress!" she shrieked at him. "And you've fucking covered me in dog bites! I couldn't wear a bikini right now if someone *paid* me to!"

He laughed. He actually laughed. "Yeah, you are definitely a no-bikini zone."

She looked down at herself and saw the truth of her own words; from her neck to her inner thighs, she was covered with Wolf's bites. He'd marked her as his.

"You son of a bitch! You were marking your damned territory!"

She reached for the first thing that came to her hand—a big, fat candle—and hurled it at his head. He displayed enough wisdom to flee. He dodged into her bedroom, grabbed his clothes, and escaped through her front door, dodging a barrage of decor.

Alone in her living room, naked and quaking, Kristin got out her phone and dialed Kevin Salinger's number. He answered on the second ring. The sound of his voice filled her with a chaos cloud of warring emotions: relief, spite, grief.

"Salinger?" she said and didn't know what else to say.

"Kristin, what's wrong?" His voice had a sudden urgency, as if he knew she was in bad shape.

"I think ... I think the pink cloud just went black. Or something. I need—"

"Are you home?"

"Yes."

"I'll be right there," he said. "Wait for me."

"Where would I go?" she asked, but he'd hung up.

It took her a moment to realize he was afraid she might kill herself. The thought made her laugh. Him, she might kill. Mad Wolf, she would have killed if he hadn't gotten out of her house. Dvorak or Tessa or Gianni or those two pricks from her freshman year in high school. But herself? That was not going to happen.

When Salinger got there, she buzzed him through the front gate, then stood in the middle of her living room with a robe wrapped around her, waiting. She started trembling again when she saw him, when he saw her. He crossed the room to stand in front of her and she could feel his eyes reading her face, trying to get her to look at him. She couldn't.

"Kristin," he said, "what happened?"

She opened the robe, displaying the red welts Wolf had decorated her with. She heard Salinger's sharp intake of breath.

"My God, what—*who* did this to you?"

She shook her head. "Doesn't matter. He's gone. I threw him out.

He *used* me, Salinger. He fucking used me!"

Suddenly, she was sobbing hysterically, and just as suddenly, she was in Salinger's arms while he hushed her and spoke gentle words into her ear. He got her to the sofa and sat with her half in his lap, her head cradled against his shoulder.

When she had let out enough of her anger and desperation to regain some semblance of rational thought, she lifted her head, tilting it back against his supportive shoulder. He wiped tears from her eyes with his fingertips, then kissed some away with his lips, and when his lips met hers, she wasn't surprised.

What surprised her was that it was as far as he went. Moments later, she slipped into an exhausted sleep, waking to find herself alone in her bed with the robe safely secured. She smelled coffee brewing.

The night flooded back into her mind. Mad Wolf and Kevin Salinger. Both men had humiliated her, each in his own patented way. Wolf had tried to possess her, to use her; Salinger had rejected her.

That isn't how it's supposed to work.

He realized he was standing in her bedroom doorway, shirtsleeves rolled up to his elbows, eyes concerned.

Fuck you.

He looked at her for a moment as though he could see what was going on inside her head—pink cloud gone, looming abyss taking its place—and he said, simply, "Coffee's ready. I've poured you a big mug. And there are bagels."

She swallowed. "Thanks, dude. I appreciate it. But I can take it from here. I'm good."

"You're not 'good,' Kristin. You're far from good. You're just better than last night."

She smiled crookedly at the ceiling. "Well, that's something. I mean it. Thanks, and all that, but I got this. You can go."

"Nope. Not going. You're going to eat and drink a very tall mug of coffee and then I'm going to drive you to the studio, where you will get into makeup and act up a storm." He checked his watch. "You've got twenty minutes, Kris. I recommend a hot shower." He turned and disappeared back into the hall.

Kristin rolled out of bed and stumbled into the bathroom, leaning on the sink but not looking at herself in the mirror. She was craving the drugs again. Just a quick blow, that's all she needed. She must have some stashed away in the house.

But no. If Dvorak discovered she'd snorted cocaine, he'd fire her. She threw herself into the shower, letting hot water course over her head and shoulders.

To hell with the bastard.

She began to wonder why she'd gotten into this project to begin with. She was going to be a star, with or without him. She wouldn't just be that anonymous woman on the magazine cover again. She could do it. She knew she could. She'd gotten on the drugs because she'd been scared that she couldn't do it, but she didn't need them, she told herself.

If Salinger could do without his alcohol—he'd told her bourbon had the greatest allure—then she could go it without coke.

Showered, she towel-dried her hair and set about brushing her teeth. Her mouth tasted of Wolf and she hated it. Her hands trembled as she wielded the brush, as though they had taken on a life of her own. She felt as though she weren't even in control of her body anymore. Salinger had called this "post-acute withdrawal syndrome" and said it could last for months—months before her body adjusted to not having the drugs in her bloodstream.

She called it hell.

An hour later, sitting in the makeup chair, the stylist concentrated her brush under Kristin's eyes, commenting that she was starting to get dark circles.

"Are you getting enough sleep?" she asked. "Fuck no."

"Try some valerian tea before bed. Tastes like wood pulp, but it works wonders for me."

Valerian tea? What planet was this woman from? What Kristin needed was Valium, Xanax, maybe some oxycodone. That would help her sleep. That would scare away that dark abyss that had opened up beneath her last night. Shit, no. Those were on the list of drugs they'd test for. She couldn't take anything stronger than melatonin, and that had never worked for her.

Kristin dragged herself sluggishly onto the set. They were shooting an easy scene that day, one where her character, Lenora, greeted her sister when she arrived at her house. She was supposed to be cheerful and supportive, sympathizing with Tessa's character Caitlin over the loss of her husband and trying to cheer her up. She would sooner have sympathized with a cockroach.

When they'd rehearsed the scene earlier, she'd nailed it, but now she couldn't even muster the energy to smile.

When the camera stopped shooting, she saw Dvorak frowning. He passed a note to his assistant who passed it to Kristin, but Kristin already knew what it would say: *Energy. More energy.*

"I need coffee," she said. "I didn't sleep much last night." Which was mostly Salinger's fault. If the jerk hadn't rejected her, if he'd only made love to her, she'd have slept like a log. But no, the man had all the sex drive of a sack of concrete.

A production assistant headed for the pot of coffee that was perpetually available on the soundstage, but Kristin gagged at the memory of the coffee at the NA meeting.

"A triple latte from Starbucks," she added, and the PA turned around and headed for the door.

Once the caffeine was coursing through her veins, they went back to shooting the scene. Kristin tried to remember how she'd performed the lines in the rehearsal, but it seemed like a distant memory now. It had floated away with the pink cloud and it wasn't coming back. She faked it, but she knew that it wasn't working. She was going through the motions. And the motions weren't very good ones.

At the NA meeting that evening she actually spoke more than a few words, talking about how she suddenly found herself unable to perform. People around the room gave sympathetic nods, and others talked about how they'd had the same problem. But the only solution they offered was to focus on her higher power. Her higher power could be God, her higher power could be the group, her higher power could be her pet cat or the cast of her movie, or someone in her life who saw her as her best self.

Her best self? There was no such animal.

She tried to avoid looking at Salinger, who'd kept his distance all day, but her eyes were drawn to him against her will. He was watching her, his eyes inhabited by a mixture of emotions she couldn't read. When she caught him at it, he looked away.

That's when Kristin knew that her movie career was going to be a disaster.

Chapter Twenty-Four

Tessa thought she must be glowing. She'd heard how boring movie sets could be, with most of your time spent in makeup chairs or waiting for the crew to prepare the next scene, but she didn't care. It was all new to her and as magical as she imagined it would be. The supporting cast were people she knew only from their faces on the screen or occasionally from attending the same parties, but she was in awe simply being in their presence—being a peer.

That uncanny sense of channeling a character whose voice she only knew from words in a script came over her again and again. Dvorak told her she had a natural talent to interpret the writer's words and the director's vision and bring them to life, that it was an ability many actors required years to cultivate. She had known from the first table read that she could play this part. She could feel it inside her. Her acting coach had told her that playing a role was like singing a song. You had to find the inner music that defined the character and flow with its rhythms. She had heard that music from the start.

As much as she hated to think it, Caitlin's music was her sister's music. She recognized so much of Kristin in the role that she channeled it effortlessly— the scheming, the penchant for manipulation, the glimpses of vulnerability that she'd reluctantly come to see as a ploy. It made her wonder, all over again, what had happened to Kristin in her fourteenth or fifteenth year that had begun to change her, and it puzzled her to the core to realize that Kristin—a natural actress if there ever was one—was unable to ace this the way she aced everything else.

Then, just before they were scheduled to start filming, something changed. Kristin began to pull herself together, sparkling with something that looked like genuine contentment, an emotion that Tessa hadn't seen often in her twin. Bitterness, yes. Cockiness and snarkiness, yes. Schadenfreude? Plenty. But contentment? That was new.

She seemed to be spending a good deal of time with the producer, Kevin Salinger. They frequently had lunch or dinner together in the studio commissary, and Salinger sometimes drove Kristin home. Tessa began to hope that she might have found herself in an actual relationship. She had used men all her adult life, but there seemed to be a genuine spark between her and Salinger. The idea of her sister falling in love, actually forming an attachment to a man, was astonishing.

Then something went wrong. When filming began in earnest, the two began spending less and less time together, and when they were both on the set, the tension between them was evident. Tessa was disappointed, but not surprised.

Dark rings formed under Kristin's eyes, and the makeup artists had to work overtime to cover them up. She started coming in late to the set, dragging her ass as though her best friend had died. Dvorak admonished her for her tardiness, yet seemed to be giving her a pass. As soon as a scene had been filmed, she would disappear to her dressing room or trailer and only return after the PA repeatedly banged on her door. Her performances seemed to have swung in a bizarre pendulum arc from manic to spot-on to flat. She sleepwalked through her part toward the end of production, which might have worked if they'd filmed the scenes in chronological sequence, but that was rarely possible.

"We'll have to edit around her worst performances," Tessa overheard Dvorak telling someone in his office as she walked past in the studio hallway. "Emphasize Tessa and Frederik as much as possible. We'll have to scrap some of Kristin's footage, but we can make it work in the context of the story. And, if necessary, we'll reshoot with Tessa in the part."

As she drew abreast of the doorway, the senior film editor stepped out into the hall. Tessa smiled at him, said, "Hi, Todd," and kept walking, pretending to have heard nothing.

She didn't know whether to feel bad for Kristin or hopeful that having her behavior catch up with her at last might effect real change in her twin. Maybe if Kristin thought she was about to lose everything she'd worked so hard for, she'd fix whatever it was in her that was broken.

Tessa felt a deep urge to help, but she knew her help would never be accepted. In the final analysis, there was nothing she could do but send up endless prayers for divine intervention. She remembered the old saw about the man caught on the roof of his house in a flood, praying for God to reach down and help him. A guy in a rowboat, a couple in a speedboat, and a rescue helicopter show up, but the man tells each one God is going to save him and they move on. He drowns, of course, and when he reaches the next world, he asks God why He didn't rescue him. "Well," God tells him, "I sent you a rowboat, a power launch, and a helicopter. What were you waiting for?"

Kristin was like that guy, spurning every outstretched hand. Tessa wondered if that had ended her friendship with Kevin Salinger. Her own impotence made her feel ill. It had been her sister's dream to be a star, someone whose name people would recognize. Why in the world would she sabotage herself like this?

The greatest irony was that Tessa was living Kristin's dream—a dream she hadn't even wanted. A dream she'd only bought into because she thought it was something they could do together and thereby salvage their relationship. Even after the trick Kristin had pulled on her at UCLA, Tessa still loved her sister. She doubted Kristin would ever return that feeling.

Somehow, despite Kristin's erratic performances, they nursed *Dark Beauty* through production. Tessa felt great about her own execution overall and was in awe of the supporting cast, but watching Kristin fall further and further into a funk finally spurred Tessa to screw up her courage and ask Kristin what was wrong.

"This stupid movie," her twin informed her, "that's what's wrong. It's going to be a disaster. I thought Dvorak was supposed to be this phenomenal director. And that *script* ... I don't know where he dug up this writer—"

Tessa, who'd intended to be supportive and positive, found herself to be unequal to the task—and ticked. "Why do you do that?" she demanded.

"Do what?"

"Blame all your troubles on everyone else. Angelica's an award-winning, much-sought-after screenplay writer, and her script was great. Alex's direction was great. What wasn't great was your performance. You were all over the place."

"I was what?"

"You were erratic, moody, angry. You know all this."

"I was hamstrung by—"

"You were hamstrung by your own carelessness, Krist. I know you started rehearsals on cocaine or something and I don't know what you're on now—Valium?"

"It's none of your—"

"It's *totally* my business," added Tessa. "I care about your mental health, Krist. You had a rough start, but you got it together. For a while there, you were doing great. What happened?" She hesitated, then ventured, "Something between you and Kevin?"

Her sister's face suffused with color and her eyes all but spat fire. "There is *nothing* between me and Salinger. He's a ... a holier-than-thou prick who thinks he's too good for ... for anyone."

As much as she would have loved to know what that cryptic remark meant, Tessa had no desire to wade any further into her sister's black mood. She gave up. She didn't admit that she was also worried about the film, though for wholly other reasons. One was the way Alex Dvorak had changed his approach to Kristin, cutting back drastically on giving her performance notes.

Tessa suspected that Salinger, who was frequently on set, was behind this. The producer watched Kristin's every move; she avoided him as if he were radioactive. She put in her time and disappeared silently at the end of the day to God-knew-where. This wasn't any version of Kristin that Tessa had ever seen, and she found it disturbing. Kristin was many things, but silent, she was not. Ever the party girl, she didn't even put in an appearance at the wrap party.

Post-production, even for an intimate live-action movie like *Dark Beauty*, was a long, drawn-out process in which the film was edited, establishing shots were inserted, and touches of CGI were added to some of the scenes. The sisters were occasionally called back in to film shots that hadn't worked the first time, or to overdub dialogue for some of the location scenes. Tessa reshot three of Kristin's scenes, stepping into the role of Lenora, if only briefly.

As the film's premiere grew near, Kristin's mood seemed to change directions yet again; the sizzling energy levels were back. Tessa suspected she was back on drugs. That would explain the strange genesis of her moods: frenetic to perfectly controlled to flat and airless to frenetic again. Despite Tessa's fears, between Dvorak's masterful directing and Todd Brewer's brilliant editing, advance reviews had been glowing, and everybody knew that *Dark Beauty* was going to be a hit. The night of the premiere, with VIP seating housing everyone from the studio executives to a limited circle of family and friends, Kristin came alone to the premiere and sat in the back of the theater. She arrived stag at the Dvoraks' after-party as well. She hadn't spoken to Tessa since the advance reviews came out. They weren't bad across the board, but they were universally puzzled by the wild swings in Kristin's acting.

As she watched the film in its entirety for the first time, as she looked for and saw the truly bright spots in her sister's performance, Tessa began to relax. Kristin would have her moment in the sun and her film career could recover. Plenty of stars had come back from disastrous first performances. Kristin would be no exception. She could still be a model. It wasn't going to be the end of her career. At least, not unless she sabotaged herself further.

On their way into the Dvoraks' Malibu home, Daniel pulled Tessa close to his side and murmured five words that made her let go of all of her worries about Kristin.

"Let's get married. Next month."

She looked up at him, stopping in the middle of the entrance hall. "Are you sure?"

"Why wait? I was doing the whole macho gotta bring-home-the-bacon thing, but I realized that it doesn't matter who brings home the bacon. As long as we *have* bacon and I'm the one who cooks it. Your kitchen skills…" He made a tippy boat gesture with one hand.

Tessa feinted a punch at his nose, then threw her arms around his neck and kissed him. She was as happy as she had ever been. She had a wonderful marriage and career ahead of her—and more joy than she could possibly imagine. This was her night; she was no longer going to let Kristin's drama shape her life.

Act 3
Daylight and Nightmare

Chapter Twenty-Five

Tessa sat in her darkened apartment and stared at the glass-topped coffee table she had rescued from her mansion before she'd sold it. Atop it, in a neat line, were the bottles of oxycodone and Valium that the doctors had given her after surgery, few of which she had taken. Next to them was a bottle of Don Papa dark rum that she'd bought and had yet to open.

The pills had proven relatively effective, at least for the problems the doctors had intended them for, but Tessa had found the opioids made her skin feel strange, as if it wanted to crawl off her body, and the antianxiety meds made her dopey. At the moment, Tessa was contemplating a different use for the drugs.

The incident that changed her life had been nothing short of hellacious. Tessa avoided recalling it as much as possible, but sometimes the memories came flooding in uninvited, as they did on this afternoon as she eyed the powerful meds on her coffee table. "No!" she screeched, covering her face with her hands as each memory that was seared on her brain flashed into her consciousness.

The acid that had landed on her face immediately burned through her skin like fire melting candle wax, along with one eye and a large section of her beautiful blonde hair. Shrieking and instinctively grabbing her face, she had seared her hands as well. She had little recall after that. She had presumably continued screaming and then passed out from the pain and shock. Following that were foggy memories of a sterile white environment, bright fluorescent lights beaming down when her closed eyes were uncovered, beeping machines, scurrying medical personnel, and serious-sounding voices. "Her eyesight ...

years of recovery ... wait, Tessa, are you with us? Give me another hit of fentanyl, stat."

She eventually learned that she had been kept in a medical coma for two weeks and, during this time, was airlifted to the burn center at Johns Hopkins in Baltimore, Maryland. Her parents had researched and found that this location might be able to do an experimental skin graft for her face. She was initially blind in one eye, but since she was so often bandaged across her eyes, she barely noticed the difference.

She got in a routine during her five-month stay there of surgery, recovery, surgery, recovery ... over and over. She'd had 112 surgeries already in two years—some of them up to ten hours long. Someone was keeping a tally—not Tessa. The dead and damaged portion of skin on her face had been removed and replaced by a skin substitute. Then skin from her back and buttocks had been grafted on top of the substitute. Several of the operations had been specifically for her damaged eye—both to help her regain her sight and to rebuild the lid and other tissue surrounding it.

In the meantime, she had a steady line of meds streaming directly into her bloodstream to keep the excruciating pain at bay. The itching itself was enough to drive her insane. She wanted to scratch her face to ease the irritation, but merely touching it brought more pain. Besides, she wore a pressure mask twenty-three hours a day to help ease scarring. Her parents visited when they could, but even though they meant well, their visits gave Tessa stress. Their voices were either overly cheerful or their conversation laced with unnatural pauses—presumably for them to control their emotions. They hinted and then outright asked if she wanted Daniel to visit. Her answer was always the same: a firm no! She was much too ashamed of her changed appearance to be able to deal with his inevitable judgment. She realized that her parents—her dad especially—were emotionally broken from the whole ordeal. And Kristin's name was never spoken or even hinted at. Tessa herself spent hours heaping evil thoughts upon her sister. Her normally upbeat personality had melted like the skin on her face. And the hours upon hours to do nothing but think about her circumstances hardly helped her delicate mental health. After the five months in Baltimore, Tessa was well enough to transfer as an outpatient to the UCLA cosmetic center. The vision in her bad eye was getting better. It would never be perfect, but the shadowy images were growing clearer with each passing day.

She had given her parents permission to sell her beautiful home so, lacking any place to live and still needing the physical and emotional support, Tessa moved in with them. They were helpful at driving her to her appointments and continued operations, since driving herself wasn't a possibility in those early months. She found it ironic to be a patient at the hospital at which she'd planned to do her residency after medical school. That dream was a distant memory now, fading like pictures in an old scrapbook.

Daniel had tried to visit at least twice a day during her stay at UCLA, but she'd refused to see him. Almost the entire right side of her face was a horrifying patchwork of varicolored tissue—butt tissue, she reminded herself wryly. She resembled a creature from Frankenstein's laboratory or a monster or villain in a superhero comic book. If the pressure mask was reducing the scarring, what would she have looked like without it? In her own view, her appearance could hardly be worse.

Pouring the bottle of Valium tablets into her hand, she counted them out in precise piles on the smooth surface of the table. She'd researched the subject carefully online and knew exactly how many pills were required to kill her, factoring in her body weight and tolerance to drugs. Of course, vomiting back up the chemicals could be an issue, but she had studied that as well and knew how quickly to down them so they would take effect before that happened. She added an oxycodone—and then one more—to ease any pain she might feel, emotional or physical, and then poured herself a glass of rum to wash all the pills down. She sighed as she glanced at the sofa where she planned to lie down and wait for the inevitable once she swallowed the pills. She'd worn her favorite dress so that she'd look good—minus her face, of course—when the EMTs found her body. The message she had composed to the 911 dispatcher sat ready to go at the touch of the Enter button. She'd send that at the last possible moment. For family and friends, she had written a different message that the police would find with her body.

Live fast, die young, and leave a beautiful corpse, she thought. At least her body would be beautiful, though arguably too thin. Nothing could be done about her face. The whole situation was ironic, really, because she'd always been a glass-half-full kind of person, which she felt should have translated into face half pretty. It hadn't. Half a face was no face at all. She had spent plenty of time chiding herself for her depression. She had never thought of herself as the depressed type and thought she could have a good attitude about any obstacle that came along. The pain and mutilation caused by the extensive burns had changed all that.

She started as her phone buzzed louder than normal against the glass top of the table. She had no desire to even see who was calling. It was probably Daniel trying to reach her again, and he was the last person she wanted to talk to. Let him find out the next day with everyone else. She hoped he'd be happy that she had freed him of any obligation to see her again. He couldn't possibly want to, with her face the grotesque mask it had become.

The buzzing stopped but started again almost immediately. She picked up the phone to switch it off but caught the name on the screen—Sarah, not Daniel. Sarah, her lifelong friend, who had given her encouragement whenever she'd needed it, who had supported her through both childhood and adult angst, was making herself available once again. In some corner of Tessa's heart, she appreciated the gesture but truly felt no emotion toward her friend. Her heart was already dead. Dear as Sarah was, Tessa's current problem went far beyond playground tattletales or breakups with boyfriends. Obviously, she couldn't tell Sarah what she had planned, but perhaps she owed it to her to have one last conversation, one last chance to tell her what she had meant in her life.

"Hi, Sarah," she said a little too cheerfully, trying to falsely mask the despair in her voice. "It's good to hear from you. How are you?"

"I'm fine, Tessa!" Sarah replied excitedly. "Do you have your computer on?"

"Uh, no. I've haven't been online much these days."

"Seriously, you've got to look at it. There's this new website called RedMasque.com and you need to see it."

"I love you, Sarah, but I'm really not in the mood for surfing the web." Tessa played with the pills on the table, twirling them and pushing them into groups.

"You will be when you see this. I'll wait while you get your laptop." Tessa sighed and put the phone down. The pills could wait. They weren't going anywhere. She could at least make Sarah happy for a moment, especially considering how her friend would react when she heard the news tomorrow about Tessa's death.

Tessa put the phone on speaker, sat on the sofa next to it with the laptop, clicked away from the message to 911, and typed redmasque into the search bar as Sarah spelled it for her. She then clicked on the link that took her to a website for a modeling agency, one called simply Red Masque. The front page of the site was filled with photographs of models, some of whom Tessa recognized. They weren't the top models in the business and none of them had ever worked with Gianni DeLuca, but they were all quite attractive. The page was fringed with an artsy border of lacy scarlet, lined with golden filigree in nineteenth-century stylings. Tessa slumped in her seat at the sight of the smiling models and grabbed her stomach, fearing she was about to vomit.

She normally would have been bothered by the tackiness of the site but had no energy for such inane concerns now. The images reminded her that her life was gone, and she eyed the pills with expectancy. Why would Sarah be so cruel and tasteless as to have her call up a modeling site anyway? To rub her face in the life that would never be hers again? Did she actually think Tessa might be able to find work there? This was insanity. Her neck and shoulders tightened into an instant tension headache.

She shook her head. "Sarah? I'm not quite sure I see—"

"The video," Sarah squealed excitedly. "Do you see that large play button in the center of the screen? Click on it!"

"Oh, really, I'm just not in the mood—"

"Click on it!"

The tone in her friend's voice was one Tessa had never heard before, one so urgent that she was unable to ignore it. She clicked on the button and a video began to play. It was an ad for the agency. Models glided elegantly past, like the figures of women in the opening credits of an old James Bond movie, as an announcer's voice extolled the beauty and skill of the modeling talent that the Red Masque Agency had to offer. Tessa watched, trying to keep her emotions at the level of dead. When the montage ended, a woman in an expensively tailored red dress appeared, perched on a vintage chair that looked like something out of the Victorian era. That was a bit odd, but what really stood out was the elaborate red mask she wore that obscured the entire upper two-thirds of her face. Only her vivid red lips and chin were visible.

A chill ran down Tessa's spine. When she and Kristin were ten years old, their mother had read Edgar Allen Poe's short story "The Masque of the Red Death" to them. The tale was about a group of rich nobles partying at a masquerade ball while a plague known as the Red Death decimated the rest of Europe. An unexpected visitor arrived in a grotesque costume fashioned to resemble a victim of the disease. The visitor turned out to be Death itself, and it took the lives of everyone at the elite ball. Poe's point had no doubt been that there is no amount of money or title or nobility that can shield you from Death if it's your time.

Yeah. Got that memo.

Although Poe didn't describe the visitor as wearing a red mask, the sisters had always imagined that he must have been. Kristin had even made a terrifying-looking red mask for Halloween one year that looked exactly like the one the woman in the video was wearing. The mask was beautifully designed with black and gold scroll work that might have been occult sigils for all Tessa knew.

Even before the blood-red lips of the woman on the video moved, before the woman spoke a word, Tessa knew whose voice she would hear—Kristin's.

"Tessa! Tessa! Are you alright?"

Tessa realized that she had zoned out for a few seconds and that the voice was Sarah's, coming from the cell phone on the sofa next to her.

"Y-yes. I'm … I'm okay. It's just that …" She paused to catch her breath, which was coming in short gasps. "That's Kristin. What's she doing in an online video?"

"Just listen. She explains in the video."

"… is the premiere modeling agency for Los Angeles's most discriminating clientele," Kristin went on. "Our line of models are the most beautiful women in the industry, with proven track records for providing the services that our clients are looking to receive. Click on the photo album image below to see photos, videos, and statistics for our models. If you like what you see, call, text, or email us today. Our contact information is provided below."

"Isn't that wonderful?" Sarah said. "Kristin has her own modeling agency! I know how worried you were about her—I mean, when she just poofed—so I thought you'd want to see this right away."

Tessa pondered with distaste the fact that her sister was back working in the modeling world. But at least her sister was all right. "This is … amazing. And unexpected. I was afraid …" *Afraid Kristin had done what you were about to do?* She swallowed. "I had no idea that Kris … Thank you, Sarah. This is … amazing."

"Then I'm glad I got you on the phone. When you're, you know, settled into your new place a bit more, maybe we could schedule a catch-up session?"

Tessa heard the longing in Sarah's voice. The desire to reconnect. The two had spoken only a few times in the last two years. "Um, yeah," Tessa said, "we have a lot of catching up to do." She couldn't take her eyes off Kristin's masked face. "Listen, Sarah, can I get back to you later?"

"Oh, of course. You're going to get in touch with Kristin, right?"

"I very likely will," Tessa said as she tapped her phone off.

Kristin at the head of her own modeling agency? It made all the sense in the world. She could no longer work as a model, but she knew the ins and outs of modeling intimately. She may have seen her only viable career move as managing other models. She had enough connections left in the industry to help her put together a stable of her own from among the second- and third-tier models Tessa recognized on the website.

She reflexively wanted to cheer for Kristin. She wanted to feel pride, and even envy … or maybe what she wanted to feel was hope. She wanted to feel all those things, but she knew her sister too well. Kristin never did anything without an ulterior motive. Unless … was it possible that the incident with Morrison had ultimately changed Kristin for the better?

Tessa saw the pills and the bottle of rum on the coffee table in front of her and realized that she had momentarily forgotten what she had been on the verge of doing. Maybe she wasn't ready to take herself out of the world quite yet.

She was surprised herself with how quickly her mood had turned. Feeling a sudden surge of energy and after checking the address on Google Maps, she grabbed her purse, hat, sunglasses, and keys and was out the door.

Chapter Twenty-Six

Los Angeles was not a city of skyscrapers. Not really. Tessa had realized this when she and Kristin had visited New York and London for photo shoots. In New York she had been awed by the towering structures that soared over her head like giant crystals fallen from the night sky to loom over the lesser mortals below. London had been a revelation, not because of its buildings' height but because architecturally stunning modern towers overshadowed and yet underscored the age of the ancient streets beneath and between. So bizarre were some of these structures that locals had given them nicknames like the Walkie Talkie, the Gherkin, and the Cheesegrater because they didn't look like buildings. They instead resembled giant sculptures.

Los Angeles, for its size, was largely flat. The few areas with skyscrapers stood out like patches of weeds in a city that was made mostly of one- and two-story buildings. One of those weed patches was Downtown LA, which had only recently become a trendy location for upscale offices and night life. The Red Masque Modeling Agency was in one of the buildings tightly squeezed into a cluster of towers. The sides of the building were made of polished glass and steel. Tessa turned away from them, afraid that she'd see her reflection looking back at her from their glossy surfaces. She wore an oversized pair of dark sunglasses and a wide-brimmed felt sun hat set jauntily on her head so that the brim covered as much of the right side of her face as possible. Her dress was stylishly retro, yet she was convinced that everyone who passed her could see her scars. She had internalized her ugliness so thoroughly that it had become a part of her self-image. She had no trouble understanding why Kristin would wear a mask.

The Red Masque Agency occupied the entire top floor of the building. When Tessa stepped out of the elevator, she found herself in the reception area, lavishly furnished with elegant decor and pictures of models on the wall. The receptionist, sitting behind a curved desk, was a gorgeous black woman with naturally curly hair that flowed like a frothing ebony waterfall over her shoulders. She didn't so much regard Tessa as she did inspect her. Tessa reflexively attributed the receptionist's arrogant glare to the sight of her scarred face, but it was more likely just the tendency most people in the modeling industry had to compare everyone they met to themselves.

"Can I help you?" the woman said in a voice dripping with "what could you possibly want?"

"I'm here to see Kristin Morgan."

"Do you have an appointment?"

"No. But could you tell her that her sister Tessa is here?"

The woman didn't hide her surprise. The tragic attack on Tessa and her twin was still in the tabloids, even after two years, and the look in the woman's eyes was a cross between horror at encountering a hideously deformed human and excitement over meeting a celebrity crime victim. No one who traded on their looks could remain unaffected when confronting a horror that could befall even them.

The receptionist hit the intercom button, mumbled Tessa's request, waited for a response, then released the button. "Your sister will see you now. I'll show you to her office." She said the words without looking up at Tessa and wordlessly led her down a short-carpeted hallway to a set of double doors.

Kristin had spared no expense in making the Red Masque Agency appear to cater to high-powered clientele. Her own office took up nearly a third of the floor, most of that empty space lined with stylish furnishings, wide-screen televisions, and a computer workstation with a curved monitor and illuminated keyboard. She glanced up as Tessa entered, registering no obvious reaction, though whatever her emotions were, they were hidden behind the mask. Her eyes appeared only as glittering silver gems from within the mask's eye holes. Her braided hair was coiled atop her head; she'd let it return to its natural blonde.

She smiled, her teeth flashing white, framed by the red of her mask and lower lip. "Tessa, darling," she said. "It's so good to see you. I thought you'd dropped off the planet."

"I did. I thought you had too," Tessa said. "Until I saw your website."

"Oh, that. It was designed by one of Los Angeles's top web developers. I hope you were impressed."

"I was impressed ... and surprised." That was the understatement of the year.

"I was surprised too," Kristin said. "I mean, to have you just walk into my office. Why?"

Tessa steeled her nerves. "Well, I'd like to say hi to my sister. And to tell you how impressed and proud I am that you've found a way to continue working in the industry. I admit, my imagination wasn't up to the task of repurposing myself. But finding you—finding this—I wondered ... if you wanted to take on a partner."

The mask tilted to one side. "A partner? You?"

"We modeled together for years," Tessa observed wryly. "We were as famous a duo as Batman and Robin, Penn and Teller, Scully and Mulder. Perhaps it would draw in a larger clientele if we ran the agency together. Who could resist that sort of human-interest story—the black and white swans become phoenixes."

The crimson lip curled. "My, don't you sound cynical. That's not like you."

"Well, I haven't been like me for a while. But I didn't mean it cynically."

"That's what you came here to ask me? If I'll take you on as a partner?"

"Yes."

"You might have saved yourself the trip. I'm doing quite well on my own. I don't need a partner."

"Fine. Then maybe you need a sister who can relate to what you've been through."

Kristin shook her head. "I'm not your sister anymore, Tessa. I'm just someone you grew up with. We no longer have anything in common." She pushed a button on her desk. "I'll have my receptionist show you out."

Tessa was speechless ... for all of the two seconds it took for anger to kick in. "Nothing in common? I think we have these in common." She lifted the brim of her hat to reveal the rough, discolored right side of her face. "We also have in common that a victim of your manipulation—or should I say *one* of the many victims of your manipulation—did this to us. You disrupted *my* life for your own selfish reasons. You dragged me into your dreamscape kicking and screaming—literally. You fucking *roofied* me, Kristin. *Used* me. Yet, when it all blew up in your face, I was the one who put myself in harm's way to try to literally save your skin. If it weren't for you, *I wouldn't look like this*! So, yeah, you're right—I'm not your sister. I've never been your sister. I've only *ever* been a convenient tool."

Tessa swung around to find the receptionist standing in the office doorway, visibly stunned and motionless.

"I'll let myself out, thanks," she told the woman and strode past her into the reception area. As she reached the door, a beautiful Latina walked in. Tessa was surprised to realize she recognized the woman from long-ago photo shoots. Juanita something? Juanita Suarez? No, Sanchez.

Tessa turned away, hoping the woman wouldn't recognize her, but she could tell from her expression that she had.

"Excuse me," Tessa murmured and moved briskly out the door and to the elevator. She wasn't interested in a conversation. Juanita Sanchez was part of a world that Tessa would never be part of again.

Back in her apartment, Tessa returned to her sofa and stared at the neat row of pill bottles and the tidy piles of pills that remained on her table. The glass of rum was right where she'd left it. All she had to do was wash the tablets down with a glass of expensive liquor and all the pain would be gone, all the anguish would be over.

And Kristin would have achieved the ultimate manipulation, said a small, angry voice from Tessa's innermost being.

The phone rang. Probably Daniel again. She almost felt as though she should talk to him, give him the chance for a final goodbye; regardless of what she decided to do with the pills and the booze, she needed him to understand that she had cut him loose. She was reluctant to talk to him, though. Daniel had always been extremely sensitive to her moods. If he even detected a hint in her voice of what she was planning to do, he would have a team of medics racing to her apartment before the pills could take effect. She didn't want to be saved at the last minute. If she still decided to follow through, she wanted to drift off to a quiet, serene death.

But the name on the caller ID again wasn't Daniel's. It was Juanita Sanchez. Tessa had forgotten she'd ever had the woman's number in her contacts list. Why in the world would the model be calling? Was she just trying to rekindle an old acquaintanceship? Unlikely; they hadn't known each other that well. Yet, on a wave of irresistible curiosity, Tessa answered the call.

"Tessa," the voice said with a mere hint of a Spanish accent. "Juanita Sanchez. You probably don't remember me, but—"

"Of course I remember you, Juanita. I'm just a little surprised to hear from you. How did you get my number?"

"From your sister's contacts app. When I saw you earlier in your sister's office, I ... You aren't working with her, are you?"

Tessa laughed ruefully. "No, I'm not. I think I can safely say that my sister and I are now officially estranged."

"Good, because what I'm calling about concerns Kristin. But I ... can't discuss it on the phone. Would you be willing to meet me in person? It's important."

Curiosity poked at Tessa again. "All right. Where would you like to meet?"

"Do you know the La Coquita restaurant?"

"I'm afraid not, but I can look it up."

"Would you mind meeting me there tomorrow for lunch? Say one o'clock?"

Tessa glanced again at the pills on the coffee table. The world was apparently conspiring to prevent her from exiting it. Maybe all one needed to stay alive was curiosity.

"Sounds good," Tessa said. "I'll see you there."

Chapter Twenty-Seven

East Los Angeles was quite different from the rest of the city. Much of it was a Latino barrio filled with a population heavy on illegal immigrants and shunned by the glitterati who made up a small but highly visible portion of LA's citizenry. Standing on a rundown street outside La Coquita, Tessa understood immediately why Juanita Sanchez wanted them to meet there; they weren't likely to run into anybody they knew.

That suspicion was confirmed when Juanita arrived, driving an older Mercedes and dressed down in jeans and a T-shirt and wearing dark, face-obscuring sunglasses not unlike Tessa's. Her thick hair was pulled back into a braid.

Inside, the restaurant was decorated in bold, rich colors and smelled deliciously of spices. The clientele was largely Latino, which was a sign that the food they served would not only be authentic but probably excellent.

The lovely model led Tessa to a dark corner booth, where they sat across from one another at a table that looked like it hadn't been painted in years. Juanita seated herself so she had the best view of the door.

"The *chile relleno* is excellent," Juanita said, removing her sunglasses.

She fluffed her bangs so they nearly covered her eyes and looked beautiful despite wearing no makeup except for a sheer wash of lipstick.

"Great. That's one of my favorite dishes." Tessa left her glasses on, arranging her hair so it covered most of the right side of her face.

A handsome waiter who looked like he might be an aspiring model himself took their order and brought them, at their request, two glasses of ice water and the obligatory tortilla chips. Juanita kept checking the perimeters of the room, as though searching for something—or someone. Was she afraid someone might recognize them?

Juanita's face was eminently recognizable. She had classically beautiful features and large, luminous brown eyes. Her beauty had allowed her to rise far above her humble beginnings in Tijuana—but only so far. There was a demand for ethnic models of all sorts in the advertising industry, but many never got beyond working on ads targeted at their own ethnic group. That was what had happened to Juanita. She had hit a kind of racial ceiling, one that Caucasian models like Tessa and Kristin had never encountered. Someone like Juanita could be trapped in a box that almost certainly meant she would be typecast as someone who could sell products to Latinas. She had made it onto a single cover of *Vogue* but that had been it.

The modeling life wasn't fair or reasonable. Juanita was not only beautiful, but she'd been easy to work with and took direction well. Tessa had never been able to understand why that hadn't afforded her a far greater reach. She remembered the last time she'd spoken to the other woman—what was it, three years ago, now?—she'd confided in Tess that what she really wanted was to be able to move her family into a nice house in Beverly Hills so she could take them to expensive restaurants and shop on Rodeo Drive. She'd wanted to give her parents and two siblings a good life. As far as Tessa knew, that dream had never materialized.

"So," Tessa said, wanting to assuage her curiosity before the rather jumpy Juanita went running out the door, "you said there was something you needed to tell me about Kristin."

"Yes." Juanita again glanced around the room. "How much do you know about what she's done in the time since your ... accident?"

"Nothing. I found out about the agency yesterday, in fact. Other than that, I know she's resourceful, imaginative, willful ... and selfish." Juanita reached into her handbag and pulled out a newspaper clipping, setting it next to Tessa's purse. "Have you seen this?" she asked.

The paper was an article torn from today's edition of the *Los Angeles Times*. The headline read "Local Photographer Reported Missing."

"I really don't know any photographers these days, Juanita. I'm retired."

"Look at the name."

Tessa glanced at the opening paragraph and a chill ran down her spine. The missing photographer was Gianni DeLuca.

At first, she didn't know what to say. Gianni had been such a central part of her life ... and now he had gone missing? That didn't sound like something a person as flamboyant and self-publicizing as DeLuca would do willingly.

"Gianni was quite the ladies' man," she said, thinking aloud. "Could… could he have run off with someone? Or maybe he went into hiding because he hit on the wrong woman?" She read Juanita's expressive face. "Do you know something about this?"

Juanita nodded again and glanced around the room. "I know a great deal about it. And it has to do with your sister."

"I didn't know she'd seen him since ... well, since we dropped out of sight. Gianni and Kristin had something of a, um, a history, but I really don't think she'd—"

"No, they are not connected romantically." Juanita took a deep breath. "*I've* been seeing Gianni. We are ... close. I thought our relationship had become serious. We were supposed to see each other the night before last, but he never showed. I was angry. I thought he'd stood me up. But when I tried to call him, his phone went straight to voice mail. Then I saw this. He has been missing for three days, according to the police."

"What does Kristin have to do with it?"

Juanita opened her mouth to answer, but suddenly her eyes shifted to something across the room. Tessa turned to follow her gaze and saw a bald-headed fortyish man in a gray suit leaning against the wall, an expressionless stare on his face, his eyes fixed on Juanita.

Juanita's face was far from expressionless. Even through her dark lenses, Tessa could read her sudden fear.

"I'm sorry, I have to leave," Juanita said, standing abruptly. She gave Tessa a chillingly direct look as she picked up her sunglasses from the table. "The website. Look for Crimson," she said, then turned and all but ran from the restaurant.

Tessa noticed the man who had been leaning against the wall gliding among the tables, toward the door, with the studied calm of a man who wanted to remain invisible. He followed Juanita out the door.

Tessa stood up and started after them just as the waiter came to take their order. "Sorry," she said. "We've had an emergency."

By the time Tessa reached the door and stepped into the street, neither Juanita nor the bald-headed man were in sight, but Juanita's car was gone.

One thing was clear, though. Juanita had been terrified.

###

Half an hour later, Tessa was back in her apartment. She now had the fortitude to gather up the pills and put them back in their bottles. Her encounter with Juanita had so intrigued her that suicide began to seem like a distant whim.

She carried the bottles into the bathroom and returned them to the cabinet. On her way out, she glanced at the mirror over the sink. For a long time, she would only look at the left side of her face—the side that had not been ravaged by Kurt Morrison's attack. Now she bravely faced the mirror straight on and saw the woman reflected in it.

Her hair was side parted and draped so it obscured most of the right side of her face from forehead to chin. The red and white discoloration bled from beneath the bright wing of hair like a piebald shadow. She raised her hand, hesitated, then pulled the hair away. A crazy quilt in the form of a human face, stretched tightly over a framework of bone and cartilage, met her gaze. She had half an eyebrow and a mottled eyelid with stunted lashes.

But I have *an eyelid,* she thought. *And an eye. I can* see *my scars. At least the ones that are on the outside. That's something.*

She knew those weren't the worst scars, though. The worst scars—the more consequential ones—were on the inside. She'd realized that with stunning clarity as she stood in her sister's office saying things aloud she had barely dared to let herself think. If she wasn't going to roll over and die, she'd need to deal with those hidden scars too.

Perhaps none of her scars were worth dying over quite yet. At least, not today. Today, she had a mystery to solve.

She let her cascade of hair fall back into place, then returned to the sofa. The rum still sat on the table. She picked up the glass and took a sip, concentrating on the sensation of the liquid burning its way down her throat. She used the heat to pull her thoughts into sharp focus: Gianni DeLuca was missing, and Juanita seemed certain Kristin had something to do with it. She had no doubt Juanita's instincts were spot on.

Okay. Next step. She picked up her phone and tried to reach Juanita, but the model didn't pick up and the call went to voice mail. After several tries, she finally left a short message: "Hey, Juanita. It was great seeing you today. Sorry you had an emergency. Call me. Let's reschedule."

Next, she opened her laptop and went back to the Red Masque website. "Look for crimson," Juanita had said. What did that even mean? Tessa watched the video of Kristin again, studying her every move, her every action. No clues were hidden in her expression, because the mask obscured her features so thoroughly that she might as well have been a statue. She checked the other sections of the website, reading each page of copy. Each model had a short biography, including a resume of her work in the industry, but nothing revealing and little that Kristin didn't already know. Each woman had a portfolio as well, with an emphasis on glamour photography, especially shots in bathing suits and negligees.

Perhaps this was the niche that Kristin had chosen for her clientele. Men's magazines and websites created a large demand for pictures of women in skimpy clothing. It wasn't the most prestigious work that the modeling world had to offer, but Kristin wasn't working with the most prestigious models.

Kristin herself had provided a lengthy bio detailing her long years with DeLuca and her role in *Dark Beauty*, declining to mention how devastating her reviews had been. She had even managed to find some review excerpts that sounded glowing when taken out of context. The message of the biography was clear: This was a woman who could not only provide work for models but provide experienced models to her clients, a woman who understood how the Los Angeles modeling industry worked and who had a vast number of powerful connections.

Kristin's claim of powerful connections was ironic. Few of the people they had known in their work—the ones who could get them jobs—had even been in touch with them since the incident. Gianni DeLuca, Jerry Lance, Charles Robeson—all had been conspicuously silent since Tessa had gotten out of the hospital. Alexei Dvorak was one who had tried to reach her a few times and had sent gifts, messages, and flowers when she was in the hospital. Kevin Salinger had sent flowers as well, and had once left a message wondering if Tessa knew where Kristin had gone when she'd "checked herself out" of the hospital early. Tessa knew that her parents hadn't heard from Kristin since her disappearance, which led her to suspect Kristin had not been in contact with anyone from their shared past.

Tessa finally found what she was looking for on the About the Agency page. Buried in the chirpy text was the sentence: *Our more adventurous clients may be interested in our Crimson services.* Nothing marked the word as different, but when Tessa ran the mouse pointer over it, the cursor changed to a pointing hand, indicating a clickable link.

Almost holding her breath, Tessa clicked on the word Crimson. An unmarked red dialogue box popped up asking for a user name and password. She tried several combinations that she thought Kristin might have used for her own username and password, but none of them worked.

Based on what she had told Tessa, Juanita at least suspected that the Crimson section of the website held the secret to Gianni DeLuca's disappearance, but without a username and password she had hit a dead end on learning what the section contained.

She finally put the laptop down and assessed her spartan apartment. She had saved only a few items from the sale of her mansion. The lion's share of the money from the sale had gone toward her medical bills, money that she now felt had been completely misspent. Tessa had refused to take much from her parents;

she didn't want to continue to drain the family coffers. She now had enough resources to live in her small apartment for another year, and then ... she had no idea where she would find the money to live on after that. Maybe she'd make another trip to the medicine cabinet, but in the interim she had to go on living.

She donned the floppy hat and dark glasses; it was time for a shopping trip. She went to Trader Joe's for groceries and Target to pick up some small appliances. When she returned home, she sank back on the sofa, exhausted. She hadn't been sleeping well in the weeks since she'd left the hospital, but for the first time, she felt a sense of purpose, which inspired her to think she might sleep better tonight. She drank enough of the rum to make herself drowsy, then fell asleep on the sofa.

The sun streaming in the open blinds woke her many hours later. She recalled restless dreams filled with images from the hospital, of Juanita Sanchez running down endless alleyways pursued by a bald man in a suit. Her sister had loomed over it all like a puppeteer, the sigils and golden curlicues on the red mask writhing like snakes. Despite the images, she felt more alive and hopeful. The sluggishness had worn off, and her tension headache had resolved.

She arose, showered, washed her hair and dressed, then made a cup of coffee in her French press. Then she settled back down on the sofa, which was the only comfortable piece of furniture in the room. In fact, aside from the coffee table and a chair, it was the *only* piece of furniture in the room.

She switched on her small television to check the news headlines. Since she could no longer afford cable TV, she tuned to a local channel, hoping to hear more on Gianni DeLuca's disappearance. She was in luck. KTLA was running the morning news with the usual stories about traffic jams on the LA freeways and other local items. A fire in the mountains north of central Los Angeles was threatening a local neighborhood.

Tessa was almost finished with her coffee when a dour-faced male anchor announced that a local Los Angeles model had been found murdered—strangled in her car. Tessa set her coffee cup carefully on the table, a sense of dread settling in her soul as she turned her full attention to the screen. The news program showed a photo of the model, one that she had also seen on Kristin's website.

It was Juanita Sanchez.

Chapter Twenty-Eight

"So you met with this woman in a restaurant yesterday?"

"Yes."

"And you're sure it was the same Juanita Sanchez who died last night?"

"Absolutely sure."

Two LAPD homicide detectives faced Tessa across her coffee table: Jayla Williams, a short African American woman in her early thirties, sat on the sofa opposite Tessa's chair; Frank Garcia, a Hispanic man in his forties, stood at the end of the coffee table.

"Is Juanita a friend of yours?" Detective Williams asked. "A colleague. We worked together years ago."

"Was there a particular reason you got together yesterday?"

Tessa considered, carefully, what she'd tell them. She wanted to be honest, but she didn't want to come across like a crank or conspiracy theorist.

"I don't know how closely your department works with others, but Juanita had been seeing a man named Gianni DeLuca and was concerned about him when he failed to show up for a date and she couldn't reach him by phone. She saw in the *LA Times* he'd been declared a missing person yesterday morning. She thought, since I'd worked with Gianni professionally and was a friend, that I might be able to help."

The two detectives exchanged glances. Their homicide case had just collided with a disappearance.

"You worked with Mr. DeLuca in what capacity?" Detective Garcia asked.

"I was a model in a previous life, believe it or not." The undamaged left side of her mouth lifted in a self-deprecating smile. The right side was mostly covered by her hair—all but the scars across the bridge of her nose and along her lips. "Gianni was the photographer who helped my twin sister and me break into the industry."

She could feel the detectives' gazes sharpen.

Williams's dark eyes widened. "You're *that* Tessa Morgan—the actress who was injured in an acid attack. That's ... horrible. I'm so sorry."

Tessa appreciated the woman's sincerity.

"Yeah. Terrible thing," Garcia said. "My wife read all about it in one of those damned tabloids she buys at the supermarket. I'm glad you came through it okay."

Okay? Apparently, *okay* was a relative concept. "Thank you," she said.

Williams leaned forward, hands between the knees of her gray pantsuit. "Can you tell us anything about this Red Masque Modeling Agency that Juanita Sanchez worked for? Were you one of their models when you were still in the business?"

"They didn't exist when I was in the business," Tessa told them. She hesitated, then added, "I just found out about them myself."

"Found out about them how?" asked Williams.

"A friend told me about the agency and gave me the URL for their website."

Garcia looked uncomfortable. "You ... weren't thinking of going back into modeling ..."

Tessa turned her wince into a tight smile. "My sister runs the agency.

My friend thought I might want to reconnect with her."

"Reconnect," Williams repeated. "You've been out of touch with your sister, then?"

"Since the attack, yes. She ... left the hospital early and virtually disappeared. Neither I nor my parents have heard anything from her since."

"And did you reconnect?"

Tessa's smile twisted toward the wry. "Not exactly. I was able to see my sister briefly, but she wasn't interested in ... in reconnecting. But I did see Juanita there, which may be why she thought to contact me about Gianni's disappearance."

Garcia looked disappointed. "So, you can't tell us much about the agency."

Tessa shook her head, realizing she could feel the curtain of her hair brushing the rebuilt right side of her chin. That was new. It felt like coming out from under Novocain after a dentist appointment. She ignored it for the moment.

"I can't tell you more than what I found on the website. It's Red-masque.com. That's masque with a q-u-e."

"Odd choice of names for a modeling agency," Garcia said, jotting something in a small notebook.

"It was from a story Kristin and I liked when we were kids." Tessa shrugged. "Kristin likely chose it because she wears a mask to cover her scars. The upper part of her face was badly damaged."

Williams shook her head, frowning. "So sorry," she repeated.

"It is what it is," Tessa said. "Like your partner said, we came through it."

Garcia seated himself next to Williams on the sofa. "Can you tell us about your lunch with Ms. Sanchez? How did she seem?"

Tessa took a deep breath, nodding. "She was uneasy. She believed that something bad had happened to Gianni. As I said, he failed to keep a date and his phone went right to voice mail." She went on to describe how Juanita had seen someone across the restaurant and had fled. She related how the man she'd seen had followed Juanita outside. "By the time I got out into the parking lot, they were both gone. And then, this morning, I heard about Juanita on the news." She swallowed the sudden tightness in her throat. "Juanita was a lovely person. She was all about her family. I can't imagine how they're—" She shook her head.

"Would you be willing to come down to the precinct today and work with a sketch artist?" asked Garcia. "A detailed description of the bald guy would be helpful."

"That shouldn't be a problem. I can be there in an hour."

The two detectives exchanged another look, then stood almost in unison.

"Thanks, Ms. Morgan," Williams said. "You've been a great help. The faster we can move on this, the better our chance of catching whoever murdered Ms. Sanchez."

"Is there anything else you could tell us?"

She came close to telling them about the Crimson link on the website, but didn't. She wasn't sure why but told herself that she wanted to give Kristin a chance to ... to what, exactly? Explain that she wasn't involved in something skeevy (as Kristin herself might say). Illegal? Evil?

Stop it, she told herself. *You're taking this whole Red Masque thing too much to heart. It was a story.*

Aloud she said, "Not at the moment, but if I think of something, I'll call."

When the detectives were gone, Tessa realized how the muscles in her neck had tensed again. She gave herself a quick massage to avoid another headache. It wasn't just having to tell them about Juanita Sanchez, and *not* telling them the details of Juanita's suspicions. She realized that other than Juanita and Kristin, the two detectives had been among the mere handful of people she'd been in close contact with that weren't in the medical community. Every time one of them had focused on her face, she'd felt the strong urge to reach up and pull her hair completely across it. How must she appear to others?

Oddly, what leapt to mind was the animated character Violet from *The Incredibles*—the über-shy teenaged daughter of Mr. Incredible and Elastigirl. The thought made her smile. All Violet was hiding was a pretty face, and Elastigirl—well, Tessa was envious of her powers. If she had them, she'd simply morph her face to hide the patchwork quilt of new skin and scar tissue.

Tessa had never cared that she was beautiful, yet now that her beauty was gone, she envied women like Detective Jayla Williams who were merely pretty. What she wouldn't give now even to look ordinary so that she'd no longer have to witness the discomfort of strangers as they fought to avert their eyes from her face.

Well, she'd promised to visit the police precinct to work with the sketch artist. She'd best get on it. She got up, went to the kitchen, pulled the bottle of rum from a cabinet, and poured herself a stiff drink. She'd never been in the habit of drinking alone, but to do what she needed to do, she needed some liquid courage.

The police artist's drawing of the bald-headed man was good. It captured the shape of his head; the long, pointed nose; and the ears that bent down a bit at the tips. This last detail was something she hadn't even realized she'd noticed until the artist began to shape the image.

There was one other detail she thought of at the last minute. "I don't know if you can capture this exactly," she said, "but it seemed to me he was bald by choice. His head was shaven; I didn't see any evidence of actual bald spots or a receding hairline. His hair would have been dark, too, judging by the five-o'clock shadow all over his head."

"You're a good witness," the sketch artist had told her.

She'd thanked him but left reflecting that she was actually a horrible witness—a witness who was withholding information from the police that she should, by all rights, give them.

I will give them that information soon, she promised herself as she walked the length of the parking lot toward her car. *But first I need to see Kristin again.*

She started the Volvo SUV, the car she'd bought just before filming *Dark Beauty*, and headed for the Red Masque Modeling Agency.

"Well, well," Kristin said, a sneer in her voice as she lounged back on an expensive-looking executive chair, swiveling lazily from side to side. "To what do I owe this privilege? Seeing my sister two times in a week? Maybe we should throw a party and invite the old gang."

"Juanita Sanchez is dead," Tessa said boldly. She stood in the center of her sister's office, taking up as much space as possible to appear larger and more confident. She held her floppy hat in her hands and tried to remember not to appear nervous by playing with its edges; she'd tucked her dark glasses into the top of her purse. She faced her twin with only the wing of bright golden hair to cover her scars.

The brilliantly red lower lip made a half moue. "And the sun rises in the east. Do you think I don't know what's going on with my employees? Even the dead ones?"

"You could show some emotion over it. Regret. Sadness."

"For all you know, there are copious tears pouring underneath this mask. But why should I care? She was just another model. There are plenty where she came from." The gray eyes glittered behind their eyeholes, but not with tears.

"Juanita was a beautiful—"

"There are beautiful women on every street corner in LA, and they'd all like to work here."

"I doubt that. And you know as well as I do that Juanita wasn't just beautiful on the outside."

"Well, Tess, you know as well as I do that inner beauty doesn't matter. It's useless and worthless, and no one gives a rat's ass if you've got it. What does matter is that I had a visit from a pair of homicide detectives just before you arrived. I don't suppose you had anything to do with that."

"I got a visit from them earlier because I called them to tell them

I saw Juanita yesterday before she was murdered. You got a visit from them because she worked for you. I did tell them about your website."

Kristin's lower lip was set in a straight line beneath the expressionless mask. "Stay out of my business, Tessa," she said coldly. "I don't want you coming around this office anymore."

"I think I can arrange that. But I have a parting question for *you*, Kristin. What does a Crimson account entitle your clients to?"

The silence that followed was long enough that Tessa was certain Kristin had not expected the question. Finally, she shrugged and said, "That's just for the select clients who retain my top-flight models. Models who do more than pose in swimsuits and underwear for JCPenney."

"Really? What more do they do?"

Kristin tilted her head to one side. "You've changed, sister mine. You've got some grit."

"Crimson?"

"Crimson is by invitation only. I give certain clients the best models, photographers, cosmetologists." She shrugged, then paused to study Tessa in a way that made Tessa's skin crawl. The assessment was made even creepier by the mask. "Did you tell the cops about Crimson?"

"No. Did you?"

"Why would they care? Why do you?" She rocked her chair upright and swiveled it to face her desk. "Now, I've got work to do, if you don't mind. Shall I call Trina, or—"

"I can see myself out, thanks." Tessa turned and strode toward the door.

"Hey, Tess," Kristin called. "About that grit. Lose it. It could be dangerous."

Tessa gave Kristin a sharp glance over her left shoulder, displaying the undamaged half of her face to her sister's gaze. Then she opened the door and let herself out.

###

Tessa stared at the Crimson dialogue box on Redmasque.com's website until her eyes hurt. What secrets was her sister hiding there, secrets so important that you needed a username and password to reach them? Maybe she was telling the truth and it just held the royal treatment for her best customers—access to higher-end services. Yet somehow, none of that seemed worth keeping under digital lock and key with no clues about how one even qualified to be invited to the club.

She pondered some more. Okay. There were a couple of ways she could approach this. She could tell the police about Crimson, and Juanita's suspicion that it was connected to Gianni's disappearance. That was legal, but possibly dangerous. Or, she could find someone who could hack the site. That would be illegal, not to mention more expensive than her current lifestyle allowed. She racked her brain to determine who she might know that could break into a website.

The answer was obvious, but she shuddered physically just thinking about it: Daniel. He was a computer genius and had hacked websites for fun in his younger and less responsible days.

But I can't see Daniel. He called constantly, but the thought of letting him see her face ... *Here, there be dragons.*

Who else could she go to? Craigslist? She had to laugh at the absurdity of that. You didn't publicly announce that you were willing to commit a crime. Programmers did sell their services, but how could she even broach the subject with them? "Hi. My name is Tessa. Can you break into my sister's website? I think she might be connected to a criminal investigation."

She poured herself another stiff drink of Don Papa. This was a habit she was going to have to break soon or she'd become as ravaged as her sister had been on the set of the movie. Tessa wanted to keep her ravages where she could see them clearly.

As the alcohol kicked in, she started thinking about Daniel again. He was smart, he was kind. He had told her repeatedly during her initial stay at the UCLA med center that he still loved her despite the loss of half her face. He declared that he would always love her.

She realized, however, that saying something, even meaning it, and living with it were two different things.

Yet, again curiosity was getting the best of her. She found herself picking up her cell phone and finding Daniel's number in her contacts list. It would be so easy to press the button and call him. When he saw her name on his phone, she knew he'd answer immediately. Her finger hovered over the button, reflexively moving to tap it, and then jerking away. How could she even think of calling Daniel? She was a wreck in more ways than the obvious. She'd become an emotional burden to him the moment she pushed the Call button.

Idiot. You're an emotional burden to him now. You've frozen him out without letting him go.

She needed this favor. She could ask it while making it clear she expected nothing more from him than friendship. Then she'd let him go. She would.

She pushed the button.

Chapter Twenty-Nine

In the 1950s, the Venice neighborhood of LA had been known as the "Slum by the Sea." Tessa found the irony amusing. Now it was one of the swankiest sections of the city that wasn't dominated by the film industry. Its streets and shops were quaint, lovely, and historic. She tried to let the beautiful architecture and nearby surf distract her from her anxiety over meeting Daniel again there.

In the early twentieth century, a clever real estate developer had bought up a large block of property near what would later become known as Venice Beach with the intention of turning it into a miniature version of Venice, Italy. He had constructed a maze-like network of canals crossed by arching bridges and lined with small homes. Unfortunately, after a rush of interest over the next few years, the Los Angeles version of Venice had fallen out of fashion and was soon, ironically, undone by its proximity to the beach.

The long pier and quirky boardwalk proved to be such a mecca for tourists that the infrastructure needed for the residents of the canal area became too expensive for the city to maintain. By the middle of the century the area had fallen into disrepair. Poor immigrants, drug use, the hippie culture, and ethnic gangs like the Shoreside Crips had caused the crime rate to soar. In the 1970s, Venice Beach was a mecca not for wealthy residents but for buyers in search of cocaine, which was so plentiful that a police station was eventually constructed on the beach itself just to curb the drug traffic.

That was when Venice had turned around. Always looking for the next old neighborhood to gentrify, young upwardly mobile professionals began restoring the houses and the canals at the turn of the twenty-first century. Venice was now one of the most beautiful and trendy neighborhoods along the Los Angeles shore. From the beach you could see the full extent of the bay, all the way to Malibu in the north, where you could watch the sun set over the mountain ridge most evenings of the year.

Then Silicon Beach had happened. Like its namesake in Northern California south of San Francisco, the area around Venice had begun attracting technology companies, and where technology companies congregated, prices soared. Venice was now probably the most expensive neighborhood south of Malibu, rivaling Santa Monica as a beach town for the upscale and well-moneyed.

Daniel and Tessa had often daydreamed about buying a home in Venice, even though the townhouses that lined the canals were tiny slivers with little more floor space than Tessa's tiny apartment. But it would have been close to the office Daniel was then planning to build. The ambience of the canals and their population of ducks was a perfect setting for a young couple in love. She remembered their duck-feeding treks along the canals with painful nostalgia.

Tessa found a seat in the outdoor dining area of a restaurant on Washington Boulevard next to an entrance to the boardwalk. She had arranged to meet Daniel there because it was only a three-block walk from his new offices. She would have preferred to dine indoors where the light would have been dimmer, but Daniel loved the perfume of the ocean breeze.

She had tilted the floppy hat so far down over the right side of her face that, combined with the oversized sunglasses, she could barely see the people around her. Yet she recognized Daniel's trim figure and confident walk as he strode directly toward her table. He must have recognized her, she thought wryly, because of the extreme effort she'd taken to hide her face. She looked like an eccentric.

"Hi, Tess," he said, and if he was nervous in her presence, he didn't let it show.

Tessa simply stared up at him through her darkened lenses, suddenly aware that she wasn't breathing. What could she say to him? She was afraid her vocal cords would freeze just knowing that he was getting his first look at her not swaddled in bandages, or at least the part that was visible beneath her improvised disguise. She was, she had to admit, thoroughly terrified.

"Daniel," she finally managed to say, her voice shaking, "it's good to see you." Given that she could barely make out his form through the sunglasses, that was a polite lie. She could hardly see him at all. She took a sip of her iced tea and lined up all the things she needed to say: She needed a favor as a friend—

just a friend. She wanted him to understand that he should feel no obligation to treat her as anything beyond that.

Daniel blew her careful presentation out of the water. He sat down across from her and cut right to the chase. "Tessa, I've been trying to get in touch with you since you got back from Baltimore. You haven't answered any of my calls or my texts. I don't care why you called me after all this time. I'm just glad you did. Whatever favor you need, I'll try to do it, but first, I have something I need to ask you. Something I have to know." He shifted uneasily in his seat. "Tessa, have you fallen out of love with me?"

She could only stare at him with her mouth open. Fallen out of love with *him*?

"No," she said. "I haven't. I couldn't. I just ... I just didn't think our relationship could continue after what happened."

Daniel leaned forward, putting his forearms on the table, hands outstretched toward her. "Not continue? Tessa, you *know* how much I care for you. That hasn't changed. I think about you every minute of every day, even when I'm up to my elbows in technical shit. Let me be real clear: I *want* our relationship to continue. I want to be with you while you ... work through whatever it is you're working through."

She thought her lungs had stopped functioning because she could no longer breathe. Sitting across from the man she'd loved since she was a college freshman was choking the life out of her. And what he'd just told her—she could barely let herself hear the words, let alone believe them. She nearly stood and bolted, but her legs felt like lead. She almost believed him but then remembered why she had kept her distance. He wouldn't want their relationship to continue if he could look under her floppy hat and her veil of hair and see what she'd become.

"Tess," he said, his voice gentle, "I was there when Kurt Morrison happened to you. I spent enough time by your bedside to know the extent of your injuries. I saw you at your most raw. The way you look now is not going to scare me off."

There. He'd done it again—known what she was thinking as if she'd said it aloud. He touched her hand—the one wrapped around the sweating glass of iced tea—but all she could do was quiver. He watched her face for a moment, then sat back.

"You said you needed a favor. What do you need me to do?"

She threw off her quakes and quivers with a will. "I need you to hack my sister's website," she said.

Even through the dark glasses she could see the startled look on his face. "Hack Kristin's website? I knew the two of you weren't getting along, but ... what ... you want me to crash her site?"

"Not crash it. Crack it. Get into its back office—its guts. It's her professional site for the new modeling agency she's started—Red Masque."

"Can I ask why you want me to do this?"

"I think something strange is going on at her agency, and I need your help finding out what it is."

"Strange? How so?"

She told him about her meeting with Juanita Sanchez and how the model had suggested that Kristin may have had something to do with the disappearance of Gianni DeLuca.

"Yeah, I saw in the *Times* that he'd gone missing. Do the police suspect foul play?"

"I don't know. But, Daniel, Juanita Sanchez was found dead last night. She'd been strangled. I spoke to a couple of detectives about it this morning and gave a description of a man who might have ... might have been the last person to see her alive."

He took her hand again. "Oh, God, Tessa! Was she a close friend of yours?"

"Not really, but I knew her from our modeling days. She told me that she'd been seeing DeLuca and that they'd gotten 'serious.'" She put air quotes around the word.

"So let me make one of my brilliant deductions here. You think Kristin had something to do with Ms. Sanchez's murder."

Did she? She took a deep breath. "I'm afraid she might. Before Juanita bolted out of the restaurant, she said, 'The website. Look for crimson.' So, I looked for the word on the website and found it on the About the Agency page. It was an unmarked link to something the site refers to as 'Crimson Services.' I confronted Kristin about it, but she claimed it was just special perks for her upper-echelon clientele. The best models, dressers, and makeup artists for example. But Juanita clearly thought there was more to it and ..."

"And what?"

"When I left Kristin, she came close to threatening me."

She felt as much as saw the shift in Daniel's posture. "What do you mean, she threatened you?"

"When I asked a few pointed questions, she suggested that my new 'grit,' as she called it, might be dangerous to me. She's ... different, Daniel. I used to see little glimpses of the old Kristin in her from time to time. But the two times I've seen her in the last several days, it was like talking to an icy stranger."

"This is like talking to a stranger for me," Daniel said, looking down at their entwined fingers. "I've missed you. God, how I've missed you. Have you missed me? Missed us?"

All she could say was, "Oh, Daniel ..."

He backed off again and shifted his focus back to the task at hand. "So, what happens when you click this secret link?"

"It opens a password-protected dialogue box. No text except field labels for username and password. I was hoping you could find a way in. Create a fake account or hack an existing one."

He nodded. "That shouldn't be difficult. I'd have to start the process at my office; we have some advanced decryption software there. We do extensive work on encryption because we don't want anybody hacking into our cars. Naturally, we have to test our encryptions."

"How soon can you do it?"

"Right after lunch. Have you ordered yet?"

Tessa hesitated. She wanted to stay in his company. She wanted to run away. If she stayed any longer, the knot in her stomach was going to become unbearable. If she left, the leaden weight in her heart would break it.

"I can't stay," she said, standing up to leave. Her breath was coming in short gasps; she hoped she'd make it to the Volvo parked half a block up the street.

"Tessa, I just got here."

"I have another appointment," she lied. "Liar. You're running away."

"Daniel ..."

"I know. I have no way to stop you." He stood and took both her hands in his and she felt as if her heart was trying to leave her chest. "I'll call you the minute I have something on the website."

For an awkward moment she thought he was going to lean forward and kiss her, but the idea was unbearable. Just the thought of his lips against hers seemed wrong, something that the universe would punish her for if she allowed it to happen. She pulled away and rushed out onto the sidewalk, leaving Daniel behind her. Once inside her car she started to calm down, but she was halfway home before she felt like she could breathe again.

Tessa's cell phone was buzzing by the time she reached her apartment, even before she had a chance to pour herself another glass of rum to steady her nerves. It was Daniel—already. She was hit with a jolt of adrenaline, but oddly, when she heard his voice, her pulse steadied. Now that she'd been with him in person, speaking with him on the phone seemed less strange and stressful. When they were just two disembodied voices, she could almost imagine that nothing had changed. They were simply Tessa and Daniel again, joined by common bonds of love and friendship. She forgot sometimes that Daniel had been more than a lover. He was a spiritual companion, a friend.

And right now, her friend was excited, brimming over with discovery and gushing technobabble that was meaningless to her. His enthusiasm made her smile.

"And what," she asked, when he wound down, "does that all mean?"

"It means I've cracked your sister's keep! Gotten over her moat. I'm into the Crimson section of her website."

"All of that in the time it took me to drive home?"

"Oh, ye of little faith. I told you we had some advanced decryption apps here. Besides, whoever wrote this website for Kristin wasn't exactly a coding genius. A precocious fourteen-year-old could have gotten through this."

"Only if the fourteen-year-old was Daniel Takashi."

He laughed. "At any rate, it was relatively easy." He hesitated. "You won't believe what I found."

"Tell me."

"No, I need to show you. I'm coming over to your apartment. Be there in half an hour."

She exhaled sharply. "Coming over? Can't you just give me the password so I can look at the site myself?"

"That would be irresponsible of me. What you asked me to do was illegal. You owe me, Tessa Morgan. So I get to call the shots."

"Daniel, honestly, I have things I need to do."

"The hell you do. You're just putting me off again, like with that appointment you didn't really have. You went straight home."

"How do you know that? I could be anywh—"

"You have a GPS in your phone, sweetheart. I'll see you in thirty, max."

Assessing the apartment, she pronounced it to be clean and tidy enough despite the lack of furniture. She grabbed something to eat from the fridge to stave off her loud stomach pangs, and ran to look through her meager wardrobe for something to wear. She'd sold off all her evening gowns and cocktail dresses and all but one or two suits. She mostly lived in jeans and T-shirts, but she wanted something nice for Daniel, which meant one of her trio of summer dresses.

She kicked herself for the contradictory messages she was sending: She wanted to dress up; she knew that it shouldn't matter—no, it *wouldn't* matter. That part of her life was done. Over.

Men, though, she reasoned, were primarily interested in bodies, not faces, and her body was still good, if a bit too thin. A pale green gauze dress in her closet with spaghetti straps, a low neckline, and an uneven hem stood out as the one to choose. Slipping her feet into a pair of sandals, she completed the outfit. She looked summery, casual, and sexy ... as long as you didn't see above her neck. She also put some effort into her makeup, using some of it to smooth out the varying shades on the damaged side of her face. Then she arranged her hair in what she'd started to think of as her "shrinking violet" style, bisecting her face with a long golden veil.

She was so tense waiting for Daniel to arrive that, when he knocked on the door, she jumped. Even traversing the ten-foot distance across the living room to the front door seemed to take forever. She opened the door so slowly that she felt as though she were some character in a horror movie prying open the lid of a crypt.

Daniel looked her up and down as if memorizing her. "It's *so* good to see you," he said.

"You just saw me less than an hour ago."

"Yeah, but after waiting this long to finally get you back in my life, every time I see you feels like I've waited forever all over again."

"That's a bit ... melodramatic." She gestured for him to enter the room.

He headed toward the couch with a laptop bag hung over one shoulder. "I really like that color on you, Tess," he said, glancing back at her. "You look amazing."

She ignored the compliment. "You didn't have to bring your computer. I've got one." She followed him to the living room, keeping her distance. "Not like this one, you don't." He took a seat toward the middle of the sofa, pulled out a sleek black laptop with LEDs rippling in multiple colors down the sides, and set it on the coffee table. Tessa noted wryly that his computer sat in the exact place she had laid out the pills meant to kill her only days earlier. "This one's loaded with an armory of things that hack and slice. Come, sit down."

Tessa landed in the chair next to the sofa.

He didn't seem in a hurry to open the laptop and instead looked her in the eye. "Tess, if you don't sit next to me, you won't be able to see what I need to show you."

Tessa hopped up, stalling for time. "Can I get you anything to eat? A drink?"

The expression on Daniel's face indicated that he was wise to the digression. "I just grabbed a sandwich at work, but what's on the drinks menu?"

"I've got some Coke in the fridge and some rum."

"Technically, I'm on office hours, so I'll take the soda. The more caffeine the better."

She strode to the kitchen and returned carrying two Cokes. As she placed one on the coffee table where it had no chance of accidentally spilling on Daniel's computer, he reached out and grabbed her other wrist, gently tugging her toward the cushion.

"Sit. Down."

Her heart was thumping so loudly she was convinced that Daniel must be able to hear it. Slowly, she took a couple steps to the side and settled on the sofa next to him.

He turned and stared at her. "God, it's been so long, Tess."

"You said that before."

"But it has been. Do you know how often I go through our time together like it was a photo album? How I start at the beginning, seeing you juggle all those books, praying you'd drop one."

"I did drop one."

"Pretty sure I owe some angel for that. I remember hanging out on the quad by that robot thing. Trying to surf at Malibu."

"You kept falling off your board," she said, unable to restrain a smile, feeling almost shy around her beau.

"Yeah, well. I was never really cut out for athletics. At least not the ones that require coordination. You know me. I've always been more of a mathematics kind of guy."

"I don't know about that," Tessa said. "You look like you've kept yourself in pretty good shape."

He was wearing a fitted knit shirt that nicely displayed the muscles of his forearms rippling smoothly below the rolled-up sleeves. She'd always thought forearms were sexy—Daniel's especially so. He was no bodybuilder, but he made an effort to stay fit. He had once told her that it was because he wanted to live forever. He wanted to stay healthy so he could see the future, because he planned to make a lot of it happen.

"Remember that time we drove up into the San Bernardino Mountains and spent the week after Christmas at Big Bear Lake?" He shot her a coy smile. "That cabin was more romantic than a five-star hotel."

"What does any of this have to do with my sister's website?"

"Nothing. I just want you to know that I think about us a lot." He gazed off into the distance, remembering. "There was a blizzard the day after we arrived. The Wi-Fi was lousy, but I didn't care." Then, looking in her eyes, he continued. "Remember how we threw snowballs at each other and watched the smoke rise from our chimney and made love in front of the fireplace on a—"

"Bearskin rug," she said in unison with him. "That was pretty wonderful," she added, charmed by the memory in spite of her nervousness. For a moment she was transported back to what it had been like to spend time with Daniel before the incident at Alexei Dvorak's party. She could almost remember what it felt like to be normal.

"We were so good together," he said, again looking away. "Good for each other. We were wonderful. We could be wonderful together again, if you wanted to be." He again gazed into her eyes. "If you just say yes." *Oh, God, no!* she thought, but, *Oh, God, yes!* She reached up and instinctively placed her hand on her face, pressing the soft hair against her jaw and cheek, surprised that she could feel the pressure. She'd called Daniel to help her break into Kristin's website, not to have a romantic chat over soft drinks.

Daniel followed the movement, gently grasping the hand she was using to conceal her scars and drawing it away from her face. With the other hand, he reached up and touched the obscuring curtain of hair.

"Don't," she said, flinching. "Why not?"

"Because you don't want to see what I look like underneath. Believe me, you really don't."

He ignored her and brushed the hair away from her cheek, tucking it behind her ear. He stared straight at her face, her undisguised half a face, and his eyes didn't flinch.

"My Tess," he said gently.

"No," she said, her features flushing through the scar tissue. "No, I'm not. I stopped being your Tess the moment that guy threw the acid in my face."

"Bullshit," he said, and she heard an undercurrent of anger in his voice. "You're the still the woman I love. You're the woman I'll always love."

She wanted to reply but couldn't. Her eyes were brimming with tears. He took her face between his hands and leaned forward to kiss her.

She didn't move. She knew that she should pull away, tell him to leave the house immediately, but she couldn't do it. The feel of his lips on hers was as gentle and yet electric, as it always had been. She found herself responding automatically, opening her mouth slightly to let his tongue brush hers. They held the kiss a long, breathless moment, then he pulled back and looked at her with as much love as she'd ever seen on his face.

"You thought I'd be terrified by you, didn't you?" he said. "Yes," she replied in a barely audible voice.

"I'm not. I see everything in you that I've always seen—the gentleness, the love, the beautiful soul. I told you that I'd love you even if you weren't model perfect, and I meant every word. I love you, Tessa. And you are still beautiful."

The tears were now streaming down her face. He kissed away the tears and put his arms around her. Then he slid the thin straps of her dress from her shoulders. She sucked in a quick breath, trembling in anticipation. "If you don't want to make love to me, you don't have to. But I want you, Tess. More than ever. I want you to know, I haven't been with anyone else. Haven't even gone on a date. What would be the point? As corny as it sounds, I was saving myself for you."

He undressed her, then himself. His well-toned body, naturally golden, was the most beautiful thing she had ever seen. For the first time since she had been taken to the hospital, she felt desire that was not for some lost memory. From the moment the acid had touched her face, Tessa had stopped thinking of herself as a sexual being, but Daniel's sensual, loving presence made the fear she had felt about intimacy evaporate like morning dew.

Daniel kissed every inch of Tessa's body, caressed her breasts, and touched her in ways she had tried to forget existed. The world seemed to slide away, and all of the dark horrors that had made her want to die fled in the face of this light. How could she have lived without this for so long? How could she have lived without Daniel's touch?

They made love right there on the sofa. The act was ecstatic, glorious ... liberating. Tessa felt as if centuries of weight had been lifted from her heart, her mind, her soul. Afterward, they lay half on top of each other, eyes closed, simply breathing in unison.

"I hate to bring this up," Tessa said at length, "but weren't you going to show me what you'd found on Kristin's website?"

Daniel chuckled. "Oh, right. You sort of blew everything else out of my mind. Funny how that works."

They both sat up, and he ran a hand through his thick hair and flipped open the laptop that had sat forgotten on the coffee table. Tessa's posture had completely changed since he'd first walked in. She now curled up next to him, her head on his shoulder. On the computer screen, the Red Masque site was open to the About page. He clicked on the Crimson link, typed in a username and password, and a new screen appeared that seemed to belong to a completely different website. Instead of the Red Masque Modeling Agency, it was called the Crimson Succubus Service.

Tessa stifled a giggle. "Succubus Service? Only Kristin ..."

Daniel made a wry face. "Yeah. Pretty old school. Like, Dark Ages old."

Some of the same models appeared on this site, but this time each was pictured in the company of at least one man, each of which were obviously male models. The women were dressed in skimpy, fantasy-themed costumes suggesting they were angels, demons, fairies, or superheroes, all wearing red half-masks that covered their eyes. It took Tessa a moment to realize that the photos were a catalogue, each one showing the models in starkly lit, melodramatic, and sexually suggestive poses—some of which made Tessa blanche. Daniel, however, was starting to get an erection.

She glanced from that to his face. "I guess these photos turn you on."

He turned and gave her a look. "Tess, we just made love for the first time in two years. You're sitting here next to me stark naked, touching me. So, yeah, these photos are giving my squirrelly little reptilian cortex ideas." Tessa arched her eyebrows. "Well, which is it, naked nerd boy?

Squirrels or lizards?"

"Squirrels. Definitely squirrels." Daniel kissed the tip of her nose and returned his attention back to the laptop. He clicked the link beneath the first photo and got a dramatically worded profile of the succubus that provided a list of the sex acts she was willing to provide, some of which Tessa had never heard of.

"FGE?" she murmured. "Do I even want to know what that is?"

"Full girlfriend experience," Daniel explained. "That's when they're willing to kiss and cuddle as well as have sex."

"And you'd know this how?"

Daniel blushed. "Not firsthand, trust me."

"Right."

Daniel put his hand on her knee, his expression deadly serious. "Tessa. Reality check. We were both virgins when we first got together and I haven't been with anyone else since, in any way. I've been all work, because that was the only way I could ..." He stopped, closed his eyes for a moment, then opened them, recapturing her gaze. "The only way I could deal."

She read his eyes, grasping at last that, underneath his careful words and his seemingly unflagging sense of humor and perspective, the last two years of his life had been as torturous as hers. She nodded and turned her gaze back to the laptop screen.

"So," she said, "it appears that my sister isn't just running a modeling agency."

"No," Daniel said. "She's running an elite fantasy brothel."

Chapter Thirty

After their passionate reunion on the sofa, Daniel had produced a handful of condoms from his laptop bag.

"Confident, much?" Tessa observed wryly.

"Just being a Boy Scout—be prepared and all that. I meant to use one earlier, but you sort of overwhelmed my—"

"Squirrelizard brain?"

"Yeah, that."

They'd made love again, ordered Chinese for dinner, made love a third time in Tessa's twin bed, then fallen asleep, holding hands. Daniel turned out to be a restless sleeper. Tessa fought for room on her narrow mattress every time he rolled over. She woke up just before dawn, not because she was in the habit of rising early, but because she'd fallen off the bed.

"Ouch!" she yipped, rubbing her hip where it had hit the floor.

Daniel rolled over, glanced down at her, and said, "This is why you're moving to my place. I've been dying to show it to you. I think you'll like it."

"You have a new place?"

"Yes. We haven't seen each other for so long that you didn't even know. It's pretty sweet."

Pinch me. "Okay by me. I'm going to make coffee. I seem to recall that you like yours with real sugar and real cream."

"Nope. If I can't get soy cream, I take it black. No sugar. Gives me the yips. If I'm going to get the yips, I want to do if for a worthy cause like chocolate or pie."

After she started the pot of coffee dripping, Tessa took a quick shower and pulled on the dress and underwear she'd left lying next to the sofa. Daniel came out of the bedroom just as the coffee was ready, naked and beautiful in the morning light streaming in from Tessa's tiny balcony.

"You want to drink hot coffee in the nude or were you planning to protect yourself in some way?"

"Shower first, then clothes, then coffee. Keep the pot warm for me."

Tessa turned on the television to the local news station, afraid that she was going to hear another report about a missing person her sister had somehow been involved with but instead heard only the usual news items. The fire in the mountains was under control, Kim Kardashian was revealing new details about her divorce from Kanye West, and of course the LA freeways were still jammed. They probably had that last item on permanent loop.

Daniel reappeared, his hair meticulously combed, and put his shirt and trousers back on. He left his black suit coat draped over the back of the sofa. "I've let them know I'll be in late for work today."

"You can be away for two days running? I guess that's one of the advantages of owning your own company."

"Honestly, honey, I've hired so many great people to run the place for me that it could practically run itself. Today, however, I'm taking you shopping."

"For a new bed?"

"For some new clothes."

"Well, God knows I could use those too."

"Yes, but these will be very special clothes."

Tessa stared at him. "Is this about the photos on Kristin's website? You're not going to dress me up like one of those hookers and—"

"No," he said emphatically. "I'm going to dress you up like Kristin so you can impersonate her."

Tessa was stunned. That had not made her list of things Daniel might propose. "You want me to pull a twin swap?"

"You've never done it?"

"No. That was Kristin's MO."

Daniel's face spasmed—a quick twist of his lips, a clenching of his jaw. His gaze dropped to his shoes.

"What?"

He looked back up at her, his lips compressed into a straight line. "I was never going to tell you this, but during the filming of *Dark Beauty*—I gather it was the day she threw that little tantrum and got sent home—she came to my office posing as you and tried to ..." He stopped, making a vague gesture with one hand.

"She pulled a twin swap ... on *you*?"

He nodded. "She tried. I realized there was something wrong right about the time she started doing a striptease for me."

Tessa was shell-shocked. "In your *office*?"

"In your living room. She was dressed in one of your favorite outfits—one I picked out for you, as it happened—and she started undressing herself the minute she stepped into your house. She was ... a little crude about it, actually. Not like you at all. It wasn't the outfit you'd worn that morning, and her hair was different. After that whole scene in college, I made a point of noticing things like that. I called her out on it and left."

"Why didn't you tell me?"

"Honestly? I didn't want you to know Kristin would do that to you. Things were tense enough between you two. I didn't want to add that to the list of things you had to forgive her for." He shook his head. "Water under the bridge. I was able to break into Kristin's website pretty easily, but whoever runs her office server is a lot better than the company that hosts her website. I've already poked at her firewall a bit; it's pretty strong. I'm willing to bet she keeps her most sensitive files on her personal computer, and after what you told me about Juanita Sanchez and Gianni DeLuca, I think we need to get a look at them. Like I said, she's got a multilayered firewall around her office network. I just called the guy I've got working on it and he's managed to get through the first layer, but he hasn't been able to penetrate the secondary ones. So, I'm thinking someone needs to go into her office and log on to her computer in person."

"And that somebody has to be me."

"You're the only person who could get away with it. So, the first thing we're going to do is buy you a mask just like the Red Masque Madame's."

###

The small costume store in Culver City was completely empty of customers. Tessa wasn't surprised. They were located just around the corner from Paradox Studios, where *Dark Beauty* had been filmed, but like most studios, Paradox kept a large costume supply of their own, most of them left over from earlier movies. And when costume designers needed clothing that wasn't in stock, they tended to buy it at thrift shops as often as at costume stores. That way the clothes looked more lived in.

Tessa showed the owner a picture of Kristin's mask. To her surprise, he recognized it instantly. "Oh, yeah. Would you believe that you're only the second customer who's wanted one of those in the last year? I got a bunch of them from Romania a couple of years ago and I couldn't sell them to save my life." He grinned. "Maybe they're trending."

"Do you remember what this other buyer looked like?"

"Hard to say. She had her face wrapped in gauze, probably just had cosmetic surgery, or maybe she was making a mummy movie. But she was about your size and build. Even sounded something like you."

He went into the back and came out with a mask that was a perfect match for Kristin's, right down to the golden filigree. "How much for it?"

"Six hundred dollars."

"Six hundred …" Tessa gasped. "Are you kidding me?"

"Hon, this is expensive hand-crafted stuff. I really took a bath on that deal."

"I can't afford anything like that."

"Just for you, then, I'll make it five hundred. But not a penny lower."

"Four hundred and fifty," Daniel said, calling up Apple Pay on his iPhone. "And I'll pay for it."

They walked out with the mask in a fancy boutique bag and went up the street to an extremely upscale women's clothing store. Tessa had a photo of what Kristin had worn in the video, but it was nothing like she'd been wearing at the office both times Tessa had visited. Kristin was unlikely to wear the same outfit to work every day, but Tessa had a good idea of her sister's taste in clothing, so she and Daniel bought half a dozen outfits and stowed them in the back of Daniel's Tesla.

Tessa felt like the character in *Pretty Woman*, whose rich boyfriend bought her an entire wardrobe of beautiful clothes while the shop staff pampered her the moment they caught the scent of his money, though they wouldn't have given her the time of day if she'd come in on her own.

Then Daniel drove them to Kristin's office, despite Tessa's protests that she wasn't ready to do this.

"Tessa, listen to me," Daniel told her as they sat at traffic light. "The guy who saw Juanita with you also saw *you* with Juanita. I know you haven't considered it, but your life might be in danger. I don't want to wait to find out."

"But what if we just forward the information on the Crimson site to the police? To their vice squad? We could do it anonymously—"

"Yeah, I think we should do that too. But today, I think we should do this."

"We? You mean me."

"I can put on shades and pretend to be your new bodyguard. If anyone asks, you tell them that since Juanita was murdered and your old photographer friend disappeared, you're taking extra precautions. Or you can pass me off as your new boy toy. Your choice. My point is, Ms. Morgan, you can do this. You did get an Oscar nod after all, and I think you know the part well."

She had to admit, he had a point.

###

The parking garage beneath the office building was down an asphalt ramp and blocked by a metal gate. Because it was an upscale building complex and housed some high-powered clientele, a guard stood watch in a booth at the top of the ramp, making sure nobody unauthorized got inside.

"Do you have an appointment, sir?" the guard asked Daniel. Tessa leaned over from the passenger seat so the guard could see her face—or, rather, her mask. She was wearing the most Kristin-like outfit of the ones they'd found at the store, though whether it was the one Kristin was actually wearing was slim. Likely the guard, whose badge said his name was Marco, didn't care.

"It's me, Marco," Tessa said. "I was just out shopping with my new bodyguard."

"Oh, of course, Ms. Morgan. I hope you've had a nice morning."

The gate ground open and revealed the cavernous parking area below. Once inside, they began cruising the parking spaces looking for Kristin's car.

It wasn't hard to find. It was the BMW she had bought while making *Dark Beauty* and had the same vanity plate: KRISTIN.

"Well, that was easy," Daniel said. "Now where do we hide?"

Tessa pointed. "There's an empty space over there. It should give us a view of both Kristin's car and the elevator."

It was just past eleven thirty in the morning. They were working on the assumption that Kristin would go out for lunch rather than stick around the office with the mere peons who worked for her. Predictably, they saw her emerge from the elevator a few minutes after noon, along with several others who set off in different directions as soon as they stepped out of the elevator. As she walked to her car, they studied her clothing.

"Dark blazer and pants," Daniel said. "Do we have anything like that?"

"That's not a blazer and pants, Daniel. That's a Dolce & Gabbana pantsuit," said Tessa, warming to the exercise. "Charcoal gray. We've got almost exactly that. Red chiffon blouse. We've got several red blouses in different fabrics. It's always been her favorite color."

Tessa turned to lift several garments from the oversized bags in the back seat. She did an impromptu striptease in the front of the car, slithering into a D&G suit that should easily pass for what Kristin was wearing.

Last, she braided her hair, which was somewhat shorter than her twin's, and pinned it on top of her head.

They waited roughly ten minutes after Kristin's Beemer headed up the unmanned exit driveway, then left Daniel's car and headed for the elevator. "Wish me luck," she said to Daniel.

"You don't need luck," he said, slipping on a pair of dark glasses and accompanying her into the building. "In that outfit you look enough like your sister that we won't have any problem getting into her office." Tessa pressed the button and waited nervously for the elevator to return. Did she really look like Kristin—the new Kristin, the one who was all style and no visible face? Kristin had easily passed for Tessa over the years, but Tessa had never tried passing for Kristin. Could she pull off her sister's walk, her attitude, her arrogance? It was strange, Tessa reflected, that Kristin's personality seemed to have remained relatively unchanged by their ordeal. Her sister was still all angles and rough edges and bitterness. Those personality traits seemed to only have gotten more pronounced.

The door of the elevator slid open and several people got out. A woman nodded at Tessa as though she knew her—maybe somebody who worked in her office or on another floor of the building. Tessa nodded as haughtily as she could and walked past her into the empty car.

She pushed the button for the top floor. With everyone in the building heading out to lunch, Tessa and Daniel were alone in the elevator as it went back up. She suspected they'd make it all the way to top within less than a minute. A panicky feeling washed over her. The door would open right into the Red Masque lobby, and Tessa, disguised as Kristin, would be face-to-face with the receptionist who'd just seen the real Kristin leaving the office.

Daniel, once more reading her mind, said, "If anyone asks, you forgot something. And I'm your new ninja bodyguard, Kaito—with an 'I' in the middle to distinguish me from that guy in the Green Hornet."

"Don't make me giggle, Kaito," Tessa said as the elevator stopped. "I'm pretty sure Kristin doesn't giggle."

"Yes, ma'am."

She steeled herself for a confrontation, but when the elevator doors opened, none came. A couple of models walked past her into the elevator, but they said nothing, only giving her a reverent nod. Probably too intimidated by their boss to risk a conversation.

The receptionist glanced up but didn't seem particularly disturbed by Kristin's reappearance, though she did give Daniel a once-over before she asked, "Did you cancel your lunch at Melisse, Ms. Morgan?"

"Just forgot a couple of important things," Tessa mumbled, though she had a feeling that her sister wouldn't have bothered to say anything at all. Talking to the hired help wasn't likely to be in her manual of managerial etiquette. She turned to Daniel with an imperious, "Kaito?" then tilted her head toward her office door.

"Yes, ma'am," he said and opened the door for her. Then he followed Tessa into the office and closed the door behind her before heading straight to the computer.

Tessa stood at his shoulder as he studied Kristin's lock screen. "Okay, I'm going to try some standard stuff for the password—words relating to her business theme, birthdates. You told me Kristin has a notoriously bad memory. If she's written this stuff down somewhere, you might be able to find it. While I'm taking a stab in the dark, why don't you search for anyplace she might have hidden it?"

Tessa nodded. Kristin's memory was awful, maybe because of the drugs she'd consumed, maybe not. When they'd been in high school, Kristin had had a pecking order of places she hid things. Recalling that fact, Tessa easily found the password for the computer login and several other logins in the first place she looked—the bottom of the retro desk's top right drawer on a bright yellow sticky note. She handed the sticky to Daniel, who typed them into the password field.

Nothing happened.

He looked up at Tessa. "Could Kristin have encoded the password?"

"Could she—yes! When we were kids, we'd pass messages in class using a simple letter substitution code. Each letter and number represented the character that followed it alphanumerically. So, a one is really a two, a two is a three, and so on. The letter A was actually the letter B. Here."

Tessa pulled a notepad across the desk and translated the password exactly the way she might've done in fifth grade.

The decrypted password unlocked the computer, and Tessa stared over Daniel's shoulder at Kristin's desktop. Daniel opened a series of File Explorer windows, looking, he'd told Tessa, for folders with names like "Data" or "Private" or, in this case, "Crimson."

"Bingo," Daniel said. "Crimson." He pulled a thumb drive from his jacket pocket and plugged it into a USB port, then copied the entire folder. Then he slipped the drive into his pocket, closed all the open folder windows, and shut down the machine.

"Need to leave everything just as we found it," he told Tessa. "So put the note back and take the top three pages of that notepad you used to do the decryption. We don't want someone to be able to lift your decryption work off it."

"Wow," she said, still feeling the fizz of anxiety under her breast bone. "I did a decryption all by myself. I'm stoked."

Daniel gave her a crooked grin. "You're easily stoked, girl. Let's get out of here."

As they walked back out past the receptionist's desk, the woman looked at her watch and said, "Did you want me to call and tell them you'll be a few minutes late, Ms. Morgan? It's a bit of a drive out to Santa Monica."

"Don't bother, Trina. They're used to me being late," Tessa said.

She didn't know if Kristin was meeting someone for lunch, though she suspected that she probably was if she was driving all the way to Melisse, which was in beach territory. Possibly one of her elite clients. But "they" was ambiguous enough that it might mean the restaurant itself. Halfway to the elevator, she turned back to face the receptionist, slipping her arm through Daniel's. "Oh, and let's not mention Kaito to anyone, all right? In view of what happened to Juanita Sanchez, the police think I might be in some danger too, which is why I hired some extra muscle. But I'd hate for people to think I was a scaredy cat." She held a finger up to her mouth. "So, mum's the word."

As they stood waiting for the elevator to arrive, Daniel shot her a surprised look and mouthed, "Nice." She was grateful that the ornate mask disguised the expression on her face, because she probably looked terrified. What if Kristin herself came walking into the elevator when they reached the parking garage?

A trio of Red Masque staff had congregated behind them, but none entered the elevator with them. Probably uncomfortable around their boss. No surprise there. The ride down took longer, because somebody seemed to be heading for lunch on every floor, but few entered the elevator with her and her Man in Black.

Kristin was not in the parking garage when they reached that level, and they returned to Daniel's car without incident. Tessa sank back in the seat and let out a pent-up breath.

"That," said Daniel, "was some Oscar-worthy acting, that was. Where'd that come from?"

"I got into the character's head. Just like in the movies. Let's go see what we got."

###

Back at Tessa's apartment, Daniel plugged the thumb drive into his laptop, which he'd left charging there. The Crimson folder was password protected. Turned out it used one of the other sequences of letters and numbers Tessa had copied from the sticky note in Kristin's office. The folder contained only seven files. All were spreadsheets except for a single TXT file. The spreadsheets were named Services.xlsx, Financial. xlxs, Bronze.xlxs, Silver.xlxs, Gold.xlxs, and Diamond.xlxs. The text file was named Maserati.txt. All were password protected and encrypted. "Well, damn," muttered Daniel when he'd tried every combination from Kristin's sticky note without success. "I'm betting that text file holds the keys to these spreadsheets. Question is, what's the key to that?

Did you see anything else in Kristin's office that looked like it might be a decryption key?"

"Imagine, for a moment, that I don't know what a decryption key looks like."

He grimaced. "Right. Um ... it would be a sequence of letters and numbers, like the passwords on the sticky note, but possibly longer. Or it could be a phrase, or—"

"Just about anything. I get it. No, I didn't see anything like that."

"Then she either carries it on her person or has a second office somewhere."

Tessa laid a hand on Daniel's arm. "The Crimson site had an address on it for some place called Le Salon Rouge in Culver City."

"That's probably the brothel itself," Daniel said, "or at least a hookup site. I doubt these elite clients all have bolt holes where they can put their fantasies into action."

"If she has an office there, how do we get into it?"

Daniel smiled. "The same way we got into the one at the agency. I think it's time you paid a visit to your elite Crimson Club."

Chapter Thirty-One

Culver City wasn't technically part of Los Angeles, but like many places that weren't technically part of LA—Beverly Hills, for instance—the amoebic metropolis had oozed completely around it. You could hardly get from one part of West LA to another without passing through it. The huge Paradox Studio buildings, slate-colored monoliths that held, among other things, the sets where *Dark Beauty* had been filmed, stood like ancient tombs along Culver Boulevard.

Le Salon Rouge was in a small alley about two blocks from the studio. Tessa wondered if locating her elite club there wasn't Kristin's subtle way of flipping off the studio in which her brief movie career had bombed—despite the fact that that implosion had been entirely her own fault. Kristin had clearly had a miserable experience during the filming, strung out on drugs, knowing that her director was cringing at much of what she was doing in front of the camera. Now she could have her own tiny kingdom within Paradox's turf where she ruled like a masked actress in a Grade Z porn film.

They drove past Le Salon Rouge a couple of times before they even noticed the place was there. "Wait!" called out Tessa. "That guy who's standing there. Might he be a guard of some type?" It turned out

285 that the guy was stationed outside the very place they were searching for. The establishment was set back in a wide but nondescript alley with understated signage. Kristin hadn't put out any neon signs to announce the club's presence, which was understandable given what was likely happening inside. From the outside, Le Salon Rouge looked like a drab dive with a red-

lacquered door set down a short flight of stairs. Two small windows in the building's narrow facade, both stained glass, clearly had seen better days.

Daniel parked the Tesla to the right of the alley's entrance so that from the front seat, he and Tessa could see the front door of the club and plan her entrance. The large African American doorman at the top of the downward flight of stairs wore a shiny athletic jacket. He was young and muscular and looked like he might have seen the pro wrestling circuit from the inside. Wearing AirPods and listening to music on his iPhone, he seemed unaware of anything going on in the street several yards away. In fact, he looked bored.

Tessa was about to open her door when Daniel called, "Wait!" in a loud whisper. He rolled down the windows and pointed at a guy strolling up the street. The young white guy wore baggy pants and T-shirt with a Dodgers cap set backward on his head. He stopped in the mouth of the alley to wave to the doorman/guard. "Hey Bruno, how's the job goin'?"

Daniel and Tessa glanced at each other, aware of the great opportunity to try and glean some information about the club.

Bruno pulled one AirPod out of his ear and gave his friend a noncommittal glare. "It pays my rent. I thought you were in jail."

"I got out for good behavior ... and smugglin' coke in for a couple of the guards. You gotta have friends in high places, you know?"

Bruno didn't seem especially interested in the conversation and was about to put the AirPod back in when his visitor asked, "Speaking of friends, how'd you like to let an old homie into that fancy club of yours?"

"It ain't my club," Bruno said. "And if you even try to go down those stairs, you gonna end up in a dumpster."

"Hey, what kind of way is that to treat a bro?"

"We wasn't never bros. Get outta here before you make me lose my job."

"Fuck you too," the man said, turning and continuing up the street. Tessa and Daniel signaled to each other that it was time to go. Daniel pushed the button to roll up both windows, and the pair stepped out of the car while Bruno was focused on his phone. They strolled casually up the alley toward him, Daniel doing his best MIB impression, dark shades and all. He'd added a red necktie to his outfit and looked professional.

Bruno saw them out of the corner of his eye and straightened up, trying to appear equally professional.

Tessa said nothing, on the assumption that her arrogant sister would take someone as menial as a bouncer for granted, but Bruno seemed eager for attention from the woman who wrote his paychecks. "Ms. Morgan," he said. "Great to see you. Who's your guest?"

"He's not a guest, Bruno. He's my bodyguard, Kaito. And we will not mention him to anyone."

Bruno's brows rose slightly at that. "Well, it's always wonderful to have you visit, Ms. Morgan," Bruno said, all traces of the 'hood gone from his voice. "Let me get the door for you."

Clearly Kristin made him nervous. Tessa could hardly blame him.

Kristin made her nervous too.

Bruno aimed his phone at the door and tapped the screen. The door latch made an audible *click* before the door swung open.

Tessa afforded Bruno a stone-faced nod, then walked down the stairs as quickly as she could, afraid that he might notice some discrepancy between Tessa's imitation of her sister and the real thing. The door at the bottom of the short flight of steps was distantly Old World—the red-lacquered wood was accented with metal fittings that looked like hammered iron. The only sign that a nightclub was inside came from a small brass-framed sign that read Le Salon Rouge. Stepping across the threshold, Tessa could see movement and red lights within, but her eyes would need to adjust to the dark before she was quite sure what kind of bizarre portal into the demimonde her sister had built in the middle of Culver City.

As her pupils widened, Tessa saw she was in a large room with a gleaming black tile floor with perhaps two dozen booths around the sides, each curtained off with sheer drapes from the rest of the area. The central floor space contained a half dozen large, circular, free-standing booths set up three to a side down the central floor, obscured by the same type of curtains. Through the sheer panels of the curtains, she glimpsed people inside, in pairs or groups. She had the impression of C-shaped sofas and central tables. The drapes swathed everything in a blurry film so whatever the people in the booths were doing was more or less discreet. The sounds were muted, barely audible above the wash of music.

Waitresses wearing red half-masks that covered only the eyes flitted discreetly from booth to booth, asking the clients if they needed anything. As Tessa watched, a masked woman melted out of the darkness to slip into one of the circular booths. She was wearing a red lacy teddy and a pair of high heels that reminded Tessa of Dorothy's ruby slippers. A Crimson succubus?

A large chandelier hung from the ceiling in the center of the room, glowing dimly with amber LED bulbs that flickered like the candles they imitated. The entire ambience of the place was a combination of softly lit discretion and an almost medieval elegance. It really did remind Tessa of the costume ball in "The Masque of the Red Death"; maybe this was Kristin's idea of what Poe's plague hideaway might have looked like before Death reared its ugly head. Although here, the partygoers weren't hiding from the plague.

A bar occupied the right-hand corner at the rear of the room, while an opaque curtained doorway lay to the left. A metal sign over the bar labeled it The Bronze in a fancy font.

She felt Daniel's hand on her shoulder. He motioned toward the curtained doorway and said, "Let's go see what's behind curtain number one. I bet it's where the real action happens."

Tessa trained her eyes on the drape. It was red velvet and covered an almost round archway. Over the arch, gleaming letters spelled out Silver Salon. A wave of nausea was building in Tessa's stomach. She shook it off and strode through the lounge like a queen, not even bothering to acknowledge the nods and murmured greetings of the hostesses. She and Daniel slipped through the curtain into a long room with a pale travertine floor. A total of twelve alcoves—six to a side—ran down the sides of the room, each fitted with a wide door made of thick, frosted, semi-opaque glass etched with an art deco motif. The interiors of the small rooms were lit to cast the inhabitants' silhouettes on the doors, creating a bizarre form of shadow theater—X-rated shadow theater.

Kristin was nothing if not clever. Here, her elite clients could flaunt their sexual prowess in a semi-public way while still maintaining anonymity. This, too, was a form of advertising, of titillation, a celebration of exhibitionism.

In front of the fourth room to their right—Salon R4, according to the gleaming neon letters on the door frame—a man and one of Kristin's succubi stood watching the shadows performing within.

"Enough watching," the man murmured, his voice husky with desire. "Let's move." He drew the woman to the end of the Silver Salon where the two disappeared behind an ornate door.

Tessa shook her head, trying to make herself follow. She knew what she sought was deeper in the building (really, how far back did it go?), but she didn't want to walk this shadow gauntlet, especially not with Daniel. She heard his breath, ragged in her ear, and felt deep discomfort that he was with her in this place.

"Don't get any ideas," she murmured to him and struck out toward the doorway.

She tried to keep her eyes straight ahead, but the sounds that accompanied the shadows tugged at her. They seemed unique to each room and focused right in front of each doorway. The men moaned, panted, growled, and grunted; the women made softer sounds: mews, gasps, exclamations, or yes! no! again!

"Speakers," Daniel whispered, his voice sounding thready and strained. "Above the doors. Your sister thought of everything."

As they passed by Room R4, Tessa heard the woman's mewing and the man's rhythmic "ugh! ugh! ugh!" She tried not to look, but her peripheral vision caught that the woman was on all fours on a low table or platform with a man the size of a small bull behind her, thrusting. As she and Daniel reached the end of the salon, the woman cried, "Oh, oh, oh!" and her companion howled like a wolf.

Her eyes on the exit, Tessa almost yelped in surprise when the last door on the left—Salon L5—opened and a man in a long robe stepped out into the corridor. His eyes lit on Tessa and he smiled. The woman standing behind him was dressed from head to toe in silver-studded black leather, though her jacket hung open to reveal her naked torso, and the pants were little more than two legs attached to a wide belt. Her shaved pubic area was clearly visible between the pant legs. She remained silent, though her eyes darted subtly toward Tessa as though to make sure she was meeting her boss's approval.

"Morgan!" the man said. "It's good to see you."

Tessa realized she recognized him, making her thankful that her surprise and embarrassment were concealed behind her mask. He was a fairly well-known producer of romantic comedies whom she'd seen around the Paradox lot. Kristin had clearly built up a large and important clientele in the short time she had been operating as a madam.

Inhabit the character.

Tessa smiled and adopted a lower voice than normal. "Good to see you enjoying yourself. I hope you've had a pleasant ... adventure."

The man ran a finger down the biker chick's body from breasts to groin, giving her an appreciative smile. "It was a riot," he said. "She was a tough customer, so I was really hard on her."

The woman smiled at the sophomoric pun. Tessa realized with a jolt that she recognized her from the catalogue on the Crimson website, and before that, from her modeling days. Her name was Theresa. She was quite beautiful, her skin olive-toned and her features Mediterranean. "I'm pleased you ... appreciate our elite services," Tessa told him. "'Pleased' doesn't begin to cover it. You have the wickedest imagination in Los Angeles, Morgan," the man said. "I've been here I don't know how many times and never repeated a fantasy. Still wish you'd do your Samantha Solar routine for me someday. I've heard the rumors—which I suspect you started."

Tessa had no idea what he was talking about. "A woman never reveals her secrets," she said coyly. "Please, *come* again."

The guy looked down at his companion. "You know what? I think I might just do that after a little refreshment. I kind of like the leather." He reached beneath the model's jacket to tweak a nipple.

She winced only a little then put on an attitude as if it were just another mask. "Come on, Ramrod. Let's get you all fired up and ready to roll again. Mama needs her tank topped off."

The guy grinned from ear to ear, and the two ambled back toward the lounge. "Will you let me give you a lube job first, ma'am?" he asked. "Please?"

Tessa shook herself and turned back toward the beckoning doorway. "Damn."

Daniel's soft exclamation made her turn back. She flushed when she saw what he was looking at. The succubus's pants also had no seat. *Yeah. Damn is right.* Tessa aimed herself back at the doorway and pushed the door open. Inside was a long, dimly lit hallway decorated to look like a haunted hotel. The ornate light fixtures and sconces—art deco in design—were covered with movie-worthy cobwebs.

More doorways. Great.

These doorways, though numbered, were made of perfectly opaque wood. They were far enough apart as to indicate the rooms beyond were large. Several corridors branched off from the main one, also lined with numbered rooms—maybe half a dozen to each side hallway.

"Heads up," murmured Daniel. He'd removed his shades and had been scanning the corridors as if he really were her bodyguard.

One of the doors had opened in a corridor to their right, and a man that Tessa recognized as a local news anchor stepped out into the hall, zipping his fly as he went. Dreading another close encounter with one of her sister's clients, Tessa quickened her step.

"Where would Kristin have her office?" Daniel whispered, keeping pace with her.

"As far from the orgy rooms as she could put it," Tessa reasoned. The main corridor opened up into a luxurious, if haunted-looking, lounge. It was empty, but on the far side was a door marked Private: Authorized Personnel Only.

"You ready?" Daniel asked. At her nod he opened the private door and ushered Tessa through.

She found herself in a reception area that was not only beautifully appointed but completely devoid of fake spiderwebs. It came complete with a receptionist seated behind a kidney-shaped desk with a wall of glass blocks behind her.

"Oh, Ms. Morgan," the woman (whose name was Tansy according to her desk plaque) said, "I thought you'd still be at Melisse with Mr. Robeson."

Robeson? George Robeson of Robeson Cosmetics? Was Kristin taking him on as one of her elite clients? The idea bothered Tessa down to her soul. After an initial coolness on his part, she'd found him to be a legitimately nice man. Conscientious, principled, and socially aware. A philanthropist. She'd loved his wife and kids too. She'd hate to think that Kristin had gotten her fangs into him.

The receptionist checked her computer. "Ah, I see that you've arranged for him to tour the club this evening. Congratulations. I know how much you wanted to bring him in."

Tessa bit back an urge to protest that George Robeson didn't belong here and said simply, "It was a very successful meeting. Now if you'll excuse me ..."

"Of course. I'm sure you have work you need to do." The receptionist gave Daniel an admiring once-over.

"Kaito," said Tessa, "this is my private secretary, Tansy. Tansy, this is my new bodyguard. No one needs to know I've hired him. You know how I hate to look ... weak."

"Yes, ma'am," Tansy said and went back to her computer.

On the back wall of the little office was a door with a polished brass plaque that read K. Morgan. Tessa stepped through into a small office, much less grandiose than the one Kristin used in downtown LA, but still impressive in its own right. That one must be largely for show, to make it look like she was running a legitimate modeling business. This would be where Kristin the madam got the real work done.

On the desk sat a computer workstation similar to the one at the other office. Daniel moved to sit in the executive chair and began searching the file folders for information.

"Okay," he said. "What I need you to do while I'm hacking her system is to search the office for a physical object she might use to hide the location of her keychain."

Tessa started to ask what to look for but stopped herself. She was the resident expert on all things Kristin Morgan. She knew her sister better than anyone.

Into her head, she told herself. *Where would Kristin hide something like that?*

She turned slowly, scanning the shelves, the credenza, and the walls for anything that spoke to her. Photos of Kristin back in the day, including stills from the movie, were carefully displayed on a shelf. Mementos and little art pieces and an armillary that looked as if it had come from a wizard's lair were on display as well. Accompanying those were several action figures: Anakin Skywalker, Kylo Ren, Darth Vader—an unsubtle progression. Tessa noted a scale model of the Maserati that Kristin had always wanted to buy but never had.

Tessa's mind double clutched. Maserati: the name of the password-protected TXT file on Kristin's other office computer. Tessa lifted the little car from the bookshelf it sat on and turned it over. She was disappointed to see no yellow sticky note under it. Realizing the tiny doors opened, she opened them. Nothing. She checked under the hood; only a shiny silver plastic engine. She tilted the model slightly to see if the engine was removable.

That was when she saw the characters written neatly on the underside of the hood in black Sharpie.

"Daniel," she said, "I think I found something."

"Me too. There's another spreadsheet here," he said and would have said more, but she set the little Maserati Ghibli down on the keyboard in front of him.

"Look under the hood."

Less than a minute later, they left Kristin's office with a thumb drive containing more of Kristin's Crimson files and with the characters from the Maserati copied onto both their cell phones and a piece of paper folded and secreted in Daniel's jacket pocket. As they breezed through the reception area, Tessa told Tansy she'd see her later. They moved as quickly as they could through the rest of the club and walked up the stairs past Bruno, who had resumed his rigid professional position. None of them spoke.

They returned to Tessa's apartment, where Daniel used the information from the model Maserati to open the Maserati.txt file from Kristin's computer.

"Bingo, baby! This is the password I was looking for, and this file contains her encryption keys for the business files. Hopefully that includes this Bloody Crimson one I pulled off of her box at the club."

"Bloody Crimson?" Tessa repeated. "Not sure I like the sound of that."

"Sweetie, I don't like the sound of anything we've found so far today."

"You seemed to like the sounds coming out of those—"

"Don't," he said holding up a hand. "Just don't, okay? Give me a minute with these."

In less than a minute he had opened all the spreadsheets.

"I imagine these filenames indicate the status level of the clients." He opened the Gold spreadsheet, which seemed to validate his suggestion. Each worksheet was labeled with a client's name. It tracked the date of each visit, what woman he'd seen, what service he'd engaged, and which services or fantasies he'd expressed an interest in. Links on a client's file cross-referenced tables elsewhere in the spreadsheet that tracked 'girls,' 'fantasies,' 'kink,' 'costumes,' and 'rooms.' It also linked to the financial spreadsheet that showed what each client was paying for his or her membership.

Daniel flipped to the lower- and higher-level spreadsheets as well. Tessa noted that the three levels seemed to correspond to the different areas of the brothel. Bronze-level members only had access to the lounge, bar, buffet, and semiprivate booths. Silver got the theater of the absurd, and Gold the private rooms beyond. Diamond members got access to part of the club Tessa and Daniel hadn't plumbed yet.

"I'm afraid to look at Bloody Crimson," Tessa said. "It sounds like maybe S&M or bondage or something."

Daniel shook his head. "No. There's a bit of that at each level, if I'm reading these right. The higher the level, the more rarified the experience, but—" He broke off as the file revealed itself. There were no tabs in Bloody Crimson, just a simple list of names with no column header. The names were: *Gianni DeLuca, George Robeson, Jerry Lance, Alexei Dvorak, Kevin Salinger, Kurt Morrison, Juanita Sanchez.*

In a second column, next to Gianni's name, was an X. In a third column were the words *the sot got shot.* In the fourth, *pervert.* In Kurt Morrison's row, the notes read *X, incarcerated,* and *attempted murder.*

The notations in Juanita's row were an X, *strangled,* and *betrayal.*

Tessa felt cold to her core and doubtful she'd ever be warm again. "Is this ... does this mean Gianni is dead too?"

"And that your sister is involved in some way?" Daniel sat back from the keyboard and wiped his hands on his jeans. "If it was only these two names, I'd think she was just tracking what happens to her enemies. But I'm thinking this could be a list of people your sister feels she has reason to hate. People she blames for ... everything. People she wants—or wanted—dead."

A shudder ran down Tessa's spine. "Why am I not on the list then?

She's been blaming me for everything for a long time."

"Yeah, but you got hurt in the same attack that injured her. She may figure you've gotten your comeuppance. And Tessa," said Daniel quietly, "no one else knows if Gianni DeLuca is alive or dead. Your sister is claiming that she not only knows he's dead, but how he died."

Tessa nodded, feeling a horrible, creeping numbness come over her. "Kristin's secretary said she was having lunch with George Robeson this afternoon and that she'd already scheduled an appointment with him for tonight to 'tour the club.' I found that thought disturbing before this." She waved at the laptop screen. "But now ... God, Daniel, what can we do?"

"Let's calm down and think this through," Daniel said, taking her hands in his. "Do you have contact info for those homicide detectives who interviewed you after Juanita was killed? I think we should talk to them."

Tessa tried to calm her breathing. "Williams and Garcia. Yes, I have their contact information."

"Then let's go see them. I think they'll want to know about this."

Chapter Thirty-Two

Daniel drove them to the precinct house—the same one where Tessa had worked with the sketch artist. They were directed to Detective Garcia's office where they sat down with him and Detective Williams so Daniel could show them the contents of his thumb drive.

"This would be of great interest to our vice squad," Garcia told them after he'd glanced over the spreadsheets. "I don't see anything here for our division."

"Look at this last one." Daniel brought the Bloody Crimson file to the top of the stack visible on Garcia's display.

"This is just a list of names," Garcia said.

"A list that includes a woman we know died—"

"A death that was all over the news," Garcia reminded her.

"More to the point," Tessa went on. "As far as anyone else knows, Gianni DeLuca is a missing person. This list says he's dead, how he died, and why. And these other men—they're all people my sister believes wronged her."

Garcia threw a glance at Williams, who was seated kitty-corner to his desk. "Ms. Morgan, I—"

Tessa sat forward in her chair. "Detective, the dead woman on this list is the one who guided me to this information, to these spreadsheets. I don't think that's a coincidence, do you?"

Garcia pulled the thumb drive back out of his computer. "Do you mind if I ask how you got this?"

Tessa froze. "I ... I had access to Kristin's computer. I was able to copy the files."

"They weren't encrypted or protected in any way?" Williams asked. She caught the look that passed between Daniel and Tessa, then said, "I'm guessing this was obtained by means that wouldn't be considered legal in the eyes of a judge, which would prejudice the judge we'd need to get a warrant from."

"Look," said Daniel his expression more earnest than Tessa had ever seen it, "I was able to set up an account on the covert part of the Red Mask website. I can give you my username and password so you can go in and see exactly what sort of business Kristin is running."

Garcia nodded. "That, we can use. In fact, if you'll give me that account information, I'll turn it over to vice right now."

"Better than nothing," Daniel said. "Having to deal with an investigation of her business might at least slow her down."

"Slow her down from what?" Williams asked.

"Whatever she's going to do to the other guys on that list."

"We don't have any proof that she's going to do *anything* to the other guys on the list."

Tessa felt the situation spiraling out of control. "Detective—" Williams held up her hands. "I'm not saying we don't believe you.

Yes, the list looks incriminating, but we have to do this right. There's a process. Like my partner said, we will turn Mr. Takashi's account information over to our vice division and let them pursue that angle. In the meantime, if you could come up with some better evidence, something we could use legally ..."

Daniel stood, a gleam of purpose in his dark eyes. "You got it. We'll be in touch. C'mon, Tess. Let's get to work."

###

Daniel took Tessa to his office in Venice, where a dozen programmers and engineers, none older than thirty, sat at computer workstations grouped around a large open office with vaulted ceilings. Tessa adjusted her floppy hat and did not remove her dark glasses before entering. To the left of the entry was a shallow skylit corridor lined with glassed-in breakout rooms; straight ahead, floor-to-ceiling windows looked out over the rooftops to the ocean; the right-hand wall was arrayed with a number of huge hi-def TV screens, while the area next to the entry looked more like an arcade than an office. A couple of young men were playing side by side at arcade machines, while two other employees—a man and a woman—were squaring off at a foosball table. Tessa wondered when they got any work done.

Glancing from one corner of the room to another, but still self-conscious of her deformed face, which she kept covered with a long strand of hair, Tessa was amazed at what she saw. Daniel had advanced so far in his career in the time they had been apart! The huge, active office full of employees was a tribute to all his hard work.

At the nearest workstation, a young woman worked on a three-dimensional model of a car. As she rotated the model with her mouse, she altered the size of the chassis, lowering and raising the roof, elongating the profile. Tessa was fascinated. The car was sleek and futuristic without looking awkwardly space-agey.

"Nyssa is working on a family-sized version of the self-driving car we're developing," Daniel explained. "We call it the Hawking, but I like to think of my prototype as the *Millennium Falcon*."

Tessa turned to look at him. "You have one of these, like, in your garage?"

"Yep. Self-driving cars aren't legal on the street yet and probably won't be for several years, so I drive it in manual mode. I'll take you for a spin in it soon, I promise. Right now, I'd like you to meet my team. As I said, this is Nyssa."

The woman smiled at Tessa over her shoulder, then returned to her work. Tessa turned her good side toward the woman and gave her a pleasant smile in return. Daniel drew Tessa over to the foosball table. "Tessa, meet Felipe and Hannah, my most trusted lieutenants. Guys, this is Tessa. She's going to marry me."

Tessa ignored the assertion and focused on Daniel's lieutenants. Both were dressed for success: Felipe wore Bermuda shorts, a Star Wars T-shirt and fisherman's sandals; Hannah was in skinny jeans and a *Supernatural* tank top that proclaimed she was "Protected by the Winchester Brothers." They greeted Tessa with smiles and shook her hand; she felt deeply self-conscious in her dark glasses and floppy hat.

"Diggin' the retro vibe," said Hannah, and Felipe added, "Any fiancée of Han's is a friend of ours."

"Han?" Tessa said, raising an eyebrow.

"She's gotta know who Han Solo is," said Felipe, winking at Tessa. "Yeah, really, dude," said Hannah, sweeping a long, straight lock of blonde hair over one shoulder. "Don't give us reason to question your taste in women."

"Okay, guys," Daniel said. "Introductions are over. Help me pull out the secret agent stuff."

"Oh, man," Hannah said delightedly. "Are we going to play James Bond down at the Santa Monica pier again?"

"Not this time," Daniel said. "I'm going to play James Bond for real."

Felipe crossed to a door virtually invisible amid big-screen TVs and pinball machines. He opened the door and beckoned Tessa inside. "Welcome to Q section," he said. "What do you need this time, Agent Takashi? The exploding pen? The hidden parachute?"

Despite Tessa's self-consciousness, she didn't detect any weird reactions from the employees themselves, which calmed her quickly beating heart a bit. Tessa followed Felipe into the room, which looked equal parts supply closet and gadget shop, and over to a wide, shallow drawer that he'd pulled open. Inside were a dozen pens, each lying in a trough in a piece of dark gray foam.

"Does the pen really explode?" Tessa asked.

"It's just a firecracker," Daniel said, coming beside her. "I need the safecracker, the signal jammer, the spy wire, and the radio tracker," he said to Felipe. "I think that covers everything."

"Are we busting into safes?" The visible half of Tessa's face appeared concerned.

"Not exactly," Daniel sold her. "But the safecracker can read the combination on any electronic lock and get us through without setting off alarms."

"And the spy wire? The signal jammer? The radio tracker?"

"They'll come in handy." His demeanor was uncharacteristically grim. "If the police aren't going to bite on the murder angle, then we need to be a little proactive. We're going to pay a visit to the next victim on Kristin's list, George Robeson."

###

Tessa got her spin in Daniel's prototype sooner than she'd expected. He drove them in it to the offices of Robeson Cosmetics as the clock was ticking up to five p.m. and waited for George Robeson to exit the underground driveway. The man was indeed punctual about leaving his office at five. They followed him up into the hills, until he pulled into the driveway of a large mansion with a wrought-iron gate that opened as his car approached. Daniel drove by the entrance and pulled over behind a stand of bamboo about 100 feet down the road.

Daniel turned to meet Tessa's eyes. She had removed the dark glasses but still wore the floppy hat. "What's our first priority here, Tess—figuring out if he's one of Kristin's elite clients as well as seeming to be on her hit list, or warning him away from her?"

228

"What are you thinking?" she asked him.

"I'm thinking we can march right up to his front door and beg to see him, or we can track his movements and try to intercept him when he's at Le Salon Rouge."

She rubbed her arms, feeling inexplicably chilled. "You make that sound so easy."

"I've been playing James Bond since college. A group of us used to break into locked spaces at night and do all sorts of interesting stuff: decorate the stadium with the football team's jock straps, move the team mascot to—shall we say—more elevated positions. Nobody ever caught us."

"You were one of the Flagpole Freaks?" The "elevation" of the UCLA Bruin had earned the group of pranksters that nickname.

He grinned. "Yeah. Bear on a stick."

"I thought I knew most everything about you! And here I thought you were a serious student."

"I was. But sometimes you can only take so much harassment before you snap and extract geek revenge."

"My boyfriend, the Bad Boy."

"Fiancée, and I considered it preparation for life in the world of corporate espionage. It's a cutthroat business, honey."

"*This*, what we're considering, is cutthroat business. Why are we talking about bears on a stick?"

"Because *you* needed to relax. You were about to implode. Now, what's it to be: Do we warn Mr. Robeson away from his meeting tonight, or do we follow him there and see what we can do?"

"If we just warn him away, who's to say Kristin won't just move on to her next target? Or try again with George? I mean, look, if we warn him and he goes to the police and tells them we were the ones who warned him, is he really going to be any safer?"

"Point," said Daniel. "Though it may make him hire bodyguards or something like that. He'd be a bit safer, theoretically."

"If he's one of Kristin's Crimson clients, I feel bad for his family." Tessa shuddered to recall what "client" meant in context with Kristin's secret business. She'd worked with that man. But ... "Daniel, if he's one of her Crimson clients, she'll have access to him anytime she wants on her turf. If what we suspect is true, she's gotten away with two murders already. She could kill George. She could blackmail him. She could ..." She took a deep breath. "I think we have to see if we can stop her."

Tessa substituted a silk scarf for her floppy hat, and they struck out through the woods that surrounded Robeson's mansion, looking for a way in other than the main gate. Daniel pointed out the surveillance cameras and showed Tessa how to dodge them as they rotated on automated pivots. "Now that particular model has motion detectors that are active within a range of about sixty feet. Which means we need to locate our point of access before we move any closer to the perimeter."

"Oooh," said Tessa wryly, "I get all moist when you talk nerdy to me."

"Hold that thought," he told her, his gaze fixed on the perimeter fence. They found a second gate in the backyard that opened up onto a hiking trail. Security cameras were posted on both sides at a height of about twelve feet. Daniel opened the little backpack he'd brought and pulled out the signal jammer. The device looked like a gun with a small satellite antenna on the muzzle. He aimed it at the cameras and pulled the trigger. The red lights on the cameras went dark.

"Won't George notice that the security cameras are down?"

"Probably, but he won't notice unless he's paying attention. We just need to hope he doesn't have a full-time security guy watching the monitors."

The gate was locked electronically, but Daniel attached the box-like safecracker to the main lock and watched it flash through a sequence of numbers until it found a combination that worked. The gate popped open.

"Now what?" Tessa asked.

"Now I place a tracker on Robeson's car. We don't want to lose him when he leaves."

They worked their way carefully to the rear of the house. The landscaping helped immensely with that. It essentially blocked their movements from the rear-facing windows. Tucked up against the house, they moved around it toward the front. Robeson's car was parked in front of the separate three-car garage, but they'd have to cross an open area to get to it. Hunkered between an opulent plumbago and the side of the house, they considered their options. Directly above their heads was the curve of a bay window that looked out on exactly the part of the artfully paved parking pad they did not want any Robesons to be viewing right now.

"Tessa," Daniel said, "stay here. I'm going to drop back and cross at the side of the garage."

She nodded and tucked herself back beneath the bay window. Daniel slipped something from the backpack into his pocket, gave her a quick kiss, then faded toward the backyard. When he'd gone about fifteen feet, he made a crouching run from the shrubbery that bordered the house to the side of the garage. Using the foundation plantings there, he made his way back up toward Robeson's Mercedes. He had rolled from the side of the garage under the front of the car when Tessa heard the front door of the house open and George say, "I'm pretty sure I left it in the car. Let me go check."

Tessa's heart leapt half out of her chest. She peered toward the Mercedes, both relieved and uneasy that the long shadows kept her from seeing Daniel clearly. She heard George's footsteps as he came down the front steps, and saw him cross the pavers to the car. She wanted to panic—it seemed like the logical thing to do—but kept herself from crying out, weeping, or leaping out of the plumbago to distract him so Daniel could get away.

George came to the passenger side of the car, opened the door, reached in, and came up with a stuffed penguin clutched in one hand. He gave the thing a fond look, then closed the car door and returned to the house. She was still watching him when she felt a hand on her shoulder. She let out a squeak that was muffled swiftly by a hand over her mouth. The hand was replaced by Daniel's lips in a kiss that was literally breathtaking.

"What was that?" Tessa whispered when he lifted his head at last. "Danger," he murmured, "is a hell of an aphrodisiac."

"Did you see what he got out of the car? The stuffed toy? He looked at it like ... He seems so sweet. I can't believe he's slipping out to cheat on his marriage."

"Shows how much you know about men," Daniel said. "Some of them don't consider paid sex to be cheating."

"You wouldn't do that."

"No, but I'm a special kind of guy. You should know that by now."

"I do know that," Tessa said. "I've always known it."

They made their way back the way they'd come in, retracing their steps back to the bamboo grove where the *Falcon* was parked. Daniel paused in the act of opening the driver side door and looked at her over the roof.

"Since we have no idea when George's meeting is, we'll just be waiting here in the car."

"So?"

"You ever made love in the back seat of a sexy prototype vehicle?"

"You know I haven't."

He grinned. "Me neither. Wanna help me do some research?"

Chapter Thirty-Three

They'd successfully concluded their research by the time Robeson was on the move. Daniel pulled out his cell phone, activated his tracking program, and set it in the dash mount. The green blip that was Robeson's car turned right coming out of his driveway—not the way he'd normally go if he were headed back to his offices. Moments later, he flew past their spot behind the bamboo going well over the speed limit.

"What a surprise," Daniel said, pulling the prototype out onto the road. He didn't speed. Didn't need to. They didn't need to keep Robeson in sight as they had to track him to his house. They just had to follow the green blip to make sure he was going where they suspected he was going.

When they passed the mouth of the alley in which Le Salon Rouge sat like a spider in its web, Robeson was walking up the alley toward the entrance. He seemed hesitant and kept looking at his phone.

"He must be meeting Kristin inside," Tessa said. "How do we get in?"

"Same way as before. We pretend to be Kristin and her significant security guy."

"Daniel, Kristin's probably already in there. Won't Bruno notice that I'm entering the building twice?"

"Damn. You're right. Let's think this through." He was silent for a moment then said, "Okay, look, he's met me, knows I'm Kristin's bodyguard. What if you repurpose your disguise a little and we'll say I'm bringing in a new girl."

"And what if we run into Kristin inside?"

"I expect she'll be with Robeson, but if worse comes to worst, we'll improvise."

Tessa took a deep breath. "Well, then I'd better make my disguise a good one."

Fifteen minutes later, with her mask and suit coat in her purse, her makeup overdone, her blouse unbuttoned to show her lacy black camisole, and her hair draped dramatically over the right side of her face, Tessa was ready to play a new role. She was Kennedy Furlong—a name Daniel pulled out of his hat and pronounced "zingy" enough for an aspiring actress/ model—a brand-new addition to Tessa's stable of talent.

She strode archly down the alley on Daniel's right arm so that the right side of her face would be facing almost entirely away from the guard. Her job was to appear scared but covering it, not wanting to look anyone in the face. Daniel would do all the talking. It was dark by now, which helped the charade.

Two guards were stationed at the entrance tonight—Bruno and a younger guy who was thin as a rail but made up for it in height.

"Hey," said Bruno as they approached. "Kaito, right?"

"Right. You remembered."

"Sure thing." Bruno turned to the younger guy and said, "This is Kaito. He's Ms. Morgan's muscle. This," he told Daniel, "is Jackson. He's on night watch tonight." His dark eyes rolled over to Tessa who was gazing off to where the wall of the club joined the building next door. "Who's the ladybird?"

"New girl," said Daniel. "Name's Kennedy."

"Yeah?" said Jackson, his eyes lighting up as he checked out the "ladybird."

"What's her specialty?"

Daniel seemed momentarily nonplussed.

"I am Borg," Tessa said with as cold and mechanical a voice as she could manage. "Resistance is futile." She followed the laconic dialogue with a mechanical tilt of her head. She looked somewhere between the two guards through her unblinking left eye, the right one hidden behind the thick fall of hair.

They stared back, wide-eyed.

"Yeah," said Daniel. "Plus, she's got this whole mechanical doll routine that ... well, it gives me goose bumps."

Jackson was impressed. "You ... like ... seen her do it?"

"Listen," said Daniel, "I'd love to stay and gab, but I gotta get the Borg Queen here into the club for a certain new client. Morgan's waiting for us."

The guards let them go inside without further ado. In the lounge, they didn't see either Kristin or Robeson, though the bartender did give her a long once-over. Daniel snapped his fingers at the guy.

"Hey, dude, you seen the boss lady? I brought her a present."

"Oh, uh, she's uh ..." He pointed toward the curtained doorway at the rear of the lounge.

Terrific, thought Tessa. *I get to run the gauntlet again.*

Daniel and Tessa stepped into the Shadow Theater and paused. She ignored the rooms on either side, focusing on Kristin, who was at the other end with George Robeson by her side. They were just slipping through the exit into the Gold-level rooms. Tessa had palmed her phone and now used it to snap a photo of them.

Aware of the telling sounds issuing from the room they stood closest to, Tessa leaned close to Daniel's ear. "Now what?"

"We find out where they've gone. I'm thinking we head for her office. If she's there we can hide ourselves until they come out. If not, we can split up and track them down. If we have to do that, though, I think you should become Kristin again."

"Okay. Can we get out of here now? I hate this place."

"This does not surprise me in the least."

Daniel led her quickly to the end of the Silver Salon and peeked around the door to the Gold area before leading her through. They headed directly to Kristin's office, ignoring any men they saw in the hallways, just as they were ignored.

Kristin's receptionist was nowhere to be seen when they stepped into her area. Her computer was shut off and her desk neat as a pin, suggesting she'd closed up shop for the night. Daniel moved immediately to Kristin's office door and pressed his ear against it. After a moment, he glanced at Tessa and shook his head. After a split second of hesitation, he turned the door knob. It wasn't locked. Another look at Tessa and he opened the door.

The office was empty and dimly lit, but a bookshelf had been slid to one side to reveal a doorway. Daniel and Tessa both crossed the office to peer through it. Beyond was an empty chamber with a thick plank floor. The chamber was large—roughly the size of the Bronze-level lounge. In the far-right corner, a curving wrought-iron banister disappeared beneath floor level. Kristin and Robeson were there, approaching the banister, their backs to Tessa and Daniel. Tessa and Daniel hid in the shadow of the door, and in the quiet of this otherwise uninhabited area were able to overhear Kristin's conversation with Robeson.

"You tricked me into coming here, Kristin," Robeson was saying. "I can only assume this is an attempt to entrap me even further. I should just leave."

"Far from it, Geo," Kristin said, her voice laced with laughter. "What I'm going to show you tonight will set you free. And if you were really going to leave, you'd have done it already."

They'd reached the top of the stairs and began to descend; Tessa snapped another photograph. She and Daniel waited until the other pair reached the lower level, then moved swiftly and quietly to the staircase. The spiral descended into a dimly lit space below.

"This is absurd, Kristin!" Robeson snarled.

The sound of Kristin's fake laughter followed, fading as the two moved away from the bottom of the stairs. Tessa and Daniel made eye contact. He nodded, held a finger to his lips, then began to descend the spiral, taking each step slowly. Tessa was impressed. He made only a whisper of sound. Knowing her heels would clatter on the treads, she pulled off her pumps and followed him down.

Nobody was in sight when they reached the bottom, but what Tessa saw around her left her stunned. They stood in some sort of ancient barroom, with cobwebs covering the walls and hanging from the rafters. Beneath and between the cobwebs were pictures of celebrities from decades ago: Bette Davis, a very young Humphrey Bogart, Cary Grant. A framed newspaper clipping announced the beginning of the Prohibition era; a red slash had been drawn across the page and the words "Nobody has to know!" scrawled below the headline. Behind the bar, aged bottles of liquor with hand-printed labels lined dusty shelves.

"This is a speakeasy!" Tessa murmured in Daniel's ear. He only nodded and did a complete 360, staring in awe.

In the dim light, the bar looked like a set from a horror movie; Tessa half expected to see the ghosts of its former patrons sitting at the tables, listening to phantom music from the baby grand moldering in a corner by the bar. It must have been left over from the 1930s, and it looked like it had barely been touched since then. The only light in the room came from flickering sconces at intervals along the walls. Tessa couldn't tell whether they were really gas lamps or only mimicked them.

Kristin and Robeson could have gone any of several different directions. A passageway to the left opened up next to the long, curving bar, and another to the right was dark except for a wan light some distance down the hall. An archway straight ahead hinted at another room beyond. "I think," Daniel said in a low voice, "we're going to have to split up."

As much as she hated to admit it, Tessa knew he was right. "I think I'll put on my Kristin disguise in case I meet any of her people down here."

"Good thought." Daniel watched as she donned her suit coat, pulled her hair back into a bun, and took the red mask in hand. He nodded at the passage to the right. "I'll take that one first."

"Okay. I'll take the path straight ahead."

Tessa started to pull the mask on, but Daniel stopped her. He turned her toward him, laid a gentle hand on her scarred cheek, and kissed her lips just as gently.

"Safety first, Tess," he said. "Don't do anything rash or dangerous."

"You mean as opposed to following a possible murderer down into a subterranean speakeasy?"

"Okay, don't do anything *more* dangerous than that." He kissed her again, then headed into the passage to their right.

Tessa slipped the mask on, took a deep breath, and pushed on toward the next room. She had to negotiate a short flight of descending stairs to do so and found herself in a large, lavishly decorated dining room. Tables, still covered with once-white cloths, were set next to graceful chairs with plush velvet upholstery. Some of the places were still set with flatware and china. The walls were hung with swags of satin and velvet in colors Tessa couldn't make out in the dim light.

The place must have been sitting underground for decades and explained why Kristin had chosen this spot for her brothel. She could have turned it into a museum or a tourist attraction, but instead she had chosen to build a nightclub and a whorehouse on top of it. She had probably borrowed many of her furnishings from it—or at least the Prohibition-era decor. Was she merely using it for spare parts, or did she have other plans in mind for this ancient piece of Los Angeles history?

Already marveling at how far this place extended beneath the city above, Tessa descended to an even lower level and toured a series of smaller salons and dining rooms. The place was huge and had obviously been very popular in its time, but she saw no sign of Kristin and Robeson. Why she had brought him down here in the first place, Tessa had no idea. To free him, she'd said. Free him from what? Extortion?

She had negotiated a series of storage rooms and was about to give up on her quest and return to find Daniel when she reached a room that had no exits except a single door on its far wall. She pondered her options for a moment, then noticed how the dust to the right of the door had been disturbed—recently by the look of it. The bottom of the door had left a fan-shaped impression where it had scraped through the dust on the floor.

She listened at the door, then opened it carefully. On the other side was another room, with a dark, dirt-floored chamber with a series of six rectangular holes that looked like graves. The first was covered over with a low mound of fresh dirt. The second was freshly dug and empty. The others were roped off by stakes and red strings, as though waiting for later occupancy.

Was Gianni DeLuca in the first grave? And was George Robeson fated to be in the newly opened one? There had been six names on Kristin's list, but Tessa had the sense that Juanita's murder was an afterthought brought on by necessity, and her body had been left for the police to find. So that begged the question as to who was slated to occupy that sixth grave.

Common sense dictated—loudly—that Tessa should return to the upper levels. Daniel needed to see this. She turned and began tracing her way back to the main rooms of the complex. When she reached the speakeasy without seeing Daniel; she considered brief tours of the two corridors in the big dining room. She knew he'd gone into the one on the right first, and footprints leading into the passageway that ran alongside the bar indicated he'd gone there next. He might still be exploring that direction. She followed the footprints, stepping into the gloom of the corridor.

Suddenly, something hit her head behind her right ear and she fell into darkness.

Chapter Thirty-Four

Tessa came to in Kristin's office, slouched behind the desk in her sister's executive chair, the mask still covering the upper part of her face. She felt as if she'd been startled awake, her ears still ringing with a loud, sharp sound. The bookshelf was back in place, but a coat closet opposite it was open, admitting a cool breeze from the alley beyond and a faint burnt smell she didn't recognize. She gathered her wits, touching a tentative hand to the lump forming behind her right ear, and tried to make sense of where she was.

Memory returned with a vengeance, making her shoot to her feet ... or at least try to shoot to her feet. She ended up back in the chair with her head pounding and her vision fuzzing out. She absolutely could not have a concussion right now. She had no idea where Daniel or Kristin or George was, and she had to find out before something awful happened—if it hadn't already.

She managed to get to her feet and staggered through the coat closet to the back door of Kristin's office, which opened into the alley. She stepped out directly onto the asphalt, which was lit by a gibbous moon and a single lamp above the door. About ten feet from where she stood, a dark, rumpled form lay in a glistening pool that she prayed was water but knew instinctively was blood. A gun lay next to the body, its barrel gleaming in the moonlight.

Tessa's lungs seized up, making breathing difficult. She tore the suddenly claustrophobic mask from her head, stumbled to the body, and bent over it. It was too dark to see the face, so she pulled out her iPhone and switched on the flashlight. She immediately wished she hadn't. It was George Robeson— she'd suspected that before the light hit him. He had been shot in the head; the entrance wound was a neat hole in his left temple, and the exiting bullet had blown the right upper half of his head away. His remaining eye stared up at her accusingly, though she had committed no crime.

Yes, you did, she argued. Her crime was not acting soon enough. She should have gone for plan A—to warn the poor man that her sister was likely going to try to murder him, for reasons she could only vaguely fathom. She straightened, her eyes on the gun. She knew better than to touch it. She wanted to run but didn't know where to go. Back into the building? What if Kristin was waiting there for her?

Reeling from a possible concussion and the combined tang of blood and gunpowder, she leaned over, hands on her knees, and struggled to take in some fresh air. She heard a sound behind her and turned, opening her eyes. A flashlight beam slashed through the darkness, blinding her. She could barely make out the figures of several policeman, backlit by the lights of their cruisers. They looked like demons advancing from the fiery glow of hell. As they drew closer, she realized she knew one of them—Detective Garcia.

"Kristin Morgan, put your hands up and back away from the gun," Garcia said. "You're under arrest."

"I'm not Kristin," she tried to say, but her voice came out in a thready whisper. She raised her hands and wept, dimly aware that she could feel the warm wetness even on her scarred right cheek.

###

She was cuffed and shoved into the back seat of a police car. There she sat until the EMTs arrived and took away George Robeson's body. Her thoughts, such as they were, revolved around the horror that had just befallen the Robeson family, fear for what had become of Daniel, and dread about what Kristin might do next. When the alley had been secured and the CSI team arrived, Garcia and Williams drove her to their precinct station and ensconced her in an interrogation room with her wrists shackled to a metal ring in the center of the table.

Just like on TV, she thought.

Time passed as if it swam through Jell-O while she cried until her eyes were dry and tried not to let the fear that Kristin had also killed Daniel crush her. She had no idea how long she'd been sitting there when Detective Garcia entered the room and sat across from her. He was carrying her purse and sipping on a to-go cup of coffee that smelled like it had been sitting in a pot long enough to turn to charcoal. He stared at her as though he were examining a specimen under a microscope, studying her bare, scarred face as if memorizing every crease.

He opened her purse and took out her iPhone, her wallet, and the red mask. "I'm not sure whether to call you Tessa," he said, tapping the driver's license on display in her open wallet, "or Kristin."

"I'm Tessa."

"Yeah, but now I'm beginning to wonder if you're not also Kristin or if you two have been in this together and just suffered a nasty breakup."

Tessa blinked at the detective, finding it hard to focus on him. "I don't even understand what that means."

"Why did you kill George Robeson?"

"I didn't. Kristin did. I think. I just … failed to stop her. Detective Garcia, do you know where my fiancé is? Daniel Takashi. He was with me tonight until we had to split up to find Kristin."

"I haven't seen him. We received a tip from your sister that you were going after Mr. Robeson, so when we found you standing over the body …"

"He was like that when I came out of the building."

"All right. Let's suppose for a moment that you're telling the truth. Why would your sister kill Robeson?"

Tessa found it difficult to muster enough energy to put one word in front of another. Her head hurt abominably and her eyes didn't want to focus. She felt as if an anvil was sitting on her diaphragm. "Kristin … the attack—the acid attack two years ago … uh, Kristin reacted as if everyone who'd been involved in our success … I think she felt they'd abandoned her. She seemed to hate them for it."

His eyes narrowed, focused on her face. "The people on the list you and Takashi found."

She nodded. "After tonight, I—" She swallowed convulsively. "I'm sure it's a hit list." She looked up at Garcia, her eyes filling with tears again. "There's a room about three—yes, three levels down from the club that has graves in it. One is covered up; the others are empty. There are six. Six graves. I think maybe Gianni DeLuca is the first one."

Garcia's gaze was assessing and shrewd. "I saw *Dark Beauty*. I know how good an actress you are, Tessa … If I check records, will I find that you and your sister co-own Le Salon Rouge?"

"No. I don't own anything but a ten-year-old Prius. And I'm not acting. I'm …"

"You're what, Tessa?"

"I'm scared. My head hurts." She raised a hand to her ear, touching the lump behind it. It had grown. She brought her hand back, her fingertips bloody.

Garcia's eyes widened. "What happened to your head?"

"Somebody hit me. While I was down in the—in the speakeasy."

Garcia rose. "The speakeasy. I'm gonna go get you some medical help."

"Yes, please," she said, then started to put her head down on her arms. She knew she shouldn't, but keeping them open simply required too much effort.

Garcia stopped her, then wrangled Williams to come in and keep her awake.

Fifteen minutes later, a medic arrived to check her for concussion, asked a litany of questions that he seemed to like the answers to, then left her with a cold compress behind her ear and a big glass of water.

"If she complains of her headache worsening or nausea," the medic told the detectives, "you'll need to get her to a hospital. You might want to get her something to eat. Keep her blood sugar up. She looks pretty spent." The detectives then left her alone in the room—Garcia seeking food, Williams responding to a call from the desk sergeant. Williams returned first with an anxious Daniel in tow. His eyes were frantic and his hair looked as if he'd been playing in a wind tunnel.

"You're okay!" they said almost in unison. "I was afraid Kristin—"

Daniel shook his head and laughed. He started to cross the room to the table, but Williams stopped him.

"Stay on the opposite side of the table please, Mr. Takashi," she said.

He nodded grimly, then slid into one of the two facing seats. Williams took the other one. She didn't stop him when he reached out and covered Tessa's hands with his own.

"Where have you been?" Tessa asked him. "I was so worried."

"Kristin. When I realized she and Robeson hadn't gone down either of those passages in the speakeasy, I went all the way back to the Gold rooms in time to see her slip out of her office and hustle all the way out the front door. So, I followed her."

"Where did she go?" Williams asked.

He shook his head in obvious frustration. "I lost her. Or rather, she lost me. The *Falcon*—a prototype—isn't exactly a run-of-the-mill car; I suspect she realized I was following her. She went up into the hills and did a vanishing act. But I saved the route I took in my car's GPS. I already mentioned this to the other guy. When I came back from tailing Kristin ..."

He tightened his grip on her hands and cleared his throat. "When I got back to the club and it was crawling with forensics people, I ... God, Tessa, I was terrified that she'd gotten you. Some kind CSI guy took pity on me and said you'd been taken to the precinct. So, here I am." He glanced sideways at Williams. "It took me awhile to get past the dragon, though."

"Dragon?" Tessa repeated.

"Some asshat named Kearney. To quote Bugs Bunny: 'What a maroon.'"

Williams glanced away as her lips quivered slightly. "You don't like him," Tessa guessed.

"He's responsible for the fact that you weren't taken to a hospital as you should have been. He said you were—and I quote—a flight risk."

Tessa laughed, but it made her head hurt so she stopped. "Yeah, I'm so dangerous, me."

Williams said, "Kearney subscribes to the theory that you and Kristin are in cahoots—co-owners of the club and co-conspirators in taking out the people who crossed you. He wants to interview you ASAP."

"Yeah," said Daniel, "so you might consider having a little swoon."

"No, Daniel. I don't want to prolong this. I want to get it over with and help the police catch Kristin."

He frowned, raising a hand to her cheek. "Are you sure? Detective Williams said you took a pretty nasty hit."

"I'm sure ... except that I'm incredibly hungry. I'd like to eat before I have to face an interrogation."

She got her wish; Garcia returned with a cup of ramen in a cardboard bowl. He apologized for the sparse fare, but to Tessa that hot bowl of noodles was the food of the gods. They freed her left hand so she could eat. The hot, vaguely chicken-flavored noodles made her feel immeasurably better. Almost ready to face an asshat dragon. She could have used a couple ibuprofen as well, but apparently it was against policy to get her any kind of medication, even the over-the-counter type.

###

Detective Lieutenant Darrel Kearney arrived just as Tessa was sucking up the last noodle. He first wanted to banish Daniel from the room, but Garcia and Williams both opined that his presence would help keep Tessa calm. Kearney agreed, but grudgingly. Daniel was afforded a seat to Tessa's right, at the end of the table. Williams sat across from Tessa, and Garcia took up a station by the door, stone-faced and watchful. Kearney perched on the edge of the table next to Tessa's chair, which allowed him to look down on her; she recognized it as a dramatic conceit.

His opening question: "The red mask you dropped in the alley—your fiancé told me you'd been wearing it. Why? Why did you want to look like your sister?"

"I needed to get into her club," Tessa answered. "All the way into her club. I needed to get access to her office."

"You had to sneak into her office? Why? You're sisters. Twins. Colleagues."

"We aren't colleagues anymore, Detective. Up until I went to see her at her legitimate business—her modeling agency—we hadn't spoken for two years."

"You went to see her, why?"

"I offered to work with her. She turned me down."

"And that made you angry?"

"It did. I yelled at her, reminded her who got us into the modeling business to begin with. I never wanted any of that. It was all Kristin. She—" She broke off, shaking her head, then grabbed it with both hands as if the slight head movement exacerbated her headache. "It's a long, wretched story."

"So, you snuck into her office to find dirt on her?"

"I snuck into her office looking for evidence that she might've killed someone and might do it again. One of her models, Juanita Sanchez, contacted me. She told me she was afraid our mutual friend, Gianni DeLuca, had—that Kristin had gotten to him."

Kearney speared her with a narrowed gaze. "Juanita Sanchez, who was murdered the same day you spoke to her."

She ignored the implicit suspicion. "Yes. I'm pretty sure Gianni is dead too."

"And you think your sister killed them?" Snide skepticism dripped from every word.

"Or had them killed. Yes, I'm afraid she did. I may have seen the man who killed Juanita. I told Detectives Williams and Garcia about that earlier and worked with a sketch artist." She blinked and met Kearney's eyes. "When I was at the club tonight, I found a half-dozen graves on a lower level below Le Salon Rouge."

He stared at her as if she'd spoken Swahili. "Really? Why have we not found this crypt?"

"Because it's at the end of a maze of rooms, the entrance to which is hidden behind the bookshelf in Kristin's office. The bookshelf opens into an old Prohibition-era speakeasy, of all things, but the underground area is much bigger than I could've imagined."

Kearney showed his teeth in what could only loosely be termed a smile. "And how do you open this magical door, Alice?"

Tessa was too tired to hide her anger. Her head throbbed. "I don't know, Detective. The first time I went through it, it was already open, and the second time I was unconscious."

Kearney turned to look at Garcia. "Pass that to the crime scene unit. Have them check it out—even if they have to destroy the bookshelf." Garcia nodded, sent Williams a pointed look, and left the room. Kearney swung back to face Tessa and leaned toward her, looming.

"You were found standing over the victim's body, the murder weapon right where you dropped it. Did you plan the killing, Ms. Morgan? Or was it a crime of passion?"

Tessa took a deep breath and met Kearney's eyes. "I didn't drop the gun," she said, her voice calm and deliberate, "and you won't find my prints on it, or my DNA because *I never touched it*. Daniel and I had been following Kristin and George through the old speakeasy. We split up, and I went deeper into the underground complex while he searched the hallways off the speakeasy. After I found those graves, I turned and went back, looking for Daniel. I got as far as the speakeasy when someone hit me over the head." She raised a hand to the bandage behind her ear. "I came to in Kristin's office. I think I may have even heard the shot that killed George. When I went out into the alley, he was lying there in a pool of blood, and Kristin was gone."

She stopped, feeling a wave of nausea at the memory. She closed her eyes.

"That's awfully convenient," said Kearney. "Where did she go?"

"I don't know. Daniel followed her up into the hills. He lost her up there." She glanced aside at Daniel. "He must have told you ... Oh, you want to make sure our stories match, of course."

Kearney gave her a look that was equal parts respect and annoyance. "Smart ass little girl, aren't you?"

Williams cleared her throat. Kearney gave her a glance that she met with raised eyebrows.

"What are you," Kearney growled at Williams, "the feminism police?"

"Something like that," Williams said. "I'd caution you about the way you refer to a witness, regardless of gender."

"A witness?" Kearney repeated, turning back to spear Tessa with his overbright green gaze. "Oh, I think Ms. Morgan here is more than just a witness. Aren't you, ma'am?"

"This is nuts," said Daniel. "Yeah, she *is* more than a witness. She's a damn victim."

Kearney turned his attention to Daniel. "Victim of what, exactly?"

"Her sister. The sister who intentionally sabotaged her medical career to force her into modeling. The sister who poisoned her own relationships with everyone, sabotaged her acting career, then turned around and blamed it all on Tess. The sister whose manipulation and abandonment of an unstable man drove him to attack her with a bottle of acid. I assume you must know that Tessa was injured because she tried to stop him. It's more than ironic that Kristin is so epically lacking in self-awareness that she feels abandoned by the people who dared try to help her."

Kearney gazed at him expressionlessly for a moment, then said, "In other words, Ms. Morgan—Tessa—has every reason to want to set her sister up to face a murder charge."

"What?" Daniel's fury ceased being quiet. He shot to his feet, flipping his chair completely over to clatter on the concrete floor. "You tin-plated son of a bitch! You have no idea who you're talking about. You don't know Tessa, Detective, so I'll cut you a little slack. Tessa isn't bitter. Tessa doesn't hold grudges. It would never occur to her to do anything to harm her sister or anyone else. That old ad campaign that cast them as darkness and light—that was dead bang on."

Kearney stared at Daniel as if unable to process what he'd heard.

Then, he snorted and grinned at Williams. "Nerd rage, huh?"

"Fuck you, sir," she murmured, just loud enough for Tessa to hear. "What was that, Detective Williams?"

"I said, 'Lucky you, sir.' I mean, you're lucky her dude's a nerd and not a ninja."

Tessa couldn't help herself; she smiled.

Kearney whipped his head back around, "What's that smug little smile for, Ms. Morgan? Are we going to find *his* prints on the gun?" He pointed at Daniel.

"I suspect," she said, "you'll find either my sister's prints or prints from the man who killed Juanita. If you find any at all."

Kearney studied her for a moment during which Tessa swore she could hear the thoughts turning in his head. "George," he said, tilting his head like a dog that's caught a scent. "You called Robeson 'George' earlier."

Tessa tilted her head. "That was his name."

"So, you were pretty friendly. Were you in a relationship with him? Is that why you were following him? Trying to catch him with your sister?"

"Oh, for the love of—" Daniel began.

"Detective, Kristen and I worked with George for years. I was trying to catch him before my sister did what I was afraid she was going to do, and I failed. *I failed.* And now George's wife is a widow and his kids don't have a dad." She raised her eyes to Daniel's angry face, tears pressing to fall. "We should've just warned him, Daniel. We should've just warned him. He might've thought we were crazy, but maybe he'd still be alive." She lost her battle with her tears and sobbed, covering her face with her free hand.

Daniel moved to her side and wrapped his arms around her. "Can we table this interrogation for now?" he asked Kearney.

"Jesus," muttered Kearney, then, "We'll pick this up later. I'd advise you to buy her a lawyer. And don't think this little play-acting is going get her off the hook or make us go easy on her. She is in this up to her eyeballs—she and her sister, both."

He left the room. A moment later, as she tried to fight her breathing under control, Tessa heard Detective Williams say, "Sorry about him. I'd love to tell you to ignore him, but that wouldn't be wise. I think he's right about one thing; you really should get your fiancée a good lawyer. Now, if you don't mind, I have some questions I'd like to ask you about your sister."

The detective placed her cell phone on the table and gestured for Daniel to take a seat. He righted the chair he'd knocked over and sat, just as Detective Garcia reentered the room.

"Kearney take a hike?" he asked.

Williams nodded. "Glad you're back. I was just going to ask Ms. Morgan about her sister, seeing as how Lieutenant Kearney didn't choose to pursue that subject. First, the route she took up into the hills ..."

"My car's navigational computer saved it. I can send you the plot." Williams turned her dark gaze to Tessa. "Do you have any idea where Kristin might go? We've sent people to her house, but if she went there, she did it in the time between the murder and our dispatching detectives to her home. We have computer forensics people going over her machines. The information Mr. Takashi gave us will expedite that process."

"Actually," Daniel said, "I might have some more information that could inform your search of the lower levels of the club. The brothel seemed to have four membership levels: Bronze, Silver, Gold, and Diamond. I was a little puzzled after we got to the Gold level where Kristin had her office, because I couldn't figure out what Diamond level might be. Then when I was searching the hallways off the speakeasy, I realized that, like in the Gold level, most of the cobwebs were fake—haunted house stuff; movie props. The dust was only on shelving and objects that didn't get moved often, and I suspect it was loose powder of some sort. The chairs and tables in the room were dust-free, and most of the tables were set with glassware that was clean. When I looked behind the bar ... well, let's just say it was a working bar. Diamond level, I'm pretty sure, is sexy, haunted Prohibition. Which means there might be more down there than you'd find in your average abandoned speakeasy."

Tessa and the two detectives stared at Daniel for a second, Tessa wondering only how she was engaged to man who could produce the phrases "sexy, haunted Prohibition" and "average abandoned speakeasy" without batting an eyelash.

"We'll pass that on to the CSI team," Williams said. "Did you see any sign of alternate entrances to the speakeasy?"

Daniel shook his head. "It was pretty poorly lit, and I didn't really have time to search thoroughly, but there sure might be."

"We'll check that." Williams turned her gaze to Tessa. "Assuming Kristin didn't double back and hide out in her haunted speakeasy, is there any other place she might go?"

"I don't know," Tessa said. "I doubt she'd go to our parents. I'm not sure they'd be willing to take her in, in any case. She burned that bridge several times."

"Any friends or romantic partners she might call on to hide her?"

Tessa shook her head. "I can't think of anyone. The one guy she connected with over any length of time was the one who ended her acting career. Kristin didn't so much form relationships as she had useful but disposable associations. I kept hoping she'd find someone who'd bring out the best in her. Bring back the girl she was, growing up. But it never happened. She's got a lot of money, though. She could go just about anywhere she wanted."

"Not without raising flags with us watching for credit card use or banking activity. And her injuries aren't easy to hide," said Garcia, glancing at his phone, which had just chirped. "Ah. According to public records, Kristin was the sole owner of the brothel. She bought the building lock, stock, and barrel, which means she put a thumbprint on a financial record within the last two years. We'll be looking into that tomorrow. We're also going to be talking to the other men on that list you found." He checked his notes. "Kevin Salinger, Alexei Dvorak, and Jerry Lance."

"Detective Garcia, will Tessa have to spend the night in jail?" Daniel asked.

Garcia and Williams exchanged glances. "That depends almost entirely on the lab reports."

Chapter Thirty-Five

Detective Lieutenant Kearney was in the process of arranging for Tessa's transfer to jail when the results of the forensic evidence came back from the lab. The DNA evidence was inconclusive, but the fingerprints on the gun were not Tessa Morgan's, nor had there been any blowback from the gun on Tessa's hands, which Garcia had swabbed when he brought her to the police station.

This resulted in Tessa being released on her own recognizance and Daniel announcing his intention to take her to his house.

"You have a home security system?" Williams asked him as they took their leave.

"Sure do. State of my art."

"That's right," Garcia said, his eyes lighting up. "You're in high tech. You got something that just leaves little smoking craters in the driveway if someone tries to sneak in?"

"Nothing quite that dire, but the entire perimeter is guarded by a charged field."

"Cool," said Garcia. "I've got a big dog."

Around one a.m. Daniel and Tessa left the precinct for Daniel's home in Malibu. The last time Tessa had been in Malibu was for the Dvoraks' party; she realized she would never look at the place the same way again. But even though she was tired enough to keep nodding off on the drive—Daniel kept rousing her to keep her alert because of the probable concussion—and her head still throbbed, a part of her was excited to see the new place Daniel called home. If his office was as stylish and modern as she had seen, what would his house be like?

Her first glance of Daniel's home was of a low-slung, split-level midcentury modern that rambled over a gentle slope. In lieu of a lawn, the house was skirted by pavers that created a large parking area bordered by succulents and dotted with citrus trees and conifers; a flagstone walkway led to the front door; solar lights, both tall and short, lit the area, giving it an almost romantic ambience. A driveway ran along the left side of the house and down to an underground garage where the Tesla was parked. He helped her out of the passenger side of the car, then fished her bag of clothes out of the prototype's back seat. It contained her own clothes plus several of the outfits they'd bought for her to impersonate Kristin.

"We'll go back to your place to get the rest of your things over the next couple of days," he told her as he drew her into the house, his arm around her shoulders.

His living room, which seemed to stretch on forever, was gloriously futuristic. The west-facing windows ran from floor to ceiling, allowing light from the landscape lighting to flow softly into the house. With a wave of his hand, Daniel turned on the interior lights; a soft golden glow emanated from beneath tables and sleek pieces of furniture, falling into the room from hidden recesses behind crown molding and beams. Table lamps magically lit, creating pools of white light amid the wash of radiance. With another wave, he raised the brightness so that Tessa could see the abstract paintings that hung on the stone pillars between the windows.

Beyond those windows she made out cypress trees waving in the breeze and the Pacific sparkling with diamonds in the moonlight. A large fireplace was built into one wall, though there was no fire burning in it. Tessa suspected that Daniel could light one with another wave of his hand. "It's gorgeous!" Tessa said, turning a full 360. "If I had to choose a place to be under house arrest, this would be it."

"You're not under house arrest. You've just been asked not to stray too far from home turf. This is now your home turf." Daniel pointed at the floor.

Tessa found the idea more comforting than she could say. She wandered toward the open kitchen, which was at the front of the house overlooking the parking area. The appliances were an ambiguous mixture of old and new, some with burnished copper finishes that had an almost steampunk appeal. Tessa seated herself at the breakfast bar and dug through the cupboards for ibuprofen. "How many bedrooms does it have?"

"There are four, if it matters," Daniel said. "But we're only going to need the one, right?" He looked suddenly unsure of himself. "I know I've been pushing you hard to rebuild our relationship. If I'm moving too fast ..."

"No. You're moving ... just right. Maybe someday I'll be able to look at my face without cringing—"

He was beside her in three strides, cradling her face in his hands and kissing her. "Don't even think about dissing that face," he told her when he broke the kiss at last. "I love that face."

"Yes, sir, Mr. Takashi, sir," she said and covered his hands with her own. She smiled, finally allowing herself to notice what had been happening with increasing frequency. "I can feel your hand on my face, Daniel. On the scarred side. And when I cry, I can feel the tears on my cheek. And when I smile, now I can feel the muscles working. The doctors told me the nerves would rebuild themselves; I just didn't believe them."

"Faith, baby," Daniel said and kissed her again, then leaned back and met her eyes. "You look like you're running on empty. Let's get you to bed."

Tessa's headache would likely improve soon, thanks to the medication, but she was exhausted. She only half-remembered Daniel helping her into the master bedroom and showing her the ensuite bath that she felt she could happily take up residence in. She brushed her teeth, braided her hair, and stripped down to her panties, not quite understanding Daniel's reaction to seeing her standing in the door of his bathroom wobbling a little. He looked appreciative, then bewildered, then uncomfortable. Then he cleared his throat, pulled a flannel shirt out of his closet, and helped her put it on. She fell into the bed, waking only a little when he climbed in with her, pulled her against his chest, and wrapped his arms around her.

Mere hours later, they were thrown from sleep by a blast of sound and light from the front of the house. Alarms went off—the home alarm and, down in its slightly sunken garage, the Tesla's. A blast wave rolled through the house, knocking items from shelves and toppling chairs and table lamps.

Daniel was out of bed in an instant, pulling on his jeans. "Call 911," he told Tessa and headed for the front of the house.

Heart pounding, mouth dry, she scrambled out of bed, shoved her feet into a pair of ballet flats, and grabbed her cell phone. She dialed 911 as she was navigating the dimly lit hallway toward the front of the house, got the dispatcher on the third ring, and reported an explosion at Daniel's address. When she stepped out of the hallway into the area between the kitchen and living room, something crunched beneath the soles of her slippers.

The floor of the kitchen and the foyer glittered as if someone had dumped a million diamonds on the flagstone floor. It took Tessa a moment to realize that every window in the front of the house had blown out and that the front doors hung open on their hinges. Daniel was nowhere in sight. "Oh my God," she murmured into the phone, able to make out the yard in the dim early morning light. "Something blew up in the front yard.

There's glass everywhere."

"Is anyone injured?"

"I don't know," Tessa said. "My fiancé just went outside to look."

She heard the dispatcher say, "There are police and an ambulance on the way, ma'am," before she hung up and shoved the phone into the pocket of the flannel shirt. She could hear car alarms going off all up and down the street, and moved as swiftly as she could to the front doors, reaching the entry only to realize that a tire and a car's front quarter panel lay in the middle of the flagstone floor.

The *Falcon.*

Tessa felt as if a cold hand had wrapped around her heart. "Daniel?" She scurried the last several feet to the doors and stared out into the moonlit parking area. What she saw was a chaotic scene of destruction. The prototype was in pieces, some of which still smoldered and burned. Part of a seat hung in a cedar tree. Some chunks had been thrown out into the street.

Daniel was near the center of the parking pad, looking at something on the ground on the other side of the largest chunk of the car's chassis. Tessa started toward him, but he held up his hand.

"Don't, Tess. Don't come out. It's ... nothing you need to see. Just go back inside." His voice sounded funny. Strained and thin. "Did you call 911?"

"Yes. They've sent police and an ambulance."

Daniel nodded. "I don't think the ambulance is going to help." He tilted his head back, closed his eyes, and took a deep breath. "I hear the sirens. Would you mind maybe making some coffee or some really strong tea?"

"Daniel," she said, not moving from the doorway. "What happened?"

"I think someone was trying to plant a bomb on the car. But it went off."

"Oh," she said, not knowing what else to say, and went to make coffee. She suspected he just wanted to keep her busy, but she had to admit a strong cup of coffee sounded really good. She was chilled to the bone despite the mild weather, and wanted something hot to wrap her hands around.

The stainless-steel coffee pot was undamaged, the grounds likewise. She set the coffee up, then, realizing police were arriving, she hurried to the bedroom to pull on a pair of pants.

Chapter Thirty-Six

Kristin sat in her car for a long time, watching the front of Kevin Salinger's house. She told herself she was coming up with a plan, but few coherent thoughts swirled through her head. She was at the end of a rope she'd uncoiled and strung up herself.

Maybe. And maybe this wasn't the end. Maybe she could rewrite the narrative or, failing that, reinvent herself again. Le Salon Rouge had been shut down. Her club now belonged to the vice squad. The alley belonged to Homicide.

Deep inside her was the urge to presume upon an old friendship—at least that's what Salinger would have called it. Friendship. Friend zone. Bile rose in the back of her throat as she recalled their last words at *Dark Beauty*'s release party. The movie done, the barrier keeping the man at arm's length was gone. He had come to her where she silently snarled and snapped at the reviews of her performance and asked how she was doing with NA. Not, "Hey, baby, I've wanted to fuck you forever. Let's go do it," but, "How's your drug problem?"

She'd lied and said NA was great. *She* was great. And he'd said, "Maybe we could get together over dinner soon."

Right, you horny bastard, she'd thought. *Now that I've been dumped on by every reviewer between here and New York, now that you think I'm needy and vulnerable and powerless,* now *you want to get together.* "Thanks, but no thanks," she'd said. "I don't need your fucking pity."

He had looked at her with those impenetrable hazel eyes and said, "I'm not offering my pity. I'm offering my support. I think you're a better person than you let yourself be. I think you need support right now; you just need to reach out and take it."

She'd frozen him out at that point and he'd gone away. *Yeah*, she'd thought. *And I was offering you my beautiful self and you just needed to reach out and take it.*

Only moments later, her beautiful self was gone and she had nothing left to offer. On some deep level, she understood that her beauty had mattered less to Kevin Salinger than her self—whatever the hell that was. She remembered, as she sat across the street from Salinger's house, that Kevin had been the name of a boy who'd befriended her in her freshman year of high school.

Kevin Cruz.

But before that was the far worse Kevin: Kevin Tomczek. Her best friend Haddi's older brother.

Both unfortunate, to put it mildly, episodes with the Kevins happened that same year: ninth grade. Haddi had been Kristen's best friend since they were little. Whereas Tessa had Sarah Hernandez, Kristen had Haddi Tomczek. Kristen and Haddi did everything together in elementary school. They always raced each other to get to the swings on the playground, climbed trees and played Barbies together, and spent hours together in Kristen's backyard swimming pool. Back-and-forth sleepovers—at Haddi's house and then Kristen's—were a given.

During junior high, they dumped the Barbies and swing set in favor of summer softball leagues and riding bikes past their friends' houses to see where they lived. They still played in the pool.

All along, Kristen had been aware of Haddi's older brother Kevin. At first, he was just a presence, like Haddi's parents—no one that she paid any particular attention to. He was sometimes kind to the girls, even building them a little jump in the backyard for their bikes so they could pretend they were riding dirt bikes. Other times he could be coerced into being something of a horse for them as they would ride on his back around the yard.

Sometime around sixth grade, Kristen began to see Kevin as a guy—a cute guy. His dark curls and manly physique was so different from the wimpy, immature sixth-grade boys. She even realized that her beauty gave her a certain power over even someone as old as Kevin, a guy about to leave for college. She realized he sometimes stared at her when he didn't know she noticed. And he had a certain smile and twinkle to his eye that hadn't been there when she was younger.

Then, of course, he was gone—off to college. She had no idea where he went to school except that it must have been some distance away since he rarely came home except for major holidays and some summers. Most times during the school year, Kristen forgot about him as she and Haddi giggled together about the different guys their age they had crushes on.

But that summer before ninth grade, Kevin Tomczek was home. He was soon to be a senior in college and had landed an internship at a Los Angeles law firm for the summer. It only made financial sense for him to live at home.

Throughout that summer, Kristen definitely sensed a difference in how Kevin saw her. No longer did he seem to view her as a little girl. She caught him eyeing her breasts in a definitely inappropriate way that she kind of enjoyed. Haddi didn't seem to notice. Her brother didn't pay as much attention to her as he had when she was younger, although he sometimes came with her parents to her softball games. She appreciated that and teased him about being the "big lawyer who actually came to my game." She would still try to climb on his back and get rides around the yard, but Kevin would appease her only when he was in the frame of mind to be bulking up.

One Friday night, Haddi and Kristen were having a sleepover at Haddi's. They stayed up late watching rom-coms until they fell asleep in front of the TV, the popcorn bowl and Reese's wrappers strewn around them.

Kristen was adjusting her position from sitting to lying down when she sensed someone in the room. "Hey, Kristen," said Kevin in a husky voice, "come here. I need to show you something."

"Huh?" she said stupidly. "Come with me. But be quiet."

Kristen's heart began beating wildly. She was instantly awake, wondering what Kevin wanted with her. Haddi was sleeping soundly, even snoring a little bit, Kristen noticed as she followed Kevin out of the room.

He brought her to the kitchen where an above-the-stove light gave the space a dim glow. Reaching into an upper cupboard, Kevin removed a dark glass bottle and from another cupboard retrieved two small drinking glasses, which he set on the counter. "Have you ever tried this before?" He showed her the bottle of Jim Beam, which Kristen noticed was actually dark liquid in a clear bottle.

"Yeah," she lied with a little giggle.

Turning his back to her, he poured two cups of the potent liquid and appeared to be stirring it for some reason. "Here you go." He set the two cups on the table.

She reached for the one slightly closer to Kevin.

"No. This one is yours," he said, pushing the other cup toward her. "Oh, okay." She giggled again, drinking in the attention Kevin was lavishing on her.

He downed his all-in-one gulp, so she did the same and came up coughing. They both laughed this time. She felt an instant warmth in her belly. Kevin lifted his finger to her mouth and gently touched her lips. "Shhhh," he said gently. When he lowered his finger, he rested it gently on her pinkie. Sparks shot through her being. He actually liked her!

Keeping his finger on top of hers, Kevin gazed deeply into Kristen's eyes without breaking the eye contact. He moved his face closer and kissed her, lightly at first and then with passion. Kristen scarcely knew what to think, but she couldn't deny that she loved the intense feelings she was experiencing. Kevin scooped her up and carried her, still kissing her, down the steps to his basement bedroom. Kristen felt a wave of unease pass through her but felt confident she could get him to stop if he tried to go too far. At the same time, and embarrassing her, was that she felt so tired. How could she be sleepy at an exciting time like this?

He laid her gently on his bed and continued kissing her. When he progressed to removing her T-shirt, she pushed his hand away. But she was so sleepy. "No, don't," she managed to get out.

She woke up on top of her sleeping bag in Haddi's room. The light streaming in the windows was bright, and Haddi was already up. Kristen heard the muffled sound of her voice coming from the kitchen.

Kristen felt a slight headache and an unusual pain "down there." She tried to remember how she had even gotten from the sofa to her sleeping bag. Fuzzy memories began to take shape. A bitter taste in her mouth reminded her of the alcohol Kevin had given her. She remembered how he had made her feel so special. Yet something in her core felt violated. What had happened? Why couldn't she remember? She realized that she had a different feeling in her soul when she thought about Kevin. She felt something beyond distaste: fear.

Just then, Haddi came bursting through the door. "You're awake!"

"Yeah. I really need to use the bathroom." Kristen dashed past Haddi. When she sat down in privacy, she noticed a blood stain on her underwear. But she had just finished her period. What was that about? And the pain in her privates was real. In her soul, she knew something bad had happened with Kevin, but she wouldn't let herself believe it.

"I gotta go, Haddi," she said when she reentered the bedroom. "I already called my mom to come get me."

For the rest of the day and for the next few weeks, she didn't even try to think about what really happened that night. She still got together with Haddi but had a much heavier spirit. She refused to stay overnight at Haddi's, making up excuses for why she couldn't. Haddi seemed puzzled and a bit distant herself, probably in reaction to Kristen's growing aloofness.

Finally, near the end of summer, Haddi made a big effort to rekindle their friendship. "Come on, Kristen. You know how we both love playing volleyball together. We can practice in the backyard and get good before we have to go back to school. And then I'll bake you those brownies you like. No one else will be home. My parents will be away for the weekend, and my brother is never around on a Saturday."

"Okay." Kristen smiled.

The girls had a great time bumping and spiking the volleyball to each other that afternoon. They belly laughed with a lightness like they used to have when they were kids. Kristen felt the joy of the fleeting summer return during those hours with Haddi.

"I gotta pee, Haddi. I'll be right back."

Kristin ran in the house, did her business, and opened the bathroom door to find Kevin standing a few feet away, blocking her path to the outside door. She stopped in her tracks. Time moved slowly as Kristen's head spun with confusion and anxiety.

"I was wondering if I'd get to see you again before I go back to school," he said slowly.

"Uh ... Haddi is waiting for me outside."

"No. She's not. I brought my friend Zack with me. They went for a little drive together. They'll be back soon." He took a step toward her. She looked down and attempted to power past him toward the outside. "Not so fast, Kristen." He stood directly in her way. "We need to pick up where we left off last time."

Kristen met his eyes for a split second and then averted her gaze. "I gotta go. My mom is picking me up in a couple minutes."

Kevin laughed. "You and I both know that's not true." He took one more step in her direction and grabbed her arm.

Kristen sucked in her breath involuntarily. Kevin scooped her up in his arms, like he had the last time, but this time Kristin kicked and thrashed. "No! No!"

But he was so strong compared to her. He carried her downstairs, threw her on the bed, tore off her clothing, and had his way with her.

A few minutes later, a tear-stained Kristin left her friend Haddi's house and never returned again.

Chapter Thirty-Seven

High school started for Kristin only a few weeks after the Kevin Tomczek incident. She pretended nothing had ever happened and stuffed the violation deep in her spirit. Unfortunately, every time she saw Haddi, she felt a visceral reaction, so she now avoided the girl like the plague. She could never have explained what happened, mostly because recalling the incident to describe it would have caused too much pain.

Kristin had felt like a fish out of water that first week of high school. She'd had virtually no classes with the few friends from middle school who'd ended up at Mar Vista High. No one had spoken to her other than to say, "Can I borrow a pencil?"

Her mother had said that the other kids—girls and guys both—were intimidated by her. And while Tessa could just breeze through, not seeming to care what other people thought of her, simply smiling and falling in with a cadre of kids who probably didn't even register how pretty she was, Kristin was too self-conscious to just let stuff happen. She cared what people thought about her. She yearned for their approval.

So, when Kevin Cruz went out of his way to talk to her like she was someone worth actually speaking to, to help her with her classwork and work with her on class projects, she'd been grateful and a little smitten.

He was her age, which seemed like a much more positive attribute than it had in the past. And he knew how to make a girl feel special, treasured, the center of his regard—so different from the other Kevin. The name Kevin grated on her, but she buried the discomfort and enjoyed feeling important to someone.

They'd been on a field trip to Yosemite for their climate science class the first time he'd held her hand. They sat on the bus together, heads close, chatting amiably. He'd bought her a pair of earrings from a park gift shop. They'd violated curfew together, too, the last night of the trip, and took a turn making out in a bedroom in his shared cabin. He'd explored her with his hands and mouth—touched her breasts, caressed her bare stomach, kissed her while he explored her with his fingers. She'd been amazed and a little frightened by the deep burning his touch caused. After her other experience, she had wondered if she would be damaged somehow, unable to enjoy a lover's touch. She could only lie back and let the exciting, frightening sensations course through her ... until they became a bit too frightening, and his exploration a little too invasive. Fearing a repeat of the past, she had pushed him away.

He'd walked her back to her cabin and kissed her good night.

The next morning it all stopped. No hand-holding, no talking. He didn't even sit with her. He sat with his guy friends, whispering and laughing. She wanted to ask him what was wrong. As soon as they got off the bus, she'd do it. But when Kevin got off the bus to greet his parents, a red-haired girl got to him first and kissed him in a way that was different from the shy, tentative kisses Kristin had shared with him.

She'd realized somewhere in the fog of rejection that she hadn't ever been a potential girlfriend. She'd been a toy. A toy that this seeming friend had played with then discarded. She had promised herself that would never happen again. She was going to be the one in control. It hadn't taken her long to realize that her beauty and her sexuality were both a lure and a weapon. She made it her goal to learn how to use them expertly.

She'd never forgotten the utter humiliation that trusting in Kevin's friendship had brought. And even the name Kevin—to have been violated in different ways from two different guys with the same name. On some deeper, hidden level, she realized with chagrin that this was why she had always found it so hard to call Salinger by his first name.

She brushed off the painful memories and summoned up her courage to get out of her car and approach Kevin Salinger's door. She had not even the glimmer of a plan in place, but she did remember how Salinger had reacted to her the night she'd thrown her old lover Mad Wolf out of her house. She'd been out of control then, too, and had to admit, if grudgingly, that Salinger had helped her get that control back.

He was clearly surprised to see her standing on his front patio. She wasn't sure he even recognized her until she said, "I need help, Salinger."

"Kristin."

She nodded, holding her breath. "Please let me in." He did.

Play it by ear, she told herself. *Improvise. See where it goes.*

He offered her food. She accepted it, trying not to let on how hungry she was. She hadn't dared stop anywhere to eat. Even at a drive-thru window, she'd be too recognizable, and she was pretty sure her license plate was on every cop's list. She solved that problem by stopping on the way over to Salinger's to swap plates with a car parked on a side street a couple of miles from Salinger's cliff-hugging home. But her face—there was nothing she could do about that. She'd switched out her red mask for a flexible neoprene one she'd found in a costume shop that catered to the studios. It covered her face from her hairline to just above her upper lip.

She'd bought several of them in beige and black. She was wearing black now, and thought she looked like Catwoman from the Batman movies.

She wondered if maybe Salinger had a Catwoman fetish she could take advantage of.

"You never take that off?" he asked her as he watched her sip the brandy she'd asked for. He sat across from her on his sofa, leaning forward, his elbows on his knees, hands clasped in front of him.

"The mask? Are you kidding? No. I can't bear to look at myself. I prefer to look mysterious."

Now that was a thought. Maybe she could hide out in plain sight by going without a mask. No one would be able to bear looking at her long enough to recognize her. She toyed with the idea of taking the thing off in front of Salinger just to watch him try not to show how grossed out he was. She studied his face, noticing, not for the first time, how graceful and strong his neck was, how smooth the muscles beneath his collarbone. Two years since she'd seen him, and she still wanted him. She'd almost come to think of her attraction to him as an abstraction. He had resisted her when she knew he wanted her, had probably fantasized about her. Now, well, that ship had sailed. Hell, it had *sunk*.

"You were in the hospital under the care of very good surgeons for over a year, Kristin. They had cutting-edge technology at their disposal. Your mom told me they worked miracles—"

Her head snapped up. "My mom? When the hell did you talk to my mom?"

"The last time was when you left the hospital and dropped out of sight. I asked for them to call me if they ever found you again. They never called me."

"They never found me." She licked her suddenly dry lips. "Why?"

"Why what?"

"Why did you talk to my parents?"

He shrugged but didn't take his eyes off her. "I asked them to keep me apprised of what was going on with you. Let me know how you were doing."

"Again, why? What could you possibly care—"

"I cared, Kristin. I still care."

"*Why?*" she demanded again, her voice quivering with emotions she couldn't name. Anger, desperation, desire, disbelief. All of them felt the same to her. Hatred and love. Sorrow and joy. Desire and anger. She wondered if she'd ever been able to tell them apart. She thought she had, but couldn't remember. Everything felt like despair.

"I honestly don't know, sometimes," he said. "I think I saw something of myself in you. The desire to excel yoked to the fear that you never could meet even your own expectations, let alone anyone else's. Underneath your flippancy and irreverence and arrogance, I saw someone who wasn't half as sure of herself as she seemed."

"You're wrong about that," she told him. "I've always been sure of myself." *Liar*. She ignored her own internal commentary and fixed him with an I-dare-you gaze, curling her lip.

"No," he said. "People who are sure of themselves don't work so hard for approval." He made a funny little gesture with his head. "Or sabotage themselves so thoroughly. I wanted … I'd hoped to get down to the real you."

"What you see is what you—"

"Which I saw when you were in the Pink Haze. The real Kristin. Kristin happy. Kristin with a purpose. Kristin freed of self-doubt … and cocaine. Kristin not undermining herself."

She stared at him. "Why? Why would you want to see that, Kristin?" He smiled—a sudden, quicksilver smile that was gone as swiftly as it came. "I thought maybe I could fall in love with her. Maybe I'd already fallen. But, of course, we were in a working relationship and, after that, she didn't want to have anything to do with me."

She laughed, a harsh, grating sound like the cawing of a crow. "Yeah, I have shitty timing—now *you* don't want to have anything to do with *me*."

He shook his head. "Not true." He just looked at her. "You mean, you still want to fuck me?"

He actually winced as if she'd struck him. "No. I never did want that. Fucking is just using. I don't want to use you, Kristin. I want *you*. I want to make love to a person, not make use of her body."

She stared at him a moment longer, then rose and moved to sit next to him on the sofa. "Prove it," she said, cursing the commanding tone of her voice. "Please," she added.

"The mask. Will you take it off?"

They sat, eye to eye, breathing in unison for a long moment before she nodded. She reached up with shaking hands to peel the edges of the mask away from her hairline; his fingers met hers and stilled them.

"Only if you want to. I'm not putting any conditions on you—on this."

"If I take it off, it's all I'll think about."

"Then it can stay. For now. I want you to think about us."

She stood and dropped her D&G trousers and her $200 panties, then straddled his legs, unbuttoning her blouse and discarding it, pulling her camisole off over her head. She'd gotten it half off when she felt his hands on her breasts, then his mouth.

"Oh, Salinger," she murmured, tossing the camisole aside, "I'm gonna wet your jeans."

He laughed, then parted his legs, which also parted hers. He reached a hand down between them to stroke her, fingertips dipping delicately into her moist recesses. She groaned, then she came, suddenly, violently, with a cry of utter surprise. She grabbed his shoulders and threw her head back, quaking until she'd ridden out the spasms. Then she grasped his head in both hands and kissed him as hard as she could, finally snaking a hand down to explore his erection.

"Salinger, you need to get naked. Right now, or *you're* gonna wet your jeans."

He laughed again and said, "It's difficult to get naked with you in my lap."

She stood. He stood. Then she stripped him with practiced efficiency and stepped back to admire his body. He was beautiful, all sleek muscle, almost hairless except for the hint of a treasure trail that drew her eyes south to his erection.

"You know, you've never called me Kevin?" he said as he pulled her back against him.

The exhilaration she'd felt teetered on the razor edge of memory. "I can't," she told him, pressing her body against his, savoring the heat and hardness of him against her belly.

"Because?"

"Because of some stupid shit high school boy who just happened to have the same name. And ... and a college boy with the same name. So, to me, you'll always be Salinger."

"I'm fine with that," he said, and kissed her.

###

It took Kristin a moment to realize that the vibrations weren't some weird after effects of her most recent orgasm, but were coming from Salinger's cell phone in its nightstand charging station. She lay atop him, her head on his shoulder, straddling him, still joined. They breathed in unison, as if they were a single creature. She had never felt anything like this. She did not want it to end.

"Don't—" she said, but he was already reaching for the phone. "Kristin, it's almost four a.m. It must be important."

"It's probably just a wrong number." She levered herself upright as he answered the phone and watched his face in the dim light of a salt lamp on the side table.

"Yes," he said, "this is Kevin Salinger. What?" He listened, a frown forming between his brows. He glanced reflexively at Kristin. "Why? What's this about?" he asked, and listened some more. At length, he said, "Well, that's not really an option. I have an event tomorrow night that I can't avoid ... Yes, that's a possibility, but I think you'd want to talk to Mr. Dvorak about that." By the time he'd said, "Yes. Of course I will" and hung up, Kristin had rolled off him to sit on the side of the bed.

He looked at her, his expression dazed, puzzled. "The police want to talk to you."

Improvise. "Yes, I know. That's one of the reasons I came here last night. I'm pretty sure I don't want to talk to them."

"Why not? They said you were a person of interest, a material witness. A witness to what?"

She sighed deeply and shook her head. "My sister, Tessa ... this ..." She gestured at her face. "It's taken a big toll on both of us, but especially on her. She was engaged to be married when this happened, remember. Now ... she's scary, Salinger. Real scary. And I think she ... she might have done something. Hurt someone. I'm not sure. But the last time I saw her, earlier tonight, she was standing over a man's body in an alley outside a nightclub in Culver City."

Salinger pulled himself up to lean against the headboard. "What man?"

"I'm not sure, but I think it was George Robeson," she said, staining her voice with tears. "And I think she's killed before."

"That explains the urgency." He sat all the way up and laid his hand on her shoulder. "Kristin, love, you need to talk to the police about this. Look, we'll go together. I'll take you."

Love. "Really? You'd do that?"

"Of course." The touch became a caress as he ran the tips of his fingers up her neck to her undamaged jawline.

She nodded and put her hand over his. "I'll go get my clothes out of the living room and clean myself up downstairs, okay?"

"Okay." He stopped her as she would have risen, turning her and giving her a long, gentle kiss. "We'll get you through this, Kristin."

"Sure," she said, and stood.

She padded downstairs, found her clothes where she'd left them by the sofa, and pulled them on as quickly as she could before slipping out of the house. Within minutes she was in her car and heading back down the hill toward the great, sprawling city, wondering where she could go next.

"I'd say your assessment of what happened is right, Mr. Takashi. It looks as if the explosion originated from a device on the deceased's person." Detective Williams sat on Daniel's back deck with Daniel and Tessa, sipping coffee and watching the forensics team work in what was left of his foyer. "Too bad about the front of your house," she added. "And your prototype."

"It's just a house and a car," Daniel said. "One can be repaired, the other rebuilt. The important thing is that Tessa and I are okay. I'm most concerned that there's not enough left of the body to ID the guy."

Williams's partner stepped out through the slider and onto the deck, phone in hand. "They found the car up the street. Three-year-old Audi."

"How do you know it's his car?" Tessa asked. "I mean, there are a lot of Audis up here."

"He had Audi keys on him—or what was left of them. It was the only Audi parked on the street that none of your neighbors could identify as belonging to someone. We broke into the car. CSI is still searching it." Garcia peered at his phone, rubbing at one eye. His five-o'clock shadow had grown a shadow of its own. "Registered to a Clifford McQueen, who has a bit of a history with the LAPD, as it turns out. Trespassing and assault, mostly. Has a lapsed PI license. Look familiar?" He turned the phone so Tessa could see it.

Tessa set her coffee cup down before she dropped it. It was a mugshot, apparently from McQueen's most recent arrest. She took a deep breath and nodded. "Very familiar. That's the guy who was following Juanita Sanchez."

"Looks like he's moved up from assault to murder and mayhem," said Garcia. "Though bombs were apparently not his forte."

Daniel looked uncomfortable. "I'm not sure it was incompetence on his part that caused the device to go off. Depending on how it was set up, it may have ... interacted with my home security system's charged field. If the device was wired to go off when the car started ..." He took a deep breath. "My system may have triggered it the moment he stepped into the field."

Williams shook her head. "Don't you even think about feeling guilty for this. The guy ended up dead because he was trying to kill you."

"I second that," Garcia said. "On another front, we talked to Lance, Dvorak, and Salinger. Lance is out of the country, but Dvorak and Salinger are in town. We've told all three men to let us know if they see the other Ms. Morgan—Kristin—or she tries to contact them."

"Will you tell them why?" Daniel asked. "If they see her, it may be too late."

"They haven't run the prints on the Robeson murder weapon against McQueen's yet," said Garcia, "but it seems most likely that McQueen was the killer, not Kristin Morgan. We're simply telling her potential victims that Ms. Morgan was wanted for questioning as a person of interest in an ongoing case and that they should call us if they happen to hear from her. We did strongly imply that their lives might be in danger, which apparently isn't enough to stop them from attending some sort of event on the Paradox lot tomorrow night."

Tessa blanched. "You couldn't talk them out of going?"

Garcia shook his head. "No, but we did get Dove Rack Productions to put on more security, plus we're sending some armed officers to help them screen people entering the studio complex. Now, if you'd like," he added, "I can take you to a hotel—"

"No need," Daniel told him. "It's almost dawn, and most of the house is undamaged. I'll make some calls—insurance, repairmen, all that—as soon as the rest of LA wakes up." He gave the detectives a wry smile. "I wonder what my insurance adjustor is going to make of this."

Williams chuckled. "I wonder what Lieutenant Kearney is going to make of it."

Chapter Thirty-Eight

Detective Lieutenant Darrel Kearney didn't like being awake at five in the morning under most circumstances; he liked it even less when an overnight break in a case brought more confusion than it did clarity. The explosion outside Daniel Takashi's Malibu home was exactly the sort of break he disliked most. That the apparent bomber was implicated in the fate of Juanita Sanchez complicated things exponentially.

They now had three confirmed murders; CSI had found Gianni DeLuca's body right where Tessa had said they would, in a grave in the hidden substructure of Le Salon Rouge. If Tessa was responsible for those murders, then it was possible that McQueen's demise had added a fourth. What better way to snip off that loose end than to instruct him to bomb Takashi's house, knowing the bomb would go off the moment it encountered the security system?

Against that was the lack of forensic evidence. Tessa seemed to have neither fired nor handled the gun that killed George Robeson ... unless she'd worn long gloves, but if she had, they'd yet to be found. No, he had to accept the physical evidence that Tessa had not fired the murder weapon. Sanchez's death was clearly a hit for hire. That left DeLuca, who appeared to have been shot as well with a .38-caliber bullet. The weapon that had taken Robeson's life had also been a .38. Ballistics had not weighed in yet on whether the bullets had come from the same gun. If Tessa Morgan was telling the truth and her twin was the murderer, he had to admit the scenario made more sense logistically. Kristin Morgan ran two fairly successful businesses and lived in a stylish residence on the proceeds. Horrifically scarred face aside, she seemed to have landed on her feet. Sister Tessa appeared to have little to her name, having spent most of her savings on medical bills, trying to spare her parents' finances. He favored the idea that the two were working together to eliminate people they felt had wronged them. They were clearly using the fact that they were twins to muddy the waters so much that the police would be unable to convince a prosecutor there was sufficient evidence to charge either or both of them.

Kearney reluctantly admitted that Tessa had made a good case for herself. Her fiancé was one hell of character witness, that much was certain.

His intercom bleated at him, interrupting his thoughts. He picked up. "Kearney."

"Lieutenant," said the desk sergeant, "I have a Kevin Salinger on the line for you. He says he's seen Kristin Morgan."

Tessa would have been unhappy with having to face Lieutenant Kearney again even on a full night's sleep. As it was, on less than three hours with a half-hour catnap, she felt nervous and gutted. The last several days had brought a series of increasingly horrific shocks, one after the other, and she had somehow been sucked into the epicenter. She was shell-shocked. She and Daniel had called her parents before going to the police precinct, had tried to describe to them what had happened in a way that made sense, but there was simply no sense to be made of any of it. Daniel had taken Detective Williams' advice and called a lawyer, Charles Handley, to sit in with Tessa during this morning's interview.

I'm not alone, she told herself, glancing aside at her legal counsel, whom she'd first met when he strode into the interrogation room and introduced himself.

Handley was a tall, imposing man with skin the color of coffee with a dash of cream, and a sprinkling of silver at the temples of his light-defying black hair. In a stylish three-piece suit, he reminded Tessa a lot of Idris Elba. Had she not been a murder suspect, she might have been a little smitten.

In a voice like dark honey, Handley advised her to answer the detective's questions honestly and in the simplest way, to answer only what he'd asked, and to take nothing Kearney said personally.

"He'll be trying to get a reaction from you that will trip you up or confuse you," he told her. "If I feel he's asked a question you can't answer—because you have no way of divining the answer—I'll speak up. If you have a question about one of his inquiries, just look to me and I'll seek clarification. And it's perfectly acceptable to say, 'I don't know.'"

Then he sat next to her to wait, while she wished fervently that Garcia and Williams would be there too.

They weren't. Kearney entered the room like a well-dressed tornado, dropping his notebook on the table, then sliding into his chair. He'd somehow found time to shave.

"Where are the gloves, Tessa?" he asked without preamble.

She sent Handley a puzzled look, then opened her mouth to ask—

"Gloves?" repeated Handley, raising a gleaming black eyebrow.

Kearney didn't so much as glance at the lawyer. "The gloves you wore when you shot George Robeson. I've got CSI poking into every sewer grate, trash can, and dumpster in that alley, so we will find them eventually. You'll save us all a lot of trouble if you just tell me where they are."

"I wasn't wearing gloves that night. I didn't shoot George. I never touched the gun." She glanced aside at Handley; he gave her the tiniest nod. He flipped open his notebook and scanned the pages. "I spoke to Kevin Salinger early this morning. He saw your sister last night. She told him, among other things, that your disfigurement has ... changed you. Your sister is afraid of you. Afraid *for* you." He waited a beat then said, "She saw you standing over the body, Ms. Morgan. She told Salinger that she thought you'd killed Robeson. She also said she thought you'd killed before." He looked at her expectantly.

"Is there a question in there, Detective?" asked Handley.

"Have you killed before, Ms. Morgan? Did you kill Gianni DeLuca?"

She met Kearney's eyes. "I have never killed anyone, Detective. The first I knew of Gianni's disappearance was when Juanita showed me the article in the *Times* about him being missing."

"That's a careful answer, Ms. Morgan. One you could make even if you arranged for his murder. As long as you didn't pull the trigger, if the gun belonged to Clifford McQueen ..."

"Detective, I don't have the financial resources to hire a ... a hit man. Or buy a gun, for that matter."

Kearney made a wry face. "You don't have the financial resources to hire a lawyer, and yet ..." He gestured at Charles Handley.

"My fiancé hired Mr. Handley."

"Ah," said Kearney, as if that explained everything. "Your fiancé, who has been right by your side through all of this. You know what I think? I think the three of you are working together to bring these people down." Tessa stared at him in complete disbelief. "Why would I? Why would

Daniel? I've nothing to gain, and he's got everything to lose."

"You want revenge. Maybe you see it as justice. It's not justice, Ms. Morgan. It's vengeance. As for Daniel, I imagine he wants to placate you so *he* doesn't end up on your hit list. He—"

"Kevin Salinger," Tessa said, a cold hand touching her soul. "You said he'd seen Kristin. He's all right? She didn't—"

"Kill him? No. Kind of strange, isn't it? Considering." Kearney narrowed his eyes. "He said they were intimate. She left about four thirty. He thought she was going to let him bring her in for questioning. But she left. Not part of your plan, was it? She was supposed to have killed him, wasn't she? But she let him live, maybe for the same reason you let your inventor buddy live."

"Detective," said Handley, "you are indulging in the most absurd speculation I've heard in many moons. Do you have some evidence to present? A line of questioning that makes sense? Or is this just what you imagine? If that's the case ..." He reached for his briefcase.

There was a tap on the door. Kearney smiled as if he'd been expecting it. "I think my evidence may have just arrived."

Detective Garcia stepped into the room, a file folder in one hand. He nodded at Tessa and her lawyer, then crossed to the table and held up the folder.

"Here's what we've got," Garcia said, his eyes on Tessa. "DNA evidence ties McQueen to the Sanchez murder. His DNA is on her body; her DNA is on a pair of gloves found in the console in McQueen's car. Which, of course, was found early this morning at the scene of the Takashi bombing. Ballistics reports that the same gun that killed George Robeson also killed Gianni DeLuca—at point-blank range, I might add. The gun in question is registered to Kristin Morgan, and while her prints aren't on the gun—which appears to have been wiped—they are on the magazine and the individual bullets." He dropped the folder on the table in front of Kearney. "I think we should thank these nice people for all their patience and let them move on. It's been a rough twenty-four hours for everybody."

###

The apartment seemed lonely. At least that's how it made Tessa feel. She realized that's how she'd felt the whole time she'd lived here. It seemed as if she'd been away for so long, but it had only been two days.

"Why don't we go sort through your clothes and pack up what you want to keep," Daniel suggested as they stood just inside the front door. "I can make arrangements to have anything you don't want taken to Goodwill or a homeless shelter."

She nodded and headed toward the bedroom. Daniel trailed behind, stopping in the middle of her tiny living room.

"Except that sofa," he said. "I think I want to keep that."

She turned around and stared at it. It wasn't a bad-looking sofa, but it was cheap compared to anything she'd seen in Daniel's house. "Why in heaven's name would you want to keep that?"

He smiled crookedly. "We reconnected on that sofa, Tess. We *reunited* on that sofa. We did the most important things a couple of people can do on a sofa; we worked together, we discovered each other, we made love. I found you again on that sofa—when I was afraid I'd lost you forever."

Tessa felt tears welling up in her eyes. "Daniel ..."

He moved to face her, meeting her gaze. "I know I seemed all bright-eyed and optimistic when I rolled in here the first time. But I wasn't. I told myself that I was going to win you back someday. I told myself that every day. But I only believed it some of the time. The day I came here, I wasn't sure what to believe."

"I love you," she told him. "Believe that."

They kissed, and he motioned with his eyes toward the sofa.

"No," she said, "I really don't want to spend any longer than I have to in this place. It reminds me too much of how wretched I was before."

She went into the bedroom and directly to the closet. Only moments later she had pulled all of her clothes out onto the bed and was sorting through them. Then she tackled the meager collection of items in her dresser drawers while Daniel gathered up toiletries and makeup in her bathroom, consigning them to a cloth tote she'd hung on the back of the bathroom door.

Last, she got out her suitcase and a smaller overnight bag and packed up what she wanted to keep. There wasn't much, but ...

"That's weird." She stood staring at the small mound of discards. "What?" Daniel looked up from where he sat on the edge of the bed. "I had another one of those big floppy hats. A tan one. It's not here, and ..." She stopped and looked up at him, feeling something cold and slimy trying to invade her insides. "I'd kept my favorite Tahari suit and a pair of Tory Burch sandals from ... from before."

Daniel's face was almost as pale as she thought hers must be. He rose slowly from the bed. "You're telling me those things are gone."

She could only nod mutely.

"Grab what you can carry," he told her. "Let's get out of here."

Tessa grabbed her overnight bag and a big JCPenney bag full of shoes and toiletries, while Daniel snagged her suitcase and the tote. Together they headed out into the living room, Daniel leading the way.

Halfway across the living room, he stopped, staring at the front door, which hung wide open.

"I closed that behind us when we came in."

Back at Daniel's house, with the security system engaged, they called Detective Williams's cell phone but got her voice mail. They called Garcia and got the same result. Finally, they called the desk sergeant at the precinct and found that the two detectives had gone home for some much-needed R&R, as had Kearney. They left the message that Kristin had been in Tessa's apartment and had taken garments and accessories intended to make her look like Tessa. They feared she might be intent on carrying out the rest of her agenda.

"She can't completely disguise herself, though," Daniel told the woman at the desk. "Her scars are quite different than Tessa's. The entire upper half of her face sustained acid burns. Tessa sustained burns to only the right side of her face. So, her disguise will have to accommodate that." As he talked, Tessa leaned against his shoulder, her feet drawn up onto the sofa. He'd turned his TV on to catch the news, but the sound was muted. She stared, unseeing, at the screen.

"Do you think she'll get the message to them?" she asked when he'd hung up.

He pondered a second, then called Williams and Garcia again, this time leaving messages.

"I feel like we haven't done enough, Daniel," she told him. "God knows what she'll do. When she has a plan, she never gives up. Never."

"She seems to have given up on killing Kevin Salinger. She was with him last night—I mean, *with* him in the biblical sense—and yet he's still alive."

Tessa considered that. "Kevin was the one person I thought might have honestly befriended Kristin. I found out after the fact that he'd helped her kick her drug habit. I thought they seemed really tight for a while, and then ..."

"You think they were having an affair while they were both involved with *Dark Beauty*? Because that would be pretty skeevy on his part."

"No. I never got that vibe from him. I think he really just wanted to see her succeed. Maybe, ultimately, he was able to reach her."

"Can we take a chance on that?"

"What else can we do?"

"I don't know," Daniel said and stretched. "I'm starving. Do you want to go out or order in?"

"Order in. I feel too vulnerable out there. I—" She cut off her thought as the TV showed a shot of the entrance to the Paradox Studio complex. She squeezed Daniel's arm. "Daniel, turn on the sound!"

He hit Unmute and the sound popped on, words leaping from the lips of a smiling reporter standing in front of the Paradox gates.

"... will be on full display tonight at the gala celebrating the official wrap for Dove Rack Productions' newest offering, *A Rare Virtue*. This promises to be a star-studded event with attendees to include lead actors Audra Alexander and Samuel Wingard, as well as the film's director and producer, Alexei Dvorak and Kevin Salinger. Festivities are set to kick off at eight p.m., though I'm sure most of the celebs will be fashionably late. This is Caroline Beecham reporting live from Culver City."

Tessa turned to look at Daniel. "What if she hasn't given up on killing Alex? The police were unable to get either him or Kevin to stay home tonight. What if she means to—"

"To get in and kill him—or both of them?" He shook his head. "Baby, the odds of her being able to sneak in there looking like Carmen Santiago ... I don't know if even Kristin's up to that. Not with the added security."

Tessa had a freakish thought. "The tunnels."

"What tunnels?"

She turned to face him on the sofa, grasping his hands in hers. "The ones that run west out of the speakeasy. They extend in the direction of the studio lots, and I have no idea how far they go. I must've gone a quarter of a mile the night—the night George was murdered."

"Sweetie, that's got to be almost, what, a mile and a half, two miles as the crow flies?"

"The speakeasy has been there since Prohibition," Tessa said. "How long has the studio been there?"

Daniel snatched up his phone and did a quick Google search for "Culver City Studios founded."

"Wow," he said as the search results appeared. "The studio that's now Paradox has been there since 1918."

"Prohibition ended in 1933."

"You always were good at history. So, what you're thinking is that—"

"The tunnels reach toward the studios. Maybe they reach all the way to the studios so that the stars featured in those photos we saw could get there without anyone knowing."

"It seems so ... wild."

"Daniel, my sister is a madwoman who wears her version of the Mask of the Red Death and owns a multitiered brothel with a freaking speakeasy under it. She roofied me into modeling and acting, made one guy so mad he tried to kill her, and she's murdered three people and plans to murder three more that we know of. Remember what I said about Kristin?"

Daniel licked his lips. "That she never gives up."

They left one last message for Detectives Williams and Garcia.

Chapter Thirty-Nine

The tomb-like darkness of the speakeasy was eerily oppressive. The faux gas lamps had been shut off, and neither of them had a clue about where the light switches might be. Daniel turned a flashlight on the photographs that Tessa had referenced earlier. They could both see it now: Some of those stars—stars of the silent movies, stars of the later "talkies"—had been photographed in this very room—a room they'd had to wait until sundown to gain access to.

With the law enforcement presence withdrawn, they'd woven their way through the crime scene tape, shadows, and sawhorses to enter through Kristin's office. The bookcase door had been open, so they'd just invited themselves in. The whole place was thoroughly abandoned and had a dejected air. Tessa wondered how many of the staff and clientele had been arrested and how many had escaped.

The made their way swiftly through the speakeasy and the dining room, then slowed as they navigated the chambers beyond. Daniel turned on the mapping app in his phone, glancing at it from time to time. In one darkened room, dusty wooden boxes of liquor bottles rose like towers, stretching almost to the ceiling. In the gaps between boxes, something moved.

Tessa grasped Daniel's arm.

"I see it," he said and trained his flashlight on the movement, then chuckled. "I'm betting *those* cobwebs are real." In the glow of his flash-light, the gossamer banners of dust looked like ghosts arising from their ancient crypts to dance in the air currents.

"I remember this storage room. I think the next room is the one with graves in it," Tessa murmured, then swallowed. "Did any of the detectives answer your last message?"

Daniel shook his head. "If they did, I wouldn't know. There's no cell phone coverage down here. All we've got is GPS."

"I don't like the sound of that," she said and panned her flashlight along the far wall of the storage room. She stopped when it illuminated the door with its fan-shaped scrape marks. "That's it. The next room."

Daniel put a hand on her forearm. "Do you want to turn back? We can just go to the police—"

"There's no time for that, Daniel. The gala starts at eight. It's 7:40 right now. If they don't get our messages or don't take them seriously, people are going to die. We need to keep going."

They did, entering cautiously into Kristin's little graveyard. It looked quite different than it had before. The police presence was obvious in the crime tape, the spray-painted markings on the floor, and the empty grave from which Gianni DeLuca's body had been removed.

Tessa stopped and stared at that grave, unable to wrap her mind around the enormity of what her sister had done. Gianni had been opportunistic and narcissistic, but in the final analysis, he had been a friend who had helped Kristin toward her goal. Kristin would probably never admit that. When the subject came up, she always insisted that she'd gotten them everything from Gianni to Robeson Cosmetics to their roles in *Dark Beauty*. Tessa had never been sure how literally to take that or how literally Kristin meant it.

In examining the room, her gaze was drawn upward from Gianni's grave to the wall behind it. She gasped, grasping Daniel's arm.

"Daniel ... over the grave ..."

On the wall of the crypt, behind Gianni DeLuca's empty grave was an effigy of sorts—a mannequin head wearing a hand-painted mask. The likeness was artful and accurate, clearly Gianni. She swept her flash to the right. There were similar effigies over the graves of Alexei Dvorak and Kurt Morrison, currently awaiting sentencing for his assault on the Morgan twins. The walls above the other two graves were empty.

"She must have just done this," Tessa murmured. "These weren't here yesterday."

"I guess she's notching her gun belt," said Daniel. His voice sounded airless and thin.

"Gianni's dead, Kurt's going to prison." She turned to look at Daniel. "She means to get Alex tonight."

"Not if we can help it. Let's move."

Through a doorway at the far side of the crypt they stepped out onto the landing at the top of a wooden staircase that disappeared into the darkness below. Daniel shone his flashlight around, revealing that the steps were enclosed in a stairwell with an arched ceiling that was roughly eight feet high.

Tessa took a deep breath and stepped on the top tread, causing it to give up a moan that seemed horribly loud in the stairwell. She pulled her foot back and looked at Daniel.

He shrugged. "Nothing we can do about it now, babe. If you want to keep going, we kind of have to do this part. Put your feet on the outer edge of the tread where it meets the riser. Less likely to stress the old wood of the tread that way."

"Now you're thinking like an engineer."

"I'm always thinking like an engineer."

She nodded, grasped the thick wooden banister, and started down again, this time placing her feet on the outer part of each tread as Daniel had suggested. The stairs made no more haunted sounds. At the bottom of the staircase, they found themselves in a broad arched hallway that was inexplicably finished—floor, walls, and ceiling—with white, red, and black marble. Pillars flanked the far end of the short passage, the capitals still gleaming with gold leaf.

The room the short hallway gave into was so vast that their flashlights couldn't penetrate the gloom as far as the walls. There were round tables arrayed at intervals through the space, a few with half-filled glasses of liquor still on top of them. Here, the dust and cobwebs were real. They moved slowly through the room, Daniel checking his GPS to make sure they were still heading toward the studios. Few if any doorways opened from the rooms they'd been in, and every one they'd checked had been a dead-end storage area.

They were perhaps halfway across the dark expanse when an anonymous sound—a clatter, a tap, a scrape—froze them in place. It was so thoroughly filtered Tessa couldn't even tell what direction it had come from. Behind? Ahead?

"We didn't imagine that, did we?" Tessa whispered. "I'm pretty sure we didn't." Daniel's voice was grim.

"Reassure me, Daniel. Tell me again about the James Bond stun gun you're carrying."

"It's a prototype wireless taser, and I'm pretty sure James Bond never used a stun gun."

"I wish I'd taken weapons training." Tessa sighed. "I could help protect us."

"Well, I saw a ratty old umbrella back there a bit. Would that do?"

"Only if we're attacked by Mary Poppins."

Daniel pressed his lips to her forehead. "I love that you can find humor in this situation. You are *so* my soul mate."

"Gallows humor."

They advanced gradually toward the edge of the room. Doors branched out in all directions, leading to private dining rooms, all dead ends. Aging paintings hung on the walls between them, remarkably unfaded in the dim light. One depicted a stately looking Franklin Delano Roosevelt, probably from shortly after his election as president. There was no sign in the photo that he was in a wheelchair.

"My God," Daniel said. "Do you suppose Roosevelt came here in person?"

"I doubt it," Tessa said. "It wouldn't look good for a president to be caught in a speakeasy. The owner probably just liked him."

"Ironic, since Roosevelt signed the act that ended Prohibition and put places like this out of business."

"You'd think they'd still draw business just out of the novelty of literally being underground."

Daniel stopped moving and swept his flashlight along the walls. There seemed to be no door. They made a quick circuit of the room, but there were no doors that did not dead end in a storage room. That left only the kitchen that had been carved out of the far wall of the large space.

They searched the kitchen as efficiently as possible but found no door there either. Daniel made a frustrated noise and stopped in the middle of the room's black-and-white tile floor. "I'm beginning to think we took a wrong turn somewhere. Although I can't imagine where. Let's head back into the dining room. There must be another hallway we missed."

"No, wait," Tessa said. "Over there. That's sort of a door."

"It's cold storage, Tess. A Prohibition-era refrigerator."

"Still a door." She crossed the room to the large metal door and opened the latch by pulling on a length of chain. Daniel was at her side in an instant, his fancy taser in hand as she opened the door.

It didn't open into a cold storage room. It opened into a long, stygian passage. Their lights showed it to be broad, high ceilinged, and with a set of narrow metal tracks running down its center.

"This must be how they moved things, back when the speakeasy was running," Daniel said. "Maybe even shuttling people. I can't imagine those ladies in their fancy gowns hiking from the studios to the dining hall. Elegant system."

"How close are we to the studios?"

Daniel checked his GPS. "We've gone a mile and a third, so another half mile, roughly."

Together they began walking along the tracks, their path illuminated only by their flashlights. Their footfalls raised little puffs of dust, which made Tessa think that it had been a long time since there had been any real traffic down here.

They followed the tunnel in silence for some time before Tessa said, "Is it my imagination or is this curving to the right?"

Daniel stopped and aimed his flashlight down the passage as far as it would penetrate. "Yeah, you're right. It is curving. You can just make out where the tracks disappear way up ahead. Good catch." He checked the GPS again. "We're close. We should keep our eyes peeled for a staircase or passage or something that might go to the surface."

Tessa shone her flashlight around on the walls and ceiling of the passage as they moved forward again. "You know, this tunnel is bored out like a big tube. I think this might actually have been an old sewer system."

"Makes some sense," Daniel said. "They could've smuggled imported liquor into the speakeasy this way, as well as their clientele—right up from Los Angeles Bay. Way safer than trying to bring it in by truck without being noticed."

Tessa was silent for a few steps, her mind turning over the history of the area in her head. "Daniel, if this is an old, defunct sewer and it was connected to the studios, then it would connect to the substructure of the original buildings, right? The old sound stages."

"Yeah."

"Which is where they're holding the gala tonight."

"Yeah. So, Kristin probably would get up into the studios from the old boiler rooms and sewer terminals."

Tessa's steps slowed. "But, think about it. Unless this is a costume ball, there's no way for Kristin to blend in. I mean, yes, she can be wearing my suit and my Peggy Carter getup, but there's no pair of dark glasses made that will cover all the scar tissue on the upper part of her face. She's going to stand out."

"So, what are you suggesting?"

"What if she's not planning on physically attacking Alexei and Kevin. I mean, personally attacking them. What if she's planning something that doesn't involve her attacking them face-to-face?"

"Like what? Gas in the air ducts? Or—shit," he said at the same moment Tessa said, "A bomb. Just like at your place."

Daniel took a deep breath. "Shit, you're right. But McQueen is dead."

"Doesn't mean he didn't leave toys behind."

"Shit," said Daniel again and picked up his pace.

They'd gone about twenty yards when they encountered a branch in the tunnel. They stopped to consider their location in relation to the landscape above. Daniel's GPS showed where they were in context with the coast, but all landmarks were gone; the phone was getting a satellite signal but no correlative data from surface stations.

"I think," Daniel said after a moment, "that the left-hand tunnel goes to the port. The right-hand one should go to the studios."

"Should?"

"Yeah ... I think."

"We could split up."

"Sure, 'cause that worked so well the last time."

"So, what do we do?"

Daniel shone his flashlight down the left-hand tunnel. Some boxes and barrels had been stowed along the side of the tracks. The sound of water dripping was loud in the stillness of the chamber.

"We go right," he said and led Tessa in that direction.

They'd gone maybe thirty feet when Tessa thought she heard a sound they weren't making. She put a hand on Daniel's arm. "Stop," she murmured. "Listen."

There it was—the sound of footfalls ... maybe. Tessa turned her head, trying to make out where the sound was coming from. Her effort was put to naught by a rumbling sound from overhead.

"What the hell?" Daniel said.

"A road, I think," said Tessa. "Maybe the one that runs north-south just east of the studios? Could we be that close?"

He glanced at his phone. "Yeah. We've gone well over a mile." He looked back down the tunnel the way they'd come. "What about—"

"Probably just an artifact of being under the road. Let's keep going." They did, with Tessa trying to estimate when they'd crossed completely under the road she suspected lay above them. When they were beneath the grounds of Paradox Studios. When they were perhaps approaching the first of the sound stages.

Once again, Tessa heard something that didn't seem to be part of the natural soundscape of the tunnel. It was a rhythmic chirp, like a mechanical bird. From the sudden slowing of Daniel's steps, she realized he could hear it too and that he was as confused as she was about where it was coming from. A sweep of flashlights into the tunnel ahead revealed four new tunnels branching from the one they were in. Each one was much narrower than the main passage and looked as if it had not been traveled for some time, though both Tessa and Daniel knew that looks could be deceiving in this place.

In the end, they were forced to proceed several yards into each tunnel to determine which one the chirping was coming from. The sound was originating from the narrower aperture just to the left of the main tunnel.

"We're assuming that chirping means something," Tessa noted. "It's an out-of-place mechanical sound that doesn't belong down here," Daniel told her. "What do you think?"

"I think that it's eight o'clock now and that if this is a bomb, she would have set it to go off when the gala was in full swing but before anyone's decided they've stayed long enough to be polite and are ready to bail."

"People do that?"

"Yes. Kevin Salinger is one of those people, in fact. He's in NA and finds parties where alcohol flows freely uncomfortable. And right now, I don't know if Kristin wants him dead or alive."

They set off down the chirping channel as fast as they could. Twenty or so yards down the new tunnel, they came to a sort of hub from which yet more tunnels radiated. The chirping was louder here and distorted by slap-back echoes from the surrounding walls. A grimy metal ladder ascended from the passage into the darkness above.

"Damn it!" Daniel swore in frustration. "Now what?"

Tessa moved to the bottom of the ladder and looked up. Her heart clenched in her chest. "Daniel, up there."

She cast the beam of her own flashlight up the ladder. Daniel's joined it. Duct-taped to the top rung of the ladder was a metal box with a line of glowing LEDs on the side that blinked in time with the chirping. As they watched, one of the LEDs went dark.

"It's counting down," Daniel said.

"In what?" Tessa asked. "Minutes? Seconds?"

In answer, Daniel woke his watch and peered at the face. "Tell me when the next LED goes out."

Tessa nodded, understanding. "Now," she told him when another LED failed to blink back on.

"Sixty seconds. It's counting down in minutes." He pocketed his phone, grasped a rung of the ladder, and started up.

"Daniel! For God's sake! What are you doing?"

"Seeing how much time is left on the clock." He reached the device. A moment later, he uttered an inarticulate sound of frustration. "There are four lights. That's four minutes, Tess." He rested his forehead against the ladder. "We should've gone back when we first suspected she might've set a bomb. We might have been able to get close enough to the surface to call someone."

"What can we do?"

He came back down the ladder in a hurry, dropping the last several feet to the tunnel floor. "Run. Back the way we came. And hope we can get far enough away not to get caught in the blast."

"But what about the studio?"

"If that's a real bomb, the studio is doomed. There's a lot of explosives taped to that box. Let's just try to save ourselves."

They ran back the way they'd come, Tessa counting down the seconds as she ran. *My God, Kristin*, Tessa thought. *What the hell have you done?* They made the main corridor in seconds, but, while Daniel might have had a chance of getting a significant distance from the bomb, Tessa wasn't at full strength. By the time they'd gotten back to the first branch in the tunnel, where the left-hand passage headed toward the port, her lungs were burning and her breath was coming in labored gasps.

She'd lost track of her count when Daniel grasped her upper arm and dragged her down that fork, shoving her to the ground behind a collection of metal barrels and stacked crates.

"Out of time," he said, and the world shook and roared.

The floor of the tunnel bucked beneath them; seconds later, a wall of flame rolled past the mouth of their corridor, seeming to suck all the air from the place. The world was suddenly in chaos. Tessa was weightless one second and slammed to the earth the next. Something struck her head, and she was submerged in inky, dusty black.

Chapter Forty

Tessa was swimming in an endless void of blackest black except for ripples of murky light. She couldn't breathe without inhaling dust. Sounds came to her: the trickle of falling dust, the settling of stone, and farther away, a high, wailing sound. Taking a quick inventory of her body, she was sore and bruised but didn't think anything was broken. She moved each limb gingerly, experimentally, then felt around for her flashlight. Of course, she couldn't find it.

She next felt her pockets for her cell phone; it was still there, amazingly intact. She woke it and turned on the flashlight, panning it around the area where she lay. She was against the opposite wall from where Daniel had hauled her to the ground, surrounded by fallen barrels and other debris.

"Daniel?"

Supporting herself against the wall of the tunnel, Tessa pulled herself upright, shining the flash first farther down the tunnel, then back up toward where it met the main passage. She saw his leg first, poking out from between two of the barrels.

"Daniel!"

She scrambled toward him, praying wordlessly, trying not to panic.

He was lying against the wall of the tunnel, a metal barrel pinning his right leg to the ground, his torso covered with the shrapnel from shattered crates. A wicked gash above his left eye dripped blood down the side of his face. He groaned in answer to her repeating his name, but his eyelids only fluttered.

Tessa gritted her teeth and tried to shift the barrel. The object was too heavy for her to lift, and the exertion left her dizzy and nauseous. She settled for pulling the debris from his chest and stomach. She tossed one piece aside, only to realize that her hand was wet. She'd shone her light on it before she realized what the wetness meant. Her fingers were streaked with blood.

Terrified, she turned the light on his body. On his left side, a piece of crate shrapnel the size of Tessa's hand had pierced his ribs.

Her breath caught in her throat and threatened to choke her. Did she dare pull it out? She had to, because she also knew she had to leave him to get help. She pulled off her sneakers and socks, folded the socks up to make a compress, then pulled the belt from Daniel's jeans. Pulling the sleeves of her shirt down over her hands, she grasped the broken slat firmly and pulled with as much strength as she possessed. Daniel gasped in pain but didn't open his eyes.

The big splinter came out more easily than she'd expected; her momentum pitched her backward. She was back up in a flash, teeth clenched, jaw set, eyes dry. She checked the wound for any additional splinters. Finding none, she pressed the sock compress to the wound and secured it with the belt, which she passed around Daniel's lean torso and cinched as tightly as she could.

She felt his pulse. It was steady but weak. She checked to make sure he had no wounds she couldn't see, feeling the back of his head for blood. There was none. But he was cool to the touch and his skin was clammy. She suspected he had a concussion and might also be in shock. He needed immediate medical attention, but how could she get it to him? She ventured out to where the two tunnels intersected, where she was faced with a choice: if the bomb had torn through the roof of the tunnel and into the studio grounds, then that might offer the swiftest path to the surface and the presence of first responders. But there would be no way to climb out of the underground. The only escape she knew had been at ground zero. She couldn't justify wasting precious time to explore in that direction, so there was really no choice after all.

She went back to Daniel long enough to kiss him and murmur in his ear that she was going for help, then she set out back toward Le Salon Rouge at her best pace, sidestepping debris and stumbling over obstacles created by the blast from Kristin's bomb. As she went, her mind worried a set of questions as a dog worries a bone: When had Kristin set the bomb? Had she escaped the blast zone? Given what her life had suddenly become—the bridges she'd burned, the doors she'd slammed shut—perhaps she hadn't wanted to escape. On the other hand, there were still names on her hit list.

The wailing sound, which Tessa had belatedly realized were sirens coming from the breached ground of the studio grounds, faded as she moved away. The thought that she might have gotten Daniel help sooner if she'd gone back toward the blast zone gnawed at her. Propelled only by her determination to save him, Tessa staggered on at a zombie shamble, marginally faster once she left the blast debris behind.

She lost track of where she was until she found herself facing a metal door. She spent a moment in confusion before she realized that, of course, this was the backside of the cold storage door they'd come through from the kitchen of the immense ballroom. She knew where she was now.

The kitchen, then the dining room, then the stairs.

She willed herself through the two rooms, navigated the short entry hall, then used the last ounces of her strength to drag herself back up the wooden staircase into the crypt. She flung herself through the door and collapsed by the closest grave, pulling out her phone. It showed one bar. That would have to be enough. She realized with a start that she could see her surroundings. There was light coming from—

"Well, hello, Alice. I see you made it out of the rabbit hole."

Tessa looked up, clutching the phone to her breast. Her sister perched on one of the saw-horses the police had set up, once again wearing the inscrutable Mask of the Red Death. A camp lantern sat next to the sawhorse.

Tessa looked up at her, too weak to move, too stunned to utter more than a single word: "Why?"

"Oh, c'mon, Tess. You're not that dense. Revenge. I wanted the men who ruled and ruined my life to pay for their fickle friendship. When I was beautiful to them, they were beautiful to me. When I was no longer beautiful, they deserted me."

"No, they didn't, Kristin. *You* disappeared. You didn't give them a chance to show their friendship. I got calls, texts, emails. I turned my back on them. They didn't destroy your beauty or mine. Kurt Morrison did that, and he's going to prison for it."

"I need him to die."

"And I need Daniel to live. He's in that tunnel, Kristin. I need to get help."

Kristin went on as if she'd heard nothing Tessa had said. "Beauty was all I had, Tess, and he took it away. Robbed me. Robbed us. And those other men, those powerful men who gave us that world, took it all back. They exiled us."

"We exiled ourselves," Tessa said. "But you rebuilt your life. You had a legitimate modeling agency."

Kristin laughed. "Do you know where the money for that legitimate agency came from? Oh, yes, my name helped me establish it, brought me good models and some good clients, but it was taking too long. I needed to get back on top ASAP. That's why I started the Crimson Service and Le Salon Rouge—because I knew that, ultimately, powerful, wealthy men like George Robeson and Alex Dvorak get along in the world by using people—using women."

"Neither of them used you. They gave you a place to show your talent, and they paid you—us—handsomely for it."

"Gianni didn't *give* me a place to show my talent. I bought it by giving him the best damn blow jobs he'd ever had. And George Robeson—*I* got us that audition by getting him to fuck me on the desk in his fancy office." Tessa had suspected that about Gianni DeLuca, but George Robeson?

"George was one of your Crimson clients?"

Kristin snorted and tossed her head. "No. George was too fucking good for me. After that first time, he was Mr. Righteous. Too little, too late."

"And Kevin Salinger?" Tessa asked. "Is that who the sixth grave is for?"

Kristin looked away for a moment. The gesture seemed reflexive and telling. "I . . . haven't made up my mind yet. He pissed me off back when we were working on *Dark Beauty*. He wouldn't go to bed with me. Not while we were working on the film. It wasn't until after—"

"Yes, I know. The police said you were with him last night. What do you make of that, Krist? When you were beautiful, he refused to use you. And now that your beauty has allegedly been destroyed, he still wants you. What has he done that merits a grave?"

Kristin was silent for a moment. When she spoke again, her voice sounded distant. "The night of the release party, Salinger asked me out. Film was done. Why not, right? I was angry. Not at him; at the reviews.

I told him to get bent. Moments. That was moments before Kurt ..." She stopped. Sighed. "Well, now it's too late. It was too late last night."

Tessa got to her feet. "Please, Kristin, Daniel's trapped back there in the tunnel and I need to get help before it's too late for him."

Kristin did another lightning change. "Oh, boo hoo," she snarled. "Do you think I give a damn about your boyfriend? I don't even understand what he sees in a gargoyle like you. He must want to puke every time he sees your face."

Tessa was wobbly. She took a step away from the grave (a grave that might yet be hers) and leaned her back against the cold stone wall. "He doesn't. And you know, I've gotten to where I can handle not covering it up." She swept her hair back from her face. "At least with Daniel. He still wants to marry me. Sounds like we both have men who want us, love us."

"I've never had a man who loved me. Ever. Nor do I want one. Love makes people stupid. As for your precious Daniel, he's just one more casualty among many. He wasn't my target—most of the people in the studio weren't my targets. It was Dvorak I was aiming at, though I don't mind that I've also managed to destroy the place where you made a fool of me in that damned film."

Tessa felt a white-hot flare of pure rage boil out of her soul. She levered herself away from the supportive wall. "You mean like you made a fool of me with that damned LSD trick in college? You stripped me of the life I wanted and I *still* tried to help you get the life *you* wanted. I wanted you to be a success so that I could bow out and go back to my life. You know who destroyed your life, Kristin? *You* did. You brought it all on yourself."

Kristin reached behind her back and produced a gun—a shiny, silver semiautomatic with a mother-of-pearl handle that must have been tucked into the waistband of her pants. She aimed it at Tessa. "I could put a bullet in you right now, *Tess*."

"Why don't you?" Tessa asked. "You've already got a grave for me."

"I want to watch you squirm a little first, the way I watched George Robeson and Gianni DeLuca squirm before I shot them. Do you know DeLuca actually thought I was going to give him a blow job before he died? Dick."

Desperation clawed at Tessa's stomach. "The police know where we are. Daniel and I told them we were going to try to stop you. They'll be here soon. I think maybe you ought to run."

"The police? Haven't you heard that there's a little emergency over at Paradox Studios? Every police officer, rescue worker, and EMT in this city has their hands full right now; they aren't coming to rescue you. Do you honestly think that the problems of one damaged young woman matter a damn to them right now?"

"One damaged young woman," Tessa repeated. "You just described yourself, Krist. Me, I'm not damaged. I'm whole in the only way that matters."

"Bullshit."

"It isn't your face that's damaged, Kristin. It's you. You're hideous on the inside. That's sad, because you didn't need to be. I'm proof of that. Twins, remember? What happened to you back in high school? Something changed you. I thought it was just that you realized how useful your looks could be, but it had to be more than that."

Kristin was silent again for a moment. The muzzle of the gun wobbled just a bit. "I'll tell you what happened, since we're in the final act here. I got owned. I got owned by this ... *boy.* A boy who befriended me our first week of school and cultivated that friendship just so he could have a playmate while he was away from his girlfriend on a fucking science field trip."

"Kevin," said Tessa. "I remember you talked about him. How nice he was."

"Yeah. Real nice. He was so nice, I promised myself I'd never let someone own me like that again."

The two sisters were silent for a moment.

"But he wasn't the only one," she said in a quiet voice. "What?"

"Someone else—also named Kevin—destroyed me. He was Haddi's brother. Remember Haddi?"

"Yes. You two were best friends. I never knew what happened between you."

"*She* never did anything. But her brother took *everything* from me."

"I'm so sorry, Krist. If I'd known ..."

"No one ever knew."

Tessa nodded. "So, I think I understand you a little better. You want to do the owning. I get it. Fine. Own me. Kill me, but don't let Daniel die. He's lying in the first left-hand branch with a metal barrel crushing his leg and a gash in his ribs from a piece of old crate. I'll trade my life for his. Help me get him out, then you can leave me in that grave. Cover me with dirt. Do whatever you want to me."

Kristin made a soft chuffing sound. "You love this man so much you're willing to die for him? Stop. You'll make me cry, and that'll get the inside of my mask all wet. You're such a good girl."

"We were both good girls. Until those boys changed you. I wish you'd said something about it to me or Mom. We might have helped you get over it. Not let it destroy who you were." Tears fell, suddenly, stealthily.

Tessa felt them on both cheeks. "I miss my sister. We were happy together. We had the whole world. We had each other."

"And look how that turned out," Kristin said dryly.

"We could have that again," Tessa said. "We're still alive. We still have a future."

"No, we don't," Kristin said. "I've killed people. You're going to be one of them. So, best-case scenario: You're dead and I go to prison forever."

"Why kill me?" Tessa asked. "Why let Daniel die? Neither of us has done anything to hurt you."

"Are you kidding? Your *existence* hurts me. You and your Lazarus routine. You and Daniel are like nails on the chalkboard of life. And like you said, after everything I did to bring you to *this*, here you fucking are, trying to save my soul. What is wrong with you?"

"I don't know. This is just me. This has always been who I am. And you ... remember, in middle school, how you protected me from that bully—what was her name—Tucker?"

Kristin snorted. "April Tucker. Yeah, so I felt I had to protect my sister. That was the kind of bullshit I believed back then."

"Why did you stop believing in it? How was it that after being loved by Mom and Dad and me and every other person in our family, you let two boys—*two boys*—make you stop believing you were loved and lovable?"

"Because ... because..." Kristin paused and pointed the gun straight at Tessa's face. "Because it was bullshit. Why are you asking me all this? You're just buying time, trying not to die. The police aren't coming, Tess."

"I'm asking you because it's important. We're identical twins. We came from the same embryo, were raised by the same parents. We were inseparable until a pair of boys convinced you that you were only fit to be used. Even then you didn't stop caring for me. Even that stupid acid trip you arranged for me was your way of trying to give me a better future than you thought I'd planned for myself."

Kristin shook her head. "I thought *I'd* have a better future. You were just a tool I used to get it."

"That's not true," Tessa said. "You loved me. I loved you. I still do."

Kristin laughed, but the muffled sound from behind the mask was more like a sob. "Love me? Love *me*? *How can you fucking love me?*"

"Because you're my sister."

"Because you're my sister," Kristin repeated in smarmy voice. "You know what a good sister I am, Tessa? I pulled a twin swap on your precious Daniel."

"I know. He told me."

The gray eyes behind the mask glittered like shards of glass. "And you're going to stand there and tell me you *love* me? Knowing I tried to fuck your fiancé?"

"Yes."

Kristin let out a shriek of pure frustration and fired the gun into the open grave at Tessa's feet. The sound made Tessa jump and cover her ringing ears. She slid down the wall to the floor, pressing her back against the cool, hard stone.

"I'm going to kill you and you still say you love me? Are you totally insane?"

"Maybe," Tessa said. "Maybe love *is* insanity. I only know what I feel. Maybe that's all any of us can know."

Kristin's laughter sounded more like choking. "Then I guess hatred is insane too, because that's what I feel. I feel hatred for everything. For life. For humanity. For ... for ..."

She stopped talking, her body sagging like a scarecrow in the rain. "For me?"

"For *myself*." Kristin dropped the gun and slid from the sawhorse to the gritty floor of the crypt, landing on her hands and knees.

Tessa's eyes followed the gun. It ended up about four feet from where she stood trembling with fear and shock. Could she grab it before Kristin could? She lifted her eyes to her sister's huddled form. Kristin's head was down, and her shoulders shook with silent sobs. When she spoke again, her voice was tear-soaked.

"I don't hate you, Tessa. I just wanted somebody to blame ... for being better at everything than I was. School, modeling, acting ..."

"Krist, I never even wanted to be an actress. You know that better than anyone. I didn't put me in that movie, *you* did. If you'd left me alone, you could have had it all, all by yourself."

The mask tilted toward her, and she could see the glitter of Kristen's eyes through the holes. "I didn't want to be all by myself, Tess. I wanted us to be a team. A team of ... of equals. But we were never equal. You were the one our parents loved best. The good girl, the one they always compared me to." Her voice took on a singsong quality. "'Why can't you be more like Tessa?' 'Why are Tessa's grades so much better than yours?' Until I messed you up, of course. Then I got about two seconds of seeing Dad look at you the way he looked at me. And you know what? It didn't make me feel any better. Then, *then*, you told them it wasn't your fault, and they believed you."

"Because I'd never given them any reason not to. Kristin, you chose your path through high school. You were every bit as smart as I was. I didn't steal your good grades or your good reviews or your goodness, period. You let those two boys steal those things from you. You *gave* them the power to hurt you. To screw you up. I *never* did anything intentionally to hurt you. *Never*."

"No," Kristin said softly. "No, you didn't. I just needed somebody to blame besides me." She picked up the gun again and got unsteadily to her feet. "I put the blame everywhere but where it really belongs. Sometimes I knew that. I did. Never more clearly than when Kurt threw that acid in my face. You didn't even know the guy. That was all on me." She shook her head. "You know, I think Salinger actually thinks he loves me. Isn't that a hoot?"

With a suddenness that was terrifying, she swung the gun in an arc around her body, pointing it at Tessa, at the grave, at the ceiling. Out of her mouth came a sound like the howl of a lonely animal. It was the most horrifying thing Tessa had ever heard—more horrifying than the explosion, more horrifying than the gunshot. It was the sound of her sister disintegrating.

"I'm a monster, Tessa! I'm a monster!" Kristin wailed. "And I was a monster before Kurt Morrison screwed up my face. He just finished the job."

With a savage yank, she tore the mask from her face. It was the first time Tessa had seen Kristin's face since they'd been splashed with acid, and she was unprepared. It was a patchwork quilt of skin grafts and half-mended regrowth. She had no eyebrows, no eyelashes, and a partially rebuilt nose. Her reconstructed eyelids drooped over her mercifully undamaged gray eyes.

Tessa's heart broke; if only Kristin had stayed the course in the hospital. If only she had faithfully worn a pressure mask. Tessa now realized the benefit the mask had given her. If only . . . Her sister's life was a patchwork quilt, too, of "if only's," of half-assed efforts to achieve something abandoned for what Kristin thought of as the easy way out—to use her beauty and charm and sexuality to get what she wanted. With that gone—

"I lost my beauty too," Tessa said quietly. "I suppose I might play burn victims or monsters on TV or in the movies. Third corpse from the right. But I had Mom and Dad and Daniel and Sarah."

Had.

While she'd stood here trying to convince Kristin not to shoot her, it was entirely possible that Daniel was dying. She felt tears wet on her cheeks. "You could have had that too," she told Kristin. "Friends, family. You said you thought Kevin Salinger loved you. You went to him when you were in trouble ..."

"And the idiot wanted to help me. Oh, I'm sure he'll visit me in prison," said Kristin bitterly. "God, he's such a freaking Boy Scout."

A sound that was not part of this tableau invaded the crypt. Tessa froze. Where was it coming from? Had she only imagined it? She had little time to focus on it, because Kristin was coming toward her, her steps unsteady. Tessa remained deathly still as Kristin knelt beside her. For a moment she was afraid her sister was going to strangle her. She didn't. Now that the mask was gone, Tessa could actually see the tears pouring down Kristin's ravaged cheeks. She couldn't even recall the last time she'd seen genuine tears flow from Kristin's eyes. Kristin looked like a zombie, a creature out of a horror movie. Yet Tessa felt no revulsion, even when her sister reached out and hugged her, placing her head on Tessa's shoulder.

"I still ... I still have you, don't I?" Kristin asked.

"Always." Tessa felt tension building up in her body like the spring in a mechanical watch. Was this Kristin surrendering, or just a new level of crazy?

"But I no longer have myself. What I was, all the things I hoped to be. They weren't just taken from me. I threw them away. I'd hoped that ending everyone who had hurt me would get me a kind of redemption, but it didn't. It got me nothing. There's only one kind of redemption left for me now." She released Tessa and stood again.

Tessa relaxed, the tension flowing out of her in one long breath. Maybe now, she could get Kristin to get help for Daniel. She started to ask, but Kristin had raised the gun again. She jammed the muzzle against her chin and pulled the trigger.

Tessa let out a scream of pure horror that was lost in the echo of the shot. Blood was everywhere, spraying from the exit wound as Kristin pirouetted like a ballerina to fall, with awkward grace, into what Tessa had feared would be her own grave.

Tessa wanted nothing more than to lie there, curled in a tight ball, giving vent to her grief. But she couldn't. She levered herself up from the floor and set herself in motion. One step after another, she stumbled across the crypt and to the door of the storage room on the other side. She was roughly halfway across when she saw flashlight beams slashing at the darkness beyond and made out the figures behind them.

She stopped, swaying, with no idea what she should do.

"Tessa?" Detective Williams's voice came out of the chaos of dark and light.

Focus, Tessa. She stopped her swaying and pointed at the doorway behind her. "Daniel," she said as forcefully as she could. "Down the tunnel. Left-hand fork. Please."

"On it," said Williams. She turned to her companions. "Frank, take Pearson and Taylor to find Mr. Takashi. I'll get Ms. Morgan out of here. Keep an eye out for Kristin Morgan."

"Kristin is dead." Tessa said the words, barely believing them. "She shot herself. She's in the last grave."

Williams came to Tessa's side and put an arm around her as the other cops filed past them with mute purpose.

"The studio," Tessa murmured. "The gala ..."

"Thanks to you, there were some injuries—some of them serious—but no deaths. Those messages Mr. Takashi left made us realize we had no idea what your sister might have planned. Given that she used a bomb on your fiancé's house, well, we shut the whole thing down before it ever really got started. The studio's a disaster, but they can rebuild."

Tessa was hit with a wave of relief so intense, her legs nearly gave out. Detective Williams kept her on her feet.

"C'mon, hon," the older woman said. "Let's get you back out into the real world."

Epilogue

The sun shone with relentless cheer over the cemetery. Several rows of folding chairs had been assembled in front of Kristin's open grave, but few guests were present. Not official ones, at least. Beyond the roped-off family-and-friends area was a bevy of reporters with cameras, cell phones, and iPads. They took photographs, narrated into microphones, mumbled notes into cell phones, and awaited the opportunity to ask questions as mourners left the cemetery. A handful of police stood guard to make sure the reporters didn't encroach on the family.

In the last week, the story of how a one-time movie actress and model had become a homicidal maniac intent on killing even her own sister had taken over the media. Kristin's funeral was the epilogue of an epic tale of tragedy and revenge.

There was a time, Tessa thought, that the story was what Kristin would have wanted. She sat in the front row of the folding chairs. Daniel—his ribs taped, his leg in a soft cast, and a crutch lying beside his chair—sat to her right, and her parents sat to her left, her father stoic, her mother sobbing. Behind them, in a second row, sat Sarah Hernandez, Alexei Dvorak, Kevin Salinger, and Jayla Williams, whom Tessa had begun to think of as a friend. There were no other mourners.

The service wouldn't be a long one. Besides the pastor of their family church, Tessa would be the only one to speak. She had thought long and hard about what to say about her twin. She wanted to talk about the pleasant past, but more than that, she wanted her parents—and the celebrity-devouring world—to know that in her last moments, Kristin had been herself again.

Daniel put his arm around Tessa as they waited for the pastor to take his place at the little podium set up at the head of Kristin's casket. Despite the tragedy of her sister's death, Tessa smiled. Daniel's ring was back on her finger, they had a marriage license, and their two families had thrown themselves into the wedding plans, defanging the past by looking to the future. Tessa felt a hand on her shoulder and looked back to see her steady friend Sarah smiling at her. Sarah was to be her maid of honor.

Pastor Avery, his shock of white hair brilliant in the SoCal sun, stood at a podium in front of Kristin's grave and began to speak. Tessa hadn't intended to listen, but she found the words comforting. He talked about the power of love and forgiveness.

"We talk about giving the people who hurt us second chances," he said. "That's a very human thing to do. But God holds out the possibility of more—of giving every soul every opportunity to be forgiven, where possible, to atone for those they have harmed, to ultimately find redemption. I believe the prayers we utter here, with heartfelt sincerity, help those who have left us on their onward journey. Let us now pray for the soul of Kristin Kerry Morgan and send her into the next phase of her existence with forgiveness and hope."

He led them in the Lord's Prayer, offered a brief set of verses about the life of the soul, then ended with: "In taking stock of Kristin's life—of all our lives—and the physical and emotional infirmities that have molded us, let us remember the words of Christian philosopher C. S. Lewis: 'I *am* a soul; I *have* a body.' Let us never forget who and what we are. Amen." He then gave the podium to Tessa. She remembered Kristin at her best, at her funniest, at her most true. "All my life," she said at last, "Kristin was the unstoppable one. The irresistible force that had never met an immovable object. I never realized until it was too late how she found ways around and under and over the objects she couldn't move. My sister learned to trick life. In the end, she ran out of tricks and met an immovable object she couldn't circumvent: herself. Kristin told me that she lost herself. It's not important what caused that loss. But know that, at the end, she found herself again. For just a moment. But I think"—she

glanced over at Pastor Avery—"I *believe* it was just long enough."

END

About the Author

Blake Rudman enjoyed a former, successful career in executive management, building his own companies from the ground up.

Success or not, Blake's heart has always been in the written word, and the myriad ideas he spent much of his spare time jotting down in notebooks, Post-Its, and scraps of paper whenever the inspiration hit him.

Now a breakout author of five noir thriller novels – all to be published in 2023 – Blake's destiny of becoming a writer of some renown is well under way.

When he's not working diligently on his next novel, Blake spends quality time with his family and tropical fish.

Follow Blake's blog at: https://blakerudman.com
Facebook: @BRudmanThriller
Instagram: @BRudmanThriller
Twitter: @BRudmanThriller

For all Blake's books, visit him at:
www.hellboundbookspublishing.com/authorpage_rudman.html

Dark Beauty

Tessa and Kristin Morgan are identical twins, exquisitely beautiful, and have the world at their perfectly pedicured feet; they are also profoundly different beneath their stunning facades.

Tessa is the laser-focused academic with her eyes firmly fixed upon a career in neurology, while Kristin exploits her striking looks and undeniable power over men to carve out a single-minded path to fame and fortune as a model and actress; an ambition she also holds for her sister.

But, on the night of the pair's debut as top-tier models, and with a high-profile movie role in the bag, tragedy strikes the twins in the form of a cruel acid attack by an unknown assailant. Thus, a gruesome chain of events begins - one that leaves a trail of blood, death, and devastation behind both Tessa and Kristin.

As Tessa fights to rebuild her life and uncover the truth behind the attack, she finds herself getting closer and closer to an uncomfortable truth about her sister and her search for the truth turns into a nightmare struggle to stay alive.

Goodbye Stranger

"As with *American Psycho*, Blake Rudman's *Goodbye Stranger* has a wealthy, successful man whose wonderful family life masks a much darker side. Throw in a once-trusting, increasingly suspicious wife, and the stage is set for twists and turns you'll never see coming!"

Danielle Harrington has the life many women envy: She's beautiful, rich, has two wonderful children, and is married to *the* Preston Harrington - the handsome, charismatic, retired quarterback who won two Super Bowls.

Unfortunately, something is very wrong with Preston. Having suffered more than his fair share of injuries and concussions, he becomes quiet, withdrawn, and distant. As Preston spends more time away from his family, Danielle begins suspect an affair without realizing her husband is involved in something much, much worse…

Following a series of tragic incidents and the return of an old nemesis from the past, things begin to spiral out of control for Danielle as Preston's dark side puts her and their children in terrible danger.

Redline

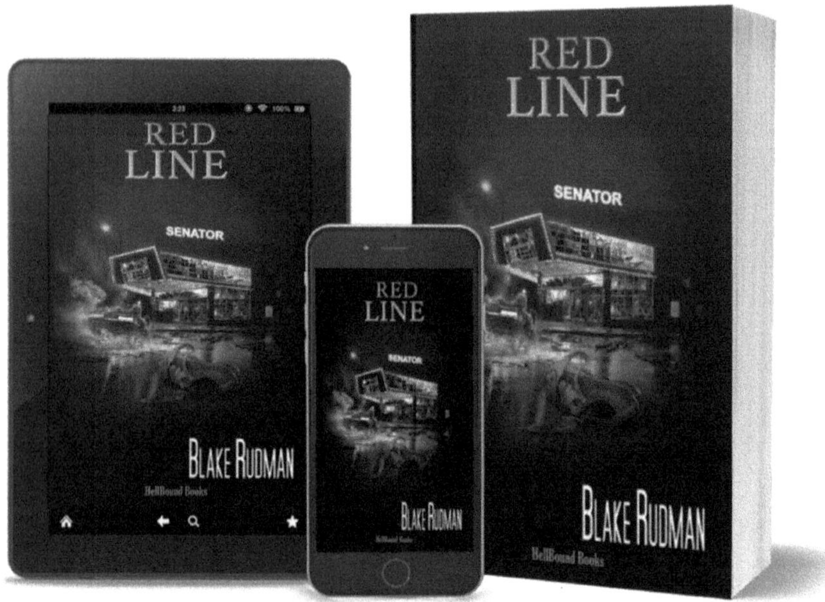

"If Lee Childs' Jack Reacher or Clive Cussler's Dirk Pitt tackled a terrorist scheme that utilized subliminal messaging to sow social and economic chaos on a global scale, it would look a lot like *Red Line*." Baltimore Police Detective Mitch Wilson wants a nice day out with his wife and son. Instead, they are all caught up in a catastrophic terrorist attack that has repercussions across the USA and triggers events that could alter the course of civilization.

Having lost everything, Mitch sets out to seek justice – and revenge and stumbles upon a global conspiracy.

On the other side of the world, renowned linguistic professor, Yasaman Karami, flees her native Iran for the freedom of the west; she holds one of the keys to defeating the terrorist organization.

Yasaman and Mitch's worlds collide as, alongside federal agents and allies, they race against the clock to hunt down the terrorist masterminds and prevent worldwide catastrophe.

Kutri

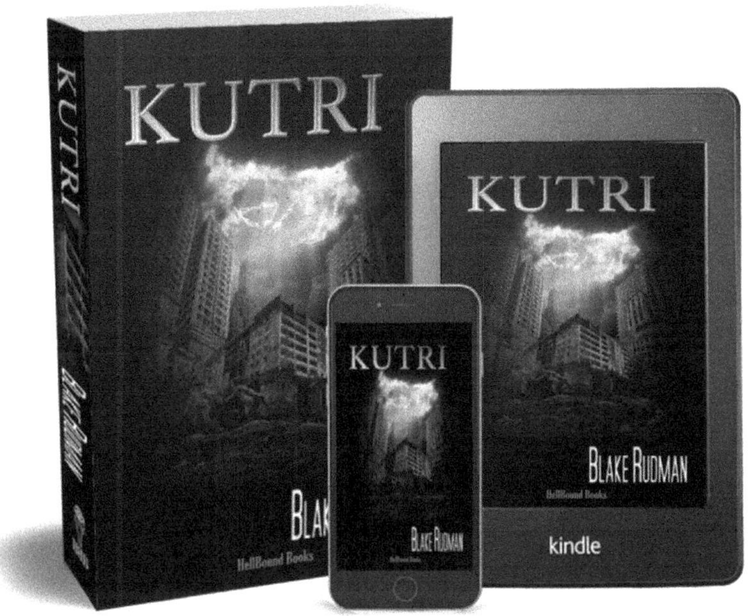

The Slow Plague killed billions of women and girls worldwide. The gender-targeting infection without cure drove the remaining, sparce female population into an insane supply and demand situation in which they are treated as valuable commodities.

Though their "market value" is high, paradoxically, women's rights take a nosedive as they have become more desirable than the most precious jewels. Women are objects avarice, awe, and worship – to be owned or won in high-stakes games.

Kutri Chandigarh, one such "prize" and a rare beauty, is shipped from her native India to Los Angeles, a shattered metropolis barricaded behind a radiation-repelling wall. Within the city stronghold, a bleak, broken society comprised mostly of men is mesmerized by the stupefying programs pumped out by Little Angel Studios: an endless parade of reality TV shows. The studio's #1 hit is "Good Breeding", in which a bevy of ethnically "pure" young women compete to marry a chosen suitor and produce a family in the spotlight of the public eye.

Like all women, Kutri has dreamed of wining the competition since her early childhood. But, when she arrives in LA and meets Jakob Freeman, her assigned matchmaker, the fantasy is turned on its head. It quickly twists into a horrific nightmare that extends far beyond Kutri and the man she chooses for herself.

As Kutri tries to escape the fate she once coveted, Jakob is swept up in events that threaten him body and soul and spark memories of a past he has deliberately tried to forget.

www.hellboundbookspublishing.com

Follow Blake's blog at: https://blakerudman.com
Facebook: @BRudmanThriller
Instagram: @BRudmanThriller
Twitter: @BRudmanThriller

For all Blake's books, visit him at:
www.hellboundbookspublishing.com/authorpage_rudman.html

www.ingramcontent.com/pod-product-compliance
Lightning Source LLC
Chambersburg PA
CBHW051123300726
48981CB00022B/528/J